They Wanted to Live

Cecil Roberts

HIS NOVELS

Scissors
Sails of Sunset
The Love Rack
Little Mrs. Manington
Sagusto
David and Diana
Indiana Jane
Pamela's Spring Song
Havana Bound
Bargain Basement
Spears Against Us
Pilgrim Cottage
The Guests Arrive
Volcano
Victoria Four-Thirty
They Wanted to Live
One Small Candle
So Immortal a Flower
Eight for Eternity

HIS OTHER BOOKS

Gone Rustic
Gone Rambling
Gone Afield
Gone Sunwards
And So to Bath
And So to America
A Man Arose
Diary of Russell Beresford
Half Way : An Autobiography
Alfred Fripp : A Biography

AND

The Pilgrim Cottage Omnibus

Cecil Roberts

They Wanted to Live

London HODDER & STOUGHTON Limited

First published . . . January 1939
Fourteenth impression . May 1949

*Made and Printed in Great Britain for Hodder & Stoughton, Limited, London,
by Wyman & Sons Limited, London, Reading and Fakenham*

To

JANÓS

CONTENTS

CHAPTER I

THE DAY BEGINS

It took a lot to depress Mrs. Brown. Throughout her life she had been an obstinate optimist. She soundly spanked the imps of misfortune who played so many tricks upon her, for she was convinced that the angels in Heaven were watching her. Her philosophy and her religion were simple and clear-cut. There was Good and there was Evil, and the Next Life possessed a flawless record of the credit and debit accounts of the candidate for immortality.

Mrs. Brown was quite sure of immortality. Though always humble in spirit, none of the cruelties of life could shake her belief in Divine Mercy. When, this bright April morning, she sang at the sink as she washed up the breakfast things—

"The King of Love my Shepherd is
Whose goodness faileth never,"

she had no doubt, whatsoever, that Divine Love would make up any deficiency in her account as a Christian.

Her singing this morning, however, had a somewhat depressed tone. Her daughter, Nellie, had told her something that had kept her awake most of the night. She had heard the trains running in and out of Victoria Station, which lay just beyond the row of grimy houses in which she lived, and she had seen the London dawn come up, and heard the clink of milk bottles as the delivery cart passed down the street. It had been just such a dawn on an April morning over twenty years ago when she had begun the first day of her widowhood, while her young husband lay at the mortuary, killed on the railway where he worked, and where now her son Jim also worked as a porter.

It was Jim, or rather something concerning Jim, which

9

had kept her awake, and added a minor tone of emphasis to her " . . . . goodness faileth never," as she sprinkled soap-flakes into the washing-up water. Jim had not come down yet, for he was on late duty last night. His breakfast now lay waiting for him on the kitchen table, with the tea in the pot all ready for mashing.

Nellie had had her breakfast and departed to work, punctual as ever. The lodger in the front parlour, Mr. Simkin, had also departed. He was an admirable lodger, quiet in his habits, punctual in payment of his rent, but exasperatingly mean. In all the five years that he had lodged with Mrs. Brown he had restricted himself to a shilling a week for gas. When the shilling's worth was spent, the fire went out ; and in the very depth of winter Mr. Simkin would not increase this allowance. The gas finished, he appeared in the kitchen with a large stone bottle, once used for ginger-beer. He would ask for this to be filled with boiling water, and then retire to his room where he wrapped up the bottle in a shawl and used it for a foot-warmer. Jim called this elderly widower, " Mr. Skinflint." He cooked his own supper over a gas-ring and read until his eyes were sore. For a long time the Brown family had felt sorry for him, and had given him titbits from their own table. Then one day Jim, who suffered from insatiable curiosity and made his mother hot with shame at his prying in Mr. Simkin's room, came out exultantly, after a forage, holding a small brown book in his hand.

" Look, Ma ! Old Skinflint's left this on the mantelpiece, behind some letters ! Just look ! " he said.

" Oh, Jim, you shouldn't—what is it ? " asked Mrs. Brown, curiosity overcoming disapproval.

Jim waved the book over her head, his merry brown eyes glowing with excitement.

" A Post Office Savings Book—and how much do you think he's got in it ? "

" Oh, Jim, you haven't looked ! "

" Of course I've looked ! Lean against me, Ma, and take a look for yourself."

Jim got behind his mother, and put his strong young arms around her, holding the open book before her.

Mrs. Brown looked and gasped.

" Three hundred and forty-four pounds ! Well, I never ! " she exclaimed.

" And you've been giving him pasties and cups of cocoa before bedtime, because he was cold and you felt sorry for him—you silly old girl ! " said Jim teasingly, pressing his cheek against his mother's.

" Three hundred and forty-four pounds," repeated Mrs. Brown, still dazed by this revelation of wealth. " It makes me feel sorry for him."

" Sorry for him ! " exclaimed Jim, protestingly.

" Yes—it's not meanness, it's a disease. He's not happy with it," said Mrs. Brown. " Money's not everything."

" Oh, isn't it ! Tell that to the Marines, Mother darling ! " exclaimed Jim. " What couldn't we do with it ! "

" There's nothing I very much want to do," said Mrs. Brown, disapproving this love of money.

" Yes, there is," affirmed Jim. " You want a new dress, and new shoes. You want a new carpet for the stairs, and you're longing for a pink eiderdown for your bed. And you need a holiday, and——"

" Jim, do put that book back—supposing he came in ! " interrupted Mrs. Brown.

" If I had all this money, do you know what I'd do ? " asked Jim, earnestly.

" Now do take that book back, please, Jim. You'll never have all that money, so don't start day-dreaming."

" Oh, shan't I ? " challenged Jim, turning his head so quickly that a lock of chestnut hair fell over one eye. He swept it back with the astonishing book. " I'm not always going to be a railway porter—not me ! "

" Jim, you won't throw up your job ? " said Mrs. Brown, in quick alarm. " It's safe, and with so many out of work——"

" Safe ! That's what's the matter with it. Now don't get worried. I might become a stationmaster," said Jim, grinning at his mother.

" Of course," agreed Mrs. Brown.

" I *don't* think ! " exclaimed Jim, with boisterous rudeness. " Chancellor of the Exchequer, more like ! "

" Do take that book back," pleaded Mrs. Brown.

" All right. Do you know what I'd do with all this money, Ma ? I'd bust it in, I'd go all round the world ! "

" And lose your job ? "

" And lose my job ! " affirmed Jim, exuberantly.

" Then it's a good thing you haven't got it. You're just a silly boy. Now do put that book back ! "

" Righto—and you're a mugwump," said Jim, planting a kiss on his mother's cheek. " I'd buy you a motor-car, before I left on the world tour."

" I don't want a motor-car. I'm quite happy as I am ! " retorted Mrs. Brown, pushing him away.

She was quite happy, but not so happy this morning as usual. Nellie's news had worried her. It was about Jim, or more precisely, about Jim's girl, Lizzie Parrish. It is difficult at all times for a mother to approve of the girl an only son proposes marrying. Her sense of impending loss is too much for strict impartiality, and Mrs. Brown was well aware that a certain amount of self-interest and the natural monopoly of an only son's affection warped her judgment. But in moments when she contemplated the future, the marriage of Jim was a desirable thing. He had been a good lad, and he would make an excellent husband. He was now almost twenty-five and had been walking-out with Lizzie Parrish for five years.

Lizzie, of course, was frantically eager to get married, and it was only Jim's modest wage that countered her constant reminder that she was getting tired of waiting. Mrs. Brown had never liked the girl. She was grasping, gave herself airs, and had a doll-like prettiness that foreboded incompetence in the kitchen. Boys never seemed to think that a woman's work with a rolling-pin, a needle, and a scrubbing-brush were much more necessary to their comfort than a complete acquaintance with dance tunes and film stars.

Lizzie spent most of her time sitting on padded cinema seats, chewing chocolates, and leading the life, by proxy, of a pampered Society girl, whose sole quest was the fierce kiss of a tough guy.

" I wonder all that mush doesn't rot her brains," said Nellie, a moderate cinema addict. " I do like a good film, but——"

" That girl's no brains to rot," retorted Mrs. Brown. " What's the matter with her is she's too pretty by half. But you can't say anything to Jim."

Well, it was high time now to say something to Jim. Any girl who went around with Henry Marriott was asking for trouble. The Marriotts lived at the end of the street, and their mode of life was a byword. They kept the fish shop, and the Marriott boy worked in a garage. He often borrowed a car, and the girls who went out driving with him were not particular.

Mrs. Brown put a rasher of bacon in the frying-pan, for she heard Jim stirring above. She was not going to say Lizzie Parrish was a bad girl, but a sense of loyalty should prevent her running around with no-goods like Henry Marriott. Lizzie always smelt too much of scent ; that was one thing the matter with her, and although she worked in an Odeon Restaurant she knew nothing about pastry that hadn't come off a tray. Now her Nellie had been thoroughly trained and would make any man happy, but the fools couldn't see it, just because Nellie was plain. If only the poor girl had had Jim's good looks, she would not be manless at thirty, with no prospects.

Mrs. Brown turned the bacon over. She had married, at twenty-five, a railway porter earning twenty shillings a week. Somehow they had managed, and been happy, far happier than folks were to-day with their cinema-going and motoring and foreign travel, if you please. Even Jim was crazy to go abroad, and said he was tired of seeing people off to countries where he could never go. He had once taken her breath away by saying that when he had his honeymoon he wouldn't go to Brighton or Yarmouth but to Paris or

Lugano. What an idea! Of course Lizzie was at the back of all that. It was a wonder she hadn't suggested Hollywood.

Mrs. Brown poured the hot fat over the rashers. Jim was coming downstairs. Should she tell him about Henry Marriott and Lizzie?

"Mornin', Mother," cried Jim, appearing. He dabbed a kiss on her cheek, and examined his face in the mirror over the sink.

"I'll soon have to shave every day," he said, rubbing his chin. "Any water in the kettle?"

"Here you are—mind, it's boiling."

"One day, with a bit of luck, we'll have hot and cold laid on, and no more kettle business, or going to the boiler with a ladle."

"Very Ritzy this morning, aren't you?" asked Mrs. Brown. "One morning, with a bit of luck, I'll have a cup of tea in bed, while the cook gets breakfast. This house hasn't been the same since the butler left."

Jim pulled the blue shirt off his head, and turned a grinning face to his mother, as he gave the belt around his slim waist a hitch.

"You've got a bruise," said Mrs. Brown, looking at her son's bare chest.

"Lucky I haven't a black eye," replied Jim, passing a hand over his muscular, hairless body.

"Oh, been running into Henry Marriott?" asked Mrs. Brown quickly, peering down at the gas stove to hide her daring.

"Eh? No, got it at the club boxing yesterday. I've put on two pounds, if you please," said Jim proudly, stretching out his arms and flexing his biceps. "Look at that!"

Mrs. Brown looked admiringly at her son, noticing the breadth of shoulders, the curve of the strong neck, the deep chest and the small belly of the half-naked youth before her.

"A regular Samson, I say," said Mrs. Brown, facetiously, to hide her pride in this boy of hers.

He turned, and ran some cold water into the tin basin. "Why Henry Marriott?" he suddenly asked.

" Oh, nothing much—only I thought perhaps you'd asked him why he was running around with Lizzie so much," replied Mrs. Brown quietly, boldly seizing her opportunity. Then, a little frightened, she picked up the teapot and milk jug and hurried out of the scullery.

Jim swilled his head and shoulders, and spluttered loudly as he took more water from the cold tap. Turning, he groped for a towel, with soapy runlets coursing down his smooth chest.

" Here you are ! " said Mrs. Brown, returning, as he squeezed the water out of his dank curls.

Jim seized the proffered towel and rubbed his head briskly. Then, pausing for a moment with a glowing face, he looked at his mother intently as she busied herself in the scullery.

" Who's told you he's running around with Lizzie ? "

" Never you mind, I'm only saying what I've heard," replied Mrs. Brown, cautiously. She was feeling uncomfortable now she had risked talking of the matter.

Jim looked at himself intently in the mirror over the shelf, pretending to examine the bruise on his chest. He set his pectoral muscle and felt it. Despite the discoloration all was well. It was as hard as iron.

" H'm—there's always someone poking their noses in other people's business, isn't there ? " he asked, after a pause.

" Meaning me, I suppose ? " answered Mrs. Brown, filling the kettle. " Is that a nice way to talk of your mother ? "

Jim laughed, and, as she bent over the gas stove, caught hold of her broad back and leaned his face over her shoulder.

" A regular gossiping old woman, aren't you ? " he laughed, and gave her a resounding kiss on the cheek.

" Oh, your hair's wet, Jim, do get your shirt on, you'll be late ! You're getting fat," she added, alluding to the plump, muscular arms enfolding her.

" Pot calling kettle. I'm eleven stone six, just right for a fellow of five foot eleven," he retorted, releasing her and taking his shirt off the hook. He pulled it over his head, tucked the tails into his corduroy trousers, and began to comb and brush his hair.

" You seem to forget, Mother, that Lizzie's a lot of time on her hands when I'm on night duty. I can't expect her to go mooning about alone," he said, dragging the comb through his thick curls.

" Perhaps so, but I shouldn't choose Henry Marriott for spare time company," replied Mrs. Brown, doggedly. " Do come along, Jim, the tea'll be getting cold," she added, passing into the kitchen. Having begun the subject she had no desire to pursue it. Her shrewd sense told her that Jim was not as easy-minded as he pretended to be.

The clock on the mantelpiece struck ten.

" What time are you on ? "

" Ten-thirty."

" There you are, bolting your food again. You'll have indigestion one day ! "

" 'Course I shall, when I'm sixty," retorted Jim, buttering his toast.

" Perhaps you'll never reach sixty."

" Bright this morning, aren't you ? " laughed Jim. " Cheer up, come to the pictures with Nellie and me to-night. ' One Night of Love '—jolly good, I'm told."

" No thanks, Jim, I can't. There's Mr. Simkin's supper."

" Let him get his own supper—or go without."

" And young folks don't want old folks with them. But it's nice to be asked. Thanks, Jim," said Mrs. Brown, kissing the top of his young head, as he read the propped-up newspaper.

" Well, I never ! " exclaimed Jim.

" What now ? "

" Lord and Lady Savery have been killed in an aeroplane smash. And he's worth half a million."

" Well, it's no good to him now, poor gentleman."

" I knew 'em both. They were always going off from Victoria. He was a sport. He once gave me ten shillings when I got his skis into the train just in time. My, she was lovely, and quite young. Those poor kids, three of 'em. Anyhow, they'll get well looked after, with all that money."

" Money won't give them a mother, poor lambs," commented Mrs. Brown, brushing her son's uniform coat. " You'll be losing a button. I'll give it a stitch," she said, getting her work-basket.

" ' Lady Savery, before her marriage, was the beautiful Miss Elsa Hofmannstahl, younger daughter of Count von Hofmannstahl, former Austrian Minister in London. She was very popular in Society, and her beautiful voice made her greatly in demand for charity entertainments,' " read Jim. " So that was it!—they were always going on the 4.30 to Vienna. It's only a month ago I saw 'em go. They're very pally with old Gollwitzer."

" Who ? "

" Herr Gollwitzer—the famous conductor. They all went off together."

" You do know some people, Jim," said Mrs. Brown, proudly.

" Oh, I know 'em all right—but they don't know me, except a few of 'em. Old Gollwitzer knew me. Funny old boy ! He's a big, fat face, blue eyes and a large green hat with a feather in it. He's got a valet called Hans, who tucks him up like a nurse and clucks over him. Old Golly, as we call him, always gives you a shilling out of a purse. ' Boy, best thanks,' he says, as he tips you, and I always look at his hand, thinking how it can make a prima-donna hang on a note till she reels."

" What ideas you do have ! " said Mrs. Brown, snapping the thread, and spreading the jacket. " It's getting a bit shiny," she observed.

" Not nearly so shiny as my pants, but they've got to last another year, and my bottom's getting tight in 'em," said Jim, standing up.

She helped him into his jacket, running her hand over his back. She looked at his pink young neck, and the chestnut hair that would not lie flat, and her mother's heart swelled with pride in her good-looking boy. He deserved something better than Lizzie, so pert and uppish.

" S'long, Ma," said Jim, turning and giving her a hasty kiss. He pulled his cap jauntily over one eye, and the familiar curl struck out rebelliously.

" You do look full of mischief," said Mrs. Brown, as he reached the door.

" I am ! " he called, gaily, standing by the area steps. Then, seizing two empty milk bottles, he clapped them together, and singing " Rum-tiddly-umtum, rum-tum ! " did a little dance.

" Oh, be off with you ! " said Mrs. Brown.

" *Auf Wiedersehen !* " called Jim, sticking out his bottom, and raising his cap with Continental gallantry. Then he raced up the steps into the street.

CHAPTER II

THE PARRISH FAMILY

I

" AND I said to him, ' You can't expect a girl to go on waiting for ever.' "

" And what did he say, then ? " asked her companion, with bright eyes, picking up the tray on the service table.

" Oh, he just looked at me and said nothing," replied Lizzie Parrish. " But it went home all right."

The two girls moved out into the restaurant, carrying their trays to the tables. The place was crammed with people. At one end an orchestra composed of unkempt young men dressed in Tyrolean costume blared across this hall of gaudy Chinese decoration a negro-Judaic jazz tune from America. The band finished its piece with a terrific crescendo that brought applause from the small tables. At one of these a lonely young man, stirred to romance by the warmth, the brightness and the noise, smiled amiably at Miss Elizabeth Parrish, as she laid out the dishes on his table. He had asked for *Wiener Schnitzel*, and she had brought him lamb chops, but he said nothing, because he was not quite sure what *Wiener Schnitzel* was, and he did not want to offend the young lady. She was so pretty that he could not keep his eyes off her. As she leaned over him he noticed her slim waist, her neat, tight breasts, and a beautiful hand and wrist. Her complexion was glorious. She exuded a faint odour that intoxicated him.

The consumptive-looking leader of the orchestra had tossed back a lock of gipsy hair and was crooning:

> " Your hair, your lips,
> Your sad, sweet eyes
> Are Paradise
> For meeeeeeee——"

The young man at the table, very properly reared in a Coventry home, had not kissed a girl for five months. Now the music, the light, the hum of conversation and the proximity of the pretty slim waitress went to his head. At the next table sat three Jews and three Jewesses, with an almost metallic brightness of hair and eyes, who rocked parrot-like on their chairs under the possessive gloating of their companions. The young man felt desperate, but in a voice of timid politeness, he asked:

" Don't you get tired in this place ? "

" Yes, I'm glad when I get away," said Lizzie, laying a fork and knife. She knew exactly what would be the next question.

" When do you finish ? " he asked.

" At eleven," she said. " The coffee now, or later ? "

" Now, please."

She went away. His hands trembled as he picked up the knife and fork. It was obvious these Jews had what they wanted. Why should he be made nearly crazy? And he would be satisfied just to talk to her, perhaps to touch her.

> " One look, one laugh,
> One short, sweet kiss
> Will be such bliss
> For meeeeeeee——"

sang the crooner, and the saxophone trembled like a jelly-fish in a sea of sentiment.

The young man began to torture himself. Supposing he dared to ask her to meet him, and she was as kind as she was lovely ? It would be terrible to go back to Coventry to-morrow. The irony of it. He found it so difficult to get on to easy terms with the girls at home. He was so self-conscious and particular. It was strange that in one evening in London he saw just the kind of girl that was his type. He had brought a car up to London from the factory where he worked, and was going back to-morrow. He thought of Edith and Jennie and Jane, and half a dozen others at home, but they all lacked what this girl had. What was it she had ? He did not know, and would not have agreed had someone told him he was attracted by novelty. He thought he had never seen anyone so beautiful.

Here she was, back again, with the coffee. He smiled and gathered his courage.

" Can I see you after ? " he asked, in a half-throttled voice.

" After what ? " she demanded, with abrupt cruelty.

" When you've finished here. I mean could I—would you like——"

She saw the back of his neck grow red. He was a fresh-looking young man, scrubbed to a polish, and full of health.

" Thanks—but I'm engaged," she said, picking up the tray and departing.

The crooner crooned. One of the Jewesses gave a parrot-like screech, and he saw the hirsute hand of her companion caressingly slide up the encased fatness of her thigh. He felt a sudden rage against the whole of Jewry. Centuries of persecution and exile from their country had not deprived the Jew of two things, money and women. He always found them, somehow. The Gentiles were supposed to despise the Jews. It was more probably the Jews who despised the Gentiles for their ineffectiveness in procuring these two essentials.

So thought the young man from Coventry, jealousy now provoking loneliness. He was a virtuous young man, made more desperate by his innocence.

The waitress was back again. Her loveliness was a torture.

But he would snub her if she said anything to him, and restore his self-respect. She hovered at his side a moment, and he was conscious of the vibration of her beauty.

"Would you like any sauce?" she asked, above the galloping fortissimo of a Middle European on the grand piano who transformed a *Rhapsodie Hongroise* into an *Epilepsie Honteuse.*

"Oh—er, thank you," he said, weakly capitulating.

"Are you a Londoner?" she asked, smiling now.

He melted at once under the warming ray.

"No, I'm from Coventry."

"I thought you weren't."

"How did you know?"

"Oh!—one does," said Miss Parrish, with a wise smile.

And then before he could recapture his senses and talk to her, she was off to the Jews' table, and smiling at them as they gave her an order.

Mr. Fred Roper did not know what the orchestra was playing, neither did he know what he was eating. It was half-past ten, and in half an hour this beautiful creature would be leaving the restaurant and going home, and he would be going back to the dingy hotel near St. Pancras, and down a long corridor with other men's and women's shoes put outside the bedroom doors; the neat and the clumsy in pairs, symbolic of the intimacy behind those doors. He was twenty-three and decent, and frustrated; a battleground of frank Nature and Nonconformist morality.

The orchestra played a Viennese waltz, every bar impregnated with sensuous vertigo. Suddenly she was back again, at the little serving table behind him.

"Anything else?" she asked, appearing at his side.

He held the menu card with a trembling hand. He must have something else.

"A Peach Melba," he said, looking up into her face.

She gave him a wonderful smile, the first warm smile, revealing the loveliest teeth between red lips.

"I'd know you weren't a Londoner. We call it Peche Melba—paish. You don't mind, do you?" she asked.

"Thank you—I expect you could teach me a lot," he said, in innocent gratitude.

"I expect I could," she retorted, coyly, and went off.

He looked at the clock. It was just five minutes to eleven. One of the Jews had lit a large cigar. Something the orchestra was playing gave him great delight. The girl at his side wanted to talk and he commanded silence with a peremptory wave of the hand. He was fat, with treble chins covered in grey-blue stubble, but the rapture on his face temporarily transformed him from an ape into a human being. The pretty little Jewess opposite to him was also enraptured. They listened and gazed at one another in a transport of delight. When the piece was finished they applauded so deliriously that the conductor gave them a special bow. It was the only serious music he had played that night, and he felt grateful to them for their discernment.

Mr. Roper's waitress had returned, but not to his table. He observed her at a distance, and thought her even more lovely. Her ankles were slim, her feet tiny, and her profile was flawless. Also her hair from behind was entrancing. She looked a lady, he thought.

Ah, now she was coming to him. She smiled. He would talk to her and perhaps——

But she asked in a business-like tone "Anything more?" and when he shook his head, pushed a folded bill against his plate, and said, "I'm going now. Good night! I'm off duty at eleven." She smiled, lingered a moment, and then left him.

He was so astonished at this abrupt finish to his dream that he could not get out a word, and saw her vanish with a sinking heart. Why had she been so nice to him? Well, he had been a fool to think anything of it. They were told to be nice to customers, and not too encouraging.

He picked up his bill. She might have waited for a tip. He would have given her a good one. Now he only gave half what he had intended, since some other girl would get it. He got up and made his way to the cash desk, where a

porter stood on guard to see that customers did not forget
to pay. He walked slowly out through the swing doors.

> " If any girl
> With a curl
> Wants a boy——"

The crooning died away as he ascended to the street level.

The crowd on the pavement made him feel more lonely
than ever. All these people were with friends, all the young
men had their girls. The theatres were beginning to empty.
He watched the limousines with their bright occupants,
men in dress clothes, expensively coiffured women in their
evening gowns, some with jewels glittering at their throats.
He felt himself to be a country cousin. He lacked aggres-
siveness. It was not enough to be a nice, pleasant-mannered
young man. He should have been more blunt with that
waitress instead of smirking and grinning at her.

He sauntered along. There was nothing to do but go
back to his hotel. Lonely young men visiting London
could, of course, go in the direction of Piccadilly—but he
revolted at the thought.

He turned up by the corner of the restaurant into a side
street which would take him back to Shaftesbury Avenue,
and towards his Bloomsbury hotel. A youth, emerging
hastily from a pair of swing doors, ran into him, apologised
and walked on. A sign above the doors said *Staff Entrance.*

He halted and stared at the doors. The waitresses coming
off duty must come out that way. She would be coming
out soon. Dare he wait and see ? He had never in his
life hung about doors waiting for girls to come out. But
for once there would be no harm in it, just to see if she did
come out, and if, finding him there, she took any notice of him.

He halted and stood up against the wall. It was five
minutes past eleven. On the opposite pavement there
were two other men, also watching the doors. They were
obviously waiting for their girls. Fred Roper lit a cigarette.
His fingers were cold, and his hands trembled. He cursed

himself for a timid fool, set his face and tried to look non-chalant. A girl came out and one of the men stepped across the road, raised his hat and gave her a kiss. They walked off arm in arm. Two more girls came out, chattering, and no one greeted them.

" And I got it for seven-and-eleven—three shillings off," said one of them.

" Well, it looks a treat ! " replied her companion.

They disappeared. Three times the doors opened and closed, but she did not appear. It was nearly ten minutes past eleven. Had he missed her after all ? He would wait until a quarter-past.

II

Elizabeth Parrish had an unshakable belief in romance. It sustained her through the drabness of her daily life, and fed her with hope of an exciting future. The twopenny library and the cinema provided a world of illusion. She did not believe in fairy princes, she believed in princes as a reality. She had never spoken to one, she had only seen one once at a distance, when he came to a workers' sports meeting to distribute the prizes, but had he stepped down from the dais and said " Good afternoon, Miss Parrish," she would not have lost her head. She would have talked to him quite naturally. For by now she was convinced that she was of a different blood from these people with whom she had to live and work.

She was careful, of course, to let them have no inkling of the difference, but some of them, the more intelligent ones, sensed it. It was once reported to her, through her mother, who had spoken a little derisively but a little proudly, that a neighbour had said, " Lizzie's got an aristocratic manner. She looks one of the toffs." Since that day Elizabeth Parrish had carefully cultivated an aristocratic manner. She never laughed loudly, she never hurried, she never stood in a queue, or fought to get on a bus. " I'd rather go without than scramble for a thing," she often said.

All this somewhat perplexed Jim. He had a liking for

standing in queues. " Oh, come on, we'll get in in half an hour," he would say, when they found a long queue waiting at the cinema. " I wouldn't wait for the Resurrection," retorted Elizabeth, scornfully. " Some people have no dignity ! " So they walked and walked, and were finally driven to sit down in a café and listen to the orchestra.

There had been one unpleasant evening when Jim had rebelled, and insisted on joining the queue. She left him and let him wait alone. By way of a rebuke she almost ruined herself by taking a five shilling seat. It not only made him look silly, but was a hint that seats could usually be obtained, at a price. When he had not called round for two days, she became apprehensive, but her courage did not desert her. An anxious week passed, and then one night he was there, waiting, as usual, for her coming off duty. Jim smiled at her nervously ; wisely, she made no comment on his absence.

It was pitiable how some people could not rise above their surroundings. And it was undeniable that blood would out. Her sisters, her brothers, and her parents were common, distressingly common. They did not know how to speak or to dress. Everything about them was dreary and untidy. She hated the way her brother Herbert always had a cigarette drooping in the corner of his mouth, and the way he coughed.

" Can't you put your hand in front of your mouth ? " she once remonstrated.

" Why ? " he asked, staring at her with his fish eyes.

" Gentlemen don't cough in the face of ladies," she replied, freezingly.

" Well, I'm no gentleman, and you're no lady, and gob's gob. So there ! " he retorted, and coughed again, with ear-splitting coarseness.

Her father, too, was impossible. He was always talking about his bunions, hateful word, and would take off his boots and rest his stockinged feet on a chair. He also had the habit of sitting about in his shirt sleeves, reading the paper. As soon as he came in he took off his jacket and sat down in his waistcoat and sleeves. He sat at the table for his meals like that.

" I shall do what I like in my own 'ouse," he declared, stoutly, on an occasion when Lizzie had succeeded in getting her mother to make a mild protest.

Alas, her own mother was no better. She was good-natured and industrious, and an excellent mother, as Lizzie was ready to admit ; true, she had lamentable lapses. She had a passion for walking about in loose slippers, and keeping her sleeves rolled up, revealing fat, raddled arms. Her good-natured face was marred by loose-fitting false teeth, and, unfortunately, she was always laughing. Worse, she had an unbreakable habit, when cooking, of putting her finger into the mess and licking it ; and her fingers were not always clean.

Many things puzzled Lizzie until one day she stumbled upon a clue, and then everything was simple, not only simple but abundantly accounted for. She was the only member of the family with any appearance. Her mother was a fat, snub-nosed woman, with an amiable face in which her eyes were too small and her ears too large. Her father was just coarse, and, objectionable as the word was, she must use it, he was beery. Not that he drank unduly, but his stockinged feet, his belching, the way he blew the juice out of his old pipe, and let the black hair on his chest emerge from his unbuttoned shirt, made him disgusting. He mocked at her, and alluded to her as " Her Ladyship."

As for Susan and Gertie, they were incorrigible. They rode on the back of youths' motor cycles. They compressed their fat posteriors into men's khaki shorts and went hiking. They were boisterously hearty, had boiled lobster complexions with untidy hair, and laughed uproariously at everything. They were always humming and chewing something. They spent every penny on their clothes, always too loud, and had dozens of " boys " who were always whistling them out.

" Can't he knock at the door and ask for you properly ? " said Lizzie, irritated beyond endurance one day when a clod had stood whistling outside the house.

"S'pose you'd wait for the Dook to send his car and shuvver!" retorted Gertie. "Can't think why you take up with a railway porter, 'im pushing a barrer all day!"

"That's none of your business," replied Lizzie, coldly.

"An' it's none of yours, Lady Elizabeth, if Bill likes to stand and whistle on the pavement for me."

So Elizabeth gave up trying to reform Gertie and Susan. Susan was just an echo of Gertie, less lumpy and boisterous. They were inseparable and worked together in a cigarette factory. It was bitterness to Lizzie to know that they earned double her wages. They had actually had a fortnight's holiday abroad, and had been to Ostend and Brussels. "Siv-ooh-play" was now the sisters' response when in a polite humour—"French for 'If you please,'" they informed Mrs. Parrish. They were generous with their money, and on festive occasions gave Lizzie presents that moved her to an unhappy state of contrition and irritation.

Bert, however, was the secret trial. Bert and Gert; how she hated those names! Herbert was a year her senior, a lout in appearance and manners. He had fat red lips and open nostrils. He sucked his teeth and coughed, and was always scratching his legs. He was crafty in earning money, for he had a gift for salesmanship and made a good income as agent for a sewing-machine company. "You can always bamboozle women, if you talk to them soft," he confided, explaining his success. "Make' em think you're gone on 'em, and you've got 'em in the 'oller of your 'and!" Thereupon he winked and hitched himself. "Sewing-machines and sex—the combination gets 'em!"

It was a strange thing that, whereas Lizzie found him odious, other girls seemed fascinated by him. He treated them outrageously, and his allure increased rather than suffered from this reputation.

Yes, looking at her family all round, they were a vulgar lot, and showed none of the innate refinements which she had always cultivated. And in physical appearance she was an unaccountable breakaway from the Parrishes. Only her mother's good complexion and hair could be found in her. He figure, her way of walking and talking, her taste and the constant attempt to improve herself put her apart from the rest of the family.

At first all this had not seemed singular to her. Living in a world of day-dream and romance, she had never really belonged to the household in Lynam Street. To most of the young men living in the neighbourhood she showed an unbreakable reserve. " Stuck-up " they called her, and she grew proud of the epithet. The young men she did take notice of had to possess social as well as physical graces. There was young Marriott, for instance. True, his people kept a fish and chip shop, which, for some reason, perhaps not unconnected with a suggestion of comedy, and music-hall jokes, was regarded in working-class quarters as in the lowest category of business. The grocer with an off-licence looked down on the fish-shop, which filled the street of an evening with greasy fumes.

Nevertheless, young Henry Marriott rose above this handicap. Despite the fact that he worked in a garage he was always well-groomed in the evening. His black wavy hair was well-greased, he shaved carefully, dressed in good taste and had suave manners. Some of them called him " The Sheik," but this was jealousy rather than criticism. His neat but powerful body, and his dark eyes and sensuous mouth all expressed a manly vigour. His somewhat heavy hands, strong from his work, had a potency felt by the girls he swung round the dance-halls and put in and out of the motor-cars he borrowed for odd excursions. He had incongruous tastes, such as all-in wrestling and playing the piano. He knew by heart odd bits of poetry and would tell you the names of the stars, but he also knew every kind of drink and every aspect of betting, whether on horses, dogs or football teams. His interest in girls was frankly animal. He left them under no illusion regarding the price of his attentions.

Lizzie found him attractive though she kept him firmly in his place. She was flattered by his obvious thrall to her beauty. " Liz, you've got no right to be so lovely, it isn't fair on a poor devil," he once said, holding her in the vice of his hands, and looking deep down into her eyes. Then he kissed her, and she smacked his face. " Cat ! " he laughed. " I'd twist any other girl's head off for that ! "

" You won't mine, Henry," she retorted.

" No, I shan't yours," he said, baffled by the hard core of resistance in her.

Jim's attraction was quite different. He was sunshine, sheer good nature, light-skinned and brown-eyed. He rippled with laughter and had a boisterous goodwill to all the earth. His hand was always ready to do something helpful. He picked up a tumbled yelling infant, or piloted an old woman across the road, or left a note for someone, or called at a shop for a neighbour. Lizzie was often annoyed to see him " put upon." " You're too soft," she often said, and the way he doted on his mother, and dragged about with him his drab sister, infuriated her. " You must love hospitals," she said once, in allusion to his frequent visits to some friend in a sick ward. " Might be there myself one day," he replied, " then would you keep away ? " " Don't be silly," she retorted.

Like Henry Marriott he had strange contradictions in his character. He had a passion for physical culture and boxing. He was always getting a bruised eye, a broken lip or a thickened ear at the Lads' Club, and all his pocket money went on strange apparatus for enlarging his chest, increasing his biceps and fetching out new muscles down his torso, which he would set like a piece of corrugated iron. " Feel here," he would say proudly. " No, put your fingers there ! " And then a hard lump would come swelling up, and his face would break into a grin of proud delight.

There was an anatomical sheet pinned up in his bedroom, with neat figures recording successive measurements all over the body. " You'll alter your shape until you'll not know yourself one day," observed Lizzie, when the advent of another quarter of an inch on some part of him was announced.

He was, as Lizzie proudly knew, a beautiful physical object, pink and white, with velvety flesh, and a boyish exuberance in the human machine he had perfected with gloves, weights, springs and bars. " He's always swilling water about," complained Mrs. Brown, mopping up in the scullery, but her complaint was really a commendation, for " Better'n swilling beer," she added.

But there were oddities and obstinacies in Jim, little things, it is true, but things that almost infuriated Lizzie with him. " It isn't pins and needles, it's pins and nails that you suffer from," she complained, for he would carry two or three symbolic pins on the lapel of his coat, a pin proclaiming membership of some League of Strength, a pin with an emblem of gloves in a ring, denoting his Pimlico Club. " It's so vulgar ! Gentlemen don't walk about with club pins in their coats," protested Lizzie. " Well, I'm not a gentleman, so what does it matter," he replied. But he removed the pins under protest while with Lizzie, and put them back when he left her. " She's funny that way," he commented to his sister, " but it doesn't hurt anybody."

To the offence of pins he added nails. He had good, filbert-shaped nails on a slender hand, but for some reason he would not cut them, and wore them provokingly long. " Chinese claws, I call 'em," complained Lizzie. He maintained a stubborn and baffling reticence regarding his nails. Lizzie never could find out why he kept them so long. There were moments when she suspected a secret cult. Her objection was weakened by the fact that he kept his nails scrupulously clean. " Must take up all your spare time," she said, acidly. " Keeps me busy between trains," he replied, affably.

She had often seen him box, deriving a certain sadistic pleasure from seeing the punishment taken by this body she regarded possessively, and she was thrilled by the dynamic ferocity with which he fought, in such complete contrast with the gentleness of his nature. She regarded all fighting displays as vulgar, and attended under a show of protest. She allowed herself to be taken to amateur displays, when Jim was boxing, but firmly refused to go to professional shows with him. " No real lady would be seen in such places," she said. "We all know the sort of women who sit at a ringside," she said, crushingly.

"Oh, they're not all bad," responded Jim. "Some of them are sports!"

"Sports!" reiterated Lizzie, witheringly. "Jim, don't use that horrid word."

"Well, I can't call 'em sportsmen, can I, and sports-women sounds daft."

"Daft—there you go again. Don't use slang!"

Next to boxing there was his passion for music and riding horses. This again tried Lizzie sorely. To please him she went to the Queen's Hall Promenade Concerts, and stood until her feet ached, listening to the orchestra. He liked the strangest pieces. "Isn't it marvellous?" he would cry, applauding deliriously. "Well, it doesn't seem to have any tune in it to me," she replied, struggling with physical fatigue and mental boredom. "Oh, but that last Movement!" he exclaimed, his eyes shining, and added, "Liz, you look lovely to-night—that green velvet just sets you off."

So you could not be angry with him, despite all his talk about "movements." At home, on the rickety old piano with a fretwork and silk front, he would pick out a "movement" and explain it. "Yes," she would say. "Yes, I see!" But she didn't see, and sometimes her pretence was too thin, and Jim would look sorrowfully at her. "I'm afraid I've no ear," she confessed. And then he leaned over, and bit her ear gently, saying, "You've the loveliest ear in the whole world," and so the awkward moment would pass. There was some compensation in the fact that going to the Queen's Hall gave them an air of distinction. "We're going to the Promenade Concert—they're playing the Emperor Concerto," she would say to the other waitresses. It proved that Jim was no ordinary railway porter.

Then there was his love of riding. She was jealous of the friendship between young Mr. Lincoln, a worker at the Lads' Club, and Jim. Mr. Lincoln was a gentleman, and his influence was all to Jim's advantage. But she was a little jealous of the world into which Jim stepped on his visits to Mr. Lincoln's house in Surrey. They went riding at week-ends, and under his tuition Jim had developed into a fine horseman and had won a cup for jumping, at a gymkhana.

His good looks were matched by his good manners; he was a natural gentleman, and gentlemanliness was a thing on which Lizzie, with her craving for refinement, and her deep instinct for the social graces, set much store. There were moments when she could see Jim, properly dressed, passing for " one of the top-drawer class " as she phrased it, but these were moments when he did not shock her by appearing with a pin in his lapel, or a bruised lip. She was proud of Jim's dog-like devotion to her, but his very patience and gentleness stirred something in her that often made her lash him with her tongue, hoping for a combat of wills. But he only smiled and gave her a quiet answer. " No doubt, old girl, you've got worked up," he would say, gently.

Yes, she did get worked up. She was no ordinary girl, and ambition for Jim and for herself burned ardently in her. It was ever a sore point that he was only a porter. With his looks and excellent manners, he was worth something better. " Well, it's safe, anyhow, and interesting—you see life at Victoria," he said, when she urged him to get something better.

The real cause behind this playing for security was his mother. She wanted his wages, safe and regular. But for her they would have been married now. She was twenty-seven and it was time she was settled. They had been engaged for three years, ever since Jim had come of age. " Wait a bit, I really can't manage it yet," he said, and it was in vain she protested that, with their joint wages, they would manage very well. " I'm not having my wife go to work," he replied, firmly. " When we've got a house you'll stay in it."

" Dear me, you talk like a Turk," she had replied, laughing.

" Well, Turk or no Turk, no woman's going to keep me ! I'm old-fashioned that way. You'll have more than enough to do with the house, and me, and the kids."

" Jim, that's not very—very delicate," she said, hesitatingly, feeling that modesty called for protest.

" No ? Well, sorry. But all the same, it won't be home if there aren't kids in the house," he replied, and then, a little self-conscious, gave her a kiss.

Lizzie never really intended to go on working after marriage. She made the gesture to reveal her growing impatience at waiting. Marrying the man she loved meant release from this work she detested, even though it entailed less money to spend on herself. She must get away from her home and its appalling atmosphere. She had not one thing in common with her family—and why should she ? For she had found a complete explanation of her difference.

Her irrepressibly romantic nature had been quick to seize certain facts and to adjust them to aid an escape from sordid reality. She had always been certain of an aristocratic strain in her nature. Everyone said she looked a lady, and she possessed an instinctive love of beautiful things, a delicacy of taste and thought that made her life in the Parrish home a purgatory. She hated the thought that the same blood flowed in her veins as in those of her loutish brother or of her coarse father. There were brief revelations of former beauty in her mother, doubtless the source of her own inheritance, but whence came this sense of superiority, of inborn, aristocratic taste ? The question had long been put, and remained without answer, until one day her mother had supplied the clue. She had been looking at the evening newspaper.

" Well now, if the Marquis of Cranford isn't dead ! " she exclaimed, pushing her glasses more firmly on her nose.

" Whose 'e, anyhow ? " asked Gertie, ironing the blouse she was going out in.

" One of Ma's old flames—going into mourning, I suppose ? " jeered Bert, probing his ear with a match-stick.

" You didn't know him ? " asked Lizzie, peering over her mother's shoulder at the picture of the dead marquis.

" I should think I did ! I'll never forget 'im ! He was a bright young man, I can tell you. Him and his pretty sister used to come and stay at the Moxfields', where I used to go in and help, when your aunt fell ill—she was cook there. He was Lord Wyford then, and I'll never forget 'ow one morning there was a telephone call—'e was in bed still, if you please, and I had to go up to his room, as Mr. Jones— he was the butler—was shaving 'isself. ' Go up and tell his lordship he is wanted pertically on the telephone,' he said to me. So I went, and down his lordship came in a dressing-gown. ' Good morning ! ' he said to me, as cheerful as could be-like, and picked up the telephone. And what do you think the poor young man heard ? His father had been killed that very morning—thrown off his horse. And there he stood, white to the lips. ' Not bad news, I 'ope, my lord ? ' I couldn't help saying. ' Yes, very bad. My father's been killed. Please ask Jones to come up to my room, and don't say anything to Mrs. Moxfield.' Mrs. Moxfield was his aunt. I've never forgotten that morning. He was such a nice, bright young gentleman," said Mrs. Parrish.

" When was all this ? " asked Lizzie, quickly.

" Oh, before you was born, when your aunt was at Colonel Moxfield's, an' I used to go in and 'elp when they 'ad company. They was so poor they'd only got two maids and doddering old Jones. It was a good day for them when 'e married Miss Moxfield."

" Who—that butler ? " asked Bert.

" No, of course not ! The Marquis."

Lizzie took the newspaper from her mother and read the obituary account. She looked intently at the portrait of the dead nobleman. Her heart thumped in her breast. The portrait made the conviction doubly sure. Her aristocratic nature was no longer a mystery. With suppressed self-control, affecting a casual tone, she said : " Was that the only time you saw him, mother ? "

" Of course not—'e was always there, when he was courting Miss Moxfield. ' Ah, Parrish,' he used to say in his cheery style."

" Did 'e ever slip you a quid ? " asked Bert.

" That's more like ! " commented Gertie, putting the iron on the rest.

" That 'e didn't ! You never said nowt about it to me, anyhow," said Mr. Parrish, sucking at his pipe.

Lizzie calculated the Marquis had died aged fifty-four. Her mother was fifty. Twenty-seven years ago they would have been twenty-seven and twenty-three respectively. Yes, it was possible. It was more than possible. It explained everything. No wonder she had nothing in common with her brother and sisters, both younger than she ; no wonder she had the manners and bearing, a delicacy of mind and taste, that made her feel out of place in these surroundings of mean streets and common people. " Lizzie, you'd be at home in a palace," Jim had said to her after she had carried off some delicate situation with grace and tact. The affair with Lord Wyford explained everything.

CHAPTER III

CHANCE

I

LIZZIE was thinking of all this as she took off her apron and cap in the staff dressing-room. It was time she ceased to be a waitress at the beck and call of any Tom, Dick and Harry. Sometimes she wondered, despite the fact that she loved him, whether she had been wise in accepting Jim. He was not very ambitious, and seemed quite content to be a railway porter. All day he saw rich people going abroad on expensive holidays, and all the wonderful opportunities for seeing the world by rail, air and sea aroused in him no thought of rebellion. His highest ambition was for them to spend their honeymoon abroad. " Perhaps in Lugano," he would say with a grin, and she knew by his voice that he had no real belief in that possibility. " You can be happy wherever you are, and wretched wherever you are. Places don't make people. I see plenty of them with more worry on their faces than luggage on my truck. They go everywhere and see everything, but they're always looking at themselves," said Jim, when she complained of the dullness of life.

" Well—I'd like the chance," retorted Lizzie. " I never want to see a tray or apron again."

But nothing she said ever stirred Jim to rebellion. You would imagine that pushing a truck with a lot of rich people's luggage on it was one of the exciting ways of spending one's life. Perhaps she had been foolish to tie herself up with Jim, for all his kindness and affection, and his attractive ways. There were plenty of young men who seemed eager to take her about, quite nice young men in good positions.

Lizzie tucked a wisp of hair under her hat, and gave her nose a rub with the powder pad. She looked closely in the mirror, which always restored her faith in herself. The young man at her table to-night had been rather pathetic in his eagerness to get off with her. He was obviously from the provinces, and lonely in London. He had a cheerful, honest face. She wondered what he was, and how much he made a week, and whether he had a girl at home. Would he be waiting at the staff entrance, as they so often were with the slightest encouragement ? There was something exciting in the speculation although she had no intention of going with him if he was silly enough to be waiting.

Lizzie said good night to the other girls, and passed out through the lobby into the street. She looked swiftly around, and there, not to her surprise, stood the young man at her table, smiling and raising his hat.

" Oh, it's you ! " she said, curtly.

" Good evening. I hope you don't mind," he began, as he walked at her side. " Perhaps you'll let me see you home—if you must go home yet," he blurted forth, with desperate courage.

" Well, I don't know as I ought to encourage you. I don't even know your name," said Lizzie. " I don't walk about with strange men."

" My name's Roper—Fred Roper. I hope you don't think——"

He did not finish the sentence, for at that moment a young man crossed the road and walked briskly up to his companion.

o his dismay the stranger, after raising his hat, linked his
rm with the young lady's.

" I never expected you to-night," said Lizzie, taken by
urprise at Jim's appearance. " I thought you were on duty."

" We changed shifts yesterday. I came off at eight,"
xplained Jim. He looked at the young man and then at
Lizzie. " A friend ? " he asked.

Lizzie did not lose her head, and she felt sorry for the
oung man, whom she had encouraged a little.

" It's Mr. Roper," she said, and then turning to him, and
ooking calmly into his eyes, " Jane'll be out in a few minutes.
he was changing when I came out. Good night ! "

She smiled, and Mr. Roper, after involuntary hesitation,
omprehended the position.

" Oh—er, thank you. Good night," he responded, and
laying up to the deception, moved in the direction of the
taff entrance.

" Well, I never ! " exclaimed Jim, with a laugh.

" What's amusing you ? " asked Lizzie.

" I thought that fellow was trying to pick you up ! "

" Jim, you do have some vulgar ideas ! I would like to
ee him try ! " exclaimed Lizzie, spiritedly.

He looked at her, a slight flush heightening the beauty of
er face.

" Well, there's plenty of Henry Marriotts around," he said,
oggedly.

She gave him a quick, frightened glance, and then recovered
erself.

" Why do you mention him—not jealous are you ? " she
emanded, archly.

" Yes, quite a lot ! "

" You silly boy," she laughed, pressing his arm.

They halted at Piccadilly Circus, waiting for a pause in the
raffic. It was a quarter-past eleven, and the theatre audiences
vere out. A line of cars, filled with ladies in furs and jewels,
noved slowly by them. It was the height of the London
eason. Lizzie looked enviously at the younger women,
hose who were just " out " and had been presented at Court.

That should have been her lot, instead of which she was
waitress, hoping to get married to a railway porter. Som
of the debutantes were such insignificant creatures, despi
their lovely clothes. And not a man among them cou
hold the candle to Jim. She glanced at him, proud of th
firm-faced, square-shouldered squire of hers. And h
catching her eye, smiled back.

"James is a long time bringing the car round. Shall v
walk?" he asked.

"Yes—it will be quite a change!" she replied, laughin

They slipped in and out of the traffic, and, gaining th
opposite pavement, he marched her ahead.

"Where are you going?" she asked, for he had not turne
the usual way they took down towards St. James's Par
where they always stood on that lovers' bridge betwee
heaven and earth, though actually between the Foreign Offic
and Buckingham Palace.

"To the Café Royal," he answered.

"The Café Royal!" she reiterated. "But we can't go there!

"Why not?" he demanded, gaily. "You can get a *ca,
au lait* for a shilling, and see life."

This was quite beyond her experience. The very nam
was frightening, as well as the lavish portals, and the pompou
commissionaire.

"How do you know?" she asked, fearfully, "you'v
never been there!"

"Yes, I have. I was there last week," said Jim, enjoyin
the astonishment this statement created.

"You! Why, who took you?"

"A gentleman," he replied, secretively.

"Why?"

"Who and why!" mocked Jim. "I suppose he liked m
face. Don't think I've joined a crook gang, do you? Now
here we go!"

He pushed her through the swing doors, piloted her boldl
through a flower-laden lobby of marble and gilt, and entere
the crowded floor of the café. They squeezed themselves i
at a table. The lights, the heat and the buzz of conversatio

verwhelmed Lizzie at first. A gentleman at her elbow addressed her pleasantly. There was an air of general friendliness and soon they were all talking freely. The amiable foreign gentleman on Lizzie's left asked her if she had ever been to Vienna. He might just as well have asked if she had ever been to the Moon, but she had the presence of mind to say " No, not yet, but I hope to."

" What a hope ! " whispered Jim, facetiously.

She gave him a reproving nudge. The gentleman was speaking.

" Oh, then, dear lady, you can't know what the gay life is. The lights, the music, the beautiful women—it brings back an echo of life in St. Petersburg, in the days of our Tsar."

" You are Russian ? " asked Jim, leaning forward.

The perspiring, bald gentleman fumbled in his pocket and brought out a small, jewelled box from which he took a card.

" Permit me, Madam," he said, presenting his card. " And should you ever come to Vienna I would be honoured ! "

Lizzie took the card and glanced at it. Her heart almost stopped. Was it possible ? " Prince Nicolai Zermizov " she read.

" That is most kind of you," replied Lizzie, passing the card to Jim.

" Charmed ! " said Prince Zermizov. " Now let us drink to our reunion there. Waiter ! Waiter ! "

Time fled on winged minutes. At a quarter to one Prince Zermizov had completed an outline of his astonishing adventures—the splendour, the hardships of a life in which he had experienced princely fortune and the exile's poverty. At last the Prince said he must go. Jim called for his bill also, and since the waiter put both accounts on one bill, there was a polite scramble between the Prince and Jim, who won. It was nine shillings, and when Jim airily produced a ten-shilling note and waved the waiter away, Lizzie's alarm was swallowed up by her admiration of Jim's bravado in the face of such a blow. He behaved like a perfect gentleman, as one should behave before a Prince.

They took leave of each other. The Prince raised Lizzie's hand to his lips and kissed it. He bowed ceremoniously to Jim, and Jim bowed back, and then he went.

Lizzie and Jim followed at a distance. They looked at each other a little unsteadily, feeling that they were treading in an unreal but expensive world.

" Nice old boy ! " said Jim, as though he met princes every day.

" Charming," responded Lizzie, catching the Prince's mode. She felt in her bag to make sure the visiting card was there. She would show it to the girls at work.

" You quite got the old boy, Lizz," said Jim, proudly.

" Don't be silly," retorted Lizzie, preening at the compliment. " I'd like to know who brought you to a place like this, and got you into such expensive habits."

" Well, if you must know—it was Mr. Lincoln. He'd been riding in a Point-to-Point, and had won. So the next night he took three of us out to celebrate and gave us dinner here. You're glad we came, aren't you ? "

The commissionaire saluted and said, " Taxi, sir ? " as they came out. Before Lizzie knew what had happened Jim had pushed her into the taxi, tipped the commissionaire and given the driver their address.

" Jim—you must be crazy ! " exclaimed Lizzie, faint with fear and excitement. Nine shillings, and now this !

He slipped an arm round her. " We must see a bit of life some time," he said, " and if I didn't take you around, somebody else might."

She had laid her head on his shoulder, her body relaxed against his in the darkness of the taxi, but suddenly she started up and looked at him.

" Now what do you mean by that ? You don't think I run around, do you ? " she asked, challengingly.

" Now don't get excited."

" Somebody's been talking—well, what have they told you ? "

He was on the point of mentioning Henry Marriott, but restrained himself. Instead he pulled Lizzie closer to him, and kissed her averted face.

" Not angry ? " he asked.

" Yes," she replied.

He held her face with his strong hand, laughed into her eyes, and then slowly kissed her, his young mouth covering hers as he held her in a long embrace. The strength and passion of him dispersed her resentful mood. She knew well she loved him as she could love no other man. There was something elemental in him, a fresh simplicity which, while it often irritated her sophisticated nature, and disturbed the aura of romanticism in which she enveloped her life, held her captive despite her keen critical faculty. There were brief moments of fright when she thought she might lose him, and when she feared her passion for improving him might arouse revolt. Beneath all his boyish ardour there was a hard core of masculinity, and her woman's instinct warned her of the limit of experiment.

So now, as she lay in his arms while the taxi glided through the empty, shining streets, she made no further allusion to his uncomfortable remark. Was he referring to that silly young man who had waited for her at the entrance, or had she allowed Henry Marriott to pay her too much attention ? She had no illusions concerning Henry and the ultimate goal to which he confidently aspired, but he communicated an air of romance, spiced with libertinism, and was always at hand with a suggestion for going somewhere and doing something. One of the many unfortunate drawbacks of Jim's deplorable work was the irregularity of his hours. She was often stranded by the vagaries of his duties, and the temptation to seek another avenue was sometimes too much. But whatever her foolishness in this matter, there was only one man who commanded her heart, and with whom her whole future was bound.

" Forgiven me ? " he asked, after a long silence.

" There's nothing to forgive, darling," she replied, pressing her cheek against his. " It's been a lovely evening—but I don't like you wasting money," she added.

He laughed, pressed her to him and kissed her again.

" What's money for ? It's only made of paper these

days, and paper's made to burn," he cried. "Why, look at our lovely Mr. Simkin, poor miserable devil! He's got over three hundred pounds in the bank and can't afford a hot water-bottle. One day he'll die of influenza or be blown sky-high with a bomb, and some relation who hates him like poison'll go and celebrate in Paris. Now, if ever I have money, I'll blow it in and get my enjoyment out of it."

"Don't say 'blow it in'—that's slang, Jim," said Lizzie, unable to let the phrase pass.

"Make it fly, then—go on the razzle!"

"Razzle—that's worse, Jim!"

"Blow, razzle, bust—whatever you like to call it, my girl!" affirmed Jim.

"And you're one of the steadiest men alive—that's why I'm marrying you," said Lizzie.

He laughed at her, and thought how lovely she was in this flitting light from the street lamps.

"Is that the only reason?" he challenged. Then his eye catching the taxi-meter, which registered three shillings and sixpence, he suddenly banged on the glass for the driver to stop. "Lord, we'll have to walk the rest! I've only four shillings in the whole world," he laughed, opening the door. "The Prince Zermizov did me in. Those hand-kissing blokes are always slick."

They alighted on the pavement. Jim parted with his last four shillings. It was one o'clock. The long Pimlico street was deserted except for a coffee-stall, a policeman and a cat. They had ten minutes' walk before them, but it was a clear and moonlit night. Jim loved this long vista of dingy porticos and fantastic chimney-pots mocking the moon.

> "The Night has a thousand eyes
>   And the Day but one;
>   Yet the light of the bright world dies
>   With the dying sun."

he hummed.

"Where did you get that?" asked Lizzie.

"I forget—but I like it, don't you?"

" Yes, Jim. You're a strange mixture. You quote poetry, you get black eyes, you're content all your life to be a porter, you dream of going abroad for your holidays, you won't save—and you won't get married ! " exclaimed Lizzie.

" Eh, what's this ? Let me tell you something," retorted Jim. " We'd be married to-morrow but for two things, one of your making and one of mine. Perhaps they're both of my making. I'm not going to let any wife of mine go out to work—I want home comforts. And I'm not going to leave Mother stranded. So until I get ten shillings a week more we'll just have to wait."

Lizzie made no reply. She knew how truculent he could be on this subject. She was twenty-seven and quite three years his senior, and three years was a long time in a pretty woman's life. She could have been married a dozen times, the restaurant provided plenty of contacts, but restless and ambitious as she was, there was only this one man she loved. His happy, easy nature held her heart, she knew the value of his steady loyalty, but she could not help waging a losing war against his serene satisfaction with life. He had no ambition, he made no mental effort to change his place in life, and yet, unfairly she felt, he was happy and tranquil, and she was worried and restless.

They parted at the door of her home. An open window on the upper floor allowed the stillness of the side street to be broken by the vigorous snoring of Mr. Parrish. Down on the basement window-sill a famished cat was licking the neck of a milk bottle left out for the dairyman. Two loose newspaper sheets were blown about by a night wind. They heard a tug-boat hoot down on the Thames. The mean street with its dowdy fronts, grim area rails and gimcrack chimney-pots filled Lizzie with a fierce hatred of life. She knew how she could blossom in propitious circumstances, how her beauty, her aristocratic instinct and her sense of society would take full advantage of a brighter scene. But with each year the hope of escape receded, her hatred of all this meanness increased.

Lizzie put her key in the latch and quietly opened the front door. Jim stepped into the small parlour, took Lizzie in his arms and kissed her.

" To-morrow—at ten-thirty then, I'll be at the staff door. I'm off duty at nine," said Jim. " Good night, my dear."

" Good night, Jim," she answered.

He heard the door close softly behind him, and walked down the silent street.

Their courtship had always been a difficult business, for neither of them had regular hours each week, and it was only seldom that their off duty hours coincided. Although she did not know it, Jim was often tempted to risk throwing up his job and to try for something else, but the force of tradition was too strong for him. His father had worked at Victoria Station, and he, too, from the day he left school, at fourteen, had worn the buttoned-jacket and peak cap of a railway servant. They could hear the trains coming in and going out of Victoria in the house where they lived, and where he had been born.

It was difficult to imagine any other kind of existence. He enjoyed the mild excitement of the life flowing about him; and Victoria Station, with its trans-Continental and Continental traffic, provided an endless variety of passengers : merchant princes, great statesmen, celebrities. He saw them all and was known to many of them. He knew the idiosyncrasies of some of them : how the old Dowager Countess of Flint always liked the umbrellas, three of them, stacked up at her side ; how the Foreign Secretary always bought half a dozen newspapers and proceeded to sit on them ; how Herr Gollwitzer, the famous conductor, tucked his ticket in the band of his hat and put on black cotton gloves. He felt a personal link with these great ones of the earth, whose luggage he handled and whose little wants he attended to. Victoria Station was in his blood. It was his window on life.

II

" Jim ! "

There was no response, and to save herself from climbing the stairs to the attic floor, where her son slept in a room

with a skylight propped open with an iron bar, Mrs. Brown
sounded the breakfast gong. This consisted of a tablespoon
hammered on the bottom of a tin saucepan.

"Jim!" called Mrs. Brown again, after a minute's tin-
panning.

There was a drowsy response this time.

"It's ten o'clock—aren't you on at eleven?" demanded
Mrs. Brown.

"Yes, coming, Mother," answered Jim.

He sat up in bed, roused from a heavy sleep. The morning
sun shone in through the skylight. His coat and jacket were
hung on the back of the chair, his trousers lay neatly folded
across it. He was a slow riser, and for a few minutes he
contemplated the bedroom and its contents. Strange to
believe that all he owned on this earth was contained in this
small attic, and would pack away into one portmanteau.
And some of the people at Victoria took away three trunks
for a short holiday.

He got out of bed, slipped off his pyjamas and stood in
front of the long mirror he had bought for five shillings in
the Caledonian market. He often wondered what that mid-
Victorian mirror had seen. It had a chipped but once
elegant gilt frame which suggested that it had once ornamented some lady's elegant boudoir. Who knew, perhaps
some fair young bride had put on her bridal veil in front of
it, or a great lady had strung her diamonds around her throat,
before departing to a Court ball, or——

He laughed at the totally naked young man he now saw
in it, who proceeded very methodically to flex every muscle
he could control. This process took ten minutes, after which
there followed ten more minutes with seven-pound dumb-
bells. Floor exercises followed all this, and then he had a
cold sponge down. The complete process took half an hour,
and he went through it with clocklike regularity. He then
descended to the scullery to shave and wash, whilst his mother,
immediately the stairs creaked, put two rashers of bacon in
the frying-pan.

"Jim, if you rush your food like this you'll have awful

indigestion," said Mrs. Brown, warningly. "Here you are again with barely half an hour for breakfast."

She glanced at the scullery clock, a small tin alarum that only went when lying on one side.

"And what's indigestion?" asked Jim, facetiously, brushing his hair in front of the mirror.

"You'll know one day—and then you'll think of me," said Mrs. Brown.

"I hope I'll remember you by something better," said Jim, patting her with the back of the brush.

There was a sudden and peremptory hammering on the front door. They both looked at one another.

"Why, whatever's that?" asked Mrs. Brown, a little breathlessly.

"Sounds like the police," replied Jim.

"And why should the police come here?" asked his mother, hastily wiping her hands on the roller towel, and preparing to go to the door.

Again there was a loud knocking.

"It's the police or the rent collector," laughed Jim.

"He came yesterday. And he's no need to knock like that, the money's always ready," retorted Mrs. Brown.

She went out through the kitchen to the front door.

"Why—it's a telegram," she said, returning, holding the thin orange envelope. There was a frightened look on her face.

"Who for?" demanded Jim.

"Brown," she read. "J. Brown—why, it's for you, Jim!"

Jim looked incredulously at the envelope his mother gave him.

"Whoever would send me a telegram!" he exclaimed. He turned the envelope over in his hand.

"Oh, do open it, Jim—the boy's waiting."

Jim tore open the envelope and read the missive. He read it twice and then looked at his mother so strangely that her heart began to palpitate.

"Oh, what is it, Jim?" she asked, fearfully.

"Have you a shilling, Mother? I got broke last night."

"A shilling—why, yes."

" Then give it to the boy," said Jim, quietly.

" A shilling ? " asked Mrs. Brown.

" A shilling."

She went to the kitchen mantelpiece, and took down a small pot in which she always kept an odd shilling for the gas meter.

" Surely twopence would do, if you must tip him," she remonstrated.

" I'd make it a pound if I had it," said Jim, reading the telegram again.

Without another word Mrs. Brown went to the door and gave the telegraph boy the shilling.

" That's from Mr. Brown. There's no answer," she said.

The boy stared at the coin in surprise and then touched his cap.

" Very good, ma'am," he said, and mounted his cycle.

" I suppose," said Mrs. Brown, back in the kitchen, " you've just received news that your uncle's left you a fortune ? "

Jim had sat down, and had spread out the telegram on the tablecloth, smoothing it with his hand.

" Pinch me, Mother," he said, " and put on your glasses and tell me if I'm dreaming."

Mrs. Brown took her spectacles off the mantelpiece where they lay tucked up behind the china dog and some clippings of recipes. Putting on her spectacles, she peered over her son's shoulder and slowly read the telegram.

" Why, whatever does it mean—are you sure it's for you ? " she asked.

" I think so—unless I'm dreaming," he responded.

" You are winner, second dividend, Bentley's Penny Pool," read Mrs. Brown, aloud. " What is Bentley's Penny Pool ? " she asked.

" It's the football results competition—you forecast the winners—I've tried for years," explained Jim. " I've sixpence on it every week."

" What, gambling ? " asked Mrs. Brown, a little shocked at this revelation.

" No, Mother—skill. I've won the second dividend ! "

"Well, very nice," said Mrs. Brown, "but why give that boy a shilling? You'll find the prize worth about two shillings. When I won that alarum clock it only went the right way up for a week, and if——"

She broke off suddenly. The smell from the scullery was unmistakable. She gave a cry of dismay and rushed out of the kitchen.

"Here's your bacon—burnt to a cinder," said Mrs. Brown, returning frying-pan in hand.

Jim got up from the table, firmly took the frying-pan out of his mother's hand, put it on the hob and then caught hold of her.

"Now sit down, Mrs. Brown," he said, quietly, forcing her down into the rocking chair. "And don't faint! Do you know what this means? It means I've won hundreds, perhaps thousands of pounds. I may be a rich man this very minute."

Mrs. Brown was about to retort, "Don't be ridiculous," when something in the boy's face bent over her told her that he was not joking.

"They send you a telegram to say you've won, and let you know the amount as soon as they've worked out the dividend on the week's bets," he explained.

"Then it is gambling," gasped Mrs. Brown.

"No, it's skill, I tell you. I've forecast the winning football teams," explained Jim.

Mrs. Brown looked at him and then smiled, smoothing back her son's hair.

"Jim, you mustn't be too excited—it might not be all you think." She glanced at the watch on his wrist. "Jim, it's ten minutes to eleven—you'll just have to have toast and marmalade or you'll be late," she added, springing out of the chair.

"I'm right off breakfast, Mother," said Jim, pouring out a cup of tea.

"Now you mustn't get your head turned. Money's the root of all evil," observed Mrs. Brown, picking up her son's cap and brushing it.

" Well, I hope it's a big lump of the root this time," retorted Jim, standing up, and swallowing a large piece of toast. He carefully folded up the telegram and placed it in his wallet. " I'll find out what this means soon—and then——" he broke off in excited uncertainty.

" And then ? " queried Mrs. Brown.

Jim gave his mother a hug and a kiss.

" I must go. And then—you can give old Skinflint notice and before he goes I'll buy the old blighter a hot water-bottle."

With another hug and a kiss, he was gone.

CHAPTER IV

PRELUDE IN PRAGUE

MR. WADDLE, Henry Norman Montacute Waddle, was known throughout the capitals of Europe as " a character." He had achieved this distinction at the early age of thirty entirely by an all-consuming passion, and a firm refusal to compromise with any of the forces that threatened to frustrate the fulfilment of that passion. He was in no way concerned with the political or social reformation of society, for he had long despaired of " the human animal," to use his favourite term. Those who busied themselves in those spheres would often soar to dizzy eminence by a vociferous appeal to the eternal discontent smouldering in the human heart. Mr. Waddle's crusade could never stir nations or draw the plaudits of thousands. Like Milton, he sought an audience fit though few—" an essentially international one, for we have the only real bond between the nations of the earth," he would declare, taking off his spectacles and wiping them.

When anyone asked what that bond was, Mr. Waddle struggled to hide the disappointment aroused by this ignorance of his incessant activity, and, carefully pushing away the coffee cup on the table, for he had the Continental habit

of living in cafés, he would say, solemnly, " to make the world
folk-dance conscious."

This, of course, entailed an explanation, which he was
always ready to give.   There were two explanations, one for
the public and another for his intimate circle.   " Folk-
dancing is one of the oldest forms of entertainment in Europe.
Folk-dances cannot die ;   they are immortal.   They have
descended through the centuries.   You will find them in any
centre where the flame of culture has been kept burning.
There are folk-dances in Palermo and Rome, in Prague and
Paris, in Moscow and Copenhagen, in Berne and Brussels—
and in London, spasmodically.   That is the shame of it.
London must become folk-dance conscious.   The stigma
must be wiped out."

If Henry Waddle knew you intimately, and it was never
long before he knew everyone intimately, for he had an
embracing gift of kindly fellowship, he would indulge in a
slightly puckish confession.   A smile would slowly enlarge
across his chubby face, and his eyes would twinkle.

" If you want to get anywhere in this life, you must fasten
on to a cause," he would say.   " Have you ever walked
down and around Victoria Street ?   It is chock-full of causes
—homes for unwanted children, lost dogs, starving govern-
esses, smoke-abatement, dental-aid, canine-defence, rural-
preservation, town-planning, invalid chair distribution, old
needlewomen's aid, convalescent homes for working-class
mothers, the decrepit gentlefolks' aid, poor widows' coal fund,
the cat-lovers' league, home handicrafts, feathered friends,
and so on.   I won't attempt to detail the societies for dealing
with our political ills.   And as for the innumerable varieties
of religion, they keep the brass plate industry in continuous
prosperity."

" Now," continued Mr. Waddle, pushing back his glasses,
" I don't deny a few of them do good, some of them are
necessary, but the majority, believe me, are quite futile.
They are only necessary to three people : the paid secretary,
his typist, and the titled chairman.   The secretary gets five,
six or seven hundred pounds a year.   He has a pleasant life,

he wears a black jacket and vest, with a tail-coat for the
annual meeting. He writes to and sometimes sees a person
of eminence, whom he has solicited for support of his cause ;
sometimes he is asked to lunch by a lonely dowager-countess
who wants to feel she is pulling her weight—often very con-
siderable," Mr. Waddle would add with a twinkle. " He
keeps the typist busy reminding laggards of their subscrip-
tions, and appealing for new ones. He keeps a watchful eye
on the newspaper, to proffer a paragraph, or insert a letter
on behalf of his society. A good secretary is as insidious as
a draught, you can't keep him out ; he gets in by the letter-
box, the doorstep and the window. As for the chairman or
chairwoman, their first qualification is a title. At the annual
meeting, followed by tea, a title is essential in the chair. We
English are fortunate in this respect. There is an unlimited
supply, and there is the utmost goodwill on the part of their
holders. They have been brought up in the tradition of
presiding, indeed they feel lost and hurt if they are not asked."

Here Mr. Waddle would pause, take a cigarette out of a
cardboard packet, offer you one, light up, and ask, " You
follow me ? " Then, smoothing the table with his hands,
shuffling invisible dominoes, he would proceed, with a mischievous smile :

" Well—when I realised I could not go on with that stupid
family tea-broking down in Mincing Lane—what a name
and what a place !—I said, ' Henry, my dear, you've got to
make your own little corner, you've got to have a cause.'
And that, in a nutshell, is how I came to found the International League for the Propagation of Folk-Dancing.
You'd be surprised how it grows, it is a very real force in
the world. We want more support, of course. I'm not yet
a paid secretary, I have to do all my own typing and write
at least twenty letters a day. But the movement's growing.
I shall make it an essential thing in English life, and it will
have important ramifications—for we have corresponding
members in every important town in Europe and in the
United States. We are, or we can become, an international
force. We are the real League of Nations. I lead a very

interesting life visiting International centres. It's unfortunate I usually have to pay my own fare—and that means travelling third-class. But one day we shall get the support we deserve, perhaps an office in Victoria Street, and a typist, and—well, who knows, a national theatre of folk-dancing."

Thus, with a light gallantry, Mr. Waddle would disclose his battle for independence. Very few knew the powerful forces he had to fight to escape from Mincing Lane. There had always been a Waddle in the business. From the first occupation of his cradle the brittle crackle of tea-leaves had sounded in his ears. Winchester and New College were but pleasant forecourts of the City prison. The dread day arrived when, in a black jacket and striped trousers, he caught the nine o'clock business train from Bromley, a newspaper tucked under his left arm, an umbrella in his right hand, a bowler hat on his head, and smouldering rebellion in his heart.

For a year he endured servitude, and then a day came, a warm spring day, when the City pigeons were love-making on the grimy office window-sills, and the plane trees put forth a bright flutter of green leaves against grey walls, when Life was stronger than tea and suburban security. A kind old grandmother had left young Henry a legacy of one hundred and twenty pounds a year. It was not sufficient on which to hoist the flag of independence, but it assisted the spirit of revolt. Henry could not live on this sum, neither could he quite starve on it. He astonished an indignant father, who gave him the ultimatum to get out or to toe the line, by accepting the first choice. A tearful mother did not shake his determination. He had already received the call. The folk-dance claimed his allegiance. He had already established international contacts, assisted by a gift of tongues, for he spoke French, German, Czech, Spanish and Italian, with the relish of the born linguist.

He left the bowler hat on the cloak-room shelf in Bromley and bought a black felt hat in Soho. This, together with an incapacity for tying a tie, gave him a slightly artistic air. Within twenty-four hours he was in Paris, in the first of those incredibly cheap foreign lodgings, in the discovery of which

he was soon to become a master. Then followed a year
of incessant travelling from Paris to Rome, Rome to Vienna,
Vienna to Bucharest. Wherever the folk-dancer could be
seen, Henry Waddle appeared, and established friendly
contacts with the dancers.

Gradually it became known that folk-dancing, the world
over, had its prophet. When the train stopped at Vilna
or Cracow, Munich or Milan, Bruges or Brussels, the local
representatives saluted Herr Waddle, smiling from a third-
class window, always with his tie up round his neck, his
shoe-laces undone, and his wallet, crammed with international
correspondence, in his hand. He had little to offer them
but conversation and encouragement, but such was his charm,
his embracing enthusiasm, he was a shower to a parched
garden. Enthusiasm blossomed, and when the train bore
off Herr Waddle, after a few minutes' halt, to a waving of hats
and cries of *Auf Wiedersehen !* *A rivederci !* or *Au revoir !*
each colony of folk-dancers felt a new baptism in the faith.

England, of course, was still largely unredeemed, and
Mr. Waddle gave long thought to the conversion of his
obstinate fellow-countrymen. The office in Victoria Street,
the titled president and the typist, not to think of the five
hundred a year as secretary, remained a dream. He surveyed the field calmly. The press was never allowed to
remain oblivious of the international significance of folk-
dancing. Any paragraph bearing the slightest relevance
to the folk-dance called forth a supplementary note, or a
letter. There was no escaping the ubiquitous Mr. Waddle.
He would pop up in Leeds, or Manchester, with the same
alacrity as he popped up in Dresden or Vicenza. Wherever
the folk-dance might shake a decorated leg, Mr. Waddle
was present.

His energy was terrific, his correspondence voluminous.
He trampled over all forms of obstruction, social, financial
or political. A clattering typewriter, its battered cover
plastered with the cloak-room labels of all Europe, and
operated with three fingers, one left-hand and two right-
hand, helped the flow of letters. Any sheet of notepaper,

from hotel, ship or café, was pressed into use. " As from,"
he wrote over the printed address. Baffled correspondents
wondered where to reach him. But the fact was that Mr
Waddle was not anxious to be reached. He preferred to
appear Messiah-like, spread the faith, bless the converts,
and disappear again.

Mr. Waddle had, nevertheless, a London headquarters,
which was modest and well-nigh inaccessible. With that
delightful humour never absent from his conversation, he
would refer to it as " The Dustbin." It consisted of two
small rooms, reached by a narrow passage between a bird-
shop and a grocer's, at the back of a high warehouse adjoining
Soho Square.

Here, to the honoured few who were allowed to know
his address—for all public correspondence, as he called it,
went to an accommodation address—he showed his restricted
but genial hospitality. He invited you to take " a dish of
tea," for morning calls were never encouraged, since he did
much of his correspondence and literary work in bed, and the
bedroom was his real office.

Entrance into the Dustbin was not easy. The visitor
picked his way over innumerable objects on the floor. Behind
curtains all the amenities of life were hidden, the gas-ring,
kettles and saucepans, a wash-bowl, a shaving mirror, brooms,
clothes, shelves of medicine bottles, boxes of biscuits, a roller
towel, files of letters, and a whole array of gadgets for sharpen-
ing pencils, making coffee, cutting corns, binding papers,
stropping razor-blades, and a dozen other singular contri-
vances Mr. Waddle had purchased in various parts of the
world. " All my life I've been gadget-minded," he would
say, as these various objects came to light when he moved
the curtains.

The living-room also held Mr. Waddle's desk, three collapsible chairs, a pile of portmanteaux, and a gallery of coloured
prints, sketches and photographs of folk-dancers performing
their characteristic dances in all parts of the world.

Those accepted into Mr. Waddle's complete confidence
were allowed a peep into the bedroom, which had long ceased

to justify its name, for he had evicted himself and now slept on a camp-bed, the lounge by day, in the sitting-room.

Mr. Waddle had a companion passion to that of folk-dancing, he collected any literature relating to ballet or folk-costume. No book was too battered, dog-eared, or mouldy if it contained any kind of illustration of ballet or folk-costume. Ten years of arduous collection, of delving in old bookshops, bargain tubs, second-hand stores, and the ever-enticing Caledonian Market, had resulted in a collection of seven thousand volumes, of all shapes and conditions, stacked now from floor to ceiling in wobbling piles that threatened to crush the incautious intruder. Even the window had been blotted out, and the semi-dark room emitted an odour of mouldy paper and crumbling leather.

" I think I've made a corner in the literature of the dance," Mr. Waddle would observe, standing in the doorway. " It's always a good thing to be the inevitable expert on one thing. They have to come to you sooner or later. One day I hope to catalogue my library and write a brochure. Oh——"

Here Mr. Waddle would break off, for the kettle was boiling over and the cat had leapt on to the table and was sniffing at the tea-cakes. " Shoo !—shoo ! " he cried. " And now take a chair—mind it's safe. Yes, that's all right. Well, it's modest enough, but it's my own, and I can shut it all up and go away with no heavy, overhead expenses. Do you follow ? I won't say it's luxurious, or even comfortable, but one must be free. I close the door, and pay a shilling a week to board out the cat, and I have nothing to worry about. Try one of those cakes. No, it's not the life for everybody—but I must be free to move. I'm peculiar, I know. You see, I come of an old but degenerate City family, but I do lead my own life, whereas most people are just puppets."

Mr. Waddle was a figure of fun to his friends, who joked at his master-passion and related his oddities with a slightly malicious embroidery, but no one who knew him well failed to regard him with real affection. He gave a fancy-dress to drab existence. His industry, often futile, had ever a note of gaiety. He always knew the date, time, place, and price of all curious and interesting performances or exhibitions. "A moment, my dear," he would say, opening his portfolio. "Yes, here's a paper about it. The Greybar Galleries, on Tuesday. I think he's a very promising artist. No Matisse nonsense, you know—the honest English line, with no Shoreditch-Jerusalem axis. I met him at the buffet in Ghent station, one morning at two o'clock. You'll like his work, I'm sure."

Those who knew him well and loved him most knew he could never be reformed. There was a hard vein of obstinacy beneath his pliable exterior. He received impressions with an easy resilience, and soon reverted to his own individual belief. The need of desperate economy had made him acquainted with the shabby world of cheap eating and sleeping places, but he brought to them his own small refinements, and the true spirit of adventure gave enjoyment to his more trying experiences.

Nevertheless, he was never far off the vortex of fashion. He turned up at Monte Carlo soon after Christmas, living in an incredibly cheap room, tucked away behind an *épicerie*. "Such a delicious perfume, my dear, every morning, when I take coffee at my window." He went every year to Bayreuth, for the Wagner season. He had struck up a deep friendship with old Frau Tischbein, a retired brothel-keeper, who let him a slip of a room—"my cabin," he called it—in a dark alley of baroque houses. His fluent German enabled him to go native, and he affected a fine scorn of the English tourists who went about in flocks, gabbling their music-jargon at café tables. Herr Waddle knew where good tea was obtainable for fifty pfennige cheaper, and *kuchen* that did not contain *kunstbutter*—a concocted cream he rejected, with withering comment on the gullibility of tourists.

Romance had touched the tender heart of Mr. Waddle. It was an episode his friends heard of indirectly, for he would never speak of it, not even in the slightest allusion. One night in Prague, leaning out of a high-gabled window down into a narrow, lamplit street, he heard a small boy singing for alms. He threw some coins to the boy, who lifted a pinched, white face, and raised his cap. The next moment he had toppled over in a dead faint. Waddle at once hurried down the dark stairs into the alley where no one had noticed the insensible figure in the gully. The boy was as light as a sparrow to lift, and blue about the lips from the intense cold of a November afternoon. In a few minutes Waddle had regained his room, warm with a wood stove, and put the boy on the bed, rubbing his hands. Presently the closed eyes opened and stared at the stranger.

"It's all right," said Waddle, in German. "You fainted —hungry?"

The boy nodded. He was about fourteen, with large dark eyes and sallow skin. He looked starved.

Waddle went to a corner of the room, made some coffee on his portable stove, and sliced a roll of bread, which he buttered, placing a strip of *schinken* between the two halves.

"There—let's see you eat this," he said, carrying a plate and coffee over to the bed.

The boy sat up with a frightened expression still on his face.

"Smile!" commanded Waddle, packing the pillows behind the boy. "I'm not the wicked witch. You eat this—and then we'll talk."

Waddle opened his bag and took out a wig, worn in a Polish folk-dance he had seen. Standing behind the bed-rail he put it on and mimed comically. The boy's solemn face was soon provoked into a grin; then he laughed aloud, and munched the sandwich.

Waddle had covered him with his overcoat, and the warmth, the coffee, and the food, set the blood running through his limbs again. They began to talk, and little by little Waddle heard the whole story. The boy, Walter Braun, of South German extraction, had been left an orphan with his elder sister. On the death of their mother they had lived on a farm with a cousin, a surly, hard-drinking fellow whose habits brought him to bankruptcy. The farm had been sold up, and his sister Martha, twenty years of age, hearing that boys with good voices were sometimes given board and education in a Moravian orphanage in Prague, had tramped with her young brother some eighty miles into the city. But the orphanage would not take the boy, and for a whole week they had slept out, under arches and in doorways. During the day the boy tried singing in the streets, hoping to gain a little money. They had had one meal in two days. The boy's shoes had almost no soles left to them, his feet were wet through. The thin coat he wore would have been inadequate in England ; here in the bitter cold of Prague it was quite useless.

" And where's your sister now ? " asked Waddle.

" She sometimes gets money for standing in a queue at the Deutches Theatre. We meet at nine o'clock."

" And then ? "

" If we have money we eat : if not, we try to sleep."

" Where ? "

" Anywhere—in a doorway out of the wind, and where the police won't find us," answered the boy.

He put down the plate and the coffee cup.

" Had enough ? " asked Waddle.

" Yes," said the boy hesitatingly.

" You don't sound as if you had. Come along, there's plenty more."

" No, thank you—but my sister would like some," said the boy, " if I could take it."

Waddle went over to the bed. The boy smiled at him, his shyness gone now. He was dark, with black eyebrows and eyelashes and his hair unkempt.

" I think a wash would do you good. Let's see what we can do," suggested Waddle.

The boy grinned and got off the bed. There was a wash-stand in a corner of the room. Waddle always travelled with his own towel, and a cake of soap kept in an aluminium box. He produced these, and the boy, taking off his coat and rolling back his sleeves, began to wash. The child was distressingly thin, the result of years of undernourishment. Waddle wondered what the sister was like. There was something attractive about the boy. Presently he began to talk, the washing finished. Waddle took out his pocket comb.

"Come here," he said, and, holding the boy between his knees, combed the long, dark locks. The boy smiled at him. He had good, even teeth. Decently dressed he would be noticeable. It was a pity, thought Waddle, he had no clothes that would fit him, and such clothes as he had were scarcely fit to give to anyone. But as he brushed the boy's hair he pondered on what he could do for this poor brat starving in a strange and snow-smitten city. This room, like those in most Continental lodgings, had a day couch as well as a bed. He could sleep on the couch and let the boy and his sister have the bed.

"Listen," he said. "You must bring your sister here and I'll give her something to eat. After that perhaps we can arrange about a bed."

He looked at his watch. It was six o'clock. He was going out to dine in a café and write some letters, and then meet a Czech who ran a folk-dance society in Bratislava.

"I'll be back here at ten o'clock. Come up the stairs and knock at the door. I must go out now," said Waddle, putting on his overcoat.

The boy accompanied him down the stairs into the street. At the corner he gravely raised his cap and went off. Waddle wondered if he would see him again, and whether the whole sad story had been invented in order to extract money. But the boy sounded truthful, and he was certainly starved.

On reaching the café Waddle ordered a frugal supper, opened his wallet, and extracted the letters he wished to answer. An orchestra began to play a lively air. The place was warm and bright, there was an appetising smell of food, a hum of conversation and an air of general prosperity. Asking for pen and ink, and a supply of the thin notepaper and envelopes on which he conducted most of his correspondence, Waddle dismissed the haunting face of a starved boy and wrote to a folk-dancer in Strasbourg whom he hoped to call upon shortly.

A little before nine, having written several letters and

scanned the newspaper provided by the café for its clients, Waddle paid his modest bill, for he was expert in deriving the maximum nourishment from a meagre menu, and set forth down Karlova-street towards his tiny lodgings of Husova-street. He could not resist making a little detour via the Karlüv Bridge. He loved the view from the many arched bridge over the Vltava. He liked the baroque statues and Gothic towers that overlooked the dark river, and the snow-sprinkled roofs and towers of this capital of ancient Bohemia.

While he thus stood contemplating the beauty of the scene before him, a clock in a tower struck the hour of ten. Mindful of his promise to be back at his lodging, Waddle hurried on. A chilling wind blew the powdery snow in his face. He thought gratefully of the stove in his room, with it delightful odour of burning wood.

It was ten minutes past ten when he arrived at the dark archway leading to his flight of stairs. He half-expected to find the boy, Walter, waiting there with his sister, but there was no one. A dim gas jet burned at the foot of the stone steps, worn by the feet of dwellers in this old baroque-faced house. It had probably been the house of a prosperous merchant ; the architraves of the old walnut doors were elaborately carved, but now it had a derelict air, and was divided into tenements. His own room was on the third floor. On the second floor someone was playing a violin with masterly skill, but here, as in Hungary, the people seemed born with fiddles under their chins, and astonishing virtuosity drew little notice.

Waddle paused, listening to the hidden executant, and for a moment, his thoughts flew back to another violinist he sometimes listened to in an Odeon restaurant near Leicester Square. That fellow was a Czech also, a consumptive-looking creature with wisps of black hair falling over a rat-face. When Waddle had talked to him of Prague tears came into the man's eyes. He had grown up there.

Strange if the fellow playing behind that door was destined to make wild music in a London restaurant, evoking, with cat-gut and resin, a Bohemian spirit in the hearts of staid Londoners! Fortune played odd tricks with human beings; himself, for instance, climbing this dark staircase in Prague when he might be in the bosom of his family at Bromley.

With a laugh Waddle reached his door, unlocked it, fumbled for matches, and lit the white-globed gas jet. He seemed to be invaded by music, for someone overhead was playing the fourth Liszt *Rhapsodie* with tremendous fervour. Perhaps it was a house patronised by poor music students. Yesterday he had encountered a man struggling up the stairs with a huge bass fiddle on his back, and he had to retire into his room to allow the man to pass.

Waddle set down the parcel of foodstuffs he had bought before going to the café. First he put some more wood into the stove. Then, for a moment, he looked out over the roofs of Prague, white and lovely in the snow and moon-light, with its centuries-old gables, towers, and spires. To make the room more cheerful he put some coloured candles in the holders on the shelf and lit them. After this he pulled out of his bag the Meta cooking-stove with which he travelled, together with a frying-pan and kettle. His equipment also included a length of flex and a portable electric light, for from experience he knew that the light in cheap lodgings was never over the bed, since landladies did not encourage reading in bed. But there was no electric light, so his fore-thought was not rewarded.

He was disappointed now that the boy and his sister had not turned up. He was going to give them a good meal, for he was no mean cook. A clock somewhere in the city struck the half-hour, followed by other laggards. Outside it began to snow steadily. Waddle began to regret he was not staying in Prague over Christmas. It had the true Christmas-card atmosphere.

Good King Wenceslas went out . . .

he began to hum, when a timid knocking on the door made him stop and listen. A violin wailed below, the piano was still being played overhead. The knocking was repeated.

Waddle went to the door and opened it. On the stone landing stood two snow-besprinkled figures, the boy and his sister.

"Come in," said Waddle, throwing back the door and standing aside.

The boy stepped forward, smiling. Behind him followed a girl, much taller, with an oval face, and shy, dark eyes. She looked for a moment at her host, and then her eyes fell. She came inside the room with a nervous smile on her face. Both of them were pinched with cold and the snow began to melt on them. Pools of water gathered round their boots.

"This is my sister, Martha," said the boy, as Waddle looked at them.

The girl gave a little curtsy. Waddle could see now, in the fuller light of the room, that she was strikingly beautiful with her pale, oval face, red lips and dark brown eyes. Her hair was neatly plaited and pinned on her head in the fashion of Czech peasant girls. She wore a thick black jacket, short and shabby, with large mutton-chop sleeves, a black skirt and bulging, laced-up boots. Her hands looked raw but were well-shaped.

He got them to take off their coats and shake them out on the landing, then he closed the door and made them sit down by the stove while he prepared some supper. As he cooked he talked to the girl, who began to lose her shyness. She was twenty, and had lived all her life on a farm. She had lost her father first, then her mother. Both were dead before she was sixteen. There had been no one but their drunken uncle to go to. Her story corroborated all that the boy had said.

"Oh, doesn't this smell good!" exclaimed Waddle, turning over the spaghetti and tomato which he had turned out of a tin into the frying-pan.

The faces of his guests shone with delight. They were warm now. The girl began to talk voluntarily. She had a soft, musical voice. Waddle put a record on his portable gramophone, to which he always shaved in the morning. The boy listened, enraptured. The meal was soon ready, and

ey gathered round the small table Waddle had pushed up
ear the stove.

"Now, we're going to be real Bohemians. We've got
ie fork, two spoons and a knife between us," he said.

They began to eat, all talking and laughing. "Oh, it is
onderful!" Martha kept repeating, her eyes shining as she
oked round the room. "It is such a beautiful place!"

Waddle laughed. It was really a rather squalid hole, but
ie candlelight hid its shabbiness and lent gaiety to the
ene. The best thing was a bed, a large affair, and soft.
ut for a shilling a day he could not complain, and it included
ood for the stove. It was actually a third of the rent he
aid for the Dustbin.

The supper was a great success. The boy and his sister
ere ravenous. When twelve o'clock came Waddle made
iem lie down on the big bed, covering them with a large
ig. They were soon fast asleep but Waddle, a little cramped
1 the couch, and wrapped up in his overcoat, lay awake for
me time, thinking. There was the problem of the morrow.
e wondered whether he could afford to take a room for
iem for a few nights. But that was no permanent solution
their terrible plight. Still pondering, he fell asleep at
st, long after the bells of the city had announced midnight.

Thus simply, by an act of kindness, it had all begun. On
ie morrow Martha, her face wreathed in smiles, insisted on
aking the breakfast coffee. Walter was dispatched for
esh rolls. The snow had fallen heavily all night, muffling
rague in a white mantle.

After breakfast the girl insisted on cleaning the room. She
ent downstairs to borrow a broom and a pail. Waddle
ondered what the landlord would say when Martha appeared,
ut there was no protest against the girl's presence. She
und some hot water somehow, and scoured all the pots and
ans. The old carpet was taken up and shaken, the board
oor was swept. The boy and his sister were so radiantly
appy Waddle had not the heart to turn them adrift. For
ie more night, at least, he would give them lodging and
ipper. He told them to return at seven o'clock. Martha

and Walter went off to a domestic employment agency wher
they called each day, hopeful that some offer would turn u

At four o'clock Waddle returned to change his shoe
which hurt him. He was stopped, as he entered, by the fa
landlord. Waddle learned that twice in the afternoon th
girl had been back, seeking him. She was in a terrible stat
said the landlord, her eyes swollen with crying. She ha
told him her young brother had been run over in the stree
and was now in hospital, seriously injured.

Waddle had to go out, he had an appointment with
director of the Czech Theatre, who was interested in folk
dancing, but he came back a little before seven. He ha
only been in a few minutes when there was a timid knock o
the door. He opened it, and found Martha there, her eye
running with tears.

" I have heard," said Waddle. " How is he ? "

She stepped past him into the room, stood for a momen
with quivering mouth, and then looked at him with inarticulat
misery.

He put his aim round the poor girl, and suddenly sb
buried her face on his chest and sobbed unconstrainedly.

" There ! there ! You must bear up, Martha. He'll ge
better," said Waddle, soothingly.

" No, no, Herr Waddle," she sobbed. " Walter is dead.

" Dead ? " he repeated, startled.

" He died in half an hour."

He drew the girl to the couch and sat down, holding he
as she sobbed her heart out.

When Waddle spoke of this episode to the chosen fe
among his friends, he would break off and say quietly
" Well, to cut the story short, the incredible thing happened
I found I was in love with that poor, destitute child, and
married her. There was no other way out of it. I couldn
make her my mistress, and I couldn't afford two rooms
We did share that room for a fortnight. I know all that th
landlord thought. He used to smile knowingly at me, an
I wanted to punch his silly, fat face. Folks wouldn't believe

of course, that we could share the same room, sleep on the same bed, and in each other's arms for two weeks, and remain wholly innocent of any intimacy. But we did. I came to love her, deeply, and to find myself dismayed at the prospect of going away without her, of living without her. Soon I had to go to Paris, and as the day drew near we were both in a state of misery.

"I haven't enough to keep anybody, I can scarcely keep myself, but you've noticed how a man finds his partner, and gets through life with her, whatever his means. Even the tramp finds someone to share his misery. So I took the chance. The day before I left for Paris I married Martha. I was never so happy in my life as in those four months in Paris that followed.

"We stayed in Paris because you can live cheaper there than anywhere else in Europe, if you know it as I do. Besides, only a few knew of our marriage. I didn't tell anyone, I didn't let my own people know, for I knew they would just have gone off the deep end." Here Waddle gave a sad little smile. "For although I exist without them, they keep a proprietorial interest in me, you know.

"I only left Paris twice during those four months—each time to rush over to London. We rarely left one another alone. I started to write a history of folk-dancing, really an achievement, for you know how incapable I am of concentrated effort. Martha was adorable. She was naturally happy. The slightest thing gave her pleasure. We found a couple of cheap rooms off the Avenue Clichy. At first we used to go shopping together, for she couldn't speak the language. But she very soon learned it. She was a good cook—but I could never get her to make tea properly! She would never wait for the water to boil. It was the only thing over which we ever had trouble. How silly of me it was—fussing over my tea like that! Yes, she was a radiant little creature, bird-like, yes, that was it—she chirped in the pretty little cage she made for us."

The rest of the story was brief and tragic. Martha caught a bad cold. One afternoon, as she had a temperature, Waddle would not let her go out shopping, and went himself.

C

When he came back he found her collapsed on the floor. He ran out for a doctor. She had a hæmorrhage of the lung. They took her off to hospital. Pneumonia followed. Waddle went day after day to the hospital. One day she seemed better, one day worse. Then water gathered in the lungs; they performed pneumothorax; the temperature went up and down. For another week the battle went on. Then consumption intervened, rapid and fatal. He saw her one afternoon, with eyes too bright and face too flushed. She was cheerful, and certain she was getting better. But that night she died. It was the eighteenth of May, and the eve of her twenty-first birthday.

Waddle's finances were severely strained to give her proper burial. He raised the money on his insurance policy. For two months afterwards he trailed aimlessly about. He had no interest in folk-dancing any more, his correspondence fell into arrears, his cheery face was not seen beaming forth from railway carriages as he passed through the European capitals, greeting the folk-dancers. He gave up the flat in Paris, sold the odd bits of furniture, keeping only a chair she loved. He returned to the Dustbin, and the chair found a corner in that crammed room, but it was never used. He tied a piece of string over the back, and crossways over the seat, and let it be understood that the chair was too frail for use. But always on the eighteenth of May it bore a vase of flowers, if he was in London.

He tried not to be in London on that date. He was invariably in Paris, so that on each sad anniversary he might visit her grave. Five years had elapsed since the close of his idyll, and the wound was not yet wholly healed. He spoke of Martha to two of his friends only, and his voice had a shake in it. " Funny you know—I never believed anything like that could happen to me. I was never very interested in women, they rather frighten me with their passion for ordering one's life."

After a time his interest in folk-dancing returned. And since it proved an anodyne for his sorrow, he redoubled his activities in the cause. He was for ever writing or tapping his typewriter. He augmented his meagre income by articles in the press, and spent it on more travel. He knew every device for obtaining reduced fares, he knew the chief Continental trains, their time-tables, their connections, and whether they carried third-class sleepers. He was adept at sitting over a cup of coffee in a German restaurant car, since it offered a pleasing respite from the hard seats of the third-class carriages. Fairs, festivals and exhibitions, offering reduced fares, were all utilized in the interest of his cause, and he never failed to suggest to the organisers that their show would be incomplete without folk-dancing. When he was successful he gleefully added any proceeds from his services to the propaganda fund.

It was a busy life, and what did it matter if certain serious-minded fellows, careerists most of them, scoffed at his industry and regarded it as an exercise in futility? He surveyed the international scene, knew all kinds of simple souls, injured no one, and was beloved by many.

CHAPTER V

ENCOUNTER IN PARIS

I

THE eighteenth of May had again seen Waddle in Paris, making his sad pilgrimage to Martha's grave at Pantin. This anniversary observed, he lingered on, for in a few days he was leaving to attend a Congress in Budapest, one of his favourite cities. Now, on the twentieth of the month, at ten o'clock in the evening, after a cheap but good dinner in the Boulevard St. Michel, he took a seat at one of the outside tables of the Dome Café, where the Latin Quarter exhibited its most curious denizens. Here, sooner or later, some French, German, Italian, Czech, Danish or Dutch friend was certain to hail him.

He was drinking his coffee alone on this pleasant May

evening when he noticed a young man at the next table pull a theatre programme out of his pocket. Waddle watched his neighbour, an Englishman without doubt, and just when he was about to screw up the programme, he intervened.

" I hope you'll excuse me, but may I have that programme ? " he asked, politely.

The young man looked at him, surprised by such a request, then smiled and said, " Why, certainly ! "

" You will doubtless wonder," said Waddle, smoothing out the programme, " at my request. But I have a friend who is making a collection of all printed matter."

" All printed matter—why, he'd soon fill the British Museum, surely ! " laughed the Englishman.

" No—you see, he collects all specimens of printing. A library of printed matter showing the styles of printing, of all ages and countries, cannot fail to be of interest. He asks his friends to assist him in this collection—hence my request."

" Well, that's about the craziest "—the young man checked himself—" the oddest thing I ever heard ! "

A waiter appeared before them. Waddle's coffee glass was empty.

" Won't you have a drink ? I see you're English," said the stranger, affably.

" Thank you—I'd like a grenadine," replied Waddle.

" An ice, a coffee and a—a—a what did you say ? It's new to me," laughed the young man, turning to Waddle.

" Grenadine—it's a syrup made from pomegranates," explained Waddle.

" Oh, thanks—you see I'm quite new to this sort of thing," said the young man, affably.

Waddle looked at him. He was a fresh-faced lad of about twenty-four, athletic and well-groomed—what he often termed " the soap and cold water " school of Old England. He had the complexion and clear eyes fashioned by wind and rain ; thank Heaven, for once he was not in that abominable English tourist uniform of flannel trousers, sports jacket and pull-over. The young woman with him was equally smart and exceedingly pretty.

" My name's Brown—may I introduce my wife ? " said the young man.

" How do you do—my name's Waddle—Henry Waddle. Is this your first time in Paris ? "

" Yes—we've been here a week. We've never been abroad before—it's all rather exciting, but we must seem stupid at times. Elizabeth has almost killed me rushing round the sights," he said.

" My husband puts the blame on me, but he's the culprit," exclaimed Mrs. Brown. " We're working steadily through Baedeker, and we're getting around, for we've only eight more things to see, and we're here for another week."

" And then ? " asked Waddle. He liked this pair of unsophisticated young things. He was always ready to play an avuncular role, particularly it if entailed a display of his knowledge of the Continental scene.

" Well—we thought of going on to Monte Carlo—and then perhaps into Italy, but this language business frightens us a little," said young Brown.

" You should never let the language question trouble you. My difficulty is that everyone practises their English on you," observed Waddle. " There's always some fellow who has tried to win a fortune in America, and who has come home again to pose as the local oracle. He waits, like the spider, for the tourist to fly into his net."

He accepted young Brown's proffered cigarette, and asked him where they were staying. Their answer assured him they were not rich or difficult to know. Mr. Brown began to ask questions. Was this the real Latin Quarter, and where could the artists best be seen ? His naïveté pleased Waddle. He found there were many things they had not yet seen. They were children at a fair. Everything delighted them. They thought Paris must be the most beautiful city on earth.

This was a challenge Waddle could not let pass.

" Believe me, Paris is by no means the loveliest," he said. " It has a few magnificent vistas ; there is the incomparable Champs-Elysées, and, perhaps, the Place de la Concorde—

I will grant you those. Oh yes, and one might add the Opera and the Madeleine—though this is only a copy of the superb Maison Carée at Nîmes. Paris is the most beautiful city to the English and the Americans because it is their first place of escape. They halt here on their flight from home—and anywhere away from home is romantic, until you begin longing to return ! "

They laughed at genial Mr. Waddle. His good-natured face, as he beamed at them through his glasses, was the friendliest they had seen since leaving England. They had attempted conversation with fellow travellers in their hotel and had received a frozen stare. The French were either very rude or very polite. It was nice to talk to Mr. Waddle so friendly, so experienced.

They were still living in a day-dream, and on waking in their room at the small hotel in a side street off the Rue de Rivoli, Jim half expected to open his eyes and see the familiar skylight in Pimlico, and his blue porter's jacket hanging over the chair back. One thousand, two hundred and ten pounds. Jim repeated the sum like a magic incantation.

For three days he had felt stunned by his good fortune and his mother had never really believed he would get the money. But the cheque came, bearing the stupendous figures, the first that Jim had ever seen with his name on it. Then followed the excitement of opening an account and having a cheque-book of his own. Every time he signed a cheque, even now, he felt he was committing forgery. It was unbelievable that you could get money, lots of it, by merely signing your name on a slip of paper. He found himself looking at shops and advertisements with new eyes. He could have most of those things they offered. He could walk into a tailor's shop, be measured for a suit, and have it sent home, all by virtue of a piece of paper with his signature on it. His first act was to draw fifty pounds.

" In one pound notes, or fives, sir ? " asked the clerk.

" Oh, fives," replied Jim, off-hand, his heart thumping.

He put the thin crisp notes into his pocket, but as soon as he got home he took them all out, felt them, let Mrs. Brown

eel them, made them crackle, held them up to the light, and
tudied the signature on them of the Chief Cashier, wondering
vhat that extraordinary man was like, whose name was on
nillions and millions of notes. Did he go home every night
vith a wad of them in his pocket, and did he eat bacon and
ggs in the morning and catch the 9.20 to the City? When
rou came to think of it, the Chief Cashier had the most
vonderful autograph in the world, and yet so few had ever
aeard of him.

Holding out one of the notes, Jim struck a match.

"Money to burn," he said jokingly.

His pretence made Mrs. Brown give a cry of alarm. He
aughed and pushed the note into her hand.

"There, go and buy yourself something, Mother, some-
hing you don't really need," he said.

But she would not take it. She warned him that money
uined people, changed their natures.

"Have you noticed mine's got soured?" laughed Jim.

"You'll be late if you don't get off to work," said Mrs.
Brown, glancing at the clock.

"Well, I can afford to be late."

"What do you mean?"

"I can pay the price!" replied Jim, with laughing eyes.

But Mrs. Brown thought he was serious. She had a dread
of what this sudden windfall might entail.

"That just shows how dangerous easy money is," said
Mrs. Brown, warningly. "You'll get uppish and lazy, and
let yourself go to pieces if you're not careful. Money turns
people's heads."

"With the result they see things they never saw before,"
retorted Jim, putting on his cap, and taking hold of his
mother. "Well, I'm not so silly as you think. But this
does alter things. You'd be surprised how many fellows at
work think I can help them out of their troubles! Well,
anyhow, I think we might have a new house, and a little car
—and perhaps get married."

"I've been thinking that was in your mind," said Mrs.
Brown, making an effort to keep her voice steady, but failing.

"Now, now, now!" exclaimed Jim, putting his cheek against hers. "It's got to be faced sooner or later, Mother. I'm going to talk to Lizzie, she'll have ideas."

Lizzie had ideas, astonishing ideas. She agreed at once about marriage and a good honeymoon abroad, but she astonished him by proposing that he should leave the railway and go into business. She knew the very kind of business. The Maddock's were retiring from their tobacco and confectionery shop in Chelsea. It was a sound business, with a turnover of sixty pounds a week, a double-fronted shop in a fine position, with a four-roomed house. The premises were held on a twenty years' lease. They wanted seven hundred pounds for the business, and to retire in August. They would give an option on it for seventy pounds.

"You see, Jim, you must get out of a groove. In a few years we can buy a second business, and gradually get a chain of shops. That's how Lord Banford began—and look at him now," said Lizzie.

"Yes, and his wife divorced him last week."

"Don't be silly, what's that got to do with business? I'll risk you divorcing me. Now be serious, Jim," urged Lizzie.

"You don't think I shall leave Victoria for a joke, do you?" protested Jim.

"I've thought it all out," continued Lizzie, ignoring his frivolous interruption. "You always said you wouldn't have me going to the restaurant after we married, but I can help with the business, relieving you at times. We get a nice house—— "

"And Mother?"

"That would always have to be faced. I suggest you allow her ten shillings a week, that would be quite generous, and enable her to carry on as she is, which is what she would really like As we don't start business until August we could have a really good honeymoon. We could go abroad, to Paris and—— "

"We always said we'd go to Lugano—when we were joking," observed Jim.

"We can go there later—you can't say you've been abroad if you've not been to Paris," said Lizzie. "I've got it all planned."

She had indeed. And here they were, talking to Mr. Waddle, only three weeks after. Lizzie had even been content with a registry office marriage, though the desire not to exhibit her family had something to do with her choice. The money had been set aside for the tobacco and confectionery business. Jim had left the railway, with some misgiving and regret. He had insisted on making a present of fifty pounds each to his sister and mother. This left a balance of about four hundred, of which one hundred had been spent in a proper outfit for them both, and two hundred was earmarked for the honeymoon. There was a hundred left in reserve. "You never know," observed Lizzie, "and let us do the thing properly while we are doing it."

They were married in the morning and left Victoria in the afternoon. Both families attended at Victoria Station to see them off on the Boat Train. It was rather a boisterous send-off, with Mr. Parrish slightly drunk and Mrs. Parrish enjoyably tearful. Lizzie, as soon as the train drew out, said, "Thank Heaven, that vulgar display is over!"

"Oh, they've got to let themselves go at a time like this," said Jim, flushed and happy as he looked at his bride. "Lizzie, you look bewitching!"

She put her hand in his. His mates had seen that they had a compartment to themselves.

"There's one thing, now that old life's over, darling, I want you to do," she said, smiling at him.

"Cut my nails shorter, I suppose?" he laughed. "Well, I have, just to please you, look! And I'm not wearing my pins, either."

"Thank you, James darling."

"James——"

"Yes—Jim is so very common. It was all right when you were a porter—but not now, darling."

"But Lizzie!" he protested.

"And I never want to be called Lizzie in public again. I hate the name. You must call me Betty," she said, her face so near to his that he kissed her impulsively.

"Gosh!" he exclaimed. "Are you out to make a gentleman of me?"

"Yes, and don't say Gosh, darling. We're travelling, and we shall meet all sorts of nice people, well-to-do people. We mustn't embarrass them," said his wife.

He had got used to calling her Betty after a week, but "James" soon became "Jim" again. He had got used to a dozen little things she insisted on. Sometimes he felt angry, sometimes he felt hurt, but she was so patient and sweet to him that he succumbed to her reforming zeal. She had an astonishing flair for "acquiring tone" and looking "top-drawer." There was an old English Colonel in the hotel, the type he knew so well at Victoria, who travelled first-class, with a "man" and excess luggage. Colonel Dalrymple-Bowen, he was called. He would sit up in the lounge until midnight on the chance of a chat with Betty when they came in. He took them to the Louvre, and showed them the Venus of Milo, and the Rubens, and the Corots. He was a great talker, and he was always paying Betty compliments. "Ravishing, my boy, she's ravishing!" he exclaimed to Jim. "Take care of her. It's lucky for you I'm an old dodderer!"

The Colonel had become a bit of a nuisance. He always accosted them in the morning with "You mustn't let a lonely old man be tiresome, but I wonder if you children would like to see——" It was very nice and kind of him, and he did know Paris, but they wanted to go about by themselves. But Betty liked the Colonel and accepted his offers. He was such an excellent pattern of an English gentleman for James to study, she said.

Jim did not give Betty a report of the café in Montmartre to which the Colonel took him one night when she retired early with a headache, and where the strangest people hailed him with familiarity. "Not my world," said the Colonel, as they left. "But it takes all sorts to make life, you know.

And it should be seen once, my boy." Jim was certain the
Colonel had seen it a good many times.

But he liked the old boy, and learned a lot from him. He
seemed connected with everybody who mattered. Then one
day his wife arrived and he became afraid to speak to them.
He did introduce them to her, but she was as hard and cold
as an icicle. Poor Colonel Dalrymple-Bowen, there was no
more waiting in the lounge for their return.

Mr. Waddle had not the aristocratic distinction of the
Colonel. His clothes were not so well cut, nor was his voice
so impressive. But he did know the places where you got
value for money, the curious things one might see, the odd
places not listed in guide-books. In half an hour they were
completely in his spell. He told them he came to Paris
every May " for a certain anniversary," but that he was
leaving in a few days for Budapest as a delegate to a conference.

" Oh—are you in politics ? " asked Betty, wondering if, after
all, Mr. Waddle was much more important than he looked.

" No—I'm in folk-dancing," he said, with an engaging air
of mischief.

He opened the portfolio on the café table, ran his fingers
over its many bulging divisions, and finally drew out a sheet.

" Oh—here's a small folder, with all particulars," said Mr.
Waddle, adjusting his spectacles. " You'll see we've a most
interesting programme—there are delegates from Roumania,
Poland, Czechoslovakia, France, England, Italy—and even
Russia. There will be some very fine performances. I,
myself, am broadcasting a little talk on the international
significance of folk-dancing."

" How very interesting," said Betty politely, reading the
folder he passed to her.

" And Budapest is, of course, the loveliest city in Europe,
to my mind. It's not yet spoilt by too many tourists,"
added Mr. Waddle. " You will be able to see some remark-
able dances. It has taken me a whole year to organise this
festival, and I have had the help of the Hungarian Government ; so there'll be no doubt about our reception there."

" What is folk-dancing exactly ? " asked Jim, suddenly.

Waddle stared at him in amazement for a few moments. If someone had emptied a bucket of cold water on him he would not have been more amazed. Then, recovering breath, he realised that here were two possible converts to the great cause.

" Folk-dancing ! " he murmured. " You want to know what is folk-dancing ? "

He opened the crammed portfolio again, and this time extracted a bundle of unmounted photographs fastened together by an elastic band.

" Now here are some of our dances," he said, pushing away the glasses and clearing a space on the table. " You must let me give you an outline of the historical significance of these figures. Now this one——"

II

It was very late when they parted from Waddle. He had almost persuaded them that folk-dancing had a deep international significance, that it was the fine flower of civilisation.

" I suppose you're honeymooning here in Paris—if I may be so bold as to hazard a guess ? " asked Waddle, at the end of his oration on folk-dancing.

" You're quite right, we are," agreed Jim. " And if ever you want an example of strange Fortune, here's as good a one as you will ever get. A month ago I was a porter at Victoria Station, reading on other folk's luggage the labels of places I thought I should never see."

His wife shifted her glass, took a handkerchief out of her reticule and deliberately blew her nose to hide her embarrassment. She could have killed him. There he went again, giving away the whole show, just as he had done to the Colonel, who had thought they were people of private means.

" Yes, and here we are in Paris—which my wife used to dream about while she was carrying trays in——" continued Jim, in friendly confession.

" I really think we should go," interrupted Betty, closing her reticule with a snap. " I feel quite cold."

But Jim could not be stopped. Waddle's obvious enjoyment of this human story encouraged him to go on.

" Yes, believe it or not, one morning I woke up to find I'd won over a thousand pounds in a football pool. It's the sort of thing we see in the films, or read about in papers. But it happened to me, and that's why we're here, as you said, honeymooning in Paris. I have to pinch myself sometimes ? "

Jim leaned back triumphantly, glanced at his wife for approval, and received a look of cold hatred.

" We really must go ! " said Betty, rising. " We've had a tiring day."

Mr. Waddle secured the bill and insisted on paying. He accompanied them to the taxi they called. No, they could not give him a lift. He had a small room quite near. There was a Basque folk-dance performance to-morrow evening. He would be delighted if they would go with him to see it— a charming thing to watch, and there was a team also from Andorra, the small Republic in the Pyrenees.

He was delighted when they accepted his invitation, and insisted on calling for them at their hotel.

Their taxi moved off, and they left him bowing and beaming, the bulging portfolio tucked under his arm.

Jim sank back into the seat.

" What a nice fellow ! " he exclaimed.

" What a nice fool you've made of yourself," retorted Betty, her voice trembling with anger.

" Now what have I done ? " asked Jim, putting his arm around his wife's waist. But she flung it away, and drew herself into the corner.

" Why must you always expose yourself like that ? Why must you tell everybody you've been a railway porter ? It's nothing to boast about ! " she said.

" It's nothing to be ashamed of, is it ? " he asked, mildly.

" Yes, it is ! Here I'm doing my best to turn you into a gentleman, I pull you out of the groove, I make the acquaintance of nice people who think we're the same as they are——"

" Oh, do they ? " exclaimed Jim.

" Well, they think I am, anyhow. I won't be dragged down and humiliated. Haven't you any ambition ? "

" I'm sorry you're ashamed of me," retorted Jim, curtly. " Perhaps you've made a mistake marrying such a common article."

" Perhaps I have, Jim, I——"

" That's better, Lizzie," he said with a smile.

She bit her lip in annoyance.

" You know I hate being called Lizzie," she said, an angry flush in her cheeks. " You look like a gentleman, you talk like a gentleman when you want. Why tell Mr. Waddle about that silly football pool, and let him know we're not used to nice things ? I've come abroad to get away from the old atmosphere. I hate mean streets and poor people, and bad food, and haggling over the pennies."

" That's very unusual, I suppose," retorted Jim. " And I wouldn't call a football pool silly when it enables you to come to places like this."

" That's not the point. The past's the past. If we play our cards well there's no knowing where we shall end."

" We shall end in a sweet and tobacco business on August the first, and if you do that High Society stuff you'll frighten all the customers."

" Slang again ! " said Betty, witheringly. " That shop is only in reserve, in case nothing better happens."

" Whatever do you mean ? " asked Jim, startled now.

" All my life I've believed a way would come, somehow. I knew I was never destined to live in a slum and carry trays in a restaurant, and I've never quite believed you would remain a porter all your days. I should never have married you if I'd thought that. I've a good reason for feeling as I do. James, there is something I must tell you, and perhaps then you'll understand I'm not a Parrish at all."

Jim stared at his wife. There was an extraordinary expression on her face, defiant, exultant.

" Perhaps you think I'm mad, but it's sober truth I'm telling you. You've never seen my father. Not my real father. You'd be quite surprised if I told you the truth about my birth."

"Oh, yes!" exclaimed Jim, derisively.

His wife looked at him with flashing eyes.

"You laugh! Very well, don't believe me!"

"How can you expect me to? It's a bit of a shock for a man to be told that his wife's—that his wife's——"

"Illegitimate—you needn't boggle at the word. I'm not ashamed of my blood. I should have thought it was very obvious. Do I look or behave like those Parrishes, like Gertrude, or Herbert, or father?" she demanded.

"I must say you've always been quite different from them. You've always looked—well, aristocratic. I've always been terribly proud of you, but——"

"But? You're not going to throw my birth in my face?"

"My dear girl, don't be silly! I don't care a damn what you are, or where you come from. You can be the Tsar's only surviving daughter if you like. Anything you fancy, my dear. But I——"

"I see you don't believe me, James."

"I know you're incurably romantic," said Jim, "and I don't mind how much day-dreaming you do, but you mustn't start reforming me. We've married one another because we love one another, and we'll take the faults with the virtues. You'll only make yourself miserable by trying to turn me into something I'm not. That's what's the matter with most people to-day. They've lost their anchors, and they want folks to think they're liners when they're only tramps. Take that fellow Waddle. You can't throw sand in his eyes. He's a gentleman, although he gets his tie up round his neck, and I remain a working man although you made me get a suit costing treble what I've ever paid before."

"You look very well, you look a gentleman. It's not how you look, it's the things you say," insisted Betty. "James, dear, it's only because I'm so proud of you that——"

Whatever she intended saying went unsaid. He drew her to him and kissed her with a forceful pressure to which she succumbed.

"It's lucky for you I'm not the perfect gentleman," he said, with a grin.

"What do you mean?" she asked, looking into his laughing eyes. She raised her hand to his brow and pushed back a curl.

"I might get too much notice taken of me by real ladies with too much time on their hands," he replied, banteringly.

She looked at him thoughtfully for a moment, and his light words awoke a faint apprehension in her mind. He was very attractive. Some women would undoubtedly find him irresistible, with his boyish freshness, his strong, good-natured face, his athletic figure. Until this moment the possibility of any woman competing with her had never occurred to her. She had always dominated him completely.

She laughed at him now, to hide her sudden alarm.

"You've a very good opinion of yourself," she retorted, lightly.

"Yes—like you, my dear, I'm not exactly what I seem. One day the railway porter might not only march off with the princess's luggage, but with the princess also. Hollywood has made anything possible. In fact it's happened already. The Prince and Princess Brown of Victoria Station have left for their honeymoon in Paris, and will return in August to their confectionery business. No bills will be forwarded."

He kissed her again, and she laughed in his arms, all her resentment gone. His good nature always defeated her attempt to change him.

The taxi drew up at their hotel.

"And now I'm going to put the Princess to bed. It's your maid's night off, I believe," he said, playfully, as the taxi stopped and he helped her out.

A sleepy night-watchman opened the door. Jim glanced at the vestibule clock. It was 2 a.m. All the shoes were out in the corridors.

As his wife slipped off her dress, he kissed her shoulder, where the pink loop of her camisole lay on the soft, warm flesh. Holding her as they stood before the mirror, he laughed at their reflected faces. Their eyes met in the mirror. She turned her head, and he laughed as his lips took hers in a long kiss.

"Why do you laugh, Jim?" she asked, breathless from his embrace.

"Is that us in the mirror?"

"Of course—why do you ask?"

"There used to be a book on the bookstall at Victoria. It had a bright picture on the jacket of a very handsome young man kissing a very beautiful half-undressed girl in a bedroom. It was called *The Night-life of Paris*. I very nearly bought it. And here's the real thing."

"I'm not sure that's a compliment," said Betty.

"Never mind, darling. I've taken you for better or worse," he retorted, running his lips down the bare arm until he came to her hand. Kneeling, he held it to his mouth, exclaiming, "Charmed, Princess!"

She laughed, touched his hair, and bent and kissed his upturned mouth. In these moods he was adorable.

III

In the next five days they saw much of Mr. Waddle. He was an admirable cicerone. He conducted them to the folk-dancing and it was almost painful to behold his anxiety for their approval of the performance. But they enjoyed themselves so thoroughly, without any need of false emphasis, that Mr. Waddle was delighted. He felt they had embraced the faith. He set his heart on enticing them to Budapest. He drew such an enchanting picture of life in the city of the Danube, of the vast palace, the hill-side restaurants, the thronged Corso, the chains of lights, the heady music, the delicious food, that they abandoned their intention to journey south.

For Mr. Waddle was very practical. He knew just the place to stay in, and the cost of everything. He worked out a plan, including a brief stay in Vienna and three weeks in Budapest. After that, why could they not go, via Lake

Balaton, the second largest lake in Europe, on to Venice, and via Milan, Lugano and Lucerne, back home ? He knew enthusiastic folk-dancers in all these places, who, on a word from him, would be delighted to look after them.

" Venice—we could really see Venice ? " exclaimed Betty, breathlessly, conjuring up a vision of gondolas on the moonlit lagoon, and all the operatic, chocolate-box pictures with which her longing had been fed.

" I've always wanted to see Lugano," said Jim. " When I went quite off my head I always dreamed of a honeymoon in Lugano."

" Well, you can see it quite easily on the way home, on the St. Gothard route. Lugano's not exactly—well—it's——"

Mr. Waddle, loathed Lugano. He was about to call it the Schoolteachers' Paradise, the Brighton of Switzerland, but he hadn't the heart to shatter the young man's eager expectations.

" It's a bit of Italy that's slipped into Switzerland," he explained, lamely. " Swiss sanitation and cleanliness, and all the arcaded, palm-tree charm of the Italian lakes. But they will play *Tipperary* in the teashops when they see you're English. And if you visit Venice, may I beg one thing of you ? Don't visit the glassworks. Don't let those Venetians wheedle you into visiting them. They're hot, dull and expensive. Venetian glass is dreadful stuff, highly coloured and spiky, and fragile. It won't travel, thank heaven ! "

Mr. Waddle smiled at them.

" You'll think I'm very sophisticated," he said, apologetically. " But I've been travelling for many years, and I think I've the right perspective at last. I can visit every place on the Continent without wanting to buy anything. I've achieved the Freedom of the Trumpery at last."

With a thumping heart, late one night at the Dome Café, when Mr. Waddle had volunteered to conduct them personally, Jim decided to go to Budapest. It was right outside all their plans, it seemed a mad thing to do, to go careering across Europe when there was so much to see close at hand. But Mr. Waddle had unsettled them with his stories of life in Hungary, and his thinly veiled contempt of the showplaces in the tourist's itinerary.

"Perhaps we're making a bad blunder," said Jim to his wife, as they went home that night. "But, after all he's said, I should always be hankering to see the place. It's perhaps an awful hole, with them fiddling in your ear all day and night. But I feel we've got to go now, damn Mr. Waddle!"

"Of course we're going," said Betty, her eyes shining. "It's such an opportunity with Mr. Waddle to take us there."

Had he overdrawn the picture, she wondered. Could life be so romantic, with midnight supper parties high above the Danube, the fashionable Corso at sunset, the delicious music of gipsy orchestras, the great plains with the herds of horses, the peasants in their brilliant costumes, and the men, the Hungarian men, so gallant, such worshippers of feminine beauty?

Mr. Waddle had not painted life in Budapest in nearly such glowing colours as she now conceived it. She had always believed that her future held promise of adventure, and had not her faith already been justified? Here she was in Paris, married to the man she loved. If Fate had beckoned her to Bagdad or Timbuctoo she would not have hesitated. She firmly believed in her star, and that there could be nothing false in the smile of Fortune.

IV

Mr. Waddle attended to all the details. He booked two second-class berths on the Arlberg-Orient Express, leaving the Gare de l'Est at ten o'clock on the following Tuesday night. He did not take a sleeper himself, indeed it was a luxury for him to travel second-class. He would sit up all night, quite comfortably, with two rubber air-cushions with which he always travelled.

The route of the train gave Jim and Betty a thrill. It was connected with that four-thirty from Victoria on which

Jim had seen so many depart, envious of the distant countries and cities through which the famous express passed—France, Switzerland, Austria, Hungary, Jugoslavia and Greece.

Mr. Waddle, well known at Cook's, by the Madeleine, had every detail of the journey at his finger-tips. He arrived at the agency's door just after it had been firmly closed in the faces of two loudly protesting American youths. " I think, perhaps, one can get in," said Mr. Waddle, smiling, and made a secret tattoo on the door. " Oh, it's you, sir ! " said the porter, when the door opened. " Yes, it's me, and two friends," answered Mr. Waddle, genially. " I fear it's closing time, but you are so obliging."

He hurried the two Americans across the main floor of the closed office.

" Say, it's mighty kind of you, sir ! " said the taller youth, with a freckled face.

" Not at all—you want that counter. I'm going to the second floor. Good-bye," he replied.

On the second floor he was greeted like an old friend, even though the office was closing down. Nor was his welcome due to the amount he spent. " In a sense, I suppose, I am Cook's. I mean I'm a kind of travelling link between their branches, a member of the family, one might say," he explained, as he obtained schillings for Jim from the cashier one morning.

Each day Mr. Waddle called and took Jim and his wife to some new place he felt they must see. But when he arrived on the day prior to their departure he had an air of excitement in his manner.

" We can lunch very quietly—and then I can tell you," he said, when Jim finally asked him why he was so agitated. So after the morning's sight-seeing he piloted them to a quiet little restaurant in a side-street off the Boulevard Haussman When he had ordered their dishes, he brushed the table with a bread roll.

" Well, my dears, this morning I had a letter from a friend in Hungary. A most extraordinary letter even to me, who has long been past surprise. The world, as you

know, has gone mad. The Great War that was to make
the world safe for democracy has resulted in its becoming
safe only for lunacy. Look at poor Austria ! "

" The letter ? " said Jim, fearing Mr. Waddle had lost
the thread of his discourse. " You were saying ? "

" I was about to say, regarding the letter," began Mr.
Waddle, raising his spoon, and tasting the soup—" I was
about to say—this soup is really excellent, isn't it ? the
French are good at this sort of thing—the letter contains a
really astonishing proposal, and since it affects you, I must
explain. But after coffee, I think. I won't spoil this excellent
luncheon, eh ? "

Mr. Waddle paused, and having finished his soup, he
selected a newspaper from several which he had been carrying
under his arm, opened it, and proudly pointed to a third
of a column reporting the performance in Paris to which he
had conducted them. " Not a long article, of course, but
it's all to the good. Keeps up the interest. And they
wouldn't put it in if they didn't know their readers were
interested. No, you may be sure of that ! "

He proudly passed the paper over to them pointing out
his anonymous contribution. In between he produced a pen-
knife and cut out his contribution, transferring it to the bulging
portfolio lying on the table. " I keep the archives up to
date," he said, with a twinkle. " And now," he added,
as coffee was brought in, and he accepted one of Jim's
cigarettes, " I can tell you about the letter from my Hungarian friend. When I tell you what it is all about, you
may think I am quite mad, or you may think our meeting
is a matter of Fate. But I'll begin at the beginning and
explain."

And shifting the coffee cups to give himself space on the
table, Mr. Waddle took a letter out of his portfolio, spread
it on the table, and began to explain. They listened with
ever-growing astonishment.

CHAPTER VI

DRAMA IN BUDAPEST

I

HERR GOLLWITZER could not sleep in his room at the Grand Hotel. He had purposely gone late to bed, late even for gay Budapest, whose life was still running strong at two o'clock in the morning. There had fallen upon him that most terrible of scourges, insomnia, and for a month now it had been sapping his vitality. He desperately tried to discipline himself, to dismiss from his mind the events of the past month, and to see in the future something worth living for, but when a man of sixty-two sees his whole life suddenly reduced to ruins there is little comfort to be derived from a store of philosophy. He cared little for fame, which had long been his in a great measure, and not very much for fortune. For the past thirty years one of the world's great conductors, he had always commanded everything necessary to his comfort. He had lived easily, he had travelled in luxury, since at all times it paid him to conserve his energies, and he had been lavish in hospitality to his world-wide circle of friends.

To his knowledge he had not an enemy. His position as a conductor had been unassailable for a great number of years. He was not deluding himself in believing he evoked something akin to affection as well as admiration in the vast audiences his name commanded. He was, in short, a very happy and successful man, living only for his work.

And now, at sixty-two, at the zenith of his fame, the incredible thing had happened. Austria had been engulfed in a seething tide of Nazi frenzy, and overnight all those Austrian qualities of gaiety, liberty and *Gemütlichkeit* had been wiped out.

He was too stunned even now to analyse how it had all

happened. He had known, they had all known, the constant
pressure of Nazi forces waiting on their northern frontier.
Herr Schuschnigg had been called over to Berchtesgaden
and there made to feel a turn of the thumbscrew. But
always there had been the hope that the disaster would be
averted, that Austria would keep its independence.

And now it had all gone. An Austrian, he felt he no
longer had a country ; a Jew, he had no political rights,
and was the mark of every blackguard's venom. His very
pleasant flat near the Stadtpark was shut up and he could
never return to it. Its rooms had been rifled on the very
morning that Hitler, speaking to the cheering thousands,
had proclaimed his sacred mission, under God, to extinguish
the torch of Austrian liberty, and obliterate a nation with
seven hundred years of proud independence.

It was impossible to believe that he would never again
raise his baton in the Opera House, where he had laid the
foundations of his world-fame. Impossible to believe that
at least one third of the members of his orchestra, whom he
loved and knew by name, who lived so passionately for
their art, were now hunted, and publicly humiliated, because
of their Jewish blood. He had never in his life thought in
terms of blood. There were good musicians and bad musicians,
there was sincere work and shoddy work ; these were the
only things that affected him.

Herr Gollwitzer turned over in his bed and looked at his
watch on the bedside table. The dawn was breaking and
he could just see the dial. It was five o'clock. Then he
had slept just two hours.

He shut his eyes, but he could not get off to sleep. Last
night he had read in the paper of some Austrian Nazis who
had dumped on an island in the Danube, just within Hungarian territory, fifty hungry and ill-clad Jews whom they
had rounded up in a village over the frontier. Three of the
oldest Jews had died of exposure, the rest were in an appalling
condition. The Hungarian authorities had denied them
asylum, and the wretched people had been returned to
Austrian territory and immediately thrown into jail.

It was the same story everywhere. The scum of the side streets, sanctified by the swastika, was preying on his defenceless race. His own immunity from the indignities visited on his people only increased his depression. His possessions had been taken from him, he could not live in his own flat, use his own goods, spend his own money, or walk the streets of his native city without exposing himself to public insult —to the inspection and questioning by arrogant officials, or even worse.

His friend Karl Warburg, for instance, the head of a great children's hospital, and perhaps the kindest soul in all Vienna, had come round to his flat one evening, a broken, unrecognisable man, his limbs shaking, his mouth quivering as he told him how the doors of his own hospital had been shut in his face. Stunned, he had gone to a Ringstrasse café, afraid to face his wife until he was calmer. Suddenly a rabble of youths had rushed in, burly louts who had seized him, forced him outside and thrust a bucket and a brush into his hands. Then, amid their jeering, he had been forced on to his knees, and made to scrub away at a " Heil Schuschnigg " notice painted on the pavement in the height of the plebiscite fervour, forty-eight hours previously.

For half an hour he had scrubbed in vain, surrounded by a jeering crowd, scrubbed with hands that had saved the lives of thousands of Viennese children. Then he had been released and given an ironical certificate exonerating him from further public cleansing for that day. He had called a taxi at the street corner, half-fainting. But the taxi-man, as soon as he saw him, had spat in his face and driven on. Poor Karl Warburg, gentlest of men and a great physician in a city of great physicians. He had blown his brains out the next day, on the threshold of his own hospital, which had again denied him admission.

Was it such a foolish thing to do, wondered Herr Gollwitzer, staring up at the ceiling of his room. He had suffered no physical indignity like poor Karl. The wound was in his soul and he felt sick unto death. He knew that elsewhere in many cities of the earth he would still be an honoured and welcome figure. There was Paris, Prague, London, Brussels, New York, Philadelphia and Chicago, where still he commanded the allegiance of great audiences. But there was only one Vienna, the city of his birth, of his own people.

He had suffered other losses. His immense library of music, all the things he had collected and loved, acquired through the years in his world travels, these he would never see again. But the material losses were not the heaviest. He did not even lament the fortune invested in Austria, which would now be sequestrated and ultimately stolen from him in the name of the State. They could not, as with others of his unhappy race, reduce him to penury. There were other countries not dead to reason or decency in its treatment of human beings, and his genius was still honoured elsewhere.

But it was not as a persecuted Jew, flung down from high honour in his native land, to the condition of an animal baited by a rabble of adventurers, that he felt mortally wounded. His name was safe with posterity, his honour unstained. He was troubled by the smaller indignities and injustices visited upon him. His home had been rifled, friendships that he thought secure against all adversities had been broken with unbelievable callousness. Two of his dearest friends had covertly sent notes begging him not to endanger their standing with the Nazi authorities. His devoted servant, little Hans, had been threatened if he, an Aryan, entered again the home of a monstrous Jew.

Unforgettable was that terrible last morning at the Polizei-bureau when, amid a herd of hysterical men, women and children of his own race, he had waited long hours in a queue to beg permission to leave the country. He could see still the coarse, leering faces of the louts who had examined him, in all the bravado of their new Nazi uniforms. His luggage had been ripped open and sorted, his pockets turned inside out, his body prodded and investigated with gloating indecency. He had witnessed women torn from their husbands, their money and jewels confiscated, their poor belongings, gathered together in the panic of flight, ravaged and picked over in an excess of triumphant officiousness. That last scene in the station of the faces of those broken men and women turned back, at the last minute, and of the poor exiles fleeing to the unknown, sitting huddled and silent as the train drew out, could never be effaced from his memory.

Until these last days of terror it had been almost a halcyon year. In his coming and going he had not noticed the sinister shadow falling over the Austrian scene. He had ignored the warnings of more timid souls. The stout heart of Austria kept off the menace couched by the Bavarian border. In his home, to which he had returned as soon as he was released from his engagements in foreign cities, there was a new interest transcending all others. An unhappy early marriage had left him a lonely man, nursing a grievance. He had craved a son and heir. Then, one day, he had perpetrated his only quixotic act. He had adopted the illegitimate child of a peasant girl, born on the train in which he travelled homewards to Vienna. How his friends had laughed at this adventure! They called it the Railway Baby, *Der kleine Eisenbahner*. At first he had arranged for the infant to be wet-nursed at Innsbruck, where mother and child were taken off the train. And now for six months there had been a strange new sound in his apartment, that of a crying infant, the crying of his adopted son.

The story of *Der kleine Eisenbahner* had gone round Vienna. Unfortunately a Viennese journalist had got the story on the train. The newspapers made a feature of it, for anything concerning him was always good news. He accepted the unwanted publicity with good humour. The baby was photographed with its nurse, finally it was photographed being dangled by Collwitzer himself. The quick-humoured Viennese public bought postcards of the famous baby.

And thereby they had found a stick to beat him with in the Day of Wrath. Should a filthy Jew be allowed to adopt a healthy Christian child, demanded a Party garbage sheet. Late one night there was a hammering on the door of his apartment, and four booted and spurred Nazis strode in and demanded the delivery of the child. Its nurse was fetched from her bed and told to produce the child. She stoutly refused, and, standing in front of the door, denounced the intruders with such vigour that they retreated shame-facedly. For the moment the enemy had been repulsed, but the situation was highly dangerous.

There was a hurried conference between the faithful Hans, the nurse and himself. The demand for the child had probably not been official, and obviously the exuberant Austrian Nazis were out of hand. But the menace might recur. They had to act quickly. At nine o'clock that morning the nurse, taking the child with her, left for a rela-tive's home in the country. Immediately they had departed he had packed two bags and said good-bye to his Vienna home, leaving the faithful Hans in charge. He had an engagement to conduct in Prague in a few days so that his departure seemed quite legitimate. Later, Hans would follow, and somehow the child might be got out of the country.

Even now, as he lay in bed in the semi-dark bedroom of the Grand Hungaria, Gollwitzer broke into a sweat at the memory of that terrible night, the hasty conference when the Nazis had gone, and the decision to leave Vienna. Hans insisted that he should go at once, before he had suffered personal violence at the hands of fanatics drunk with power.

There had followed the indignities at the railway station. For a time it seemed likely that they would not let him go, but he was the great Gollwitzer, with an engagement in Prague, and finally they consented. As the train drew out he knew he would never see his beloved Vienna again, and when he crossed the frontier it seemed as if something had snapped within him. He actually burst into tears as the last Austrian village receded out of sight after passing the Customs, but he did not make himself conspicuous thereby, as many of his fellow passengers were in a similar state, and there were harrowing scenes when some of the refugees were turned back at the frontier.

He had collapsed in Prague, worn out by the stress of

the past ten days. He cancelled his engagement to conduct
unable to face an audience. For three days he never left
his hotel bedroom. He felt terribly old. Then, on the
fourth day, he decided to leave for Budapest, a city he had
always liked. The faithful Hans had telephoned to him
on the second night, but he told him nothing of importance
It was obvious he was afraid to speak, knowing the wires
were tapped. But he did learn that his correspondence had
been seized, his apartment closed and placed under seal. Hans
said nothing about the child. He did not dare to ask.

He had been a fortnight here in Budapest. He had seen
a few friends. Fortunately he had some money in a New
York bank, for his money in Vienna could not be trans-
ferred. He had given liberally to fellow exiles in extreme
poverty. His worries were not financial. He was broken
in spirit, the zest had gone out of his life, his work offered no
solace. His mind went over and over the events of the
past weeks. And now he was tortured by insomnia.

He had written to Hans begging him to join him. There
was no response. After four days of terrible anxiety he
learned why. His devoted servant, on some pretext, had
been locked up, pending investigations. What investigations ? What could his devoted Hans have done to be thus
summarily shut up ? The cousin who wrote to him could
give no reason and, fearing the censorship of the mails, made
no suggestion.

Gollwitzer could not sleep, he could not eat. He felt
overwhelmed by the tragedy of Austria. There was nothing
worth living for. He began to play with the idea of suicide

The thought frightened him at first. He knew it was the
sign of an unbalanced mind. He was not without food or
money, as so many other poor devils, but there were worse
things than hunger and poverty ; he no longer felt equal to
the daily battle of life. He was too tired to hope for anything. Ambition had fulfilled itself, and his quiet world of
music had suddenly been invaded by the din of political
doctrines, the extravagances and brutalities of madmen
bellowing their blasphemies against the light.

At nine o'clock Gollwitzer rose, bathed and dressed. He ordered coffee and rolls, but scarcely touched them. Retaining his dressing-gown, he sat at a small writing-table near one of the windows of his corner room. From his window he looked out on the blue-grey hills where Buda rose above the broad Danube, its heights crowned by the citadel and the vast grey pile of the Royal Palace. Below him, the wide Corso, the scene of Budapest's evening parade, was deserted. He opened the *Pester Lloyd*, but he only glanced at the head-lines. It was folly to read newspapers these days, they contained the same endless accounts of futile conferences, groupings of big and little nations, professions of peaceful policy allied with staggering expenditure on munitions. The dictators shouted at Europe through their microphones. Spain writhed in the agony of civil war, and a Non-Intervention Committee, energetically doing nothing, made the world break into ironic laughter. The moribund League of Nations awaited its next session of pious futility, the red carnage swayed to and fro across China, and Russia, not to be outdone in spectacles of blood, embarked on a new orgy of executions.

Gollwitzer pushed the paper aside, and stared out of the side-window opening on to an annex of the hotel. Opposite, in full view on a balcony, a young man was kissing the nape of a woman's neck as she sat enjoying the morning sun. She turned, laughed, and smoothed the young man's face with her delicate hand ; a honeymoon pair, Italian in appearance. Gollwitzer would have enjoyed this little scene, in normal circumstances. Now he looked at them impatiently. Were they going to bring children into this mad world ?

He wondered where Friedl, his adopted son, was at this moment. Every morning, immediately after breakfast, he had gone into the pleasant room overlooking the Stadtpark, which he had had fitted up as a nursery, and interviewed the nurse. He watched the baby bathed and weighed, laughed at it and shook his big head over the cot, heard news of the new tooth, and let Friedl curl his tiny hand around one of his fingers.

"He knows you, Herr Gollwitzer," said the nurse.

"Of course he knows me!" responded Gollwitzer. "Don
you, *kleiner Eisenbahner*?" he asked, shaking his head a
the laughing baby. Every morning that had been h
custom, when at home. If only Hans were free, to sen
him news of Friedl.

The *Pester Lloyd* said that the Austrian Nazis had behave
badly, breaking into apartments, pilfering their content
sacking shops and treating Jews as political enemies, an
that the persecuted had been grateful for the presence o
disciplined German Nazis, who had checked these outrage
What had come over the kindly Austrian people, with thei
ready laughter, their light-hearted indifference to othe
people's views and habits? The murderer of poor littl
Dolfuss was now turned into a national hero, and the criminal
who had let the poor little Chancellor bleed to death in th
room in the Chancellory, were now fêted and honoured b
the State.

Gollwitzer put on his coat and hat, and left his room
Down in the vestibule the concierge brought him five letter
which had just arrived. Not one of them bore the Austria
postmark. He sat down, his heart heavy, and opened them
A concert agent in Paris wished to obtain engagements fo
him. There were two appeals for help, written from Zuric
and Milan, from members of his Viennese orchestra, fugitive
both of them, starving with their families. He knew ther
well, and they must be helped. Every day he was sendin
money to someone in dire distress. He had some te
thousand dollars in a New York bank which would las
him for some time. Fortunately he could always mak
money.

Yes, there was an Austrian letter. He opened it eagerly
It came from his solicitor. The engagement with the Sal
burg Festival had been cancelled. Well, he had expecte
that, and would not have gone in any case. He read on
He had been dismissed from his directorship of the Oper
House and the College of Music. The bank had written t
say that no money from Herr Gollwitzer's account could b

nt abroad. He had expected that also. His old friend
ranz Wertheim had shot himself, also Hans Erhardt.
Gollwitzer read on, but the news in his solicitor's letter
ad no further effect on him. The old life had gone for
ver, and he was too old to nourish any hope of making a
ew life in some foreign place. The solution of it all was
ery simple. Franz and Hans and Karl had not hesitated
 quit a life so monstrous, to put themselves beyond the
dignities of existence.

He read the remaining letters, and thrusting them into
s pocket, went up to the hall-porter's desk, with the in-
ention of asking the address of a gunsmith. But he checked
imself. That would never do. There had been three
icides in Budapest hotels in the past forty-eight hours,
ll of them refugees.

"A beautiful morning, Herr Gollwitzer," said the hotel
anager, bowing as he passed. "You are taking a walk?
here is the flower market this morning."

Gollwitzer went out through the revolving door, into the
uiet street behind the hotel. The flower market! No,
e was not visiting the flower market. At the end of the
reet he turned left towards the busy Váci-utca, on his
rrand to buy a pistol.

II

Gollwitzer lunched late on the terrace of his hotel, sitting
nder the awning. The Corso was almost deserted. A few
eamers passed along the dun-brown river, which had long
ased to be, if it ever had been, the blue Danube of Johann
trauss. Across the street the immense pile of the Royal
alace, with its central bronze-green dome, and long façade
f windows, shimmered in the afternoon sun. It was a dead
ile of royal splendour, a palace without a king. Surely
e ghost of the wayward, lovely Queen Elizabeth walked
s silent chambers! The Hapsburgs had vanished, their
mpire had vanished.

Gollwitzer remembered a dazzling reception in the great

Audience Hall, with King Franz Josef, his Queen, and th
Court, assembled in magnificent array, as the nobles, th
statesmen, the soldiers and notables passed and made obei
ance to the wearer of St. Stephen's crown. He was a ver
young man then, commanded to his first State performanc
It was all as a dream to-day, only the backcloth of the grea
scene, that palace, remained. The assassin's dagger foun
the breast of the beautiful Empress, the son died violentl
in the mystery of Mayerling, the heir to the throne fell t
a Serbian bullet, the old Emperor watched his Empire'
death agony, his successor died in poverty and exile. An
now nothing remained of that proud Empire establishe
for seven hundred years. How could his fellow-countryme
exult in the obliteration of their native land, cheer the or
coming of the conqueror, and offer eager hands for th
shackles of Nazi servitude !

At five o'clock Gollwitzer took a long walk. He wa
strangely calm now. He surveyed the world about hir
with quiet eyes. He had finished with life ; the turmo
and the anxieties would continue, but he would be beyon
them.

The oddest things passed through his mind : that the
of his personal luggage on the way to St. Petersburg—h
had conducted at the command performance of *Fidelio* i
the borrowed dress-clothes of the President of the Duma—
shot a week later ; the frozen Lake Michigan seen from hi
suite at the Commodore Hotel in Chicago, on a winter
afternoon ; the surprise on the young clerk's face in Cook'
London, when he had given him a five-pound note to cele
brate the birth of a son, to which the young fellow had shyl
confessed ; the box of cigars King Edward had given hi
after dinner at the Marlborough Club—so strong he coul
not smoke them ; a little girl's face, so lovely and caln
after having been run over in a Warsaw street—he ha
picked her up, dead—dead twenty years ago ; and his wif
and the unhappy marriage ended after two years. He re
called how, in a passion, she had hit the top A on his Stein
way piano as she stood by him, storming. She had smashe

the hammer, and the repairer had to be brought all the way to their summer villa on the Attersee.

He regained the hotel a little before eight o'clock. The orchestra was playing in the dining-room, but he was in no mood for light music, and, after hesitating on the threshold, he decided to have some food sent up to his room. But when it came he had no appetite, and in half an hour he rang for the servant to take it away.

He took off his clothes, changed into pyjamas and a dressing-gown, and sat down at the writing-table to write letters, his last letters ; one to Hans, to be held for him by a friend in Paris, one to his solicitor, and one to his niece, living in Geneva, who would inherit the remainder of his estate after he had made provision for his adopted son and left a legacy to Hans. All of this would come out of his investments in America and Switzerland. His fortune in Austria had been stolen from him by the Nazis as a penalty for fleeing from the horrors of their persecution.

His eye caught the telephone on the writing-table, and he had a sudden impulse to ring up his apartment in Vienna. It would be interesting to know what would happen. He lifted the receiver and spoke to the hotel operator.

" I want a call to Vienna, Stadtpark 262114," he said.

" Very good, Herr Gollwitzer."

He put back the receiver, and went on writing.

In a few minutes there was a tinkle.

" Your Vienna call," said the operator.

" Hello," said Gollwitzer. " Who is that ? "

" Stadtpark 262114," answered a voice.

" Is that Herr Gollwitzer's ? " asked Gollwitzer.

" Yes."

" Who is speaking ? "

" Herr Gollwitzer's servant. Herr Gollwitzer is away— can I take a message ? "

" You can indeed. This is Gollwitzer speaking from a place you blackguards cannot get at me. I know you are tapping all calls to my apartment. I have no servant with a voice like yours."

He put back the receiver. It had been as he expected. Yesterday he had met an American, with a villa at Salzburg, who told him his telephone had been tapped by the Nazi agents six months before they marched into Austria.

The clock on the mantelpiece struck nine. Gollwitzer, his letters written, telephoned down to the reception clerk.

"I shall be leaving early in the morning. Will you please send up my account at once; I will settle it now," he said. "No, no, by car," he added, when the clerk inquired what train he wanted to catch.

While the account came up, Gollwitzer packed his things. He stood in front of one of his leather portmanteaux, thinking how odd it was that he had no address label to tie on. He had left instructions for all his personal possessions to be held in store for three months, and if not claimed by Hans they were to be sold and the proceeds given to local charities.

There was a tap on the door. A servant entered with an envelope containing the bill. Gollwitzer opened it, gave the man the required amount, and a twenty pengö tip. He retired all smiles and bows. It was a quarter-past nine. On the bedside table lay a small parcel. Gollwitzer had been a good shot in his youth, but he had little experience of pistols. This Mauser was infallible and simple enough.

He took the weapon out of its box, loaded it, and crossed the room to the dressing-table near the window. There was a clear space in which he could fall. His hand did not shake, his mind was calm, his face, seen in the mirror, betrayed no agitation.

"God forgive me," he said, quietly, and placed the nozzle of the pistol to his temple.

The next moment there was a sharp, loud report.

CHAPTER VII

MÁTÁNY INTERVENES

I

THE first thing Gollwitzer was aware of was the astonishing fact that he was not dead. The mirror at his side had been wholly shattered, but not from his pistol, which had not been fired. The window was cracked, star-fashion, across its centre. It took Herr Gollwitzer, now trembling, a full minute to realise that he had been shot at by someone outside his room, who had fired through his window.

He put down his pistol. The perspiration stood in beads on his forehead. Now the tremendous moment of his resolution had passed, he felt terribly weak. Perhaps it was the shock of this incomprehensible attack, more than the reaction from intended suicide, which exhausted him. He sat down, drew out a pocket handkerchief and wiped his face. Then he stared for a moment at the splintered window through which the unknown assassin had shot at him. The bullet had missed him by only a few inches, had travelled across the room, and smashed the long wardrobe mirror into fragments.

There was silence, except for his own thudding heart, and the sound of *Aida*, coming up from the well of the hotel wing under whose glass roof the orchestra was playing in the dining-room. In a few minutes the hotel staff would come up. It was impossible for the shot and the crash not to have been heard.

Pulling himself together, Gollwitzer got up from the chair, picked up the pistol and hid it in the dressing-table drawer. He collected the letters he had written and put them out of sight. The police would make inquiries, and he did not wish it to be known now that he was on the verge of committing suicide.

But who could have desired his death? The shot had come from the opposite wing. Switching off the light, he went to the broken window and looked out. There were lights in three of the rooms opposite, two of them had their windows open.

Heavens, how he was trembling now! He should have been dead a few minutes ago, and here he was, wondering who had attempted to shoot him. What possible motive could there be? He had no personal enemy, he had pursued no vendetta against anyone.

A sharp tapping on the door made him start, although he expected to hear it at any moment. They had come, and he must be very careful what he said. He was just preparing for bed when he was shot at. That must be his story.

He quickly surveyed the room, and then unlocked the door. To his surprise there was only one person there—a dark young man in evening dress.

" Herr Gollwitzer ? " he asked, calmly.

" Yes."

" You have just been shot at—may I come in ? "

Before Gollwitzer could answer he had entered the room and closed the door. He was tall and dark, with glossy hair brushed back on his neat head. He was perhaps thirty years of age, well-groomed and self-possessed in manner. He had quick, sharp eyes. It seemed impossible that he could be a house detective or a member of the staff. He had the bearing of an officer, with his well-set shoulders, and brisk manner. He wore a monocle in his left eye ; there was a gardenia in the lapel of his dress-jacket. He was typical of the young men in the smart set of Budapest. His clothes were certainly English in their cut.

He stood now in the middle of the room, looking at the splintered glass on the floor, and the long, cracked window. Then, his examination finished, he turned to Gollwitzer with a slight air of embarrassment.

" This is most unfortunate," he said. " May I introduce myself ? I am Count Tibor Mátány. I have the honour to be addressing Herr Gollwitzer, I know."

He bowed slightly, and again looked at the shattered glass in the wardrobe door.

" I suppose you heard the shot ? " asked Gollwitzer.

Count Mátány stepped forward, took Gollwitzer by the arm and led him to a chair.

" Please sit down—it must have been a very great shock. Permit me."

He pulled out a flask, went to the carafe on the bedside table, and poured out some brandy.

" Please drink this," he said, advancing with the glass. "I can recommend it. Bisquit Dubouché. I brought it from Paris last week."

Gollwitzer took the glass with a shaking hand, and drank. Count Mátány watched him, with an approving smile.

" Somebody, for some reason, has just tried to shoot me —are you next door ? " asked Gollwitzer, feeling more self-controlled. The drink was a stiff one.

" No—and you are mistaken," said the Count, quietly. "I did not try to shoot you. I shot at your mirror."

" You ! It was you ? " cried Gollwitzer, in astonishment.

The Count pulled out a gold cigarette-case and offered Gollwitzer a cigarette, which he declined.

" May I ? " he asked, and when the other man nodded, lit up. " You are astonished, of course," he went on. " It wasn't an easy thing to do. Fortunately I am considered a crack shot, and the mirror gave me just the right target."

Gollwitzer stared at the imperturbable young man.

" I don't understand—why you—for what reason——" he stammered.

Mátány made a gesture with his cigarette.

" May I sit down ? " he asked.

" Oh, certainly—excuse me," said Gollwitzer.

This fellow was mad. He wondered if he still carried his pistol. He looked across the room at the bell-push by the bed. Mátány must have read his thought.

" Please," he said, smilingly. " You can trust me implicitly."

" But can I ? " queried Gollwitzer. " You've just confessed to an attempt at shooting me ! "

" No, I have not said that, Herr Gollwitzer," replied the Count. " I shot not to kill you but to save you, if you will forgive me making such a claim. I must apologise for interfering in this manner. Most men have a perfect right to do what they like with their own lives. I have no scruples in the matter of suicide—who knows, perhaps I may find it necessary myself, when I lose faith in my lucky star. But you are in a different category, Herr Gollwitzer. It's enough that those stupid Nazis should drive you out of Austria. It's intolerable that they should drive you out of existence. You belong to the whole world. It has only one Gollwitzer. If I may say so, in a temporary aberration, you were taking too severe a revenge on society. I have often been to the Metropolitan in New York, to the Scala in Milan, to the Festival in Salzburg. You have always been the reason—and I'm not terribly musical. But there are others to whom your art means—how shall I put it ? Men of genius are above these silly racial spites. Beethoven, Wagner, Verdi—all that matters in history is that they have lived and enriched the world. Oh, pardon me, I am talking nonsense, I fear.'

" It is very comforting nonsense, Count Mátány," said Gollwitzer. " I see I need hide nothing from you. As you know, I am a refugee from my own country, which is in the hands of fanatics to which nothing is sacred, nothing in art or science, if it comes from my own race. They have a mandate from the mob to destroy us. We are powerless. I am an old man, and everything I care for has been stripped from me. A few minutes ago I was on the verge of suicide—a decision you have seen fit to interrupt."

" Forgive me, I obeyed an impulse," said Count Mátány, smoothing an ankle with one hand as he sat, one leg crossed over the other. " I was always impulsive ; it has been my downfall."

" Your downfall ? " reiterated Gollwitzer.

" You see before you a ruined but quite cheerful young man whose relations are sorely tried by him."

He spread his hands deprecatingly, and laughed.

Gollwitzer laughed too. There was something ludicrous in this situation.

"You've not told me, Count Mátány, how you came to shoot at me—the reason, you have just told me, and I thank you for the compliment," said Gollwitzer.

"That is very easy," replied Mátány. "You omitted a simple precaution. You neglected to pull your blind, and you stood right under the electric light. I have a room in the opposite wing, directly in line with yours. I was changing, and I couldn't help watching you. It is the penalty of fame, Herr Gollwitzer, that you must always be watched, even in your most private moments, if you are careless enough to permit it. Well, there was a moment when you took me by surprise. You took a pistol out of a box and loaded it. It's a significant fact, Herr Gollwitzer, that people who go about with pistols almost never carry them in the boxes in which they bought them. I wondered at once. And I got the answer at once. The suicide of three well-known Austrians was in the paper this morning. I would have been a fool not to guess your intention. What could I do? You won't suggest that I should have sat there and watched you shoot yourself, if I could possibly have stopped you? There was no time to rush round to your room—I didn't even know the number. It was useless to ring down to the management; they would not have got up in time. I keep my pistol handy. It is a family habit; my father was shot on the Chain Bridge by the Bolsheviks in 1919, but not before he had finished off three of them. We were brought up to shoot. The second I saw your hand go up, I shot. I chose the mirror shining just behind you— you were not really in danger, there was a margin of some inches. Now I'm wondering how one can account for the mess!"

He laughed pleasantly, showing good teeth. Gollwitzer felt steadier. The young man stood up.

"Well, I must beg your pardon for what I have done— I shall not say a word about this to anyone, of course," he said. "And if I can be of any service to you, Herr Gollwitzer—in a different fashion," he added, shrugging his shoulders whimsically, "I shall be delighted."

"Sit down, Count," said Gollwitzer, abruptly. "You already know so much, you shall know the rest. You were quite right. You shot at the moment I was attempting suicide. Insomnia is now added to my other worries. I am probably unbalanced. You see, what has happened to me doesn't belong to a sane world. I've lived in Vienna for sixty years. It's my native city. I've always had an honoured position in its public life. I can say, without boasting, that my name stands for something in the music world—an international world. Will you believe me when I tell you that my Jewish origin is something, in a very busy life, which has never been of the slightest significance to me ? I am not even concerned with defending the Jews. We have our defects. As with all oppressed peoples, liberty may have developed an ostentatious arrogance among a section of my race. But we are loyal, thrifty, hard-working. I will say no more of this aspect of the matter. I have suffered public insult, my home has been invaded, I have been forbidden to follow my calling. Every day I receive news of some friend who, persecuted and impoverished, has been driven to suicide. I fled from Vienna, but my heart is there, there *in der schönen Stadt*. At my age, Count, the roots go too deep for these drastic upheavals. Call me a coward, if you will. A man of sixty-two asks nothing more from life than an honourable and peaceful close in the place he loves, among the friends he cherishes. I can have only one home, one country. I thought my art would sustain me— but it's not enough, Count Mátány."

"And Fame ? Surely there's a consolation in that ?" asked the Count. "It's an Open Sesame wherever you go."

"One tires quickly of Fame. It subjects one to the attack of every bore. True, it makes a thousand people ready to be kind to one, but it is kindness at the price of reflected glory. It may seem strange to you, Count Mátány, you are a young man with life before you, but for me the world has become too silly to live in. I have lived to learn, at sixty-two, that since I am a Jew there is no merit in anything I have done. My country repudiates me. I am not fit to keep the child I have adopted."

"Ah! *Der kleine Eisenbahner?*" exclaimed Mátány. "The baby you adopted on the Express! Where is it now?"

Gollwitzer sighed, and regarded the back of his hands as they rested on his knees. The management would be here now at any moment. He still had no idea what explanation he could give them.

"Pardon me, you are very tired," said Count Mátány. "I shouldn't question you like this. I will go."

He stood up, but Gollwitzer motioned for him to sit down again.

"Please stay," he said. "I feel I must talk to someone, and I find you sympathetic. You asked about my adopted boy. One night, very late one night, the Nazis came to my flat and demanded custody of the boy. I was so stunned that I would have let them take him, but my faithful servant Hans and the nurse put up such a strong resistance that the Nazis finally retired. We feared they might come again the next day, so the boy and his nurse were hurried into the country, to some place known to my servant. I do not know where the child is. Hans implored me to leave Vienna, while I could. I left the next day for Prague. Three days later I learned that Hans had been arrested."

"Why?"

"I cannot conceive, except that he was known to be my servant. My flat was rifled. The whole——"

A sharp rat-tat on the outer door checked Gollwitzer's words. The two men looked at each other.

"I'll deal with it, leave it to me," said Mátány, rising, for he saw that Gollwitzer was trembling.

He went boldly to the door and opened it, but instead of the manager, a small pageboy stood there, wearing a pill-box hat and bearing a salver in his white-gloved hands. On it there was a telegram.

" Herr Gollwitzer ? " he asked.

" I'll give it to him," said the Count, tipping the boy. " Don't wait, we'll 'phone down if necessary."

The pageboy retired.   Mátány closed the door and gave the telegram to Gollwitzer, who opened it with a shaking hand.

" Released. Writing. Hans. Schulerstrasse 272."

The expression of joy on Gollwitzer's face was immediate.

" Good news ? " asked the Count, pushing aside some glass with his foot.

" My servant Hans has been let out of gaol ! Look ! "

Gollwitzer passed the telegram to the Count, who read it. Then, handing it back to the elder man, he asked, smiling—

" If that had come half an hour ago would your intention have held good ? "

" No—I know now I was temporarily unbalanced. Our talk has done me good," said Gollwitzer. " I wonder why they have released my servant."

" They may be using him as a decoy duck. You mustn't go back—and I don't think they'll let him leave Austria," replied Mátány. " They know about this telegram, of course, and they'll read what's in his letter. Their organisation has no flaws. Austria under the German Nazis will learn what discipline and method mean. I think they have released your servant for one purpose only—he knows where *Der kleine Eisenbahner* is hidden away. They think he is bound to write to you about the baby, and in that way they can place their hands on it."

" *Mein Gott*, you are right ! The villains ! " exclaimed Gollwitzer.

The Count lit another cigarette, and smoked it in thoughtful silence.

" Two things are obvious. You can write nothing. Every bit of correspondence will be scrutinised. And *Der kleine Eisenbahner* must be spirited out of Austria, somehow," said Count Mátány. " We must arrange a little kidnapping. It will divert your mind from your sorrows, Herr Gollwitzer."

The Count laughed, his dark eyes glowing with excitement at the thought.

" But how ? " asked Gollwitzer. " You couldn't——"

" Oh no ! I shouldn't know how to hold the baby if I found it," laughed Mátány. " But I have an idea."

" What is it ? "

" At the moment it's a little immature—I'd like to sleep on it."

Count Mátány glanced at his wrist-watch. It was a quarter to ten. Across the Danube Old Buda glittered with lights. They jewelled the hillside, up to the Palace and the high Citadel. The real life of the Hungarian capital was just beginning.

" I wonder if you would be my guest, Herr Gollwitzer ? At ten o'clock I'm due at *The Green Cockatoo*, where I've a dinner-party for six—including Princess Solenski, lovely, very lovely, and, unlike many very lovely women, she has brains and makes no attempt to impress the fact. And Count Zarin—you'll like him, I'm sure, reputed to be the wickedest man in Budapest ; which means that so many people are jealous of him that they'll say nothing nice about him. He has the kindest heart and the coolest head of any man living. Then there's Frau Rubenstein, a little hunchback American, who talks vile German but is so comprehending that she's become an international mother-confessor to all the waifs and strays of Europe. For the rest there is——"

Gollwitzer interrupted the volatile young Count.

" Thank you," he said, " but I am in no mood for company to-night."

" You do not understand, Herr Gollwitzer," replied Count Mátány. " You must be out of this room while the mess is being swept up. Let us leave word down at the hall-porter's desk—no explanation. They're too tactful to ask for any if you don't challenge the bill. And I have a price for my services—I am vain enough to crave the honour of presenting you to my dinner-party ! "

Gollwitzer looked at the suave, ingratiating young man who stood smiling before him.

" Very well," he said, after a pause. " I suppose that in a world that's gone mad there's nothing unreasonable in a man who wanted to die at nine dining at ten ! "

" Nothing at all ! " assented Mátány, shifting more glass with his patent shoe. " Now, if you will excuse me, while you are dressing I'll go back to my room. If I come back in twenty minutes——"

" You'll find me clothed, and in my right mind," replied Gollwitzer.

He grasped the hands of the young man standing before him.

" Let me say very simply, ' Thank you,' " he said, in a husky voice. " You've given life a changed face with your friendliness to me. I begin to hope again."

A moment later his surprising visitor had left the room and he began to dress himself.

II

Count Tibor Mátány had three master passions. He loved fine horses, English clothes, and lovely women. He always regretted he had not become a diplomat, but his regret was mitigated by the reflection that diplomats do most of their work in foreign countries, and he loved Hungary. For under his gay manner, his restlessness, his love of bright society, he nursed a constant passion for his country. It was a flame that burned in secret, for, shy in nothing else, he was shy in exhibiting the wound he felt whenever he contemplated his lacerated fatherland.

In the country house where his widowed mother lived, between the immense flat Puszta with its great herds of horses, and Mount Tokay, on whose slopes lay the famous vineyards, he had made a great collection of books dealing with the proud, varied history of the Magyar race. He had had an ancestor who fought at Mohács in 1526, and was killed in that wholesale annihilation of the Hungarian army, with its king, five bishops and two archbishops, when Sultan Suliman and his Turks advanced on Buda, to sack the city and leave the land desolate. His great-grandfather had been a chamberlain at the court of the Hapsburgs, a devoted courtier of the beautiful Empress Elizabeth, who brought back the ancient splendour and gaiety to her beloved Budapest.

It was at the Viennese court that Count Kálmán Mátány, his father, had first met the lovely Countess Ilynski, the youngest of the three daughters of the Polish Minister, whose beauty ravished the hearts of all the Viennese bucks. To the surprise of all Vienna, Count Kálmán, a notorious spendthrift and roué, carried off his lovely bride, and, jealous of the attraction she created, he retired from court life to his vast estate at Tiszatardos on the edge of the great Hungarian plain. Here he created a family of four sons and three daughters, wild, dark-eyed boys, and vivacious lovely girls, bred horses, cultivated the Tokay vines, and quarrelled violently with everyone. He was killed by Bolsheviks in Budapest during the terrorism of Béla Kun.

Two of Tibor Mátány's brothers were soldiers, one was a chemist in the University at Graz. Tibor, the youngest, deeply attached to his mother, tried everything in turn. He, too, joined the army, but the discipline irked him, and the indigestible food turned his stomach He thought of the law, but a month's study made him impatient of its fastidious processes. He turned to politics, but could not succeed in hiding his contempt of the democratic formula. His mother's proud blood, as well as his father's uncompromising spirit, were united in him.

In one sphere only did he command immediate success. He was a great favourite with the smart set of Budapest. Witty, good-tempered, staunch, men liked him and women adored him. He spent money liberally while he had it, and then retreated to the country for long periods of recuperation. His patrimony had long been dissipated, but at thirty he still had a good supply of loving and aged aunts whose successive deaths helped him to overcome each crisis in his affairs. Judged by every standard, he was a spendthrift, a drone in the human hive, but everything was forgiven him, for the gods had endowed him with irresistible personal charm, and this engaging quality flouts all the virtues, and wins easy and undeserved victories. It is a painful truth that it is usually the more solid and reputable members of society who fall most readily under the spell of volatile creatures like Count Mátány. "You'd be the favourite boy in any Rotary Club," once said a candid American friend.

There was always a crisis in the affairs of Count Mátány. Adept in raising money by mortgaging his various assets, he had come to the end of that method of income and was now wholly dependent upon an allowance from his widowed mother. She was well aware of her son's extravagance and gave him only a subsistence allowance. He had a passion for travel, and she did all in her power to keep him at home. The most troublesome of all her children, she adored him, a victim of his charm. It was the same throughout the Countess's large estate ; the peasants and the servants would do anything for Tibor, who treated them in the high-handed fashion of a feudal aristocrat.

He was fond of his great rambling home, of the life on the farm and in the vineyards, but he could not exist without the gay diversions of the great capitals. He knew Budapest, Vienna, Berlin, Paris and London intimately. He had cultivated the society of the most varied types in the countries he visited. He had hunted in Leicestershire, bringing over some superb Hungarian horses, and was a popular figure at the point-to-point races. He always contrived to sell his horses at handsome figures. They liked to help the dashing, hard-up Count, with the winning smile and beautiful grey Magyar eyes.

He had been the guest for six months, in Kentucky, of a rich American family. Everyone prophesied a marriage that would restore his fortune, but although the Count loved many he could not bring himself to love anyone exclusively. A brilliant shot, he was always to be found, in the season, at the most exclusive châteaux in France. His mother, by no means a snob since she came of one of the best families in Poland, could not refuse to supply the money for these excursions, and through her sister, married to a French Duke, Tibor had the entrée everywhere.

But his social activities were bizarre. He had lived for four months on a Rhône barge, eating and sleeping with a dozen tough bargees, owning little more than a pair of trousers, a jersey and a shaving outfit. He left the barge at Mâcon with a tanned body and the muscles of a prize-fighter. His friend Pierre, a Lyonnais youth, whose account in a local bar had inspired the adventure, accompanied him to the station and burst into tears as the train carried away the engaging Count.

A love affair with a German trick-rider in a travelling circus, a flat-nosed, blue-eyed creature, whose charm lay in a singular ugliness and a seductive body, took him round the smaller manufacturing towns of the Rhineland. In this manner he learned those equestrian acrobatics with which he astonished and delighted his friends. When he visited his *csikós* in the Puszta he took the breath away even of those lads born to the saddle, the far-famed horsemen of the great Hungarian plain.

He could ride, he could swim, he could shoot, and above all he could make love, with an absorbing but easily terminated passion. His singular nature displayed other and more incongruous gifts. His knowledge of English, French, German and Italian poetry was by no means ephemeral, for he could always cap a quotation in any of these languages, and he had a speaking knowledge of Polish, Russian and Spanish, in addition.

The long winters in the utter seclusion of his mother's house, unless he had been fortunate enough to devise a means of escape, had been spent in the cultivation of two of his passions, in embroidery and the compiling of a book on Hungarian folk-dances. It seemed unlikely that the book would ever be completed, as the Count was lost in a vast accumulation of manuscript notes, and the embroidery, an enormous tapestry illustrating an event in the history of the Mátány family, progressed at the rate of a yard per winter. It was designed to cover a wall of sixty square yards. He had trained six assistants, peasant girls on the home farm, to help him in this great undertaking, but they never knew when their tutor would vanish to foreign parts.

It was his interest in folk-dancing which had brought

him the fruitful and singular friendship of Henry Waddle. Though belonging to entirely different worlds, and in so many ways the antithesis of each other, they were devoted friends. Every year they contrived to meet, three or four times.

Henry had been on a visit to Tiszatardos to bless a folk-dance congress organised by the Count. He had made at once a complete conquest of everybody, from the Countess down to the stable boys. Everyone knew of his presence within an hour of arrival, and he was a popular figure on the whole estate within a fortnight. He now came at least once a year and presided over a local dance festival. It was an unforgettable thing to see Henry Waddle dance the *csárdás* with a terrific energy that made the sweat pour down his florid face.

What adventures they had had, and in what strange places they had been together! Henry had always flatly refused to move in social circles. Mátány could see him now, his tie up round his neck, his shirt collar unbuttoned, because he had long grown out of his shirts, a shoe lace undone, and the inevitable crammed portfolio under his arm. He was a fellow not only of infinite jest but also of infinite resource.

Mátány was thinking of Waddle now, as he lay in bed at the Grand Hungaria, his morning coffee on the bedside table. He had brought Gollwitzer home at two o'clock in the morning. After dinner they had gone to a cabaret show. He had already seen it, but he said nothing about this to Gollwitzer. The poor old fellow must not be allowed to think, and it was his determination to take him back to the hotel so tired out that he would put his head on the pillow and go to sleep at once.

" And in the morning I'll come to see you, and outline my plan concerning *Der kleine Eisenbahner*," he said to him, as he left him at the door of his bedroom.

The more Mátány thought about the business of smuggling the Gollwitzer baby out of Austria the more excited he grew. It was a wild idea, but wild ideas, such as shooting past the nose of a world-famous conductor, to prevent him committing suicide, had always been a part of his life.

Henry Waddle was really to blame. He had received a

letter only yesterday in which Henry had announced, almost with a note of triumph, that he was bringing a honeymoon couple with him from Paris.

" They are very young, very unsophisticated, and thrilled at being abroad for the first time. Mr. and Mrs. Brown by name. That is plain enough, but there the plainness ends. He is a good-looking lad, a fine product of our freshwater school, teeth that munch apples, a hand that makes you wince, and a lad to be with in a tight corner. He says he can ride, and his face lit up when I talked of your horses. Mrs. Brown is ravishingly beautiful—yes, I say it and fear no competition from your Magyar beauties. She aspires to being social, I fear, new from some dreadful kind of bondage whose nature is not to be disclosed. She keeps a firm eye on Jim, calls him James, and wants to improve the lamb. I am a little bit afraid of her. Line up the princes, counts and barons, and let them kiss her hand—they will gladly queue up for the purpose—and she will like Budapest better than Hollywood. But joking apart, they are charming children. I shall show them Vienna, and then we will come on. We shall motor-bus from Vienna, for the pleasure of arriving in your mauve dusk, when the hills of Buda are festooned with lights, and Pest lies like a tray of gems in the lap of the night. You must be in Budapest, of course, when we make our advent. You might meet the bus, with flowers. Or are you too old to experience the pleasure of watching starry-eyed children gasp at their first sight of your Aladdin's cave ? I suppose you have gathered that what I really suggest is an invitation to Tiszatardos ? That, with your feudal splendour, the *tzigány* fiddling under the lanterns, the *csikós* riding valiantly, and the peasants dancing the *csárdás* to the fury of violins, will crown the honeymoon. But you must not make love to Mrs. Brown. I suspect Jim has a nasty uppercut. To correct my portrait of the bride, she is quite domestic. She has undertaken to darn six pairs of socks which I have just washed in my little hotel here, despite the injunction against home laundry-work."

When he had first read Henry's letter he had felt a little

impatient with the crazy fool for linking up with a honeymoon couple. Henry was always taking lame ducks under his wing, hoping for converts to the sacred cause. He would drag the poor wretches to every meeting of the Folk-Dance Congress. But now he blessed Henry, for the Browns were a heaven-sent pair. The more he thought about it, the more feasible it became.

Drinking his final cup of coffee Count Mátány picked up the telephone.

" I thought I saw Mr. Charles Sebright in the foyer last night. Is he staying in the hotel ? " he asked the desk clerk.

" Yes, Herr Graf, Room 192."

" Put me through to him, please."

" Hello ? " said a voice in English.

" Charles—Tibor Mátány speaking."

" Tibor ! How are you, my dear fellow ? I got here last night. All Melton Mowbray sends its love. Where are you ? " asked Captain Charles Sebright.

" In the hotel, Room 321," replied Mátány. " Charles, are you up yet ? "

" No, haven't had my bath. I've just breakfasted in bed."

" Would you do something frightfully urgent ? I've got an idea, and my ideas won't wait. Can you put your hand on your passport ? "

" Yes—but why ? " asked Sebright.

" Then do—and relieve my mind. If you have a British passport, and you are married, and you have a wife and a child, a baby in fact, do you all have the same passport, and is the baby's photograph in it ? "

" Good Lord, how should I know, Tibor ? I haven't a wife and a baby," exclaimed Sebright. Tibor was always a bit mad. " Are you in trouble, in the family way ? " he added, laughing.

" Please, please look at your passport, nice, kind English-man, and end my anxiety."

" Very well, but I've got to get out of bed, damn you ! "

Mátány heard the bed creak. After a few moments he heard the receiver picked up.

" Well, here you are," said Sebright. " There's a place for the wife's name, and for her photograph. There's nothing for children, except a line headed ' Children ' and there's no photograph of them required. Why should there be ? All babies look alike ! "

" Oh, no, you have no maternal instinct, Charles. But a thousand thanks, my mind is at rest."

" You're not in any trouble—baby-farming or anything like that ? " asked Sebright.

" No, nothing like that. Just a little plain kidnapping."

" Plain what ? " demanded Sebright.

" I'm being indiscreet, don't press. Shall I see you in the bar at one o'clock ? " asked Mátány.

" Yes—what about lunch on the terrace ? "

" Splendid. And Charles—— "

" Yes ? "

" Not a word about this—but I love your Foreign Office for not bothering about babies. Good-bye," said Mátány, putting down the receiver.

He stared up at the ceiling for a few moments, thinking hard. Then he glanced at the newspaper on the coverlet. It was now the twenty-seventh of May. There was just time to write to Henry before he went to Vienna. It was important for him not to let that honeymoon couple slip out of his hands. Henry had a habit of suddenly tiring of people.

Count Mátány got out of bed, collected his fountain-pen, a blotter and some notepaper, and got back into bed. He outlined his proposal to Henry, saying he would be in Vienna on the thirty-first.

It was half-past ten when he had finished the letter. He was meeting Gollwitzer at eleven. He leapt out of bed, and turned on the bath water. Then he went to the window and looked across at the other wing of the hotel. Yes, there was the evidence still, a sheet of glass with long cracks radiating from the spot where his bullet had penetrated the window. If the world's music lovers knew what they owed to him, mused Count Mátány, slipping off his pyjamas and stepping into the bath, they would give him an illuminated address and pay all his debts.

CHAPTER VIII

ONKEL HEINRICH

I

"WE are drawing into Vienna now," said Waddle, peering out of the window, as houses began to take the place of forests and fields. "I wonder just how much it will have changed under German rule. You'll never persuade me they can make the Austrians stand to attention and mind their p's and q's. The Austrians are the Irish of the Continent, they'll always be ' agin the Government.' "

"They all look very charming," said Mrs. Brown, very tired, but too excited to let anything slip by unnoticed. There had been that exhilarating moment at Innsbruck when, looking out of the window of their wagon-lits, she had seen the first Austrian in native costume, with embroidered braces, leather shorts, and white stockings with flowery " clocks " running down them. He was an impudent-looking young man, with bronzed throat and thighs, who, seeing her at the window, ogled her with his beautiful blue eyes. She drew back, her heart beating faster. On the same platform were two *Dirndl*, in pleated muslin frocks, small embroidered aprons, and black velvet corsages laced tightly over their white bodices with half sleeves. They had little hats, broad-brimmed and decorated with flowers, perched on their blonde hair, neatly plaited and drawn up severely from the neck. They seemed to have come straight off the stage.

But then the whole panorama since daylight had been theatrical. The great mountain ranges gathered around them, their heights crowned with the shining snow-fields, their lower slopes covered with forests of firs and pines, so straight, so dense that they seemed like an army on the march. And between these dark forests the closely shaved upper pastures shone with their vivid, green turf, so fresh, so shining, high up there in the morning sun, that it was as if a spotlight played upon them. The flower-rimmed balconies of the mountain chalets made Betty catch her breath. She kept turning to Jim, her eyes shining, her cheeks flushed with excitement.

" Oh, I'm so glad Mr. Waddle made us come ! " she had cried at that first glimpse of Austria. " It's more wonderful than anything I'd imagined ! "

" I don't believe any of it's true—we'll wake up with a terrible bang. Is this really Mrs. James Brown ? " asked Jim, standing behind his wife. He held her waist, and leaned his face on her shoulder. " Or will you suddenly vanish, and I'll find a barrow in my hands ? "

She laughed, and kissed his cheek.

" Oh, do forget that—and I do wish our name wasn't Brown. It doesn't go with all this," exclaimed Betty.

" Nothing goes with all this except a Strauss waltz. They'll begin playing the Blue Danube soon."

He swung her round and kissed her. " Excitable child, aren't you ? " he asked.

She laughed happily, her arms around his neck. Paris lay behind her, Vienna before her, and her lover was holding her now as the express raced through these Alpine villages. It was far more than ever she had dreamed of. She had always kept an unshakable faith in a romantic ending to her rebellion against circumstances. It was more than a stroke of chance that brought her here, out of bondage ; it was the reward of faith.

" Lizz—you're the——" began Jim, with shining eyes.

" Betty ! " she corrected.

" Betty, you're the loveliest thing here or anywhere else. Happy ? " he asked, holding her to him. " You won't desert me for some wicked Prince prowling about in Vienna ? "

" Idiot ! " she laughed, her cheek pressed to his. " What Prince is going to take any notice of me ? "

" Everybody takes notice of you—look at that awful old Russian in Paris."

" Oh, him ! " laughed Betty.   " Poor old man ! "

" Dirty old man ! " retorted Jim.

He was still angry at the thought of that incident.   An old man sitting in a restaurant had stared and stared at Betty.   Then he sent his card across, with a rendezvous scribbled on the back.   Betty could not hide her excitement. The name on the card was that of a Grand Duke.   Jim tore up the card, put it in a wine glass, and sent it back to the audacious old roué.   He vanished in a few minutes.

Everywhere they went Betty drew this unwelcome attention.   Their new life had added a vivacity to her face which increased its striking beauty, so that one could not wonder that men everywhere found themselves attracted to her. It was a new experience for Jim to feel a pang of jealousy and apprehension.   Now, as they drew into Vienna, he began to wish they had chosen a secluded retreat for their honeymoon instead of this musical-comedy city of wine, women and song.

The red and white swastika flags began to appear on the buildings.   Waddle gave a cry of impatience.   " I expect we'll have propaganda pushed down our throats night and day.   I went through all that in Germany—the novelty's worn off there.   These Austrians are at the height of the fever.   Well, it's not for us to object.   Who was it said ' Every country gets the Government it deserves ? '   And I'll say this for the Reich—it does support folk-dancing. Ah, here's the station—now you stand at the window, Mr. Brown, and I'll slip out on to the platform and get a porter. You can pass your bags through the window—that'll get us ahead of the scrum."

Waddle vanished, to appear below the carriage window, with a porter in tow.   He commanded the fellow with a friendly fluency.   No one, seeing him now, would believe he had sat up all night since leaving Paris.   In the taxi which bore them away his face was wreathed in smiles.

" Oh, I love this place—nice people, these Austrians.   All a little bit mad, I think, but then so am I.   Look, this long street is the Mariahilferstrasse, a shopping place, so-so."

Mr. Waddle, perched on the small seat, began to talk with the taxi-driver. It became very intimate, judging by the way the man kept turning to say something. Jim wished they would stop. There were perilous moments of collision.

"Oh—here's the Ringstrasse!" exclaimed Waddle. "Lovely, lovely—it goes all round old Vienna—it was originally the old fortifications around the city. The Emperor had them swept away and made this circular boulevard. There's the Hofgarten ahead, with the Royal Palace—oh, what a place!"

"What does the taxi man say?" asked Jim.

"Hush!" admonished Waddle, putting a finger to his mouth. "I fear he's not a good Nazi. In fact I'm sure he's a good Communist. He's very rude about the German visitors."

"But he's wearing a Nazi badge!" said Betty.

"Of course!" replied Waddle. "It's what you call in the jungle 'colour-protection.' Now, look, there's the Opera House. Oh, what memories, what memories!"

Mr. Waddle swayed on his seat, with half-closed eyes, as he invoked the past. The long, tree-lined boulevard stretched before them. They turned left and began to enter a narrower street filled with shops. The pavements were crowded with people.

"Nothing but uniforms!" commented Waddle, sorrowfully. "This is Kärntnerstrasse—Vienna's Bond Street. In the last three years there's been more English money spent in this street than in any other on the Continent. And most of it's gone into the pockets of the Jews."

"You're not anti-Jewish, are you, Mr. Waddle?"

Waddle gave them his embracing smile.

"Am I? I wonder! When I walk down Coventry Street and Leicester Square and get pushed off the pavement by a solid block of East End Jews, I become very anti-Jewish. Do you realise you can't see a decent German film because the cinemas are owned by Jews, and all the films outside of Germany are made by Jews? And it's a sad fact, for which they are in no way responsible, that so many of them are physically repulsive—coarse jowls, thick necks on squat bodies. That's why it's so easy to stir up feeling against them. When they succeed they exult in public. they wear too bright colours, smoke too big cigars, and load their fat women with too many jewels. But there's the other side—they're loyal among themselves, their charity extends to Christians without favour, they're born bankers, and a great deal that's worth listening to, and much that's worth reading, has been written by a Jew. I've many friends among the Jews. They own most of the shops in this street—because we Christians are no match for them in business. They fill most of the orchestras—because we're no match for them in music. They've suffered for so long with fortitude that, in misfortune, they always come out on top. You see, they survived defeat in Germany after the Great War—they rallied together and bought up everything. That's what's behind the attack on them now. There's envy added to venom. What I can't stand is the cruelty of it all. It's the Middle Ages come back. with the rack and the thumb-screw. And that's why, at the moment, I'm on every Jew's side in Germany and here. Oh !—now there's a sight for you—the Cathedral ! Your hotel's just behind that."

II

It almost seemed as if Mr. Waddle owned the König von Ungarn. From the moment that they stepped in under the wide-arched doorway he took command of the place. There was a sudden uproar of welcome. The concierge was the first to exclaim " Herr Waddle ! " A waiter rushed out of a side door, serviette in hand. rushed back again, and signalled frantically, announcing to the inner room the advent of Herr Waddle. The cry ascended the staircase, and was re-echoed through the courtyard around which the hotel was built. Smiling chambermaids came running down the stairs, and arrived breathless, Lisa, Julie, Martha, Greta, Anna, Mitzi, Paula, all curtsying, all exclaiming " Ach, Herr Waddle ist da ! " Waddle presented them all in turn to Jim and his wife.

" No. 154 ? " asked Waddle, as the concierge took a key

off the indicator board. " The Graf von Esslinger Zimmer—
no, no ! They must have the corner room, with the nice
bathroom—the Graf von Lescbetizky Zimmer."

" Alas, Herr Waddle," moaned the concierge, " it is occupied ! "

" That's very naughty of you," reprimanded Waddle.

The poor man looked anxiously over the board.

" If we had only known, Herr Waddle——" he began.

" But I telegraphed you," asserted Waddle. " From Paris."

" We haven't had any telegram."

" Now I'm sure I did," said Waddle, reflecting. " *Himmel*,
no ! I didn't ! Forgive me, my dears, I meant to," he
said, turning to Jim and Betty. " So much correspondence
these days, you know. Now what's to do ? "

" No. 121—the Fürst von Baben Zimmer—very nice,"
said the concierge.

" *Schön, schön*," chorussed the chambermaids, all smiling.

" Yes—excellent, at the end of the landing. I know it,"
exclaimed Waddle. " With the cut-glass chandelier, and
the glass-panelled door into the bedroom, and the porcelain
stove."

Waddle's fingers drew a picture of it in the air.

" Ach, Herr Waddle knows it ! " laughed the excited
chambermaids.

" Let us proceed," said Waddle, imperiously. " Hans,
pay off the taxi."

" *Ja*, Herr Waddle ! " shouted the porter.

Led by the concierge, Waddle took the procession up the
stairs.

" You must understand," he said, pausing on the half-
landing, " this was the lodging place of the old country
aristocracy. So it scorns a lift. When the count came to
Vienna to attend the court, he took rooms here for the season.
The rooms still carry their names—painted on the doors,
amid arabesques of flying cherubs and garlands of flowers.
Look ! "

He pointed to a bedroom door, painted in the florid Viennese
manner. " Graf von Limberg Zimmer " they read. They

passed on, beyond the " Ritter von Erlach Zimmer," to a door bearing the legend, surmounted with a coronet, " Fürst von Baben Zimmer."

With a smile, bowing, the concierge unlocked the door and threw it back for them to enter. The chambermaids and the porter brought up the rear.

Waddle advanced and then turned triumphantly, standing under an enormous chandelier.

" Truly a museum piece," he said, addressing Jim and Betty. " Those beds, in all their brazen glory—only the Austrian Empire could have supported them."

Jim and Betty gazed, wide-eyed, at the shining brass rails, the towering canopies, the gilt chairs, the ormolu side-tables, the incredible, vast gilt mirror with a veritable waterfall of nymphs and cherubs.

" Do you think this age of Electro-Hollywood will weather like this ? " asked Waddle, and then answered his own question. " Of course not, it will never achieve the *patina.* Imagine the history of this room I The beautiful Empress Elizabeth reigns at the Hofburg, the Court is sitting, the streets are full of glittering uniforms, the horses go clattering down the Graben. At midnight there is a gala ball given by the Emperor and Empress in honour of the Tsar, preceded by a banquet. In that bed, resting before his valet dresses him, lies the haughty Prince von Baben. In this bed lies the even more haughty Princess—die Königliche Hoheit Prinzessin Sophie von Teplicz-Hohenlohe. I hope it was the Princess—it might have been someone else, I fear, more naughty than haughty. Since their day they have knocked a hole in the wall there—to make a bathroom. And the twentieth century gives you a bedside telephone. Will this do, do you think ? "

" It's like a dream," said Betty, sitting down on a chaise-longue.

A clamour of bells came into the room. The clocks of Vienna struck eight.

" At nine I shall call for you and we'll have dinner. I must now go to my attic in the Graben," said Waddle. " Oh, the price," he added, and turning to the concierge he began a long, good-natured argument.

" There—they've taken five schillings off the price. Morning coffee and honey inclusive," said Waddle. " And *Auf Wiedersehen* until nine ! "

III

It was not an attic in the Graben to which Waddle went on leaving the Browns. It was to the fifth story apartment of Doctor Hermann Kummer. He had known the Kummer family for ten years. To Elsa, Pauli and Karl he had long been Onkel Heinrich. Der Tanzmeister Waddle was, indeed, a member of the family for whom the little room behind the doctor's consulting-room was always ready. Sometimes he came for a night, sometimes for a month. Elsa, the lovely, vivacious Elsa, aged twenty, was a student at the Dramatic Academy. Pauli, a year her junior, worked in a bank. Karl, the eldest, aged twenty-one, was a medical student at the University.

It was of Karl that Waddle was thinking as he went up in the lift to the Kummer apartment, for Karl had been a source of worry to a united family. A year ago the police had suddenly appeared at Dr. Kummer's door, demanding Karl. They were not satisfied that he was out until they had brusquely searched the flat. It was then that the doctor and his wife learned that Karl was associated with a secret Nazi organisation. There was an order for his arrest on the charge of subversive activity.

At midnight Karl had not returned to the flat. In response to his wife's appeals, the doctor went round to the Police Headquarters. They had no news of Karl. Four days passed : four days of harrowing anxiety, and then, at last, a letter came from their son. He had escaped across the frontier into Bavaria and was now at Munich, in the Austrian Nazi Legion. " When you see me again we shall have triumphed in Austria," he wrote.

" When ! " commented the doctor, bitterly, a staunch member of the Patriotic Front. " God save Austria from these young hot-heads. But I never believed Karl would join those brigands and murderers."

" Oh, Hermann ! " cried Frau Kummer.

" Karl was always a bit crazy, Papa," said Pauli. " It'll do him good to have Prussian officers drilling him."

" Pauli, how can you say such a thing—just think of your poor brother ! " protested Frau Kummer, tearfully. " He thinks he's doing right."

" I suppose they thought that when they murdered Dollfuss. They're thugs."

" That's enough," said the doctor. " Remember he's your brother."

" He's crazy—he always was," persisted Pauli.

" Not another word ! " commanded the doctor. " I'll have no strife in this house."

But from that moment on the home was divided. Frau Kummer corresponded secretly with her son. The doctor would not talk of Karl, who had recklessly ruined his career. Elsa was pro-Nazi, and gloried in Karl's escapade. There were incessant quarrels between Pauli and his sister, quarrels quelled by the doctor and heard by the dismayed mother.

Waddle, aware of this disturbing situation, wondered what had happened now. Had Karl returned with the triumphant invading army ?

On the landing he paused, putting down his bag. The entrance lobby was in darkness. For a moment he had a pang of apprehension. What if they had gone ? He suddenly remembered that Kummer was in partnership with a Jewish doctor. There was the name still, on the same plate, Dr. Jacob Neumann.

Waddle rang. To his joy a light sprang up in the lobby. They must have been listening. A moment later the door was flung open and Elsa stood there. She sprang into his arms.

" Onkel Heinrich—*wie herrlich !* " she cried.

Holding each other they marched in, Elsa shouting for her mother and father. They came out of the sitting-room, joy on their faces.

He answered their breathless questions. They were dismayed when he said he must go out to supper, he had brought some English friends to Vienna.

" And Pauli ? " he asked.

" He is out with a friend."

" And Karl—what has happened with this—this change ? " asked Waddle.

" Karl's here—in barracks with the S.S.," said the doctor.

" Then you see him ? "

There was an awkward pause. Frau Kummer looked at her husband.

" No—I've forbidden him to come home. It's all very difficult, now, Heinrich," said the doctor, sadly. " We have a lot to tell you. Ach, how good to see you, old friend ! Sit down, sit down, your room's waiting for you."

Waddle sat down. Frau Kummer looked at him with sad eyes. The doctor had lost his jovial air. Only Elsa reflected the old spirit of the place.

" I want to hear everything," said Waddle, quietly. " I have been wondering how you have fared in this turmoil."

The doctor spread out his hands.

" Well, they're here. Austria is no more. Most of the people like it—for the present. You can't imagine what that last twenty-four hours in the history of Austria was like. When our Chancellor declared a plebiscite the atmosphere was electric ! We all knew it was the hour of Fate, that Hitler was waiting over the frontier. There had been dark days, mysterious negotiations, wild rumours. And then suddenly the Chancellor turned and defied the menace."

" Would he have won his plebiscite ? "

" Yes, yes ! The Nazis knew that—you see, no one under twenty-four could vote. That cut out all the young hot-heads. Youth always wants a change at any cost, but we older people were content to struggle on. Austria was getting stronger, slowly. Then one evening we were paralysed—the eleventh of March, at seven-thirty, our Chancellor spoke to us over the wireless. We were released from our vows to the Fatherland, the Nazis were entering Austria ! At six o'clock the next morning we were invaded

—and it was the end of Austria. It was wonderfully done, wonderfully, I have to admit——"

"The planes overhead, droning, droning, droning—the air shook with them, Heinrich," interposed Frau Kummer "You couldn't sleep! You opened the window and the room was filled with the noise!"

"And the armoured cars and tanks down in the streets,' added Elsa. "A stream of them, on and on! And then the soldiers, and everyone delirious, and all Vienna out in the streets, waving flags and cheering—you couldn't speak for the noise!"

"The place went mad. It was magnificently done, overwhelmingly done. The soldiers were the pick of all Germany," said the doctor. "Even I, knowing the meaning of it all felt the thrill of that scene. The whole city became a fair the boulevards were thronged for miles. You would have thought it was Austria's most victorious hour—that rattle of armoured tanks and artillery, the drone of battle planes the tramp of marching men, the crowds cheering themselves hoarse, the bands playing everywhere, the passionate broadcast speeches. I was here when Austria declared war in 1914, but never have I seen anything like this. It swamped us like a tidal wave. We know now not a detail had been overlooked, for months they had planned for this hour. There was, there could be, no opposition. Not a single voice was raised."

"But the Fatherland Front, the Schuschnigg supporters, the Socialists—did they all go over?" asked Waddle.

The doctor turned over the palm of his hand.

"Like that, my friend, like that. On Friday they shouted for Schuschnigg, on Saturday they shouted for Hitler. I'm a moderate man, there are faults on both sides, and Austria's nerves have been on the rack a long time, but I can't understand the passion of men, their swiftly changing loyalties —if one can use the word. On Saturday afternoon we began to know what the change meant. Our exiled Nazis came back. They started looting the Jews' shops, they rounded up former opponents. Men began to shoot themselves in terror. My

olleague Neumann, a Jew, rang me up and said he daren't
ome round to the surgery. They had turned him out of
hospital ward that morning, and forbade him doing any
nore operations. I went round to see him at once. He has
ground-floor flat. All of his windows had been smashed.
He had been called in to see Professor Heinemann's son—
shy lad of eighteen—four Nazis had thrashed him in a
estaurant where he went for lunch. The lad's face and
eck were lacerated, they had beaten him with *Stahlruten*,
teel whips."

" Steel ? "

" Yes—collapsible steel whips—it's beneath the dignity
f the Germans to thrash people with *Gummiknüppel*—
ubberjacks, and our Nazis follow suit. Well, Neumann
ent to see the poor lad ; he was in a terrible state. On
is way back, going down the Burggasse, he was stopped
y four Austrian Nazis—mere boys—and told to get into
car they had. He could do nothing but obey them, and
or all he knew they might be taking him away to beat him
o death. My colleague's a delicate fellow, fifty-six years
ld, and the kindest soul breathing. In the Kärntnerring
hey stopped, hauled him out and forced him down on to
is knees in front of a *Kruckenkreuz*—our Patriotic Front's
ymbol—painted on the pavement for propaganda. They
rought him a bucket of water and a brush, and for half an
our, while a crowd jeered at him, they made him scrub
ut the cross, beating him over the head whenever he stopped.
You won't believe it, but there was not a single decent
Austrian in that crowd to make a protest. Finally, they
eleased poor Neumann—and he reached home and collapsed,
nd was in bed for three days. And Heinrich, I tell you—
hey'd put corrosive acid in that water so that the skin
eeled off his hands ! We are a Christian people, a race
vith a civilisation a thousand years old, famed for our pride
nd our culture, but we do these things to our fellow country-
nen ! My own son—the boy we have reared in love, and
ducated to the limit of our means—our own Karl, is one
f these hyenas ! "

"No, no," said Frau Kummer, "Karl is not like tha
Papa, I cannot believe it."

"We cannot help believing it, Anna," replied the docto
"These lads are crazy, drunk with their idea of patriotism
Heinrich, I daren't talk to anyone here, as I am talking t
you now. I'm attending to some of Neumann's patient:
and any moment one of these insolent young monsters ma
take it into his head to beat me up for betraying ' the Cause
as they call it."

He put a hand on Waddle's arm, smiled sadly at him
and then looked from his wife to his daughter.

"I'm afraid, Heinrich, you'll find all of us a little difficul
these days. I think none of us is normal just now. Why
I found myself ' listening in ' to the Führer the other nigh
and approving! Sometimes he is so right, sometimes
feel we want discipline, to be led out of a morass of incom
petence and apathy. His men look so splendid, the organisa
tion is superb, and then, suddenly, one of them is seen fo
what he is—the hooligan in uniform. Well—that's enough
I'm sure. Where are we all going, where will it all end
Does anyone know ? Our very families are divided agains
themselves. Karl is a passionate Nazi. Pauli calls then
traitors. I have to forbid Karl entering the house or the
will be at each other's throats."

Dr. Kummer pulled out his watch.

"I must go, my friend," he said, rising. "I've all Neu
mann's patients now. I foresee trouble for myself there
soon. Will you be staying long ? "

"Three or four days—then I go to Budapest," answered
Waddle.

The doctor left them. Frau Kummer took Waddle t
his room. There was a posy of flowers on the small table
He loved this little room with gabled window looking ou
on to the old tiles and chimney-pots of Vienna. It wa
dusk. The sky was red overhead. Somewhere a cloc
struck nine, with a bold, reverberating clamour.

"*Himmel!* I've to meet my friends at nine," crie
Waddle.

" Here are some towels—and the door key," said Frau
Kummer. " Oh, Heinrich, it's so good to see you again !
t'll do Hermann good to talk to you. I'm terrified that
he'll be saying something indiscreet, and someone will
report it."

" Nonsense, my dear," replied Waddle, reassuringly.
" Hermann is no fool. In a month or two you'll find everything will calm down."

Frau Kummer smiled sadly, paused in the doorway and
asked : " Everything you want ? "

" Everything, thank you."

The door closed. Waddle took off his coat and waistcoat,
and undid his collar. He would be late, but he had not had
a proper wash since he left Paris.

Ich tanze mit dir in den Himmel hinein.

he sang, turning on the hot water. Let Nazis come or go,
one couldn't help singing in old Vienna.

CHAPTER IX

VIENNA IS SO GAY

I

JIM was the first to wake in the morning. For a few moments
he stared up at the ceiling of the dim room. To-day was
—what was to-day ? He had lost all count of time these
last two weeks, and he could fix the day only by the oddest
reaching back. Yesterday they had arrived in Vienna,
one night he had slept in a train, for the first time in his
life, and the night before that he had slept in Paris. They
had left Paris on Tuesday, which was the thirty-first of May,
and his mother's sixtieth birthday. He had bought her a
lovely work-basket he had found in a shop in the Rue de

E

Rivoli. To-day, therefore, must be Thursday, the second of June. They had still a long honeymoon before them. Paris had been delightful, Vienna seemed likely to prove just as exciting, and after Vienna there was Budapest which, according to Henry Waddle, was the jewel of cities.

Jim wondered who the people were who had slept in this bedroom. He stared up at the heavy glass chandelier which glimmered in the curtained half-light. The Prince of Baben, whose name had been given to this room—what had he been like, when had he died, how had he lived ? Had it all ended tragically or in sadness, had he died young or in venerable old age, still powerful or in poverty ? Had he survived the downfall of the Austrian Empire, or had he been fortunate enough to precede it ? And whence came his fortune ; from vast estates, rich mines or an advantageous marriage ? Which brought Jim to speculation upon the Princess. Was she beautiful and proud, had she children, was she faithful to the Prince, or did she conduct sly little intrigues with the gallants of Vienna ? Perhaps, poor child, she was married to the Prince, years older, and never loved him, and waited for him to die, and then died first, cheated of everything she wanted. Or perhaps she was very ugly, a heavy, domineering woman who never let the Prince out of sight, and always came to Vienna with him, and lay in the next bed, and——

In the next bed there was a movement. Jim started, and turned. It was Betty, her lovely head deep in the big square pillow, her delicate face pink and white against the linen, her hair loose and golden about her brow. He raised himself on one elbow and gazed in the half-light at his bride, deep in sleep. Why wonder about Austrian princes and princesses ? There could have been nothing in the life of the Fürst von Baben one half as wonderful as his own good fortune. A month ago he was a porter carrying other people's luggage at Victoria Station, and now here he lay in the Fürst von Baben Zimmer in a Viennese hotel, his wife at his side, honeymooning across Europe.

It was difficult to believe that at the end of this journey they would go back to grey old London, to bus-catching.

and cinema-going, and a tobacco and confectionery business in the King's Road. His mother would be taking old Simkin his breakfast now, up to the front bed-sitting-room with its plush mantel-board, black bow-grate and rattling Venetian blinds. If only old Simkin could see him now in the Prince's glittering bedroom!

Betty's white hand and arm lay outside the coverlet. He put out his own hand and grasped hers, his fingers closing over the plain gold band he had slipped on her finger. She sighed, stirred slightly, and then slowly opened her eyes. He leaned over and kissed her, lying there with his head on her bosom.

She was awake now, and smiled at him.

" Has the Princess von Baben slept well ? " he asked.

" Very well, your Highness."

" Am I exiled, or may I enter your Highness's domain ? " he asked.

She made no answer, but her smile was assent.

He slipped out of his bed and in under her bedclothes, her soft, slim body nestling against his with a little sigh of happiness.

" Is it very early ? " she whispered, still drowsy.

He answered her with a kiss. They lay in silence. Somewhere down in the street there were strange noises, a cart rattling over cobbles, a door hinge squeaking, a woman calling something in a foreign tongue. And then a bell tolling slowly. Someone in the next room was running water into the wash-bowl.

Betty opened her eyes again and looked into Jim's.

" I don't ever want to get up," she said, sleepily.

" Then don't."

" But, darling, we must ! "

" Why must we ? " he asked. " It isn't every day you can lie in the heart of Vienna, under a gorgeous chandelier."

" It's a monstrosity."

" I think it's beautiful."

" Darling, you can't ! " she protested.

" But, darling, I do—we'll never live in a room with a

ceiling high enough for a thing like that. We get all that
for twelve schillings a night."

"Silly darling," she laughed, running her hand through
his hair. "And now we must be serious."

"Why?"

She played with the button of his pyjama jacket, not
answering for a few moments.

"I think Mr. Waddle's hypnotised us," she said, at last.
"I like him awfully, he's very kind and very persuasive
—and that makes him dangerous. I've never quite realised
until we got here just what he really wants us to do about
that baby. He wants us to run frightful risks, to make a
false entry in our passport in order that he can get a Jew's
baby out of the country."

"It's Gollwitzer's baby—I like old Gollwitzer," said Jim.
"I'd like to help him."

"But we'd run the most frightful risks. He's no right
to ask us to do such a thing. Darling, we simply mustn't!"
she cried.

"I'm not worried about the entry in our passport—next
year it might be true," he said, with a mischievous smile.

"But how could it ever be——"

And then, her eyes looking into his, dancing with the
playful light she knew so well, she gave an embarrassed
laugh, and felt his eager lips on hers.

She pushed his young head away after a few moments.

"Darling, we must be serious! We must tell Mr. Waddle
we can't do it. And he hasn't found the baby yet," said
Betty.

"Poor Waddle will be heartbroken. He's set on getting
Gollwitzer his baby," said Jim. "Betty, let's take a sporting
chance."

"No—do you know what might happen to us if we were
caught?"

"That's what makes it exciting. I hate the way they're
trampling on these wretched Jews. You heard what Waddle
told us last night about that doctor friend of his? They
shouldn't have it all their own way."

" It's too big a risk, Jim."

" Very well, if you won't——"

" I won't."

" Very well, that ends it," said Jim, resignedly. " But I'm sorry for Waddle—he'll feel let down."

" But we never promised him anything definite. He's a hypnotist, Jim. When you think of it, in the clear light of morning, the whole idea's crazy."

" The whole world's crazy just now—and the light's not clear in this room."

She shook his tousled head, and kissed him.

" Now go back to your bed," she said.

" That lecture over ? And if I refuse to move ? "

" I shall get up."

" That's what a good wife should do—and turn on the bath, and ring for breakfast. Thank you, darling," he retorted.

" Will you go ? " she asked.

" No."

She raised one arm and touched the bell hanging overhead.

" Now you'll get up—the maid'll be here in a minute ! " she threatened.

Jim did not move. He held his wife tightly, feeling her heart beating against him.

" Jim ! Jim ! " she pleaded. " The maid will be here ! "

" Bravo ! "

She began to struggle with him, but he held her in the vice of his arms. There was sudden tapping on the door. Betty gave him a desperate look.

" Come in ! " he called, triumphantly, enjoying the panic of his bride.

There was a voluble outcry in German beyond the door.

" Silly darling," said Jim, slipping out of the bed. " Didn't you know I shot the bolt last night ? "

He laughed delightedly at the trick he had played on her. Then he put on his dressing-gown, went to the door, and opened it. The fat chambermaid stood there, rocking with laughter. A pantomime followed.

" *Frühstück, bitte,*" said Betty, sitting up, busy with a phrase book.

" *Ja—mit Kaffee und Honig?* "

" *Mit Honig und Ei, bitte schôn.*"

" *Danke schôn!* " cried the smiling chambermaid. " *Die gnädige Frau spricht sehr gut Deutsch!* " she said, turning to Jim, and, shaking with laughter, bustled out of the room.

" Now, whatever have you done ? " he asked.

" I've ordered breakfast, coffee, honey and an egg. And the maid, let me inform you, says I speak very good German, mein Herr ! "

Jim sat on the side of the bed, and, holding her jubilant face between his hands, kissed the tip of her nose.

" I knew when I married you I'd chosen the prettiest and cleverest—and most obstinate woman in London," he said, with shining eyes.

II

They did not see much of Waddle all day. He was very apologetic, but he hoped they would understand. There were delegates to the Folk-Dance Congress at Budapest already in Vienna, and naturally he had to see them. Then, at midday, he had met the Belgian delegates arriving at the station. At four o'clock he broadcasted a ten-minutes' talk on the international significance of folk-dancing and its bearing on peace between the nations. At seven o'clock he had called on the editors of some of the Viennese newspapers. " Just sowing a little of the good seed, you know," he said, when he met Jim and Betty, later, at their hotel. He was excited in manner, full of energy, his portfolio bursting with papers, his tie higher than ever round his neck.

" We'll dine together in a little place I know, cheap but quite good, and then we'll go to one of the cafés. I don't know what the night life is like now—this Nazi business may have changed everything. We'll go to a café in the Schwarzenberg Platz where all the most interesting people go."

Waddle looked round their bedroom, where he sat talking to them.

"You're quite comfortable?" he asked. "I want you to meet the Kummers, a charming family. And I've good news for you. Count Mátány is here—and he's asked us to lunch with him to-morrow at a restaurant in the Stadtpark. I saw him for a few minutes this afternoon and he was very excited about our little plot. It seems Herr Gollwitzer has been in a terribly depressed condition, but the idea of getting the baby back has given him new hope. There's a scheme also for Hans, his valet, you know, to get into Hungary also, and the Count has found a delightful flat in Buda where Gollwitzer's going to live. Mátány's seen Hans, and the whole business will be quite simple. We leave at two o'clock on Sunday by the motor-bus that starts from the end of the Kärntner-Ring. In the morning a box containing the baby's things will be delivered here, addressed to you——"

"Mr. Waddle, I'm afraid we're going to disappoint you," said Jim, interrupting him. "After thinking it over very carefully, my wife and I have decided we really can't do this job—it's far too risky."

"But I assure you there's no risk!" exclaimed Waddle, in dismay. "Oh, you can't realise what it means to Gollwitzer—he thinks the whole thing is going through. That's why Mátány's here. Now, please—why have you changed your mind?"

"Well, I'll be frank. You rather rushed us into this business before we knew what we were doing," replied Jim. "You've a very persuasive way with you, Mr. Waddle. What we really dislike about it all, is that we should have to make a false entry in our passport."

"Which is a very serious thing," added Betty.

Waddle smiled blandly, and nursed his portfolio.

"The entry need only be for twenty-four hours—we can erase it again. It's really very simple. No one is going to raise the slightest question. You are a young couple travelling to Budapest, with your child. Why should they suspect anything?"

"But if they do—if we're caught smuggling out Goll-witzer's baby? On your own admission they are deter-mined he shan't have the custody of it. What do you think would happen to us—our own Consulate wouldn't help us," said Jim.

"I admit all that," answered Waddle, blandly. "But don't unusual difficulties call for unusual methods? We're trying to outwit these people in the perpetration of a monstrous injustice, on behalf of a man of genius whom all the world —all the sane world—reveres. I'm not a brave man, my dear Mr. and Mrs. Brown, but if I had it in my power to tilt the scales just a little in favour of people I see being mons-trously persecuted, I shouldn't hesitate for a moment, no matter what it involved—forgery, perjury or imprisonment. Of course, I'm a wretch of no principles whatsoever. I come of an old but degenerate family, which makes it easy for me. Perhaps I should not have persuaded you to do this thing—I'm sorry; after all, I have no claim whatsoever on you. But it happens that you are the only and very easy solution of something I very much want to do. It would be striking a blow for liberty against tyranny; it would be serving a man of very great genius who is being monstrously ill-treated. Dear me!" exclaimed Waddle, breaking off apologetically, "I'm getting too persistent! Forgive me. You've a perfect right to draw back. We'll all be very upset—just when we're on the verge of success. Mátány has arranged everything brilliantly. But if you say, 'No,' then 'No' it must be."

He looked so unhappy as he said these words that Jim looked from him to his wife, half hoping she might change her mind. He was ready for the adventure, but since they were both involved he would not urge her against her will.

"Mr. Waddle, I can understand everything that you feel. But you do admit we should be running a very serious risk?" said Betty. "If there was a slip no one knows what the consequences might be. No, we can't do it."

"Very well, my dear. That's the end of it," replied Waddle. "You must forgive me if I led you on a course

hat is too dangerous. My enthusiasms do run away with
ne. I'll have a bad ten minutes with Count Mátány, but
I'm sure you'll find him just the same delightful fellow.
Now, shall we go? Our little restaurant's about twenty
minutes walk, if you're not too tired."

III

Waddle dived suddenly out of the Mariahilferstrasse down
a steep flight of steps into an underground restaurant. It
consisted of numerous curtained boxes, dimly lit with old
brass lanterns. Somewhere a string orchestra was playing
waltz tunes. The place was like a conspirator's den. A very
fat host showed them into a box, followed them in, and drew
the curtains behind him. A long vivacious conversation
between Waddle and the host ensued. What it was all
about Jim and Betty had no idea, but there was an air of
conspiracy about the conversation. Their voices were
subdued, and their host, who could see over the top of the
curtained box, kept looking from left to right.

" And now," said Waddle, picking up the long menu
sheet written in faint blue ink, " what shall we eat ? "

The debate took on a louder tone, and became positively
pantomimic. Mine host explained his dishes with a wealth
of gesticulation.

" Will you leave it to me ? " asked Waddle, peering over
the top of the long menu at Jim and Betty. " This is the
home of the very best Viennese cooking, at prices to suit
poor artists.

They agreed to leave it to Waddle. It was obvious he had
command of the place. After a prolonged debate mine host
withdrew.

" I must explain," said Waddle, shifting his knife and
fork across the plain, board table. " That is Richard Scherer.
He was once a magnificent tenor at the Opera House, an
idol of Vienna. He married a little ballerina, a veritable
fairy he could almost hang on his watch-chain. He wor-
shipped her. She spent every penny of his money ; she

treated him in the most outrageous way, flirting with every man that looked at her. But he never believed the warnings he received. It was natural for men to lavish attention on her. One day he received an anonymous letter saying that if he watched a certain flat, during the hours that it was known he was rehearsing, he would find that she was visiting a lover. So one day he cancelled his rehearsal and watched outside the flat. Presently his young wife arrived at the apartment house, and went up to the flat occupied by a famous painter. His suspicions confirmed, he kept watch on his wife's movements, until it became clear, beyond doubt, that she was involved in a love affair. One night, when he was singing in *Faust*, with his wife dancing in the ballet, he noticed that her lover was in one of the boxes. He watched from the wing, and when the young man leaned forward to applaud her, Scherer shot him through the head. You can imagine the sensation! But there was another sensation at the trial, for it transpired that the little ballerina had committed bigamy, and the dead painter was her first and therefore legal husband. In court her counsel stated that she had visited her legal husband under compulsion. He had returned after a long absence, having deserted the ballerina, and had insisted on resuming relations with her, although he was quite content that she should pass as Scherer's wife. Of course there was a big pro-Scherer and a big anti-Scherer party. Scherer was found guilty of murder. The country rose against the verdict. An appeal went to the Chancellor, and then to the Emperor. Finally, the sentence was commuted to imprisonment for life, but after seven years he was pardoned. He couldn't go back to the stage, so he opened this restaurant, which is patronised by the opera artists. That was all thirty years ago."

"What happened to the ballerina?" asked Betty. "Did she——"

A waiter appeared through the curtain, bringing bread and cutlery.

"In a moment—he may know English," said Waddle.

The waiter, hearing the warning, laughed.

" Oh yes, I know English, sir. I was four years at the Savoy Hotel in London, before the war. Ah, what days they were ! I used to have a young lady at Hounslow—a lovely girl."

" And you didn't marry her ? " asked Jim, amused by this fat smiling fellow with a long black moustache.

" No, sir, I wasn't able to—I was interned, and when I came out I was deported. She married a baker, and years later sent me a portrait of herself and three children ! I like the English, sir. I like everything English except the beer ! "

He laughed merrily and withdrew.

" The ballerina ? " asked Jim.

Waddle pulled the curtain on one side, revealing a vista of the long room, with the orchestra on a dais at the far end.

" Do you see that cash desk in the corner ? " he asked.

They looked in the direction indicated by Waddle.

" Yes," said Jim.

" The fat lady ? "

Jim and Betty looked and they saw the woman to whom Waddle alluded. She sat at a cash desk, dressed in a bright green bodice, in Tyrolean style. Her enormous arms bulged from the short sleeves, and her tiny face rested on tiers of chins, each set back from the other. She was probably a woman nearing sixty, but there were still vestiges of the pretty doll she might once have been, and her peroxide hair, built up in elaborate curls, gave her an absurdly babyish expression.

" That lady is the ballerina," said Waddle. " She met Scherer at the prison door, and they started this business together. For years she did all the cooking, and made the place famous for its food. But this is not the end of the story. Scherer is an old friend of Gollwitzer's. Count Mátány tells me that it's their daughter who is nurse to Gollwitzer's baby, and it's our friend Scherer, and his wife, who've now got the child hidden away somewhere in the country."

The waiter was returning carrying soup-plates.

" Oh, here's the *Nudelsuppe*," broke off Waddle. " I hope you'll like it, and after that I've ordered *Gänsebraten mit Reis*—roast goose with rice, a speciality of the house."

They began to eat while Waddle continued with an endless repertoire of Viennese stories. From time to time Herr Scherer appeared, anxious to learn whether the food pleased them. It was indeed excellent. The warmth, the food, the soft light, the gay lilting music, and Waddle's conversation, produced in Jim and his wife a feeling of complete benevolence to all the world, and it was with reluctance that, after much handshaking with Herr and Frau Scherer, they allowed Waddle to take them forth to his favourite café near the Schwarzenberg Platz.

They walked along the Ringstrasse, under the linden trees. It was a warm June night, and the fresh green leaves shone under the lamplight and made a delicate patchwork on the pavement. Taxis and trams swirled by, the promenaders, chattering and laughing, passed in an endless stream before the open-air cafés, at whose thronged tables Vienna gossiped and discussed the political situation. The world was in the melting-pot again. The Duce and the Führer in Rome had toasted their mutual greatness, the bombs were falling on Barcelona, the red tide of war flowed over China, the French were creating another Government, the English appointing another committee, and the walls of the babel fortress of Czechoslovakia were ominously cracking. Vanished Austria, now swinging a little giddily on the Rome-Berlin axis, devoured its newspapers and began to look dubiously at the overwhelming preponderance of their German overlords in this old city where *Gemütlichkeit* was to be disciplined by the swastika.

But of these speculations and glimmering apprehensions, Jim and Betty knew little. They only felt the beauty and gaiety of this warm, heavy night as they strolled along the leafy boulevards towards the café patronised by their cheerful companion.

IV

Waddle's favourite café was not one of the large, resplendently lit places that occupied a corner of the Platz. The prices of these fashionable rendezvous frightened him. " And more than the prices—the people. You meet the English and Americans, thick as bees, all wearing Austrian hats and comparing notes about hotels," said Waddle.

Jim wondered whether Waddle cherished the illusion that he had succeeded in disguising himself. Those shapeless flannel trousers, and that bulging old sports jacket could only have come out of England, and of their kind they were truly vintage, matured through many seasons. Waddle was the archetype of all those English travellers who do not care what they look like and who, carrying only a bulging portmanteau, make Europe their inexpensive playground, experts in third-class travel, second-class hotels and first-class entertainment.

They turned out of the Platz into a quiet street and stopped in front of a smaller café. Waddle pushed open the door and led the way into a plush-upholstered room, lit with white globes hanging in triple clusters. The Herr Ober rushed up and greeted him warmly. Waddle carefully selected a table not too near the pianist, who was playing with astonishing virtuosity. The café was half full, it had a sad air of tawdry splendour, with its plush seats, heavy gilt mirrors and formidable oil paintings of scenes of Tryolean beauty. Jim and Betty wondered why Waddle made this his haunt ; it had none of the cosmopolitan gaiety of the cafés they had passed.

But it soon became clear that Waddle was at home here. As soon as the order for coffee had been given, the waiter returned with a large writing-blotter, a pot of ink, and a plentiful supply of notepaper and envelopes. Having deposited these he collected a number of newspapers affixed to large sticks with reading handles, and stacked them up beside Waddle.

" You may think the coffee dear in Vienna," explained

Waddle, " but you must remember you pay for much more than the coffee. You are supplied with pen and paper, and a great collection of newspapers to read, and in winter you can sit here for hours and save the cost of heating at home. I conduct all my correspondence from this café—they're most friendly people. It's a favourite place for poor musical students—some of the greatest geniuses of the musical world have come in here from their lodgings, to warm their frozen fingers when they couldn't afford fires. One of them you have certainly heard of—it was the favourite haunt of a lonely young Pole named Paderewski, when he came to Vienna to study under the great Leschetizky."

The waiter brought them coffee, and a revolving tray of cakes, each locked up in a separate glass partition.

" Oh ! " exclaimed Waddle, delightedly, revolving the roundabout of cakes. " Isn't this a good idea—none of our fly-blown, fingered cakes. Watch ! "

He took out a small coin and pressed it into a slot over the desired cake, which unlocked the cover.

He insisted on making selections for Betty and Jim.

" I've a weakness for gadgets. There's a glorious automat café here in Vienna, where I often dine. I should be very happy in the United States, they tell me all these things come from America," said Waddle, stirring his coffee. " And now, if you'll excuse me, I'm going to write a few urgent letters," he added, opening his crammed portfolio. " You'll find some interesting illustrated papers in that pile. By the way, there'll be two hundred and sixty-four delegates at the Folk-Dance Congress, representing twenty-four countries. There's even a delegate from Chile ! "

" Are you going to address them ? " asked Jim.

Waddle looked startled by the idea.

" Address them—oh, dear me, no ! I always work behind the scenes—you know, a little word here, a little word there, and a suggestion for something. There are always plenty of people ready to get up and talk. That's the disease of the age. I'm not a politician."

" You prefer to be a diplomat," suggested Betty.

Waddle beamed.

" Well, that's perhaps somewhat flattering," he said.   " I have been called an intriguer for the Cause.   I've always enjoyed pulling wires.   And now, my dears, if you'll excuse me."

He picked up a pen, extracted the nib and supplied one from his waistcoat pocket.   Then he began to write.   Neither the exuberant pianist, now embellishing a Strauss waltz, nor the general hum of conversation disturbed him.

Jim and Betty worked steadily through the illustrated papers.

The café had filled up.   The pianist, taking a well-earned rest, went round with a collecting plate.   Waddle stopped writing for a moment to make a contribution.

" Ah ! " he smiled, pushing up his glasses on his forehead. " Two more letters and I'm finished."

" Go on, we're quite happy," said Jim, lighting a cigarette.

And then, so suddenly, as though a hawk had flung its sinister shadow from a serene sky, there was a tense hush. Not a word was spoken, no one moved, but all turned and looked in the direction of the door.   Four strapping young men, top-booted and wearing uniform, with the swastika red-and-white cross blazing on their arms, stood inside the door.   They surveyed the café with hostile eyes, slowly ranging the whole length of the room, examining each customer.

Waddle, made conscious of something unusual by the sudden hush, looked up from his writing.   Then he calmly put down his pen and watched the men.   Betty's heart began to thump.   Something told her they foreboded evil. There was arrogance and challenge in every line of their powerful bodies.   Their aggressive jaws were emphasised by the peaked caps from beneath which they glowered.   The waiters went deathly white.   The pianist ceased playing.

Two of the S.S. men walked thunderously down the café, leaving their companions on guard at the door.

" All Jews stand up ! " barked one of the men.

There was a moment of frightened hesitation.   Then about

fifteen men rose at various tables, their dark eyes shone, the pallor of their faces deepened. The proprietor, paralysed with fear, broke into a sweat. He tried to open his mouth, but no words came.

The two Nazis stood in the middle of the café, glaring at the customers who had risen at their command.

" Jewish swine are only allowed in their own cafés," said the taller Nazi, a young man of about twenty-four. He turned to a middle-aged Jew standing near. " You know that. How dare you come here ! "

The terrified man tried to say something, but before he could utter a word the Nazi struck him across the mouth. The Jew tottered, and sank into a chair.

" Stand up ! " bellowed the second Nazi.

The Jew stood up. Blood began to trickle from his cut lips.

They turned to a thin youth shaking with fear.

" Your name ? "

" Jacob Wassermann."

" Why are you here ? "

" I have always come here," answered the youth.

" Oh, have you ! " cried the Nazi.

The next moment he struck him across the head and face, making savage blows with his flexible steel stick.

Jim rose from his seat, but Waddle's quick hand pulled him down again.

" You'll make it worse for them. Keep quiet," whispered Waddle.

One of the Nazis turned to the proprietor.

" Your place wants washing down after these swine have been here," he said. " Take two of these Jews and give them buckets and brushes. We'll have the floor and windows washed."

He pointed to two stout, elderly Jews who had been playing chess.

" You'll do for the job," he said.

" I have rheumatism," said the Jew, his eyes starting out of his head.

The young Nazis roared with laughter.

"Then we'll give you some exercise. Come out here!"

"No, please," pleaded the man.

"Come out here, you filthy Jew!"

The man advanced fearfully.

"Touch your toes!"

"But I can't!"

The two Nazis looked at each other, then caught the Jew between them and forced his head down towards his knees. The man began to struggle, when one of his tormentors suddenly jerked up his knee, catching the Jew violently in the ribs. The victim shrieked with pain and collapsed on to the floor. They let him lie there.

"I can't stand this!" said Jim, getting up.

Before Waddle could stop him he was walking down the café. The Nazis at the door drew their revolvers. The two Nazis in the café turned and looked at him angrily. They said something to him.

"I'm English. If you put your dirty hands on me, I'll knock you for six," said Jim.

They did not understand him. He walked past them to the Jew moaning on the floor, picked him up, and half-carried him to a seat. All the café watched in absolute silence. Jim went back to his seat, ignoring the Nazis who said something to him.

The waiters had brought two buckets and brushes. These were given to the Jews, who, under command, went down on their knees and began to scrub the floor. The first Jew who had been struck was being attended to by another Jew.

"Leave him alone—go back to your seat," cried the Nazi.

"You've broken his nose."

"I'll break your neck if I have another word from you!" shouted the young Nazi.

"Let's go. Ask the waiter for the bill," said Jim to Waddle, rising. "If I don't get out of here I shall go for these blackguards."

They got up from their table. Not a waiter moved. They stood petrified. The Jews were scrubbing the floor.

The steel stick whistled over their shoulders when they did not scrub hard enough. Then Waddle created a diversion. He suddenly bolted for the door, and pushed past the obstructing Nazi guarding it. Jim and Betty saw him go, with amazement. Had he lost his nerve?

Jim paid the waiter. The four Nazis glared at him as he led his wife towards the door. Just as he reached it Waddle came in again, with two more Nazis. One of them was an elderly man with a monocle, in a German S.S. officer's uniform. He took in the situation at a glance. The Austrian Nazis stood to attention. He spoke to them curtly, and ordered them out of the café. He commanded the Jews who were scrubbing the floor to stop, and stand up. He looked at the two men bleeding about the face, and at the man who lay crumpled up in the chair where Jim had placed him.

" You can get them a doctor if necessary," said the German officer. " I shall report these men. Tell your Jewish customers to go home quietly."

He saluted the proprietor and Waddle, and marched out, followed by his companion.

" Please, let us go," cried Betty, very white, as Waddle began to talk with the customers.

Jim put his arm under hers. They hurried out into the street. Waddle hailed a taxi. They got in. He ordered the man to drive to the hotel. For a few minutes none of them spoke.

" Who was that fellow with the monocle you brought in ? " asked Jim.

" A German officer—these Austrian bullies have quite lost their heads. I saw him going by the window and rushed out to get him," said Waddle.

" Do you think those men will get punished ? " asked Jim.

" No—every young blackguard in Vienna is now getting his chance. I would never have believed it, if I had not seen it," said Waddle.

" Nor I," added Betty. " I thought the Austrians were civilised."

" They are—that's the paradox of it," commented Waddle.
" It's a virus that gets into their blood. But you've not had
the shock I've had."

They looked at Waddle inquiringly.

" I knew one of these fellows—one of them by the door.
He saw me and had enough shame to pretend he didn't.
I've known him since he was a boy. I used to take him
riding roundabouts in the Prater fun fair. He's my host's
son, Karl Kummer. Just think of it, that boy Karl behaving
like a thug."

They did not speak again for a few moments. The taxi
passed down the brightly lit Kärntnerring. Betty was the
first to speak.

" Mr. Waddle, I want to do one thing now, and I know
Jim will agree. We'll risk anything to get Gollwitzer's
baby out of Austria. It would fill me with joy to outwit
these gangsters."

" I'm with Betty. God, how I'd like to trick the devils ! "
exclaimed Jim. " It made my blood boil to sit there so
powerless."

Waddle put his hand on Betty's.

" That will be a beautiful revenge, my dear," said Waddle.
" I'm glad you feel like that."

A few minutes later he left them at the hotel, promising to
call on the morrow. Then he walked slowly back to the
Kummer apartment. The sight of Karl indulging in that
ghastly Jew-baiting had been a severe shock. He had loved
the lad. They had had many delightful outings together.
He remembered how he had told the two brothers thrilling
good night stories as they lay in their twin beds, and how he
had taken them swimming and sailing one summer on the
Attersee. Karl had always been the Adonis of the family,
with his fresh boy's face and wavy, blond hair, his slim
athlete's body, his skill at every game, his infectious spirits.
And now, believing himself to be a fine fellow, a patriot, he
had developed into a bully in uniform. Was there an
ineradicable sadistic streak in the Teutonic race ? Or was
it common to humanity once the restraining traditions had

been broken down ? Perhaps civilisation was only a very fine crust over the volcano of human passion.

As Waddle mounted to the Kummer apartment he decided that he would say nothing regarding Karl's participation in the raid on the café.

CHAPTER X

WADDLE SPEAKS OUT

I

" I HEAR you were at Scherer's last night," said Count Mátány, addressing Waddle.

The sun was shining, the orchestra was playing softly, the beds around the raised terrace of the restaurant were gay with flowers. Mrs. Brown was one of the prettiest women he had ever seen in his life, and he liked the young husband at sight. The luncheon was already a great success. He had lost all apprehension regarding Waddle's protégés, who were apt to be the most singular creatures.

" This morning," continued Mátány, " I had a visit from Hans."

" Do you think we ought to talk here ? " asked Waddle, glancing around him.

Mátány laughed. " I suppose we are conspirators," he answered. " Mrs. Brown, if I may say so, you look like the fair spy in the film story."

" What film story ? " asked Betty.

She was radiantly happy in this Viennese setting. There were well-dressed people all around her, the orchestra played seductively. The wine glinted in their glasses, and before her on the table stood an enormous basket of delicious fruit, tied up with large blue ribbons. The striped awning had been drawn against the sun, the smartly groomed waiters moved deftly among the crowded tables. Before them

stretched the vivid parterres of the Stadtpark. Beyond the
trees they could see the upper storeys of the buildings lining
the Parkring. The sound of trams occasionally broke in on
the music. Below their terrace there was a large enclosure
covered with small tables where the Viennese gathered for
the *thé dansant*.

Betty felt it truly was a setting for a film. Anything
could happen. There was unreality in the events of these
last few weeks. When one of the waiters disappeared through
a swing door she was reminded of another swing door through
which she had carried trays. It did not perturb her. Those
days of bondage were no longer real. Here she sat, having
eaten food beautifully cooked and served, on the terrace of
a Viennese open-air restaurant, the guest of Count Mátány,
whose eyes flattered her every time he spoke to her.

" What film story, you ask ? " said the Count. " In every
spy story there is always a lady so lovely that the most
discreet men make incredible fools of themselves. I've never
understood the psychology of this. I should have thought
men would have been on their guard against the fair enchant-
ress. I once knew a lady, a Polish lady, who was a professional
spy. She died true to type. She was shot by a Russian
firing squad—by White Russians in Archangel, but she had
the most formidable squint. It helped when she ' went
native ' she said. She had a most astonishing and successful
history, until that last slip. No one would ever credit such
an ugly woman with such dangerous activities. Not all the
resources of Hollywood could have made her credible—women
spies must possess a fatal charm, according to fiction."

He turned, beckoned a waiter, and asked for the bill.
Betty noticed what beautiful hands he had, lean and brown,
with perfectly shaped nails. He drew a thin, leather wallet,
gold-tipped, from his coat, and extracted some notes. He
was perfectly dressed in a dark grey suit of English cut.
His hair and his Magyar eyes apart, he was the kind of well-
groomed young man one might see walking down Bond
Street any morning. Betty found it hard to credit him with
many of the exploits told them by Waddle.

" I suggest we now go back to my hotel, where we can develop the plot in safety," said Mátány.

Outside the Stadtpark he called a taxi, and in a few minutes they had reached Sacher's Hotel, where the Count had a suite of rooms.

" My aunt pays," he explained as they entered, and Waddle exclaimed on the luxury of it. " I once came to Vienna and lived in a very cheap hotel. The old dear was so horrified that I should lower the family reputation for extravagance that she volunteered to pay for my lodgings in Vienna on all future occasions, providing they were expensive enough ! She's very rich and very eccentric. Unfortunately she has ten nephews and nieces, and I am by no means the favourite one."

" If this is what she does for you, I wonder what she would do for the favourite one ? " asked Jim, looking round at the luxurious room. He went to the window. " What building is that ? "

" The back of the Opera House. Sacher's, as you know, enjoyed the patronage of the Hapsburg scions. The hotel has a happy proximity to the stage door," explained Mátány.

" If these walls could talk ! " said Waddle.

" They would be pulled down at once," answered his friend. " And now let me tell you what I have arranged with Hans. He came to see me here this morning, in answer to a telegram I sent him. His one idea is to get to Goll-witzer, but it is going to be very difficult. No Austrian can get out of the country. So we are going to manufacture an aunt who lives at Györ, who will be seriously ill and send for her dear nephew. With this pretext he may get permission to cross the frontier. On Sunday morning Scherer's daughter will bring *Der kleine Eisenbahner* to town. On Saturday night Hans will leave at your hotel," said the Count, turning to Betty, " a parcel containing the baby's clothing, from which, as a precaution, all Austrian trade labels have been removed, in case the officials became inquisitive. The idea is that you should lunch at Scherer's on Sunday, and leave afterwards with the baby, you and Henry and Mr. Brown. We must get rid of the hotel people somehow."

" I'd thought of that," said Waddle. " We'll say we are leaving by the 11.40 train for Budapest, and take the taxi to Scherer's."

" Excellent. Now at the other end. I've arranged for a nurse," said Mátány, opening a large box of chocolates and passing it to Betty. " I told Gollwitzer he could not go on living at that hotel—he'll feel more homelike in a flat. So he's taken one, with a lovely view, up in Buda. We've fixed him up with a housekeeper and a man, until Hans joins him. There's a room for the nurse, and another that'll make a nursery. I'm leaving by the morning train on Sunday to let Gollwitzer know everything's all right, for we mustn't write to him. I shall meet your motor-bus and we'll go straight to Gollwitzer's. How does that all seem to you ? " asked the Count, stubbing his cigarette.

" I see no flaw—if Scherer does his part," answered Waddle.

" Hans assures me he's quite safe," said Mátány.

" There's one thing worries me," said Betty.

" The passport ? " asked Mátány.

" No. My husband doesn't think that is at all difficult. It's the baby—he must be fed."

" Ah, so ! " laughed Mátány. " I can't help you there."

" The baby's weaned—he's nine months old," said Waddle. " He's certain to have a feeding bottle."

" I think we ought to have a group photograph when we arrive," said Jim. " Honeymoon, complete with baby—how the tongues would wag at home ! "

" James, dear ! " cried Betty, crimson.

" And where will you be staying ? " asked Mátány.

" They're going with me to the Pension Balaton," said Waddle. " I think they'll like that."

" Frau Balaton's ! " exclaimed Mátány. He turned, smiling to Betty. " It's not a *pension*, it's a menagerie. She captured a poor devil of an Englishman and married him, to qualify for an English legacy."

" It's quite respectable, I hope ? " asked Jim, and then realised too late he should not have asked such a question before Waddle.

" If you want to squander money there's always the Ritz," retorted Waddle.

" We're sure it's very nice, Mr. Waddle," said Betty. " It will be a great advantage for us to be with you."

" And it's quite near to Gollwitzer's. You'll like the old boy, I'm sure," said Mátány.

" I know him, I always used to——" began Jim, but before he could finish the sentence Betty gave him a warning look. " Of course he doesn't know me," added Jim, hastily. " But I often saw him in London."

" I imagine when he knows what you've done for him he'll adopt you both," said the Count.

When they left Mátány Waddle walked a little way with Jim and Betty. Then he parted from them. He had to call upon some delegates at their hotel.

II

Waddle found his delegates, six blue-eyed *mädchen* in a little hotel in the Mariahilferstrasse. They came from Würzburg and Munich. Three of them were old friends, and there was an effusive scene of reunion with dear Tanzmeister Waddle. They showed him their dresses for the folkdancing, which he appraised with the eye of the connoisseur. He examined their headdresses, and expatiated on their legendary significance, so that their blue eyes opened wider at his astonishing omniscience. Out of this portfolio he produced badges and programmes. He gave them advice upon the right *pensions* to stay at, the cost of everything, the sights to visit. He thoughtfully asked after Herr This and Herr That in their home towns. He announced impending visits in the near future. He was planning a congress in Stuttgart for next April ; he was broadcasting a small talk on the movement from Munich in October.

They talked and laughed until an hour had fled, and then he made a courtly farewell, leaving them charmed with his friendliness, his enthusiasm, and his care for their comfort in Budapest. " Heil Hitler ! " they said, as he went. " Heil Hitler ! " he responded, flapping his hand.

He wrote some letters in a quiet café, and then decided to go back to his room. He wished to change his shoes before going on to the hotel, to take the Browns out to dinner in the Prater. As he opened the door of the flat Frau Kummer came into the hall. At once he knew something had happened. Her face was deathly, her lips bloodless.

" They've just arrested Hermann," she said, quietly.

He followed her into the room. Pauli and Elsa sat at the table, which had been laid for supper.

" They've taken Papa, the brutes ! " cried Pauli, flushed and angry. " Six of them ! They walked right into the surgery. They wouldn't let Mother see him."

" But why ? " asked Waddle. " What has he done ? "

" Papa would attend to Dr. Neumann's Jewish patients. He was warned not to," explained Elsa.

" Warned not to ! The insolence of it ! Of course Hermann attended to them," cried Frau Kummer.

" It was silly of Papa, when he knew," said Elsa, stoutly.

" I suppose you told them," cried Pauli, glaring at his sister.

" Pauli ! " said Frau Kummer, reproachfully.

" Where have they taken the doctor ? " asked Waddle.

Frau Kummer spread her hands despairingly.

" They wouldn't let him take a thing with him. There were six patients waiting in the surgery. He might have been a murderer. If I'd had a gun, the swine ! " cried Pauli.

He shook with passion, his hair fallen over his brow. His sister looked at him, in cold control of herself.

Waddle sat down on the sofa with Frau Kummer, and put his arm across her shoulder, comfortingly.

" Perhaps they'll release him soon," he said.

The bell rang. They all looked at each other apprehensively. Then Elsa got up and went into the hall. They heard the door open, and voices. Elsa reappeared and stood for a moment in the doorway.

" It's Karl," she said, standing aside.

" Mother ! " cried Karl, coming into the room.

Frau Kummer stood up, white and trembling. Karl put his arms round her.

" I've just heard—a friend in the Marokkaner Barracks told me. They've taken him there. I'm sure it'll be all right. They'll only question him."

" You seem to know the habits of your charming friends," said Pauli, his face white with defiance, as he confronted his brother.

" Pauli dear—I can't bear this, I implore you ! " cried Frau Kummer.

" Why does he come here ? He ought to be with his gang. There's plenty of people they can beat up without fear of retaliation. Ten of our fellows at the bank are in hospital, after their tender persuasion, because they weren't prepared to turn their coats and scream for Hitler. Haven't you got me on your list ? " mocked Pauli.

" Pauli, don't be silly—can't you think of Mother ? " asked Karl, quietly.

" Don't take any notice of him, Karl," said Elsa.

" Children, I can't bear this quarrelling, please, please ! " sobbed Frau Kummer, the tears streaming down her face.

She released herself from her son's arms.

" Karl, you had better go," she said, quietly.

He stared at her. His young face quivered.

" But Mother——" he cried, hoarsely.

" I mean it, Karl," she said, crushing the handkerchief in her hands. " There's been no happiness in this house since you joined the Nazi Party. I care nothing for politics. I care nothing for Austria——"

" Mother ! " interrupted Elsa.

She turned to her daughter.

" I care nothing for Austria—sometimes I think you patriots are the curse of the world, with your blind egotism, your intolerance ! I care only for my home, for the husband I love, the children I have borne. Yes, Karl, that is my faith. What has Hitler done for me ?—he has caused my

daughter and my sons to be flying at each other's throats,
my poor husband to be arrested. Karl, leave us alone ! "

" You mean that, Mother ? " asked Karl, quietly, all the
blood gone from his face.

" Yes, Karl," she answered, desperately. " And God
bless you, my poor boy."

He picked up his hat with a trembling hand. For a
moment he stood still, then suddenly he caught Frau Kummer
in his arms, pressing his cheek to hers.

" Mother ! Mother ! " he said, with tears welling in his
eyes.

For a few moments they clung to each other, and then
parted. Karl turned to his brother.

" Good-bye, Pauli," he said, quietly.

Pauli did not answer, and looked at him with hostile eyes.
Karl turned away. Elsa gave him a swift embrace.

Waddle, an impotent witness of this miserable scene,
looked uncomfortably at Karl, who now approached him.

" Onkel Heinrich—can I have a word with you, privately ? "
he asked.

" Certainly—come to my room."

Karl gave one desperate glance at his mother, crying in
her chair, and then resolutely left the room. Waddle followed
him, closing the door. They crossed the hall and entered
the bedroom.

" Onkel Heinrich," he said, quietly, his intense face level
with Waddle's, " I want to explain about last night."

" Won't that be difficult, Karl—why bother ? "

" I'm sorry you are hostile, too. I can understand—but
I am not all you think. I'm not a blackguard," said Karl,
earnestly. " I feel ashamed of what happened last night.
I don't wonder you think me contemptible. I got carried
away. We've been the under-dogs so long, have had to hide
and run for our lives so hard, that now the tables are turned
it goes to our heads at times. We raided that café on impulse.
I'd no idea those fellows would act like that—beating up those
Jews. I confess it was horrible."

" Then why didn't you interfere ? " asked Waddle.

Karl was silent for a moment. He looked at Waddle uneasily.

" It would have been difficult—the others—the others——' he floundered.

" It would have been less cowardly. We agreed not to recognise each other. Your judgment was not at fault in that. I never, never expected to feel ashamed of you, my dear Karl."

The boy flushed, and then looked at Waddle miserably. His eyes began to fill with tears.

" Onkel Heinrich, you can't think——" he began, and then turned his face away.

Waddle grasped him by the arms, and looked into the boy's swimming eyes.

" My dear boy," he said, kindly, " you may be right in all you believe and stand for. I won't judge of that. After all, I'm a foreigner, and perhaps I'm in no position to assess the rights and wrongs of it all. But why sully your cause, why tarnish so much self-denial and discipline, so much burning patriotism, with a want of chivalry, with intolerance and cruelty to a cowed minority ? Your father—why should he be arrested ? "

" He's attending to Neumann's Jewish patients."

" And why not—is it a doctor's function to inquire into the racial origins of those who are suffering and need medical help ? "

" You don't defend the Jews, Onkel Heinrich ? " asked Karl.

" I neither defend them not accuse them. You feel aggrieved because you see them entrenched in law, medicine and business. Why are they there ? Let us be honest— because they're prepared to work harder than we Christians. While you students are duelling, and sitting in beer gardens, they're hard at work in the libraries. They stand together, their family ties are insoluble—qualities you Nazis are always emphasising."

" The Jews are only part of the problem. What hope is there for Austria standing alone ? We've been cut to pieces, trampled on by the Treaties, kept down in grinding poverty.

They did that to Germany, and the Führer raised them from a rabble of Socialists into a powerful nation. He will do that for Austria—he is doing it now ! The world will listen to us again ! " said Karl, with shining eyes.

Waddle looked at him. The boy believed, passionately. It was something to see a faith so strong in these days of negative tolerance, when the faint approval of liberty covered a distaste for self-denial and discipline.

" For Austria ? " repeated Waddle. " Where is your Austria to-day ? You've opened your frontier to what—to the German invasion ! You are no longer master in your own house. You were a proud Empire long before the petty states of Germany were fused into one people. For seven hundred years you've given the world a pattern of social order, a long line of kings and emperors, a great aristocracy, a high tradition of manners, a splendid legacy in music and the arts, a proud record of statesmanship. The Austrian nation stood for all these things. And to-day it does not exist ! You call in the German broker, you cheer the bankruptcy of your national pride—after standing so splendidly defiant at the threatened barrier. You've not even the sad excuse of having been conquered. You have not been compelled to surrender your birthright—you young fellows, honourably no doubt, but mistakenly, I am certain, have gone out and assisted in the undermining of your own defences —for what purpose ? "

" To make the Reich a power in the world, to make the nations respect us."

" To give the Reich more power, I agree," retorted Waddle. " But you are sadly mistaken if you think you can ever enjoy control of it—one day you may have to march and fight at the bidding of that power. You will march as Germans."

" Why not ? "

Waddle looked intently at the young man before him.

" Karl, I have no answer to that question. A German can ask it with justification, but only an Austrian dead to all that he has inherited, impoverished it may be, but still sacredly his, could ask such a question. Don't think me blind and hopelessly prejudiced. There is much I admire in your Nazi creed—its readiness to make sacrifices, its self-discipline, its tremendous industry, its achievement in bringing a nation out of murderous feuds and chaotic politics. I can admire all this, but I detest its intolerance, its violence, its mediæval creed of blood, its cult of martial power, its reduction of the individual to a unit of mass hysteria. I will die in a ditch, or be driven beyond the farthest frontier of civilisation, before I will part with my right to say ' Yes ' and ' No ' to questions that a man must answer if a soul survives in him ! There, Karl, I don't want to be a doctrinaire. I don't doubt your honesty, your good faith in this business. But since you take this course—and it means suffering for all, as we see here to-night—try to bring some tolerance to your creed. I'm not so good a democrat that I believe a thing is right because fifty or sixty million people can be induced to shout the same thing. Well, I've had my say—you've been very patient with Onkel Heinrich. We part good friends, I hope ? "

Karl gripped Waddle's hand, and the words he wanted to say choked in his throat. He gave Waddle a long look, in which the man was aware of the contrary emotions surging in the boy's heart, and then, quickly, he turned and was gone. Waddle did not move. He heard Karl cross the hall, and the door closed after him.

For a few moments he stood contemplatively, then with a deep sigh, he sat down and began to change his shoes.

CHAPTER XI

ON TO BUDAPEST

I

AT eleven o'clock on Sunday morning, Waddle arrived at the König von Ungarn Hotel ready for what he called " the Flight into Egypt." To his surprise he discovered that

Betty was the calmer of the two. She had made up her mind to go through with the business, and dismissed all of Jim's misgivings. The fictitious child of Elizabeth and James Brown had been entered in the passport, on the line reserved for children. " You know they could give me time ' for that," said Jim, lugubriously.

" You can say you did it under strong feminine compulsion—or, if you like, you can say I did it, and you had a shock when I produced the child," retorted Betty.

" I can't think what's come over you ! " exclaimed Jim, admiringly. " I never knew you could be so war-like."

" I can still see that terrified Jew with the blood on his mouth," replied Betty.

When Waddle came he brought good news with him.

" They released Dr. Kummer yesterday evening. He refused to be intimidated, and said he would attend every patient who required his services," said Waddle. " When they found he couldn't be shaken, they let him out. Some of his colleagues at the hospital made a hullabaloo, and they got frightened, I suppose. And now are you all ready ? We officially leave for the station in a few minutes. As soon as we are out of sight of this place we'll go and leave the luggage at the motor-bus station, in readiness, and then we can walk slowly on to Scherer's. I said we'd be there about twelve for lunch. Did Hans leave that box last night ? "

" Yes," answered Betty, " there it is. I've been through all the linen. There's one funny thing—do you realise I don't even know the name of my own baby ! "

" James Henry Brown, of course," said Jim.

" Its real name—what is it called, Mr. Waddle ? " asked Betty.

" Good heavens, I don't know; I've never heard its name. Everyone calls it *Der kleine Eisenbahner*."

" It must have a name—but as it can't talk it doesn't matter," laughed Betty. " Do you think it's going to scream all the way to Budapest ? I know no German baby-talk, Mr. Waddle; you really have found me an extraordinary job."

Betty stood in front of the mirror and put on her hat. It was an Austrian one, a small felt shape, trimmed with flowers which she had seen in a shop and found quite irresistible. It gave a slightly audacious air.

" It's sheer musical comedy ! " commented Jim, as she turned, tucking a curl under the hat.

" Like it ?   No, not in front of Mr. Waddle," she laughed, as Jim attempted to kiss her.

" My dear children—I'll hide my face in a corner if you like," he said.   " Now, can I ring for the porter ?   I warn you, the whole hotel will line up to wish us *Auf Wiedersehen.*"

" I'm all ready for the great adventure ! " cried Betty, flushed with excitement.

Jim looked at her sparkling eyes and marvelled at her high spirits. His hands were icy, and he knew he was a bundle of nerves. He had only one longing now, to be safely over the border.

The Restaurant Scherer had not filled up when they arrived. There was an effusive welcome from Herr Scherer. He produced his long menu card and assisted them to make a selection. He had given them a box in the far corner of the restaurant. His fat, good-natured face showed not the slightest consciousness of the business on hand. Only when the assistant waiter had departed, and Herr Scherer was placing a bowl of flowers on the table, did he speak to Betty in his excellent English.

" My daughter is here—in our sitting-room. After lunch you will see her, gnädige Frau ? " he asked in a low voice.

" Thank you.   The baby——"

He spread his hands, and as he smiled his ears were buried in his fat cheeks.

" *Fabelhaft !* " he exclaimed.   " Ach, he is loffly ! "

Herr Scherer straightened himself up, and pulled at his moustache. The waiter was returning. With a bow, he withdrew to attend to new customers entering.

The lunch was excellent : a minestrone soup, Wiener schnitzel, some asparagus, and wild strawberries and coffee.

It was a quarter-past one when they finished. Jim had recovered his spirits, and, as a demonstration of coolness, selected a small cigar. When he asked for the bill Herr Scherer returned to their table, expressing a hope that they had enjoyed their lunch.

"If the gnädige Frau will follow me I will present my wife and daughter," he said.

Betty got up and let Herr Scherer escort her through a door and up some stairs. From the landing they entered a small sitting-room. Frau Scherer and the Fräulein rose to greet her. They could not speak English so Herr Scherer interpreted. And there, lying on the sofa, lay *Der kleine Eisenbahner*, a chubby fellow with enormous black eyes that looked at Betty with the utmost seriousness.

Laughing and talking, Fräulein Scherer picked up the infant and fondled it, then she gave it to Betty to hold, while Frau Scherer clucked and tickled its cheek, and cried "*Wie reizend !*"

"What's his name?" asked Betty, holding the little fellow to her bosom. His black eyes searched her face wonderingly.

"Friedrich," said Herr Scherer.

"Friedl! Friedl!" exclaimed Frau Scherer, shaking one of the baby's feet.

Mother and daughter talked vivaciously.

"What do they say?" asked Betty, pressing Friedl's tiny face to hers. The baby smiled at last, and began to bubble at the lips, to the fresh delight of the women.

"My daughter says the baby never cries, gnädige Frau," explained Herr Scherer.

"Why, that's unnatural!" laughed Betty. "And when do I feed him?"

There was another animated conference.

"Friedl has just had his milk. He should sleep soon. At four o'clock he can have some more milk. My daughter will give you his feeding-bottle. At six he has his last milk with a biscuit, and is put to bed. My daughter has written a letter for his nurse," said Herr Scherer.

F

Friedrich began to clamber over Betty's shoulder. Yes, he was a strong baby. He was already crawling. What beautiful black hair he had, what lovely eyes. *Fabelhaft!*

Herr Scherer now began to explain the arrangements for handing over *Der kleine Eisenbahner*. It was better, he thought, for his daughter and the baby to go first to the motor-bus station. There she would hand over the child, and it would seem, to anyone observing, that it was the nurse or a friend who had been in charge.

Betty rejoined Jim and Waddle. Herr Scherer had escorted her downstairs. He told her some stories of the early days when he and Gollwitzer had been musical students together. Days like that would never come again. His poor friend Gollwitzer, so gentle, so kind, so great a genius.

" I'm a good Austrian, gnädige Frau, yes, but I am a good friend too. When I was in great, great trouble, Gollwitzer did not desert me. No, that I shall never forget, never! "

The big fellow paused on the landing as he recited this to Betty. There were tears in his eyes, and he blew his nose lustily to hide his emotion.

" *Lieber Gott! Ich bin ein Idiot!* " he muttered, following her down the stairs.

II

They found Fräulein Scherer waiting for them by the long green motor-bus which made the daily journey between Vienna and Budapest. It left the corner of the Kärntner-ring at two o'clock. There was always a curious crowd to watch the departure of the tourists. Poor students, with satchels under their arms, stood gazing enviously at these mortals for whom the whole earth seemed a playground. Jim looked at his fellow passengers. There were some Austrians, two very *chic* Frenchwomen, an American family bursting with merry vitality, a group of English tourists in the charge of a bespectacled clergyman who beamed on everybody, and a large fat lady, with an Alsatian dog, who had a fierce argument in German with the conductor, who refused to take the dog.

Waddle had booked three seats. He superintended the bestowal of the luggage. It began to drizzle with rain. There was the loud noise of a band coming down the street, and of men marching. There was always a noise of men marching these days in Vienna, complained Waddle. But the first enthusiasm was wearing off. The men and women on the pavements now let them march by without any acclamation. In some cases they watched the massed Nazis go by with a sullen air. " They'll soon be tired of all this," said Waddle. " It's not the good fun they thought it would be. The Germans will make them work harder, get up earlier, and toe the line. Vienna won't be so *gemütlich*, you'll see ! "

The conductor began to shepherd the passengers into his bus. Betty took the baby from Fräulein Scherer. She said something in German and forced a smile to her face. Tears were not far away. The child had been in her charge for almost six months, and she was attached to it.

At last they had started. The motor-bus began to run through the suburbs. Jim and Betty sat side by side. The route lay over a dull plain. It passed through Hainburg, a quiet, country town. Waddle, in the seat behind, began to doze. The weather had cleared again. The baby lay very quiet in Betty's arms. They had been travelling about an hour when they came to a black-and-white barrier swung across the road. The motor-bus stopped.

Waddle woke up, and leaned forward, tapping Jim on the shoulder.

" The Austrian frontier," he said. " Or, more correctly, the German frontier now."

The moment had come. Jim's hands felt moist. He looked anxiously at Betty, who gave him a confident smile. Through the window they saw two soldiers standing on the steps of the Customs House. The people in the motor-bus got up and began to prepare for the examination of their passports.

"Mrs. Brown can stay in here—she's on your passport. We'll have to declare our money too."

Jim followed Waddle out and joined the queue. Two officials examined the passengers' passports and checked over their money. They had let Betty remain in the motor-bus.

Jim's turn came. A lean-faced official opened his passport, glanced at the photographs and then at him, then he banged the rubber stamp on a blank page, handed the passport back, and turned to the next person. It took a few minutes for the next official to check over his money and compare it with the form Jim had received on entering the Reich.

At last he was outside the building again. It had only taken a few minutes. There sat Betty and the baby. All his apprehension had been for nothing. How simple it was! He climbed back into the motor-bus, which began to fill up again. Waddle came in, smiled at them, and took his seat without saying a word. The conductor shut the door, the driver started up the engine. The black-and-white barrier pole swung upwards into the air. The motor-bus moved forward across the frontier. A Customs officer saluted as they passed.

They travelled about five hundred yards and came to another barrier, red, white and green. The motor-bus slowed up.

"Whatever's this?" exclaimed Jim, with a return of anxiety.

Waddle laughed. He, too, had felt anxious at the frontier, now he felt jubilant.

"This is Hungary, my boy—this is the Hungarian Customs and Passport Office. We'll all have to get down, for they'll insist on examining our luggage and reading through our passports. They look terribly fierce, but they're charming, really. Now, Mrs. Brown, let me hold the baby while you get down. We'll be quite twenty minutes here. Put your feet on Hungarian soil."

As Waddle had predicted, the Hungarian officials were

slow and meticulous. They looked at Jim, and Betty and
the baby. They carefully entered up all their money. But
not for a moment did Jim feel any anxiety. Gollwitzer's
baby was safely in Hungary. They had taken a risk and
succeeded.

The formalities completed. Betty sat on a bench outside
the Customs House, and nursed the baby in the warm sunshine. " Friedl ! " she whispered, and the child, attempting
to stand in her lap, made a chuckling response. He really
was a lovely baby, with his plump arms and legs and dark,
luminous eyes. Betty wondered for a moment where the
peasant girl-mother was. Waddle had told her how the
baby had been born on the Arlberg-Orient Express, in which
Gollwitzer had been travelling, and how he had bought it
from the girl-mother struggling to get home to Austria after
the death of her lover in Paris. Waddle believed Gollwitzer
was paying the mother a small pension. Poor mite, born
on a train, and now smuggled out of Austria ! What next,
wondered Betty.

They climbed into the motor-bus again. The conductor
closed the door. They began to move. The baby nestled
down and went fast asleep. For a time Betty looked at this
new land in which she travelled, but it was very flat and
dull, with a straight, dusty road bordered with acacia trees.
Presently the bus had stopped again. They were in a town,
and had halted at an hotel fronting the wide high road, with
a bridge opposite.

" This is Györ," said Waddle. " We've half an hour's
halt, and we can get coffee in the hotel garden."

" Give him to me," said Jim, holding out his arms for
the sleeping child. " This is good practice." He laughed
at his wife's sudden blush. " I'm going to hold you up
to the passport. I can't rub it out ! "

Waddle had already ordered coffee and cakes.

" Ah," he sighed, " I've been in this garden at least three
times. I used to go to Budapest by train, now I go by
motor-bus so that I can enjoy the drive into the city. I
hate being thrust into a place suddenly, after rushing past

sidings and gasometers. This isn't much of a place—but, to tell the truth, no town in Hungary is, except Budapest. The country seems to have put all its jewels into that show-case. This place has seen a lot of fighting in its time. The Turks once took it, then the Hungarians won it back, to lose it to the Turks again, and, of course, Napoleon was here, twice. My dear boy," broke off Waddle, " you make a most paternal picture with that infant in your arms ! "

" Let me take him, Jim," cried Betty.

The baby opened its eyes as he passed Friedl to her.

" Hello, Herr Gollwitzer ! " cried Jim, shaking his head over the baby. He felt very gay now the ordeal was over. Betty had been marvellous.

" Well, what an adventure ! " he exclaimed, pouring out some coffee. " Here we are, married, on our honeymoon, baby-snatching, and drinking coffee in a Hungarian inn. I'm going to write home and tell my old mother all about it as soon as I can get pen and paper. And it's all due to football ! "

" And to Mr. Waddle," said Betty.

" And to Mr. Waddle," said Jim.

" Oh, my dears, I only hope you'll never regret running into me," said Waddle modestly.

Soon after leaving Győr the road bordered a wide river, with low banks and swampy islands in mid-stream.

" The Danube," said Waddle. " Czechoslovakia lies on the opposite bank.

" But it's not blue ! " cried Betty.

" I've never seen it blue," replied Waddle. " A friend assures me it's blue in the Schwarzwald—nearer its source. Strauss's waltz has caused a great number of people to be sadly disappointed in this river."

They kept close to the river for the next hour. Its desolate banks, the flat islands, the muddy-coloured water, disappointed Jim and Betty. The villages, too, were rather miserable-looking places. The side roads seemed to be just tracks of beaten earth. The highway running through each village had a deep ditch on either side, in which flocks of geese floundered. They waddled lazily across the road and held up the traffic. Most of the children ran about bare-footed. Life here was in a primitive stage; it was the world of the poor peasant wringing a scanty livelihood from the soil. The houses were white-washed cabins, with gable ends turned to the road so that their fronts looked into an inner courtyard. It gave a secretive air to the villages. The travellers glimpsed nothing of the home-life of the inhabitants.

They passed few motor-cars. All the carrying and move-ment between these quiet villages seemed effected by long, horse-drawn carts. They had no springs, and the driver on the backless front seat was mercilessly shaken as the cart bumped over the uneven road. Black seemed the prevailing colour of the people's dress. Mud, dust, white cabins, acacia trees, wandering geese, and jolting tracks, seemed to characterise Hungarian life.

They passed a few gipsy encampments, out of which some filthy rapscallions poured, waving violins and beckoning the travellers to linger at their festooned open-air cafés, but the places were obvious tourist traps. Was Budapest going to be a bitter disappointment? There was certainly nothing in this dreary approach to suggest the enchantment of the Hungarian scene, the wild music, the superb horses, the lovely women, the handsome men, of which they had heard so much.

They left the bank of the Danube, a glaring expanse in the afternoon sun. To the left the dim shape of mountains began to rise. On a far hillside they saw a building with a massive dome, standing in isolated splendour. Even against a background of mountains it was an impressive pile. Was it the first glimpse of Budapest?

No, said Waddle, it was the cathedral at Esztergom, built high above the Danube; once the capital of old Hungary, the birthplace of Stephen, Saint and King, and the seat of the Prince-Primate of Hungary. " And for the rest a rather miserable place," added Waddle, with brutal candour.

" I'm beginning to lose heart about Budapest," said Betty, now feeding Friedl from his bottle.

" Don't ! I sometimes think Nature purposely designed this dreary entrance to heighten the effect," said Waddle. " Look at these ranges rising up."

The country was beginning to change. They entered a fold in the rising masses of porphyry and limestone rocks. In the play of light and shadow on these high, barren hills there was some exquisite colourings—amethyst-blue, vine-yard-green and deep purple.

They began to enter the outskirts of Buda. The road was blocked with the long rattling trucks coming in and out between the city and the market gardens. There was a grim journey through a factory district, over noisy cobbled roads, and then, swerving left, a sudden view opened up of the Danube, with Pest lying on the opposite side. The river ran now between splendid embankments, and flowed under a magnificent suspension bridge. But it was an immense pile of buildings with a central dome and massive wings, and innumerable windows glimmering with the crimson of the setting sun, which commanded the eye.

" What is it ? " asked Betty, overcome by this sudden sight of the Gothic edifice. " Is it the Royal Palace ? "

" No—it's the Parliament," replied Waddle. " It covers over three and a half acres. Some of us like it, and some of us don't. But it does stand well, with that great flight of steps down to the river. The palace is in front of you, on this side, but you can't see it yet. That bridge is the Lanczi-Hid, the Chain Bridge, one of the largest in Europe. It was built by a couple of Englishmen."

The motor-bus came to the end of the embankment and turned to cross the bridge. Betty and Jim had a fleeting view of the immense river, up and down stream, and of a long embankment opposite, lined with a leafy promenade and towering hotels.

" That's the Corso, where everyone goes at seven o'clock, to walk, or drink and gossip," said Waddle. " I know of only one thing in Europe to equal it—the Piazza at Venice. Well, we'll be there in a moment."

They crossed the Danube, turned in and out of some quiet

streets, and suddenly came into a large square, and halted
before a café whose customers had spilled over on to the
pavement, where they sat listening to an orchestra.

For the next twenty minutes they were in a whirlpool
of sensations. Count Mátány was there, with a friend, both
holding great bouquets of flowers. They waved them with
ecstatic joy at the sight of Betty carrying *Der kleine Eisenbahner*.

"Bravo! Bravo!" cried Mátány, vigorously shaking
Jim's hand. Then he bowed low to Betty.

"Let me present Count Zarin," he said.

A tall, dark young man of about thirty bowed and kissed
Betty's hand. Waddle, now holding the baby, was looking
round.

"Where's Gollwitzer?" he asked.

"The poor old man's so agitated we thought it better
to keep him at home," explained Mátány. "We've got
our car here and we're going straight to him."

The Count and his friend presented their bouquets. Betty,
flushed, and so pretty in her excitement that Count Zarin
could not believe his eyes, thanked them, feeling for a moment
like a film star receiving public acclamation.

Jim went to the end of the motor-bus to claim the luggage
being handed from the roof. Over a babel of voices and
waltz music he identified their bags, which were promptly
claimed by Count Zarin's chauffeur, a Mongolian-faced youth
whose mouth seemed set in a permanent grin.

They got into the large saloon car, Count Zarin sitting
outside with his chauffeur, who deftly slipped through the
traffic. They roared back again over the great bridge,
and entered a long illuminated tunnel whose echoes stunned
the ear, and then, emerging into daylight again, they swept,
twisting and turning, up the steep hillside. They halted
in front of a tall block of new flats. Herr Gollwitzer lived
on the sixth floor.

They ascended in the lift, stepped out, and paused in
front of an iron-grille door. Mátány rang the bell. Betty
felt her heart thumping with excitement. Friedl, wide-awake,

stared about him with his dark, wondering eyes.   His chubby hand clutched at a chain on Betty's neck.

There was the shadow of someone on the grisaille panel of the door.   Then a servant opened the door, asking them to enter.   At the end of a corridor, coming out of a room, Jim saw Herr Gollwitzer, big, leonine-headed, his eyes glowing as he hurried to greet them.   The last time, reflected Jim, that he had seen Herr Gollwitzer was when he had carried his luggage at Victoria Station to the four-thirty Continental Express.

III

" No one dreams of dining before nine o'clock in Budapest," said Count Mátány, as they went to the Pension Balaton. " Se we'll call for you then."

The car turned into a precipitous street, paved with enormous cobble-stones.   The character of the place had suddenly changed, they were in the older streets of Buda terracing the steep hillside of the Vár.   The houses had a Turkish air, with their shuttered over-hanging windows, and internal courtyards guarded by old wooden doors, under deep baroque arches.

The car stopped in front of one of these fortress-like entrances.   The chauffeur got out and pulled a hand-bell that created an uproar behind the closed gates.

" Here we are," said Waddle.

The heavy doors swung back, and a little, middle-aged man in a red-and-brown striped apron, and a black velvet waistcoat, came out.   He helped the chauffeur to carry in the luggage.   Waddle had been swallowed up in the inner darkness, whence came a woman's excited voice greeting them.

Mátány kissed Betty's hand.   Zarin followed suit.

" At nine o'clock!" said Mátány.   " Good-bye, Mrs. Brown."

They formally shook hands with Jim.   The chauffeur got back into his seat.   The car moved away, but not before

Zarin, leaning forward, gave Betty, burying her face in her bouquets, a smiling farewell bow.

"Did you ever see anyone so handsome?" asked Betty, turning to Jim.

"He's the wicked Count all right," laughed Jim.

Waddle reappeared, with a stout lady.

"Madame Balaton—our landlady. She speaks quite good English."

"A little. Herr Waddle is so kind. Please, come in. I haf your room on the first floor."

They followed her up a dark, creaking staircase. On the landing a trim, chubby-faced servant stood aside for them to pass, her face wreathed in smiles. They went on down a dark passage. Jim began to wonder in what kind of a place Waddle was lodging them.

Madame Balaton opened a door, and paused for them to enter. Jim's fears were at once dispelled. The large double-windowed room was furnished in the most modern German style. The twin wooden beds had small tables and reading lamps. There was a comfortable lounge. A thick carpet covered the floor. On a writing-table there was a large bowl of vivid hibiscus blooms. The window-boxes were gay with marguerites and petunias. There was the unexpected luxury of a private bathroom opening off the bedroom.

"Nize?" asked Madame Balaton, who had the air of a *grande dame*, and somewhat overawed her visitors.

"Oh, charming!" exclaimed Betty, who had feared the worst as she mounted the dark stairs.

The little servant girl appeared with towels, and threw open the windows. The view made Betty catch her breath. The chimneys and roofs of Buda fell away below them. Across the Danube lay the buildings and streets of Pest, fading into the deep mauve pall of evening.

"We are high here, yes?"

"That is your luggage. I will send you a key that to-night you can come in. Please be comfortable," she said, withdrawing.

The door closed. Betty and Jim looked at each other.

"Well, what a surprise—my head's in a whirl with it all. Oh, look at this view!" cried Jim, going to the window. "Jove, what a place!"

"I'm going to love Budapest," said Betty, joining him.

Jim laughed and slipped his arms round her.

"What alarms me is how Budapest's going to love you. Count Thingamy's eyes simply devoured you. I distrust him, he looks a swift lad."

"Count Zarin? Jim, I think he's the most wonderful-looking man I've ever seen, and such charming manners!"

"He'd charm the tongue out of a parrot. He's a killer all right. Now what's become of Waddle?" asked Jim, leaving the window and beginning to unpack.

Betty sat down by the window.

"Tired?" asked Jim. "I expect our day's only just beginning when those bright boys come round for us."

"Tired, and oh so happy," answered Betty, watching the light fade over the city lying in the plain. "I liked Herr Gollwitzer tremendously. I'm so glad we got his baby out of Austria. Poor man, he cried when he tried to thank me."

"I noticed that. He looks much older than when I last saw him. I suppose he's lost everything—except his genius. What did you think of the nurse he's got for the child?"

"She looks a sensible woman—but, of course, I couldn't talk to her. She kept on swinging poor little Friedl up and down, exclaiming, ' Reizend! Reizend!' whatever that means."

"Let's look," said Jim, finding the small German dictionary they carried with them. "'Reizend—charming, delightful, delicious, bewitching.' Well, that's true enough about the poor little beggar!"

Jim opened the wardrobe and hung up his suits. Then he carried toilet things into the bathroom.

"I wonder what all this is costing us? Being a Waddle place, I expected something cheap—but I'm beginning to doubt."

"How much money have we left?" asked Betty, beginning to take frocks out of her luggage.

"Nearly a hundred and thirty pounds—there's no need to worry, my girl. We can last out on that!" said Jim. "I've lived on that for a whole year—and found a girl to love me!"

Betty laughed happily. He was proving a perfect lover, and she noticed how he was losing the gaucheness which had irritated her so. Yes, Jim was improving, but there were still some little things he blundered over.

"James, dear," said Betty, pausing on her way to the wardrobe, "you mustn't say 'Thank you' so often."

"Why ever not?"

"It sounds a little too humble—an occasional 'Thank you' is all right."

"Oh, anything else, duchess?" asked Jim, good-naturedly.

"Yes—you don't mind, darling? They're just little things. Don't call the Count 'Count' so often—call him Mátány occasionally."

"You're a bit slow there—he calls me Jim, so I'm calling him Tibi—short for Tibor he tells me," answered Jim. "I like that cove!"

"That what?"

"That cove—or fellow, whatever you like!" cried Jim, seeing his wife's reproving look. "He's a grand lad—but I don't like the boy friend—he's a parlour sheik."

"You've no right to say that. We haven't known Count Zarin for more than an hour. Men aren't bad just because they're handsome. I like him."

"I know you do. Women always fall for men like that," retorted Jim.

Betty broke into a peal of laughter, caught Jim by the coat, and gave him a kiss.

"I believe you'll be fighting a duel over me! That would be a compliment!" she cried.

There was a tap on the door. Jim opened it. The porter in the red-and-brown striped apron stood there.

"I've brought you the key," he said.

"You talk very good English," said Jim.

"I am English," replied the porter.

" Good Lord ! What are you doing here ? " asked Jim.

" Oh, I happened to get here," he said, evasively. " Anything you want ? "

" No, thanks."

" Thank you," said the porter, and withdrew.

" Now I wonder what his history is ? " exclaimed Jim.

There was a tap on the door again.

" Come in—*herein !* " called Jim.

It was the porter again. He had a faint smile on his face.

" You'll excuse me—but I can't help asking. You haven't by any chance an English cigarette on you ? That's what I miss most here. You'll excuse me asking ! "

The little man smirked apologetically.

" Why, yes," said Jim. " I've some left—a moment."

He searched among his things and found a tin of cigarettes. He took out half-a-dozen.

" Here you are," he said.

" Oh, I won't take all those," said the porter, nervously.

" Take them," commanded Jim.

" Well, since you're so kind," answered the little man.

He put them carefully inside a note-book, which he replaced in his breast pocket.

" My wife doesn't like me smoking, so I'll enjoy them on the quiet. Thank you ! " he said, and disappeared again.

" I've got it,' said Jim. " I'll bet he was taken a prisoner and stayed on here and married a Hungarian. That accounts for it."

" Did we fight on the Hungarian front ? " asked Betty.

" I don't think so—but things got pretty well mixed up. Look at our fellows on the Rhine. A lot of them——"

There was another tap on the door.

" Don't give him anything more," said Betty.

" Can I come in ? " asked a voice, as the door opened.

It was Waddle. He had washed and put on a clean shirt, and for once his tie was well down under his collar.

" I hope everything's all right ? " he asked.

"It's really delightful, and just look at our view!" cried Betty.

"Have you any idea what the room costs?" asked Jim.

"Oh, yes. I fixed it beforehand. One always should, you know. Of course this is one of the best rooms," explained Waddle. "It's ten pengös—about seven shillings."

"Including bathroom?"

"Bathroom and breakfast."

"Good Lord! We'll stay here for ever," said Jim.

"Well—I don't advise that. You would get tired of even Budapest, like poor Mr. Bowling," observed Waddle.

"Mr. Bowling?" queried Betty.

"Madame Balaton's husband, who's English."

"You don't mean that beaten-out looking fellow in the striped apron?" exclaimed Jim.

"Yes—that's Percy Bowling. He's an Englishman. He got away from home, he says, because he grew sick to death of his grasping relations. He earned quite a nice wage in the Rolls-Royce works in Derby. Then he drew a matured Life Policy, and heard his people plotting to spend it for him. That made him revolt. He put his money in his pocket, threw up his job, and without letting his people know, set off to see the world."

"Sensible chap!" commented Jim.

"Well, yes and no," said Waddle. "He didn't get very far. On the Continental train he met a Hungarian widow, Madame Balaton. She had inherited a legacy in England, which under the Enemy Debts Commission, or something like that, she couldn't collect as a foreigner. So she took hold, in her forcible way, of poor little Bowling and married him, thus getting her English status and her legacy. He says she dazzled him with the lights of Budapest, and before he could see properly she'd hooked him. That's his version," said Waddle, "but I guess he's a poor fish, anyhow, since he couldn't deal with his relations. Madame Balaton said she'd take care of his capital in her business. So he's parted from that. He might just as well have stayed at home, poor devil! Still, he's happy in a way. He slips out of his apron and gets round to a café where he's collected a few cronies. He's been here for a year, but he doesn't know much Magyar yet. I don't suppose he ever will. In a way, he's in love with Madame."

" But why is she Madame Balaton if she's married to Bowling ? " asked Betty.

" Oh, she refuses to change her name—says it would be bad for business. She's quite well off, what with this *pension,* her legacy and Bowling's money."

" She sounds a vampire. She looks a formidable old mare," said Jim, lighting a cigarette.

" Yes—there's no nonsense about her," agreed Waddle. " But she runs an excellent *pension.*"

" Excellent," said Betty.

" Well, my dears, what I really came to say was this— I hope, after to-night, you won't feel hurt if you see very little of me," said Waddle, almost timidly. " But I'm going to be terribly busy with this Congress. I've over a hundred letters waiting for me here, and to-morrow I have to begin sorting out nearly three hundred delegates. And then there's all the programmes to work out with my colleagues. So that altogether, you see——"

" Oh, please, Mr. Waddle, don't worry about us," said Betty, seeing he was really concerned. " You've been wonderfully good to us. But for you——"

" You wouldn't have smuggled *Der kleine Eisenbahner* into Hungary," joked Waddle. " Well, for the risk you took over that, my dears, I am sure Gollwitzer's face this evening repaid you."

" It certainly did, the poor, dear old man," said Betty.

" Well, now," said Waddle, looking at his wrist-watch, " we've got an hour before we dine at *The Green Cockatoo.* I'll leave you, and come back just before Tibi calls for us."

" What is *The Green Cockatoo*—a restaurant, or a night club ? " asked Jim. " Dinner jacket ? "

" No—that's not necessary. I suppose it is something of a night club. You see, no one dreams of dining before nine o'clock in Budapest," explained Waddle. " If you arrive before that you find the waiters laying tablecloths. *The Green Cockatoo* is the smartest of these places, with delicious food. It's Count Zarin's party in your honour. I suppose he's the richest bachelor in Budapest, and the wildest. I don't know him very well, I'm not in his world at all, but he's a great friend of Tibi's. Well, I'll call in for you just before nine," said Waddle, and left the room.

" I feel this place is going to be exciting," said Betty.

" Oh, James, look at those lights all beginning to twinkle ! "

" I'm pretty sure of one thing, we'll not leave this city without rings under our eyes—it's the kind of place you never get to bed in," said Jim, gazing out of the window where Budapest began to glitter with a thousand lights.

CHAPTER XII

COUNT ZARIN

" Lajos ! "

" Excellency ? "

The valet placing the onyx studs in his master's silk shirt turned towards the bathroom door.

" They know I want the corner table, in the garden ? "

" Yes, Excellency, I asked for the corner table."

" Have you unpacked those records from Paris ? " called Count Zarin, putting another handful of verbena bath salts into the water.

" Yes, Excellency."

" Then bring the gramophone in here, I want to hear them."

The valet put down the shirt, went into the sitting-room, and carried the portable gramophone and a box of records into the bathroom. Count Zarin lay in the steaming, scented water, smoking a cigarette in a long, amber holder.

" Put one on," he said.

He had a monthly order with a shop in Paris for the latest dance music. The valet plugged in the gramophone and put on a record. The bathroom was filled with a strident jazz fox-trot. Count Zarin lay back, listening with lazy pleasure. He rested his black head on the small air-cushion.

Tu es si charmante, si douce, chérie !

crooned a voice to the accompaniment of a saxophone. The words coincided with his thoughts. He was looking forward to his dinner-party. Tibi had given him no idea how really lovely this English woman was. It was a pity they were a honeymoon pair, for they might still be obsessed with each other. The husband was a good, solid-looking boy, undoubtedly stupid. She might be stupid also, he had had no opportunity to talk to her at old Gollwitzer's. He knew how seldom a pretty face went with a pretty wit, and, unfortunately, he liked women who talked intelligently, even while they flirted.

" Lajos—another record. And the pin-stripe blue suit, and the car at ten to nine."

" Yes, Excellency," answered Lajos, returning to the bathroom.

" I'm ready," said Count Zarin, standing up in the bath. " Wipe the mirror."

Zarin carefully surveyed his lithe, brown body in the long mirror. At thirty-five he had still the athlete's figure, wide in the chest, slim-waisted, his flesh spare. The sun had tanned his skin a deep bronze. He knew he was certainly the handsomest young man in Budapest.

Lajos wrapped him in the bath-gown. He sat down holding his head over the wash-basin. The valet took the stopper out of a pint bottle of eau-de-Cologne and poured it over his master's head. Then he slowly massaged the thick, black hair. The gramophone blared away on the side table. The valet interrupted his labour to change the disk.

" Rather a poor lot," commented the Count.

" Very poor, Excellency," agreed Lajos.

He now spread a white cloth on a small table and began to manicure the Count's nails. They were strong, beautifully shaped hands, an inheritance from his mother. They handled the reins, the gun, the bobsleigh, the running tackle, the control of a plane, with the same sure skill as that with which they made a woman thrill to his touch. It amused him to know that he was called the " Wicked Count," more enviously than maliciously, merely because no one imagined that, with so many assets, he would be negligent of opportunity. Naturally, he had been married young, and divorced early.

At twenty-four, rich, inexpressibly gay, tireless and hospitable, he had already attracted the interest of the prophets of doom. He would come to a bad end, they said, meaning that one day some outraged husband would shoot him. When the years passed, without any attempt at shooting him having been made, he achieved a reputation of sinister astuteness. He was too sharp for them, it was declared.

All this increased the glamour of his reputation. The young women shunned him, the middle-aged women rushed to him. He drove the smartest horses and the largest cars, and gave the noisiest parties. Everybody thought he had a wonderful life.

Zarin was an odd mixture. He had publicly thrashed the conductor of a *tzigane* orchestra who had ignored his request for a certain piece of music on behalf of a cocotte he was entertaining. The next day he sent the bruised fellow a violin worth two thousand pengös. He was mercilessly exacting with his valet Lajos, but when the man fell seriously ill with pneumonia Zarin cancelled his departure for winter sports at Davos, refused to send him to a hospital, and sat up for three nights nursing him through the crisis. Yet Lajos was so miserably paid that he stole his master's money consistently, which Zarin as consistently ignored. " The fear of discovery keeps him loyal," he explained.

Count Zarin looked at his valet now as the fellow bent over his hands. Twenty years ago Lajos had tramped into Budapest from a village in the Plains, one of thousands of starving peasants who had fled to the city after the end of the Great War, when the country had been looted by the successive waves of Czechs, Roumanians, and finally that terrible scourge of Bolshevik Jews, who made a shambles of

Budapest. He had rescued the starving lad from the hands of a couple of Bolsheviks who, having shot him down in a back street, were stripping the only good things off him he possessed, a pair of top-boots. Zarin brought down the Bolsheviks with a couple of shots, from the cover of a shop door, picked up the bleeding, unconscious youth, and carried him back to the small room he lived in behind the Opera House.

Zarin was then seventeen. He had left his home near Debrecen when he heard that his father, a discharged officer back from the Italian front, had been murdered in Budapest by Bolsheviks. He had a favourite spot in the doorway of a hairdresser's shop behind the Ritz Hotel, where Béla Kun and his foul crew rioted with the prostitutes. They often came out fuddled with drink. He picked them off with ease, until one day they laid a trap for him. He retreated into the shop. The protesting old shop-keeper was riddled with bullets. Zarin escaped up his stairs out on to the roof, and got away with only one bullet through his leg.

He looked at his brown thigh now, where the bath-gown had slipped from it. The scar was still there, would always be there. But there was a deeper scar in his mind. He could never forget the plight of Hungary in those black years —the ravaged countryside, the looted houses, the daily shootings in Budapest when Béla Kun released and armed all the criminals from the gaols. And every day there was fresh news of Hungary's woe. The Roumanians had seized Transylvania, and were pouring down over the plains. The Czechs had ravaged the land to the north. The Bolshevik scum had seized power in Budapest, and only the Polish mud held up the Russian hordes. Then, at last, the French came, and the mission of the Entente and Allied States, and the White Russians.

By this time Zarin's resources were ended. There was no possibility of communication with his home. For a week he starved in his unheated room, and nursed the wounded peasant lad. But he still had bullets left to pick off Bolsheviks. His bag now numbered thirty-four.

One evening, walking up and down the Corso, looking

hungrily into the restaurants where the Allied officers were dining with their lady friends, a French officer spoke to him. He was delighted to find he understood French, took him back to his suite in the Hungaria, gave him a bath and clean underlinen, and then took him out to dine. The Frenchman's eyes opened wider and wider as Zarin told him the story of his Bolshevik hunt.

"*Ma foi! c'est magnifique!*" he exclaimed. He was a middle-aged man, a captain with the Croix de Guerre, and seven wound stripes. Zarin saw the Frenchman every day after that, and the money that was forced on him went to provide Lajos, now slowly recovering, with good food to eat. But at the end of six weeks the French mission departed, taking with it the genial captain, for whom Zarin now felt a real affection. Things were better. The Bolsheviks had been crushed. Béla Kun had fled.

But the terms of the Treaty of Trianon began to assume menacing shape. Hungary was being carved up. Dreadful news of oppression, pillage, shootings and torture came from the newly ravaged provinces. In Budapest a vast unemployed population shivered in hunger and misery, slept in cellars, on river barges and in discarded railway trucks. Out of the tumult of their misery rose the determined challenge of the dispossessed Hungarians, "*Nem, Nem, Soha!*" "No, No, Never!" roared the frenzied population, defying this monstrous dismemberment of their race, the butchery of their ancient kingdom.

Zarin as a youth had passed through all this. When at last calmer days followed the tumult of Treaty-making, and of Allied Commissions, and when Admiral Hortny had grasped the reins of a plunging kingdom, he slowly made his way back home on foot. Lajos accompanied him, carrying a bag with their belongings. The two youths slept in the peasants' huts or in cattle shelters.

When Zarin arrived back at his home he found it shut up. It was an enormous, rambling house with a long colonnaded portico on the south side, consisting of more than sixty rooms. The Countess Zarin, his mother, after drunken

Roumanian soldiers had occupied the house and pillaged it, had fled to Szeged, to join her married sister in the comparative safety of that town near the Jugoslavian border.

Zarin and Lajos now camped in the immense, lonely house. All the servants had vanished. There were no horses in the long stables, no linen on the beds. The Roumanians had left the place in terrible disorder. Gradually the servants returned, and the peasants began to bring their tribute of stored corn and vegetables, for money was practically unknown. The Hungarian spring gave place to the glorious summer. The vines were dressed. Young Zarin asked his mother not to return until conditions became normal. Then, one day in July, she arrived, and was met at the station by her son in the family carriage, with Lajos driving on the box-seat, black streamers to his hat, and wearing the black-and-green frogged jacket of the Zarin livery.

Lajos had never left his master after that. They had been together for eighteen years. They went to Paris, London, Berlin and Vienna. There were no secrets between master and valet. The Zarin wealth had been much reduced by the war, but they were still one of the richest families in Hungary, with three vast estates, and, through the Countess, large interests in Polish coalfields. The death of a childless uncle brought even more acres to Count Zarin. He had experienced, therefore, the extreme of poverty and wealth, known hardship and hunger as well as great luxury.

Lajos finished the manicuring and brought his master his silk underclothes and the newly pressed suit. Count Zarin dressed leisurely to the music of the gramophone. He began to plan in his mind the menu for the evening. It would, of course, be an essentially Hungarian meal for these English guests. He had a great contempt for German food, and he did not think Austrian food was much better. The Hungarian plain was a larder unsurpassed by any other country in Europe.

He could give them, to start, a palóc soup made from french beans, bay leaf slices of paprika, carroway seeds and sliced onions, boiled together with a leg of lamb, and served with a froth of beaten cream. Next might follow a delicious *fogas* fresh from Lake Balaton, and then, of course a real gulyás-a magnate's gulyás, made from braised beef with mushrooms, peas, young carrots and parsnips, together with sliced tomatoes, dried paprika and a *tarhonya* dressing. And drink ? He would start them with a *barack*, an apricot brandy braced with spirits. They would want to drink Tokay, of course, whose pellucid gold brought sunshine to the table, but he would not allow them to drink it, as was the habit of vulgarians, until they came to the dessert. They should start with a 1921 Villány Furmint, a good, dry white wine, and then progress to an Imperial Tokay Aszú.

He heard the door-bell ring just as he was putting a pin into his tie. It was Mátány who came forward into his dressing-room.

" Am I late ? " asked Zarin, turning.

" No, it's twenty to nine," answered Mátány, sitting down —while Lajos helped the Count into a pair of shoes.

" Tell me—your curious English friends——" began Zarin.

" So you think them curious ? " asked Mátány, smiling. " I wondered what the verdict of a connoisseur like you would be. They're very, very English."

" You mean we shall be examined most carefully ? "

" No, on the contrary, my dear Károly, they're in that stage of Continental travel in which they are excited by everything they see—a state you and I lost many years ago ! It's our duty to be Hungarian to the utmost. I'm sure that if you got up and danced the *csárdás* in the middle of dinner Mrs. Brown would believe it was our customary habit. She's very disappointed that the Danube isn't blue. It would be terrible if she came to think the Hungarians are not Hungarian ! "

" What's the history of Mr. and Mrs. Brown ? " asked Zarin, selecting a silk handkerchief from the box held by Lajos.

" Waddle discovered them somewhere in Paris. I confess, when he wrote to me, telling me they were on a honeymoon trip, I saw them only in the rôle of *Deus ex machina*. They were the means of getting *Der kleine Eisenbahner* out of Germany."

" Who ? " asked Zarin.

" That's the public nickname of Gollwitzer's adopted infant."

" So you evolved the plot ? "

" Yes. Rather good, wasn't it ? " asked Mátány. " I feel a burning desire to inform the Nazis, they are such ardent plotters themselves."

" By the way—why did you plunge into this extraordinary business ? " asked Zarin. " I never knew you knew the famous Gollwitzer."

" I didn't until I was forced to make his acquaintance in a rather hurried manner," replied Mátány.

He related the shooting incident at the *Hungaria*.

" After that, having saved one life, as it were, I had to do something about the baby."

" I hope you're at the end of your trouble," said Zarin, with a smile, now completely dressed, and putting a camellia, which he ordered for every evening, into his lapel.

" Why do you say that ? " asked Mátány, surprised.

" I don't know, except that I have a feeling—how shall I put it ?—that your odd Mr. Waddle gave you a little bit of a shock when he produced his fair conspirator," said Zarin, with mischievous eyes. " Tell me, are they very devoted ? I admire your Mrs. Brown."

Mátány laughed and stood up.

" So long as you confine your feelings to admiration, I shan't be apprehensive—otherwise I shall feel it my duty to watch you," he said. " I'm not going to let you ruin a very pretty honeymoon. I've got too great a liking for that English lad," he said.

" And more for Mrs. Brown ! Oh, what a nice kind man you are, Count Mátány ! " mocked Zarin. " Well, let's be going. Our party consists of the Browns, Waddle, Julietta Molnay, Lotte Lederer, and Zoska Bratiascu—that nicely balances us."

" Zoska ! Do you think——" began Mátány, doubtfully.

" She will shock our dear Mrs. Brown ? " exclaimed Zarin, giving his friend a slap on the back, as they left the room.

" On the contrary, Zoska will portray just that flamboyant wickedness for which, very unfairly, I think, Budapest has such a wide repute. The car, Lajos ? " he asked, as the valet gave him his hat.

" Waiting, Excellency," answered Lajos, crossing the landing, and ringing for the lift.

It came at once. They descended to the street where the high-cheek-boned Toni, with almond eyes, stood holding open the door of his master's car.

II

Jim, Betty and Waddle were waiting when Count Zarin called for them, a few minutes before nine. Mátány came upstairs to fetch them, and as he entered their room he had to suppress his surprise at Betty's appearance. She had always looked pretty, but now, attired in a long, salmon-coloured dress, cut low, with wide, cardinal sleeves, she was a ravishing picture of fresh English beauty, with her small red mouth and exquisite colouring. Her dark eyes shone with excitement, her abundant hair was banded with a simple spray of artificial Tyrolean flowers, another purchase in Vienna.

And turning from her, after his courtly greeting, to the young husband at her side, he felt how splendidly matched they were. Jim wore a smart, blue-flannel, double-breasted suit, with a broad blue-and-white striped shirt. His ruddy, fair skin glowed with exuberant health, the tumbling chestnut hair had been vainly brushed back from his well-shaped and intelligent brow. His face had a wind-swept freshness which Mátány associated only with island-dwellers, where the sea winds blew over white cliffs and emerald-green headlands. It was a boy's face, lit with that eager expectancy which is of the essence of youth, unconscious of charm and careless in grace.

As they stood together now, Mátány experienced a momentary sadness at the thought that the years must tarnish such a picture of morning freshness. Looking at his guests, he had an intuitive sense of their inexperience of life. In no way gauche, they gave him a feeling that Daphnis and Chlöe, wafted from some Illyrian meadow, had assumed modern dress to make discovery of this later, sophisticated world. They did not belong to this scene, and his quick eye had detected at once that they were what the English picturesquely called " working class." He liked them the better for it, his own aristocratic origin increasing his admiration for a more virile class. Like Waddle, he disregarded the social barriers in his quest of an interesting life. The quick Károly had remarked : " Not—not—I think ? But delightful, Tibi, delightful ! " He knew Károly would never allow them to be embarrassed for a moment.

As for himself, they were Daphnis and Chlöe, round-eyed, hungry for adventure, for whom he would try to make Budapest a city of enchantment.

But they knew nothing of these thoughts racing through his mind as he greeted them, and escorted them down into the lobby where Zarin stood.

CHAPTER XIII

PLAY, GIPSY

FROM the moment that they got into the car Zarin's chauffeur drove like a demon. They roared through quiet, dimly lit streets, they traversed long tree-lined avenues, they seemed, within the darkness of the lurching car, to be climbing a precipitous cliff. Once or twice Betty gave a little cry of alarm, for a collision with the traffic, darting around them, appeared inevitable.

" He's very safe—please do not be alarmed," said Zarin, sitting on the small seat facing Betty. " We are going, first, to show you something I hope you will like."

The car went into a lower gear and roared upwards through the night. The houses had disappeared, the streets gave place to bold escarpments of rock jutting forth at every turn.

A road had been cut, twisting and turning towards a summit. Far below them, lights began to twinkle. The air grew sharper, then the car slowed and stopped.

"We get out here," said Zarin, slipping from his seat, and handing out Betty, a little frightened by this wild journey.

The Count led them across a small terrace to a low boundary wall. Jim and Betty, following, gave a gasp of amazement, and Mátány and Zarin looked at each other smiling. This was, they knew well, the *pièce de résistance* in the experience of the tourist in Budapest. Nowhere else in Europe was there such an overwhelming vision of nocturnal loveliness as now met the eyes of their guests. Far below them, so remote that no sound of life ascended to the height on which they stood, to remind them that this city was as mortal as it was radiant, lay the dark curve of the Danube, a steel-blue scimitar, barred with jewels where the illuminated bridges, their towers and sweeping chains picked out with fairy lanterns, swung from bank to distant bank. They were renewed again in the reflective flood that ran so majestically between its jewelled banks. Were these bridges, or were they ropes of luminous pearls hung across the dark throat of the night? Even that darkness was not space, it had a velvet quality, as though the hand might touch and feel its softness.

Betty counted four bridges, and Mátány named them; the Franz-Josef Bridge to their right, the Elizabeth Bridge immediately below them, the Chain Bridge by which they had crossed from Pest, and far up the river, glimmering more faintly, the Margaret Bridge.

They could not speak, either to question or to exclaim, for the first few minutes of that overwhelming revelation. Then behind them they became aware of the plain walls of a fortress, the Citadel, crowning the mount on which they stood. To their left, lifted from its surrounding tiers of lights, there loomed, unlit and immense, a dark pile of buildings, dominant above the shining river, with one high dome of green bronze flooded in light. It was the Royal Palace, said Zarin, they could not see it here in all its colossal length. Behind, its undulations picked out by the street lamps, lay Buda, with its valleys and hills.

Lovely as this panorama was, touched with the sense of the green leafiness of long boulevards, through which the lights twinkled intermittently, it was the illimitable floor of the plain lying below, across the shining river, that held them in a trance of unfathomable beauty. There, in the plain of Pest, latticed with avenues and streets, lit to the far rim of the impenetrable night, it seemed as if all the stars in the heaven had fallen to earth. The hills to their left, spangled with lights, hung like an embroidered curtain, at whose hem there ran the wide, dark river. Across that flood, on whose full bosom, like fireflies, flitted the steamers with their red and green lights, there was a long belt of incandescent fire which caught the façades of the buildings facing the river embankment. It marked the line of the Corso, said Zarin, and ran from the Chain Bridge to the Elizabeth Bridge. The buildings were the chief hotels and restaurants.

A strain of music came through the air as they stood looking at the magic of the night. A little behind Jim, a figure had silently come up, and, bent low in the shadow of an acacia tree, was playing a violin. He played it with more of the skill of a ventriloquist than of a musician, so that his instrument gave plaintive voice to the beauty of the night.

" This is too——" began Betty, and then, knowing the inadequacy of her words, lapsed into silence, letting that piercing music express the weight of beauty on her heart.

" I thought this would delight you," said Zarin, quietly.

They moved along the parapet. The starry world beneath them seemed to turn on its axis. The light-festooned bridges speared the dark river ; the soul of the city pulsated in that jewelled darkness. The musician followed at their heels, making little quips and trills, now mocking, now pleading. He followed them the whole length of the terrace. Mitány tipped him and told him to go. He receded, soft-footed, into the darkness whence he had come, his violin singing a plaintive farewell.

" Shall we go ? " asked Zarin, after a few more minutes

contemplation of the myriad-lighted city of the plain. " You will remember this sometimes, and love Budapest ? " he said gently.

" Never, never can we forget it," replied Jim, finding voice at last. " Perhaps we ought to go now, knowing it only by night, and never see how it will look by day. It will remain a dream for us then, something we can never believe was real."

" Oh, but there's another Budapest," said Mátány, as they went towards the car. " You will find it along the Corso, when the day is fading behind the Royal Palace—but we mustn't boast. Perhaps we love our city too much, and are vain ! "

" It merits all your pride in it—oh, it is lovely, lovely ! " said Betty, taking a last survey of the far plain, where earth and night merged in one star-spangled panorama.

Count Zarin looked at her shining eyes and animated face. She took new beauty from the things that stirred her. Her pleasure was so quick, so radiant. He began to foresee rich entertainment in the parade of things evoking her fresh enjoyment. So many of the women he knew had lost the naïve charm evoked by novelty. They had seen too much, experienced too much. Their world was no longer a happy playground, it was a mine for their exploitation.

The car whirled them down the tortuous drive towards the lower plateau. It stopped opposite a doorway lit with Turkish lanterns and guarded by a massive attendant in a green uniform, with a frogged jacket, gold epaulettes, and a Cossack's hat, in which a slender, white feather stood stiffly up.

A crimson drugget covered the pavement and the interior hall. Led by Count Zarin, they walked through a number of rooms and corridors in which the waiters bowed to their patrons. An orchestra on a dais was playing strenuously, in a room so hot, so noisy with music, and heavy with the smell of food, that Betty and Jim were glad it was not their dining place. There was another corridor, and here, with a tremendous clucking of delight, the head waiter greeted Zarin and Mátány, and gesticulated and bowed strenuously to Betty and Jim. Then, waving obstructing waiters aside, he led the way, his arms spread out as if announcing a royal entry. At a turn they were in a large, open courtyard, framed in terraces, with illuminated tables under the spreading leafiness of trees through whose branches shone the clear starriness of the night.

"There'll be no delegates to worry me here," whispered Waddle, into Jim's ear. "They'd all faint at the expense I've never come here without feeling weak at the knees, and then I've always been a guest!"

It was certainly the rendezvous of the smart set. Lovely women, with their escorts, sat at the little tables, most of them tucked away in vine-screened alcoves. The linen, the Bohemian glass, the well-groomed waiters, reflected the chic standard of a cosmopolitan restaurant where the experienced gourmets of the Continent found a menu to satisfy them.

As ordered, the Count had been given his favourite round table in a corner of the garden courtyard, in full view of the central dancing floor and the gipsy orchestra seated on the dais at one end. Above them there was a vine-pergola whose leaves were mingled with the immense heliotrope blossoms of a clematis. Around the courtyard the trees rose towards the open sky, their trunks floodlit with coloured spot-lights. The dancing-floor was dim, only the reflection from the small tables, and the lantern festooned alcoves providing sufficient light for the dancers. They moved to the languorous music of the string orchestra, dream-figures under the starlit canopy of the sky.

The round table, with a large bowl of salmon-pink and white azaleas filling its centre, had been set for eight persons. While Count Zarin was arranging the seating of his guests there was a perceptible stir as two ladies, escorted by the proprietor, came towards them along the edge of the dancing floor. Jim noticed that the hum of conversation was lowered for a few moments, that the most engrossed couples paused and watched the transit of the two women who were being conducted towards the Count's table.

The foremost of these women was, indeed, a breathtaking

ight. She was tall, with a full figure emphasised by the
ress that clung to her limbs. It was made of an emerald-
reen cloth, cut daringly low in the corsage, sleeveless and
ackless, except for two slender shoulder-straps, and covered
ntirely with green sequins. Its clinging scaliness and
idescence made her look like a mermaid, but the arresting
ffect of this luminous dress was wholly outshone by the
azzling whiteness of her bosom and shoulders, her high-
ploured cheeks, with their thin, arched eyebrows, the fiercely
carlet mouth and heavily kohled eyelids. All this would
ave been arresting and bizarre in a woman of such imposing
tature, as she sailed majestically past the watching tables,
rithout the crowning asset of her astonishing appearance—
flaming aureole of hair so red that her white flesh and green
ress seemed to burn with a reflection of its fire.

She came forward, confident in the sensation of her advent,
er hands and arms encased to the elbows in crimson gloves,
nd received the salute of her host, Count Zarin. It was then
hat Jim saw her eyes. They were a brilliant green, matching
he colour of her dress exactly.

With her was another guest, a woman of about thirty,
rith fair hair and a soft, warm complexion. She was dressed
uietly in a dark green velvet frock with tight-fitting sleeves.
round her waist she wore a girdle made of silver medallions,
nd from the high-fitting collar of her tight bodice hung a
ouble rope of pearls. She had none of the high colour of
er companion, but her intense personality was in no way
warfed by the red-haired woman. They were presented to
he company as Mademoiselle Zoska Bratiascu and Madame
otte Lederer.

"Madame Lederer is one of our Opera stars," explained
arin, " and Zoska—well, Zoska is indispensable at any
arty."

"Károly darlin', it is zo nice to meet your Engleesh
riends," said Zoska, giving Jim and Betty a flashing smile.
I lov to talk Engleesh zo badly ! "

As she seated herself she pulled off the long crimson gloves.
ler beautiful hands had magnificent rings.

" You have been long here ? " she asked Jim, her neighbou
" About three hours," he answered.

The lucent green eyes scanned his face, and he felt he
interest deepen in him at once. He became self-consciou
and defenceless before her keen scrutiny, like a small bir
observed by an owl.

" Ah—but 'ow wonderful !—it is first time in Budapest ?
exclaimed Madame Lederer. " It is leetle town but ha
beeg—beeg—oh, 'ow do you say, I am zo silly with Englees
speech ! " she ended, with charming dismay.

" Lotte, your English is ravishing," said Zarin. "
couldn't help asking you here for the pleasure of hearin
you talk it."

" He tease me," complained Madame Lederer to Betty
" He is so clevair, it is cruel ! "

She picked up a rose from the table, smelt it, and smiled
Her teeth were perfect, her grey Magyar eyes were magicall
soft.

The last of the guests arrived. The company rose for her
Had Zarin chosen them for the colour of their hair ? Fo
the new-comer had the dark beauty of an Italian. She wa
olive-skinned, with black, burning eyes. Young, slender an
small, her frock of white matt crêpe had a softly gathere
waist-line, long sleeves and a high neck, with an open V i
front. On her dusky throat hung a large ruby, matchin
her wine-red lips. In her thick black hair a ruby-and
diamond comb had been jauntily stuck.

Jim, bowing a little giddily, did not catch her name. Sh
was his left-hand partner at the table. Her small brow
hands had the longest crimson nails he had ever seen.

The dinner-party began, with everyone talking, with th
band playing so plaintively, so piercingly that it seemed tha
at any moment the violins would break into sobs. Th
waiters moved noiselessly, there was the soft slither of fee
on the polished dancing floor, the ever-changing kaleidoscop
of women's dresses, of fair and dark faces, of athletic youn
men, bronzed, faultlessly groomed, threading their delicat
partners through a maze of gliding bodies.

Zoska was having a flashing wordy duel with Count Zarin, her neighbour, relapsing at moments into what must be Magyar, so incomprehensible was it. Jim found himself talking easily with his ruby-throated companion.

"But you talk English perfectly," he exclaimed. "You are Hungarian?"

"Half Hungarian, half Italian. My mother was Italian, my father was half Polish. I'm a mongrel. I had a Scotch governess—the most respectable thing I can claim. I once went home with her, to Aberdeen, and nearly died of the cold—and the food. Is that too unkind of me?" she asked. "Are you Scotch?"

"No—so you can say anything," replied Jim. "I'm a Cockney—if you know what that is?"

"Of course—born within the sound of Bow Bells!"

"Then I'm not—you know too much. I was born within sound of Victoria Station."

"Oh, where the buses stop—I love the London buses!" exclaimed his companion. "And I love even more the young conductors—they are so no-nonsense-like, and healthy."

"And not the policemen?"

"Not the policemen—they are not so talkative," she said, with a mischievous flash of her dark eyes.

"And the railway porters?" asked Jim.

She clapped her hands together vivaciously.

"You are a wizard!" she cried, looking at him with her glowing, dark eyes.

"Why?"

He looked into her eyes, wondering for an unfaithful moment what it would be like to be the lover of this flashing, vivacious creature; then abruptly he smothered the query.

Her hand rested, soft as an alighting bird, on his sleeve, while she spoke to him confidentially.

"Oh, it was terrible! I was never forgiven by my poor Scotch Nannie," she said, with big, pleading eyes. "I was very young, seventeen, and I found that your porters smelt——"

"Smelt?" queried Jim, aghast.

G

" Oh—you think it dreadful! Yes, it was! But I was fascinated every time I went to a station. I smelt and smelt and smelt them!"

" But why—do they——"

" Corduroy—corduroy waistcoats and trousers! Your streets smell of beer—yes, on street corners at ten o'clock," she said, " and your porters of lovely corduroy. I shock you!"

" On the contrary—you make me think."

" Yes?" she asked.

" But I can't tell you what."

" Oh," she cried, reproachfully. " And now it is so sad. The last time I was in London, full of excitement on arriving, and thinking of my poor old Nannie, no longer there to scold me, I found many don't wear corduroy any more. I was so sad!"

" You don't sound at all sad, Julietta," said Mátány. " You're enjoying yourself immensely, monopolising Mr. Brown. I am boring Lotte, who wants to talk to Henry— I claim a little of your attention."

Zarin was talking to Betty. Zoska turned to Jim.

" I haf heard how you bring *Der kleine Eisenbahner* to Budapest. How gallant that is!" she said, her green eyes smiling at Jim. " I am excited to hear you are making a honeymoon—she is so ver' pretty your wife, Mister Brown. How long you stay?"

" Two or three weeks."

" An' you go journey into the country? You must see Mezökövesd, where our dresses are so pretty, and Lake Balaton—with leetle bathplaces all down the shore. And you must see the Puszta—so wide, with oh such 'igh 'igh sky, and all the cattles and horses. Károly must take you— or, better, Tibi, who has a lovely home where he lives with his mamma. When I was leetle, every autumn we go to the Puszta. You ride and ride and ride!"

Jim wondered how Zoska would look on a horse. He could not imagine her riding; the restaurant and the night-club seemed her setting. How old was she? She had the fresh skin of a baby, so smooth and veinless, but he noticed there were lines under her eyes. Her eyelids were painted a faint mauve. What was her history?

In ten minutes he learned that she had been everywhere. Vienna, Paris, Berlin, Madrid, Athens. She had something to relate of all these places.

"And London—you have been there, of course?"

"No—I haf not ever been to London."

She gave a little laugh, toyed with the *fogas* on her plate, and added, "For you English I am bad woman an' cannot kom there!"

He looked at her with such a startled and serious face that she laughed again, popping the *fogas* into her beautiful red mouth.

"I am spy-woman, not forgiven! You English have long memory!" she said. "You are slow but you do that, sudden."

Her jewelled hand spread its fingers in the air, then came down sharply on the table, clenched.

"I was spy for Austria, in Schweiz," she said, smiling again.

"Schweiz?" echoed Jim.

"*Igen*—yes—how you call Schwizerland. In Genf. I make so much trouble for ver' nice but stupid Englishman."

"I suppose you made him fall in love with you?" ventured Jim.

"Yes—that was joost it!" she answered, radiantly.

"And then?"

"I did the beeznis I was there to make," she said, with a little smile. "Your Meenistar one night at Berne, at a party where we meet, he said, oh zo nicely, ' Mademoiselle, we are deeply indebted to you.' Oh, so nicely he said it, with cold, cold eyes, and I reply—' One bullet will cancel the debt.'"

"You've led a dangerous life," said Jim. This, he reflected, was like a page out of a spy story. Such books could be true, it seemed.

"No—not vair dangerous for me," she replied. "I look so much a wicked spy woman, with these eyes, thees hair, that no man think it possible I do such beeznis. The nize Englishman, he laughed often and said, 'My dear Zoska, you haf not dog's chance!' No, I have not—I haf cat's chance. Poor man, he was nize."

" Can I ask—what did you do exactly ? "

She looked at him full in the face, a reflective light in her extraordinary eyes. Then she laughed lightly.

" You can ask, oh yes, but I do not say—not all. He stole someding in my room, someding I wanted him to steal. How sad—for we lost the war, and zo all those lives I cost you it was for nodding."

She was silent for a moment, then she looked at him with a light in her eyes that surprised him.

" Life is sad—no, not life, but the seeliness men make it," she said, slowly. " Why should nize boys like you, nize boys like those "—she indicated the young men dancing on the floor—" be killed to make some future trouble, for nize young men again ? "

She shrugged her white shoulders. At that moment Zarin asked her to dance. She rose and went on to the floor. The heads at the surrounding tables watched them ; Zarin, handsome and possessed, Zoska, brilliantly bizarre, dancing with a smile on her face.

The partner on his left spoke to Jim.

" I overheard Zoska confessing her past," she said.

" It sounds—fantastic," replied Jim. " As fantastic as she looks."

" It's quite true. I think she is the most wonderful woman in Europe," she said. " What a head she has ! "

" It's breath-taking," agreed Jim.

" Oh, I don't mean looks, I mean——" she tapped her temple. " She owns a group of the best hotels in Hungary, and was penniless when she came out of a French prison."

" A French prison ! " exclaimed Jim, really startled.

" She received a sentence of twenty years for espionage. She was released in 1920. You should ask Károly to tell you the story. She was then mixed up in the *putsch* of our King Karl."

Mátány was now dancing with Betty. The floor was crowded.

"Will you give me the pleasure?" Jim asked.

She responded at once. Her slim, svelte figure slipped into his arms. She was marvellously light. Her delicate scent pervaded him, the red ruby swung on her tawny throat.

"I do not know your name. I'm afraid I never hear names when introduced," said Jim.

"Julietta—after my mother—Julietta Molnay!"

"And mine's Brown—James Brown."

"Jim, for short?" she laughed, her sparkling eyes looking into his. She danced superbly, they moved as one to that rhythmical music. Then, in the pure enjoyment of the dance, they ceased to talk. Her soft, yielding figure took every line of his own. When the band stopped she gave a little sigh of regret.

"How well you dance," she said, as her hand slipped from his.

"I was thinking the same thing," he replied, escorting her to the table. Betty and Mátány had returned. The waiters were serving dessert. Glancing at his wrist-watch, Jim was astonished to find it was half-past eleven. All the people around were still dining. The leader of the *tzigane* band was wandering from table to table, and in some extraordinary manner, however far off he was, however softly he played, the band followed his lead with perfection. He was a small, black-haired gipsy, with a sallow, unhealthy face, and dark, mouldering eyes. He visited the tables and hung over the chosen lady, playing close to her ear his soulful lamentation.

"That is László Tonay—one of our best *tziganes*. His father used to play for our King," said Zarin to Betty. "All the members of his band are gipsies. The best of them migrate here, where they earn good money, the very best go to Paris or New York, where the women spoil them. They are children—they must be scolded and petted. You'll find them all over Hungary. There are gipsies living in every village—often very filthy, but always playing their violins. The children begin at five—at ten they can make

their instruments talk. They play for money, and yet it i
not for money, if you understand me. They will play to ;
beautiful lady until their eyes are full of tears, they will pla
for wine or flattery, but when they only play for duty, the
they are dull and bad. They can't read music, they wi
repeat anything you hum to them, and make elaborat
improvisations."

He raised his hand and beckoned the *tzigane*. The gips
came, cat-footed, up to the table, his fingers dancing on th
strings of his violin. He leaned, still playing, over Zarin
who spoke to him in Magyar. Then he stopped, and turne
to Betty, looking at her with tired, black eyes. He had
thin, bloodless mouth, sensual and sensitive. The blac
hair straggled over his damp brow. He bowed low, and then
with a faintly derisive smile, he leaned very close over Bett
as she sat at the table. His bony, white hand brought th
bow over the strings. Softly he began the theme, and a
softly, as if its name had been whispered across the garden
the orchestra on the distant dais took it up.

It was a lament, rising to piercing long-drawn notes. Th
violin pleaded, narrating some tragic tale that wanted n
words to express its despair. Then, quickly and fiercely, i
developed the theme, passing to a passionate declaration
and rising triumphantly into a *fortissimo* gallop, supporte
by the whole orchestra in strenuous ensemble. Then again
as though a stormy gust had smitten the players and lef
them prostrate, the soft pleading of the solo violin repeate
the opening theme. The violin sang, with undertones c
playful embroidery, exulted briefly, and passed again to it
first lamentation, the violin ceasing in a *pianissimo* sob.

The *tzigane* smiled slowly, his intense eyes, now afire
holding Betty's. A little embarrassed by this attention, sh
laughed, and thanked him.

" That was beautiful—what is it called ? " she asked Zarir

" That is the *Song of the Lost Hussar*," he said, and turnin
to Tonay, " Play it again—the theme—slowly," he com
manded. The gipsy put the violin to his chin and begar
while Zarin supplied the words.

" Oh, my István, beautiful you were as you rode by,
    Your hair danced in the sunshine like ripe corn ;
    You will be brave in battle, you will conquer,
    And I will take the oxen to the meadow,
    Waiting, waiting.

    Oh, my István, the long years have ridden by,
    My hair is white with sorrow like the snow ;
    Soon I shall ride the black horse to the meadow
    Where all the ghosts rise up—will you be there,
    Waiting, waiting ?

    Yes, my István, my beautiful lover, so long lost,
    Your hair will dance, your eyes will shine for me.
    I shall feel then your arms so strong go round me—
    That will crown the long years I've been faithful,
    Waiting, waiting."

He quoted the words slowly, softly, to the accompaniment
of the violin and the distant orchestra ; then there was a
moment of silence in which he smiled at Betty.

" Thank you," she said, her breath coming quickly.

" You will please László greatly if you toast him in wine,"
said Zarin, " if you give him a glass to drink from."

He filled a glass with wine and passed it to Betty, who
toasted the gipsy and gave him the glass. Having drunk,
he said something to her in Magyar, and again put the fiddle
to his chin. This time he played for her solely, unaccom-
panied, as she sat there, his instrument so near to her face
that she could see the powdered resin under the bridge, and
his long filbert-nailed fingers quivering on the strings as he
played with double-stopping, ending the piece on a thin,
high note, so high up the neck of the fiddle that it was only a
ghost of a sigh. Then, with a dazzling smile, he bowed and
was gone.

" That was a great compliment. It was the *Rose Song*,
played only by a *tzigane* when he wishes to make tribute.
You cannot buy it from him," said Zarin, and added quietly,
" I wish I could play it, Mrs. Brown."

The dinner came to an end at last. Madame Lederer
had given Waddle an opportunity to get on to his favourite

topic. They were discussing the Hungarian dances, with great animation.

" Oh, you know them zo well. Pleese, 'ow know you all zo ? " she asked.

" It's my life study. Here is a real bond between nations. How can they quarrel if they dance together ? " said Waddle, warm with food and wine, riding his hobby hard.

" Yes, I tink so. Music, painting, dancing, zey are a— how do you say—a one-language," said Madame Lederer, wondering whether she should tell him his tie was over his collar.

" More," continued Waddle, firmly, " dancing is much more a universal medium than music or painting. Our dancing is a folk-dancing, it belongs to the people, it is of the soil, it is born of undying, unquenchable tradition."

" Oh zo ! " exclaimed Madame Lederer, overwhelmed by this sudden flood of words from her dinner partner, who had eaten heartily and silently for so long.

Count Zarin rose and addressed his guests, who had now grown to over a dozen.

" Shall we go ? " he asked.

The party moved down the dance floor.

" Where are we going ? " asked Jim, bewildered.

" To the *Arizona*—eet is vair good time to arrive," explained Zoska.

" Arrive ! " repeated Jim, dismayed. His head ached with the noise of the restaurant, the strain of trying to follow foreign speech, and being affable and watching that he made no slips.

" We're all going on to a night-club—it doesn't really warm up until twelve," said Mátány.

Outside, Toni was waiting with the car. He had the great gift of immediate sleep and instant awakening. Zoska, Madame Lederer, and Julietta Molnay went off ahead of them with their friends.

" If you don't mind," said Jim, as soon as they were seated in Zarin's car, " Betty and I would like to go home. It's been grand, but we've had a heavy day."

" Oh—we're not too tired to see more," expostulated Betty, casting a quick look of disapproval at her husband.

" I'll get you a drink at the *Arizona*—you'll feel better then," said Zarin, a little annoyed.

" Thanks, but I do want to go home—I'm dog-tired," persisted Jim.

There was an awkward silence for a few moments in which Zarin and Mátány exchanged glances.

" Certainly, if you wish it," said Zarin, with cold courtesy.

He turned to the chauffeur and gave him an order. Then, recovering from his annoyance, he smiled back and spoke to Jim.

" You must excuse me. My enthusiasm runs away with me. I've tired you. One should not see too much at once."

" I could go on all night. I'm not a bit tired—you're such a wonderful host, Count Zarin," said Betty, ashamed of her husband's churlishness.

" Well, there's plenty of time to show you more of the place," observed Mátány, aware of a change in young Brown's mood. What had gone wrong ? He looked at Waddle, who, at that moment, either from diplomacy or need, put a hand up to his mouth and yawned.

" Yes, one has to get into training for late hours. If you really don't mind, I'll get you to drop me also," said Waddle. " We were up rather early this morning, and kidnapping's exhausting."

" Of course, of course," answered Zarin, politely.

They drove on in silence until they had arrived at the Pension Balaton. They waited at the great door while it was unlocked by Bowling, half asleep. Zarin bent low over Betty's hand and kissed it.

" It has been delightful—perhaps to-morrow we may meet ? " he asked, smiling. " I will telephone in the morning." He turned to Jim and shook his hand. " My apologies, if I have tired you."

He waited with Mátány until the door had closed on them.

" Sorry if we've got you up," said Jim to Bowling.

" Up—I'm always up—but to-morrow you can have a key. No one's in yet," he replied.

He turned on the staircase lights for them, waiting until they had reached their landing. Waddle groaned as he climbed the stairs.

" You can never get to bed in this place," he said. " Ah, here I am. Good night and bless you ! "

Jim unlocked the door of their room, switched on the lights, and sat down heavily on the bed.

" Oh my ! So this is the gay life ! " he said.

Betty made no comment for a few moments.

" I think you were downright rude," she said at last, slipping out of her frock. " You might have made an effort, knowing I wanted to go to the *Arizona*."

" But surely you'd had enough ? " cried Jim.

" I can never have enough ! And now it wouldn't surprise me if Count Zarin never asked us out again."

" Oh, he'll ask you—don't you worry ! "

Betty gave a sharp look at her husband.

" What do you mean ? " she asked.

" He's a hand-kissing sheik, right enough. You've got to watch that fellow," laughed Jim, rising from the bed.

" Don't be vulgar ! " retorted Betty, angrily.

" I am vulgar. There's no doubt about that. And I'm something else," he said, taking hold of her, " I'm jealous, too."

She laughed at him, as he kissed her. She was still angry, but she knew that there was little to be gained by openly opposing him.

CHAPTER XIV

MUSIC BY NIGHT

I

THEY slept late. When Jim arose and pulled up the blind the brilliant sunshine came flooding into the room over the gay window-boxes. There was a cloudless blue sky, the air was warm. He looked at his watch and was astonished to find it twelve o'clock. Betty blinked as he drew up the blind, then she sat up. At that moment there was a gentle tapping on the door.

" Yes ? " called Jim.

It was Mr. Waddle. Were they awake ? It was terrible, but he was due at noon on a judging committee for some of the folk-dance competitions. He must rush off at once. Did they remember that at half-past one they were all lunching at Gollwitzer's ? He would meet them there.

" But where ? I don't know the address," cried Jim; opening the door a few inches. The street names were quite unpronounceable.

Waddle scribbled an address on a piece of paper and rushed off.

" The question now is, does one have breakfast when lunch is so near ? " Jim asked his wife.

" I think we might have coffee. I have a headache," said Betty.

Jim rang the bell. It was answered in a short time by Mr. Bowling, in his striped apron.

" Do you think we could have some coffee ? " asked Jim, at the door. " Or are we too late ? "

" Too late ? Of course not ! Most of our guests are only just getting up," replied Mr. Bowling. " Coffee—rolls and butter, for two ? "

" No rolls, thank you," said Jim, closing the door. " You heard that—most of the guests are just getting up !—so we weren't the only night-birds."

Betty put on a kimono and began to brush her hair. Jim went into the bathroom, and had to emerge again to take in the breakfast tray. Bowling was perspiring.

" I'm always rushed at this time," he said, plaintively.

" Are you full ? "

" Very nearly—it's not the numbers, it's the babel of tongues that gets me down. We've two Japanese students, a Dutchman—always soaked—five Englishmen, a German, three Hungarians, a Frenchman and his Javanese wife, a

Cuban, a Roumanian countess, doped most of the time, and a young Russian Prince who won't come out of his room till four, and leaves it like a pigsty," grumbled little Bowling. " All you want ? "

" Yes, thank you."

Jim carried in the tray.

" This isn't a *pension*, it's a League of Nations that functions," he called, returning to the bathroom. " I wonder what Madame Balaton's doing all the time that he's running up and down with breakfasts."

" If you'll come to this window, you'll see," answered Betty, looking out over the cobbled street, as steep as a roof.

" Can't—I've got nothing on ! " called Jim.

" She's just driving away in a very nice open car, with what looks like her bathing things," said Betty, watching her smart landlady depart. Madame Balaton, robust and self-possessed, was setting out for Margaret Island, one of Budapest's bathing resorts, where she lunched in the alfresco restaurant.

" And that poor fellow ran away from home to find liberty ! " commented Jim.

There was another tap on the outer door.

" I'll answer it," said Betty.

The door had a little trap in it through which the room occupant could speak with anyone in the corridor. She opened it to find Bowling there again, red in the face and out of breath.

" Count Zarin's on the telephone—he wants to know if you will lunch with him to-morrow, at the Palatinus, on Margaret Island, at two o'clock. He'll send his car," he said.

Betty looked at Jim, standing in the bathroom door. He smiled knowingly.

" Ha ! Ha ! What did I say ? He's after my wife ! " he exclaimed. " Well—are we to go ? "

" Not unless you'd like to," answered Betty, tactfully.

Jim hesitated. Then he smiled and put his head out of the bathroom.

" Thank the Count and say ' Yes '," he called to Bowling.
The trap door closed. Bowling was gone. Jim turned
on the bath water and began to shave. Presently he hummed
a song, and Betty, singing in the bedroom, joined him. After
all, jealousy was so silly. He had stamped on it with both
feet. That Zarin fellow was probably quite harmless for all
his sheik-style. Betty had got her head well screwed on.
Nevertheless, it wasn't their set, and although his wife took
to it like a duck to water, for himself he felt like a cowboy
in a drawing-room.

" Darling, do hurry in that bath," said Betty, looking in
at her husband's strong back and white-lathered head.

He turned with a merry laugh, his face covered in soap.

" Come in and share it ! " he said.

II

A little after one o'clock they emerged into the street.
They could now see the place clearly in daylight. The
Pension Balaton was built on the steep hillside, so that it
had four storeys at the bottom end and only two at the
top. Every window-sill was gay with boxes of petunias and
geraniums. Opposite, there was an old house with a baroque
gateway. The oak door was heavily studded with iron.
A pretty, squat-faced young woman leaned out, dressed in
a white bodice with a richly-embroidered neckpiece. She
caught Jim's eye. He smiled at her, and she smiled back,
laughing, and turned to talk to someone in the room.

" How friendly everybody is ! " said Jim. " I should
think if we go down there we'll find a taxi. Thank heaven
I've got Gollwitzer's address written down—I couldn't
pronounce it."

" Give it to me," said Betty. " I'll try it on the taxi-
man."

They descended the cobbled street, and came to a flight
of steps. At the bottom they found a long avenue. There
was a glimpse of the Danube between the buildings. A
taxi came along and they stopped it. Betty read out the

address. The man seemed to understand at once. They got into it.

"Now how did you manage that? I didn't understand a word," he asked her, proud of her cleverness.

"I'm learning Magyar—the Count gave me a lesson last night. You say 'cs' as in 'chop' and 'gy' like 'd' in 'dune,' and 'á' with an accent as in Mars, 's' is 'sh' and 'sz' is plain 's'," said Betty.

"Clever little woman! I don't know how you do it," he said, catching her hand in his. He noticed how quickly she picked up a little French in Paris, and German in Vienna. Evidently she had a gift for languages. But she had a gift for most things. Last night she had never betrayed an embarrassed moment, whereas he had to hang behind cautiously and watch, a little bewildered by all the cutlery and glasses. He had mistaken a fruit-knife for a fish-knife, but had made a surreptitious change over while Julietta Molnay talked to him.

"I suppose it's coming back to me," answered Betty. "When generations of one's people have travelled and spoken languages——"

"But your people have never been out of England!"

"Oh, I don't mean my father and mother," answered Betty, cryptically.

The car began to mount the hill. They came to a square, and saw a beautiful church with a delicate Gothic façade and spires, a large circular rose-window, and sloping roofs of red, green, pink and lavender tiles. Jim stopped the taxi.

"What is it—the cathedral?" he asked the driver.

The driver answered, but not a word of it could Jim understand. His wife asked, and again the man repeated the unintelligible name, putting his cap on and off, to indicate something.

"I've got it!" said Betty. "It's the Coronation Church. I read about it in Baedeker. It was once a Turkish mosque and is now the cathedral."

They told the man to drive on. In a few minutes they were at Gollwitzer's apartment. The servant showed them into the long room overlooking a line of acacia trees. Their host came forward to greet them in his broken English.

"You must see Friedl—he is ver' goot they tell me. He sleeps, he eat, he cry a leedle. I haf goot nurse, I think— she is Magyar girl who speaks German."

He rang a bell and asked for the baby to be brought in. A sturdy young woman, with a good-natured peasant's face, came in, bearing Friedl. His chubby feet and legs were bare. Jim waggled the pink big toe, and Friedl, after a moment of serious contemplation, gurgled with delight. Gollwitzer then took him, and it was an odd sight to see this big, round-faced old man shaking his head and making faces at his adopted son, whose tiny hands took a perilous grasp of a few wisps of the conductor's hair.

At that moment Count Mátány arrived, so bright that no one would have believed he had not reached his bed until half-past four. He, too, made noises at Friedl, who was now in Betty's arms, and asked questions of the grinning nursemaid. Then Waddle arrived, in a great flurry. He was very hot, very excited. His shirt was undone at the neck, as he had outgrown it. He clung to his portfolio. He greeted Gollwitzer in fluent German, apologised for being late, and began to unfold some Hungarian newspapers, triumphantly pointing out the long description of the Folk-Dance Congress.

"You Hungarians have a right appreciation of these things," he said to Mátány. "You realise the importance of the Folk-Dance—even more than the Germans. But I've always said you are a very intelligent people."

"You haven't greeted Friedl," said Betty, holding the baby towards him.

"Oh, Friedl! *Wie geht's, mein Junge? Du bist sehr lebhaft!*" he cried, tweaking the baby's toe. The baby stared at him. "Thinks I'm the funny man, my dears," said Waddle.

"You are, Henry—that baby's never seen anything like you before!" chaffed Mátány.

Gollwitzer dismissed the nurse, with Friedl. He poured

them a *barack* each. The servant announced lunch. This furnished apartment evidently belonged to an opera singer. There were portraits of her in different rôles. Jim, looking at these more closely, recognised Madame Lederer. He turned and asked Tibi a question.

"Yes. She's hard up just now, poor dear. She was glad to let the flat—I arranged it between her and Gollwitzer. So she's off to Carlsbad soon for a cure, but nothing'll cure her of frightful extravagance, poor dear," said Mátány.

The lunch was simple and good. Betty, sitting at her host's right, fell under the charm of this world-famous old man. He had a tremendous personality. She thought of the thousands of people in all parts of the world who would envy her this intimate contact with the *maestro*. He was so kind and simple, with his fame resting so modestly upon him after a lifetime of public adulation, that she wondered again at the intolerance of the Nazi philosophy.

It was soon four o'clock. Waddle had to go. He had a very busy evening before him. They were electing an international committee. He was full of anxiety, and alluded vaguely to " distressing heresies " introduced by the Russian delegates. He took an elaborate and courtly farewell of his host, despite his lateness. Count Mátány suggested that Jim and Betty should go with him to see Margaret Island.

As Betty was leaving, Gollwitzer smiled and drew her back into his sitting-room, while the others crossed the hall.

"Please—a moment, dear Mrs. Brown," he said, a little nervously. "How shall I thank you so much? You and Mr. Brown haf given me happiness again. I—I——"

He faltered and his voice grew husky. Betty pressed his hand.

"We did very little, Herr Gollwitzer—we did only what anyone would be honoured to do for a great man like you," she said.

He put his big left hand into his coat pocket and brought out a leather case.

"My dear young lady. I haf here for you a leedle memento of your kindness, your bravery for me and my

Friedl. I will be most happy for you to take it—eef you like it."

Surprise crossed her face as he made his little speech. She opened the small case he pushed into her hand. It contained an exquisite wrist-watch, set in small diamonds. She gave a cry of delight.

" Oh—Herr Gollwitzer, how beautiful it is ! "

" I am glad you think it so," he said, beaming.

" I shall always, always treasure it," she said, closing the leather case.

He escorted her out on to the landing, where Jim and Mátány waited for the lift, and did not leave until they had descended from sight.

Betty's face, with its flush of excitement, made Jim wonder what Gollwitzer had said to her, as she lingered behind. She told them, showing them the watch.

" And to think that that great old boy was driven to such despair that he tried to shoot himself," said Jim. " I hope he lives to a hundred, and conducts an orchestra of Jews in Berlin ! "

III

At eight o'clock in the evening, Count Zarin could generally be found in his favourite place at the Ritz. It was in a corner, outside the bar, of the long, open dining-terrace that fronted the Corso, that gay, tree-lined promenade where, in the early evening, all Budapest took the air.

A more enchanting parade ground could not be imagined. A long line of hotels bordered the wide avenue on which no traffic was permitted. The terraces of these hotels were covered with the small tables of open air cafés, each with its string orchestra, so that everybody promenaded to the music of successive bands. On the opposite side of this leafy Corso, thronged for some two hours each evening, there was a parapet overlooking the wide Danube. The customers at the café could watch the constant stream of promenaders, listen to the music, gossip, and see before them a panorama unique in its impressive beauty. Across the Danube rose the great hills of Buda, a natural wall which had for centuries held up the invading Turkish hordes; they captured it eventually, to be expelled again. Now its height was crowned by the long, noble pile of the Royal Palace, where the beautiful Empress Elizabeth, deserting her husband, once held court with the Hungarian nobles about her.

Zarin, sitting at his favourite table, could see this enormous palace, high above its terraced gardens, with its eight hundred and sixty rooms, its mansard roofs, and its green copper dome. At sunset it stood in black silhouette against the glowing light of the departing day. In darkness, brooding under the stars, high above the myriad lights clothing the hills of Buda, and linking the long river embankment and the slender bridges, it was even more impressive in its grandeur. That floodlit dome rose serenely above the long panorama of spires, terraces, bastions, and houses' built on the slopes of ancient Buda.

This palace-covered height was the Marathon of Hungary. Here all that the Magyar race had fought for was typified. Here Attila had set his camp, commanding the vast plain towards the Carpathian mountains. Here the Tartars and Mongols, from the frontiers of China, had halted, striking terror into the heart of western Europe. Here that Christian King, Stephen, built his palace and his churches, and left a legacy of peace and law, until the janissaries of the Turkish Sultans brought bloodshed and ruin, sacked the fair hill-city, converted the cathedral into a mosque, and sent down the Danube in their galleys the gold, the silver, the cloths and the statues as trophies to Stamboul. Here, finally, the dark invaders were pushed East again, and Buda rebuilt its ramparts, bastions, towers, stairways and streets, so that by night the glittering site of the ancient city recaptured again its mediæval beauty.

Count Zarin was a man who lived easily and lavishly, as his wealth permitted. Under his slightly cynical air few divined the flame of his patriotism. It was perhaps symbolic that he chose his seat, holding court with his friends, drinking cocktails, exchanging gossip, and planning some fresh excursion in frivolity, within sight of the palace-crowned hill where now no king kept court, no dynasty reigned, and a Regent waited for some distant day when a ravished country should regain its territories and renew its splendour.

He chatted now with his friends, glancing from time to time at his watch. Three days ago the Browns had lunched with him at Margaret Island. This evening they were dining with him, together with Tibi and Julietta.

His table was already filled when, prompt to the minute, Betty and Jim arrived. He presented them to the company and called for more chairs and drinks. He placed Betty so that she could see the saunterers along the Corso, and, across the river, the dark hill with the majestic Palace crowning its summit. At the next café a *tzigane* orchestra was playing, with a small crowd halted before it.

The Corso parade was a delightful compound of idleness, vanity, curiosity and flirtation. The men, well-dressed in the English fashion, escorted their ladies, or strolled in two's and three's, under the amused scrutiny of the spectators sitting at the cafés. A few of the ladies, very self-consciously attired to arrest the eye, were without cavaliers, but walked in the obvious hope of soon finding them. Along the wall of the parapet lounged a few wastrels, and some women from the Danube barges, in their billowing skirts, with coloured kerchiefs on their heads, and bright Bosnian shoes. They stood apart from the fashionable throng, and watched the pageant with round eyes. Officers, monocled and gloved, carried their swords and took the salutes of neat young cadets.

Towards nine o'clock the throng on the Corso began to grow thin. Lights now twinkled all over the hill opposite, leaving only the Palace in brooding darkness, but its countless windows caught faint reflections of the waning sky. Then, suddenly, the high, bronze-green dome leapt into light, its pillared façade picked out by the floodlights. A Danube steamer with a red lamp on its port, and a white one shining on its masthead, glided noiselessy downstream. The tables had emptied. It was dark under the trees. Zarin's friends took leave of him.

"Let us dine here—on the terrace," he said to Jim and Betty. "The next hour is the loveliest in Budapest."

He selected a table where they could look across the Danube to the Vár with its palace, steeples, and ramparts.

"What is that?" asked Betty, pointing to a high terrace over the river, with conical towers, shining white in a flood of limelight.

"That's the Fishers' Bastion, and to the left there is the St. Gellért Mount, with the huge statue of the Saint-Bishop who converted the Hungarians. He ended, poor man, in being put into a spiked barrel and thrown into the Danube. There's an hotel near by, with a rather amusing open-air swimming-pool," said Zarin. "It's got artificial waves, and one end runs into the rocky cliff, where they've made arbours and terraces. But if you take a tour of all the baths you'll be busy for a week. We've got hot springs all over the place, and each one is supposed to cure you of something."

He glanced at his watch. It was nine o'clock. A warm wind stirred the branches along the Corso.

"Ah, here's Tibi, with Julietta. Now we can eat," said the Count.

He called for the menu.

IV

"And now," said Zarin, when they had finished dinner, "I suggest the *Café Ostende*—for you to hear the gipsy boys' orchestra. You can no more come to Budapest without hearing the gipsy orchestra than you can cross the Line without meeting King Neptune. You must get it over!"

"Thirty little demons tearing at their catgut," commented Julietta. "And how they want washing!"

"I think it's very unfair to suggest our guests are as sophisticated as we are," expostulated Mátány.

"I'm sure we shall like it—clean or dirty," replied Jim.

Somehow, the remark seemed wrong. He saw a swift glance pass between Mátány and Julietta, and a smile glimmer in the Count's eyes.

"Don't be alarmed," he said, affably. "The orchestra is kept at a safe distance."

Jim knew that the Count was sneering at him, for all the smoothness of the remark. Betty's foot had kicked him under the table. He had a swift suspicion that an alliance was being formed against him, that Betty found him a clod beside this suave cavalier who lost no opportunity of flattering her with his attention. It was not jealousy which made him uneasy, it was a growing sense of menace.

Mátány, quick to detect a note of discord, began to talk about a letter he had received from a friend in the Sudeten-German district of Czechoslovakia. The Nazi propaganda was growing intenser, day by day. It was bound to lead to an explosion soon.

"After Austria—Czechoslovakia," commented Mátány.

"And after Czechoslovakia—Hungary will have something to say," added Zarin. "Our time's coming."

"Károly—I can't stand all this political talk. It never ends! Do let's go!" cried Julietta.

"I'm sorry!" said Zarin, rising. "But Tibi started it."

"Guilty!" laughed Mátány, knowing he had bridged a difficult moment.

The *Café Osterde* seemed enormous. The head waiter, who, of course, knew Zarin and Mátány, escorted them through a sea of packed tables, and placed them at a round table immediately facing the orchestra.

The gipsy boys, whose ages ranged from ten to fifteen, sat on a platform rising in tiers towards the ceiling. Some of them, the bass fiddle players, were scarcely as high as their instruments. They had dark, honey-coloured faces, with large, brown eyes and dank, black hair. They looked unnaturally old, and in need of fresh air and sleep. They wore sleeveless vests of red velvet, white shirts with wide bishop's sleeves, and gold-braided blue trousers. They were

playing as Zarin entered. A diminutive child, the *primás*
or leader, was conducting them through a frenzied *finale*.

As soon as the party was seated they were each presented
with a long sprig of fine, white grass.

"What is it?" asked Betty.

"You wear it—it is *árvalányhaj*, which means 'The
Hair of the Orphan Girl,' and it comes from the Puszta,"
explained Mátány.

The orchestra began to play again. It was a lament,
with passages of double-stopping and elaborate bow work,
performed by a tiny boy. Betty closed her eyes. The
music, the setting, the excitement of this new life, ravished
her. The head of Count Zarin, now turned away so that his
profile met her opening eyes, was of a piece with the romance
of this city. She looked at her husband, his fresh, young
face intent upon the band. He was so very English, calm-
tempered and safe, but in this atmosphere his self-possession
prevented him from experiencing the complete emotional
appeal of this Hungarian scene. His feet were planted
firmly on solid earth. He would never know her own soaring
flights of imagination, her faith in a special destiny.

At half-past one, with the music still in full spate, and the
café crowded to its limit, Zarin suggested they should leave.

"Now we'll go to *The Eagle's Nest*—where we can dance
to a small but very good *tzigane* band," he said, when they
were in his car.

Jim looked at Betty, but she was talking animatedly
to Mátány. If he insisted on their going home there would
be a scene later. He was conscious that he had disgraced
himself already this evening. So he made no protest and
sank back in silence while the car, driven by a demon chauffeur
with pointed ears, raced across the city.

So this was the gay life, to which so many aspired, this
drinking, over-eating and gossiping. He was envious once
but now he pitied them. He was aware of the awful boredom of doing whatever one liked, of getting up when one
pleased, of having no discipline imposed by necessity. The
rescuing of Gollwitzer's boy had given a zest to their honey-

moon, with its element of danger. These people did nothing but rush about, eating too much, talking too much, and sleeping too little. The strange thing was that Betty exulted in all this. If he confessed to her that he was beginning to long for the sight of a London bus, to think fondly of a discarded porter's cap, and to miss the bustle of the Continental Express leaving Victoria, she would think him mad. Incredible though it was, he was wondering if Fortune had been kind in smiling upon him. A honeymoon at Brighton, with a fortnight's pay and a regular job to return to, began to seem preferable to dinner tables with too many knives, too much hospitality he could never return, and the constant strain of trying to be something he was not, and had no desire to be.

Moreover, he was made unhappy by a growing consciousness that there was something wrong in Betty's mentality. She spoke of poverty as revolting, as if it were a vice into which weak characters fell. She expressed a dislike of " common " people, and had no loyalty to her own class, which she disowned. Yet she had wonderful qualities. She was far more intelligent than he would ever be; she had taste, and courage in reaching out for what she wanted. But she had no deep enjoyment in anything existing in her own world. She wanted life to be a fairy-tale in which she was discovered as a princess in disguise.

What would happen when she suddenly found that Cinderella generally remained Cinderella and never got to the ball, that the kitchen and not the ballroom was the place for a working man's wife ? He thought of his mother, faithful to the kitbrush and the ovencloth, so handy with the iron, and quick with the needle, so rich in the lore of cooking, jam-making, hemming, turning, renovating, and a hundred things by which an accomplished housewife made a man's home his castle. Enticing and lovely, Betty had none of these arts which she scorned. Instead, she had learned how to give an order to a servant or a chauffeur she would never possess, and to make the " common " people feel common. And yet how lovable she could be, how gay, how swift and bright in movement !

All this passed through his mind as he sat back in the car while she laughed and chatted with Mátány and Zarin.

" You are very quiet," said Julietta Molnay. " Are you tired ? Budapest never goes to bed. You'll get used to it."

Jim roused himself out of his gloomy thoughts.

" I'm sorry—no, I'm wide awake—but I don't seem to have your marvellous energy," he replied. " I couldn't keep going like you folks."

" Oh, you'll get wound up and find it easy. There's something in the air of this place—like New York," laughed Mátány.

" I find it intoxicating—look at those lights ! What a lovely place ! " exclaimed Betty, turning in her seat.

Lights danced beyond the windows. Their own head-lamps flung a dazzling beam on strange doorways, shuttered shop fronts, leafy trees, all rushing backwards into the darkness again. They had crossed the river and were now climbing steadily. Up and up they went, turning and turning. The street lamps had long ceased. Their way was lined with overhanging rocks. They passed through a grove of acacias, and caught their scent. Then, before a faintly lit, trellised portico, they stopped.

" *The Eagle's Nest*," said Zarin.

They entered a large restaurant, with windows on three sides. The place was built roughly of logs. Stags' heads decorated the walls. Beyond the windows there was a wide terrace roofed in with a vine pergola, and trellised arches hung with small coloured lights. Most of the terrace was a dancing floor. At one end, in an alcove, there was a gipsy orchestra of a dozen players, dressed in short green velvet coats, with wide, white sleeves. They were playing very softly a Viennese waltz to which about twenty couples were dancing.

Zarin selected a table on the outer side of the terrace, and Betty at once knew why the place was called *The Eagle's Nest*. Far below them lay Budapest, visible only because of the lights shining in that black expanse. The jewelled city seemed to glitter as far as the horizon.

" We must come here in daylight, you can see the great Hungarian plain. I've seen the snowy peaks of the Hohe Tátra from here. That small hill below is the Vár, with the Royal Palace. There's a faint glimmer of the Danube to the left," said Zarin.

He pointed downwards, over the slopes clothed with beech-woods. Betty's eyes began to discern details, the hill with the Palace, and a stretch of long linked lights that marked the river's embankments.

Zarin ordered wine. His table was soon crowded with friends. The orchestra, after a short rest, began to play again, very softly and languorously.

" Let us dance," he said to Betty.

He led her on to the floor. There was only the dimmest light coming from the coloured globes among the vine leaves. The music had a dreamy intoxication, and the gipsy *primás*, leading it, played as if in a hypnotic trance. Jim, with Julietta Molnay for partner, had never before felt himself moving with such effortless rhythm. Perhaps it was the music, perhaps his partner, who floated over the floor with effortless grace, that dispelled his mood of unrest.

" This is perfect ! " he said, quietly.

" You like dancing ? " she asked. " I have danced here until sunrise. Then we have breakfast under the beech trees in the garden. The foreigners don't come here."

" That must keep it nice," he replied, banteringly.

She pressed his arm, and raised her face and laughed at him.

" That was tactless of me—I mean this dance band isn't spoilt. We are severe judges. This is perhaps the finest *primás* in Hungary. When he plays our national airs he brings tears to our eyes. We are a strange people and most happy when we are most sad. We dream of our past, and dream of our future—and perhaps we really enjoy the sadness of our present."

" But I don't find you sad," said Jim. " Budapest seems a city of lights and laughter, and no soul."

" Yes—it appears so," agreed Julietta Molnay. " But

that is only a façade. Always we have fought for liberty, and lost it—we fought the Turks, to keep Western Europe free. They ravaged us, pillaged our country and left it a ruin. But we rose again. We threw them out. Then the Austrians enchained us, and we struggled and struggled   Then came the Great War, and after it the hordes of Bolsheviks, the Roumanians, the Czechs, the Serbs. And then the Treaty of Trianon ravaged our frontiers, gave away our Carpathians to the Czechs, our Croatia to the Serbs, our Transylvania to the Roumanians, some of our counties to Austria even, and a great port like our Fiume for the Jugoslavs and Italians to quarrel over, and ruin with their jealousies. Two of our university towns went to the foreigner, Pozsony to the Czechs, Kolozsvár to the Roumanians. It was as if your Oxford had been given to the Germans, and your Cambridge to the Russians. Oh, but I become tiresome. The world is very tired of our grievances," she said, breaking off. " Let us dance and be happy ! "

" No, go on, tell me more," urged Jim. " I know nothing of all this—in England we have no frontiers."

" You have your navy—you are a happy people. But be very careful, for many are jealous of you. They would like you to be broken. They plan for it. And I think you are too easy, too supercilious, perhaps too lazy and comfortable in your long freedom. Why are you so careless ? You've offended Italy, you've offended Japan, and you're being hoodwinked in Spain, and all the time the Germans march and march. They've swallowed up Austria and——"

" You're afraid they'll swallow up you ? " asked Jim.

He was amused by the intensity of his partner. She talked with her whole body. As with all these foreigners, politics and not sport was their master passion. Now, as he asked his question, she almost shook him in passionate repudiation.

" Hungary—no, no, no ! You blind English ! Hungary will wait—she must wait. One day Germany will march south—through Czechoslovakia towards the Ukraine, to the Roumanian oilfields, and then we shall pick up what we can," said Julietta Molnay.

" I think it's all very silly," replied Jim, smiling at her intensity. " I can't see much difference between human beings. We all want to eat, and work, and play a little. It's the politicians and newspapers that work people up. You know, you don't look very oppressed here," he added, banteringly, " not with all these folks dancing, and corks popping ! "

At once he knew that it was the wrong remark. She flashed her eyes at him.

" Are you a Bolshevik ? " she asked, bitterly.

" I'm not anything at all except a fellow who has to work every day to feed himself. It's not a bad thing, either. It keeps folks busy and out of mischief."

The band stopped. They went back to their table. His partner took no pains to show that she resented what he had said. He began to feel reckless. Betty was dancing continuously with Zarin. He claimed her for the next dance.

" After this we're going home," he said to her.

" Oh, no—it's marvellous here. The Count's been suggesting we should——" began Betty.

" We're going home," repeated Jim, firmly. " I'm in disgrace, anyhow—so we'd better get out of it."

" What have you done now ? " asked Betty, dismay in her voice.

" The Count's girl friend thinks I'm a Bolshevik."

" Do you mean Fräulein Molnay ? "

" Yes—she seems upset because I won't get excited about Germany gobbling up Austria, and——"

" Don't say ' gobbling '—it's slang," said Betty. " Why can't you behave like a gentleman ? "

" Because I'm not ! " retorted Jim. " These people get my goat."

" Goat ! Really ! " exclaimed his wife.

" They eat and they drink and they chatter,' went on Jim, ignoring her exclamation. " And what's it all about ? Some new way of spending money, some new place to eat at—or why she runs after him, or he won't live with her. God Almighty——"

" Don't swear. You make me hot with shame."

" That's nice, coming from my own wife," he said, quietly.
She made no answer. They danced on in angry silence.
Two red spots glowed on her cheeks. The floor was crowded,
the place was hot, the music became more and more frenzied.
It was past two o'clock. When the band stopped he made
one more attempt as he led her back to their table, now crowded
with Zarin's friends.

" Betty," he pleaded, " say you're tired and let's go home."

She gave him an angry stare. He could not help noticing,
even in her present hostile mood, how beautiful she looked.

" Isn't it obvious to you that we can't go until our host
wants to ? " she said, witheringly.

At that moment Zarin, approaching, introduced her to
a young man who talked broken English. She gave him the
next dance.

Mátány's sharp eyes had seen that all was not going well.

" Had enough ? " he asked, quietly.

" Too much," replied Jim, with brutal frankness. " I'm
sorry, Tibi—but I want to go."

" Very well," replied Mátány. " I'll get hold of Károly."

Jim saw Julietta Molnay sitting alone at their table. He
went up to her and sat down beside her.

" I'm sorry—I must have seemed rude to you. I'm—
I'm——" he began, floundering.

" You were very rude," she said, a smile lighting her
face. " But you were quite right in what you said. Do
you think I don't know ? This is your honeymoon ? "

" Yes," he answered, a little surprised at her remark.

" Mrs. Brown is very beautiful—and a beautiful woman
has every Hungarian at her feet."

She said this very quietly and, their eyes meeting, they
looked at each other for a few moments of silence.

" I feel that's a warning—thank you," he said, thoughtfully.

A little later Zarin led them out to his car. The sleeping
Toni was alert at a touch. They ran down the silent streets.
At the door of the Pension they said good night to their host,
and Julietta Molnay and Mátány.

"It's really good morning," said Jim, as he unlocked the door, glancing up at the sky where the first flush of dawn was spreading. Betty made no answer. But when they had gained their room she turned on him.

"I suppose you realise you've behaved like a bounder in front of those people? I wanted the earth to swallow me up!" she cried, flinging her hat on to the bed.

Jim made no reply. He took off his coat and hung it in the wardrobe.

"Going to sulk now, I suppose," said Betty, tauntingly.

"On the contrary, I'm going to talk now, my girl," replied Jim, going up to her. "You've just said I've behaved like a bounder. Quite right. You're not the only one who's noticed it."

"What do you mean?"

"I suppose you thought we were getting away with it finely, didn't you? You were so busy rolling your eyes at that hand-kissing Count——"

"Don't be vulgar!"

"I'm going to be what I really am—very vulgar, before I've finished, my girl," retorted Jim, trembling, in his suppressed anger.

"Don't call me 'my girl,' I hate the expression," said Betty. She turned away from him and went towards the dressing-table, but he followed her, caught hold of her, swinging her round, and looking down into her face.

"You needn't add brutality to vulgarity. You are hurting me," she said, in a voice of icy contempt.

He ignored the remark and kept his grip on her.

"P'raps you didn't——" he began.

"Perhaps," she corrected.

"P'raps," he repeated, obstinately, "you didn't see the looks those bright birds were giving each other across the table last Sunday night, during our high-life act, did you? I got hold of the wrong knife and the red-headed cat twigged it and sniggered. And all the time that smug-faced dago was whining in your ear with his violin, and you purred like a cat that's found cream, those women were watching you and reckoning just how long it would take the Count to hook his new fish."

" You're crazy ! " retorted his wife.

" We're both crazy ! We thought we were getting away with it. I was as dazzled as you until I heard something Zarin asked Waddle the other day. That brought me to earth with a bang. ' Where did you find them ? ' That's what I overheard in the cloak-room while you women were powdering your noses. I'd half a mind to knock him down.'"

" What if you did hear it—there's nothing in that remark to take offence at."

" No ? "

" Unless you're quite blind with jealousy," snapped Betty. " Do take your hands off me. You behave and talk like a prize-fighter. If you knew how ugly you look in your present mood."

" Betty," said Jim, hoarsely, his anger subsiding as he looked into her eyes, " don't you see we're making awful fools of ourselves ? They saw through us in a flash—they know quite well what drawer we've come out of, only they're too polite to let us know they know. We haven't the clothes and we haven't the manners. Old Waddle's a good sort, but I'd no idea he was letting us in for anything like this. We'll finish our sightseeing, and then we'll get out."

He held her and looked earnestly into her face. Her eyes met his in frank hostility.

" Won't we ? " he asked, wishing to be reassured.

" You can go if you like. I'm staying," answered Betty. " I don't understand you. I'm just beginning to live as I've never lived before, among the kind of people I feel at home with—refined people instead of the awful herd——"

" You picked me out of," interjected Jim, bitterly.

" I picked you out of, if you want to know the sober truth," retorted his wife.

" And why, I wonder ! "

" Because I thought you'd got something in you—a natural instinct for the best society, for——"

" Society ! " laughed Jim, derisively. " So you think you'll et me into Society, do you ? I could tell you something about those women at that party to-night. I got hot in the head like you, and was doing a little flirting myself under the influence of wine, women and fiddling. I found one of them pressing my leg under the table——"

His wife swung round and gave him a glance of withering contempt.

" You're an inexpressibly vulgar cad," she said, and, crossing the room swiftly, entered the bathroom, closing the door after her with a bang.

Jim was about to follow her, and then, changing his mind, began to undress, slowly. He wound up his watch. It was three o'clock. He changed into his pyjamas and still his wife had not come out of the bathroom. Her pyjamas lay on the bed in their initialled, silk case.

He went to the bathroom door and tapped. There was no response. Then he tried the door. To his surprise it was unlocked and his wife stood before the wash-bowl, her back towards him, dabbing her face with a sponge. He went towards her, looking over her shoulder, and the mirror told him that she had been crying. Contrition smote him.

" Betty, old girl," he said, softly.

She took no notice and continued dabbing her face.

" Betty," he repeated, " I'm sorry if I've upset you. But I couldn't stand them laughing at us. They meant well, I know. We'll go off on our own, we'll enjoy ourselves much more, you and me——"

She turned round quickly, her eyes swimming with tears, her face distorted with anger as she shouted at him.

" Go away—go to bed ! I hate you ! You can go and wallow in the mud, and lead your low life, and push your silly barrow at a railway station, and get black eyes prize-fighting, and wear your silly club pins ! Your smart Mr. Lincoln's tried to make a gentleman of you—God knows why—and I've tried, and you're just common clay, and like being common clay. But you won't drag me down ! I shall make the friends I can, and go where I'm invited—and you can amuse yourself as you like, but leave me alone ! "

" You mean that ? " asked Jim, white-lipped.

" I mean that. Now get off to bed ! " she replied.

He was so stunned that for a moment he stared at her open-mouthed. It was a Betty he had never seen before, had never imagined could exist. The revelation frightened him more than it appalled him.

He said nothing in reply. The anger in her eyes was like a knife in his heart. He left the bathroom and got into his bed, and lay on his side, his face deep in the pillow. Presently he heard her come into the room and move about. After a few minutes she got into bed. The light went out.

He lay in the darkness, his mind in turmoil. Through a gap between the blind and the window-frame he saw a cold, bright star. A car climbed up a hill somewhere, breaking the pool of silence. There was silence again, save for the ticking of their travelling clock, a wedding present from fellow porters at Victoria Station. Then he heard an unmistakable sound, his wife sobbing quietly into her pillow.

He raised himself on one elbow and listened. The sound was unbearable. He slipped out of his bed and crossed to hers.

" Betty," he cried, softly. " Betty ! "

He stooped and put his hand under her shoulder, and tried to turn her towards him, but she resisted and kept her face in the pillow. Then, with sheer force, he lifted her in his arms, and pressed his face against hers, her wet cheek to his.

" Betty, darling, I'm sorry. I only want you to be happy," he said. " I'm so fond of you, darling ! "

She did not answer, but continued to cry, her head on his shoulder. He lay on the bed, holding her to him, his hand stroking her hair as she sobbed convulsively. The minutes passed, and she grew quieter.

" Sleepy ? " he asked.

She made no answer, but this time their lips met and her hand passed through his hair, caressingly. There was silence again, and he lay awake, wondering at this strange night in Budapest.

" I'll leave you now, darling. Good night," he whispered
after a time. " Sleep well."

They clung to each other in a long kiss that dissolved all
their anger with each other. Then he lowered her head on
to the pillow, drew the sheets up over her, and silently
regained his own bed.

But not for immediate sleep. He lay thinking and thinking. There was now someone in his life united with his
own, who was, nevertheless, a stranger, living apart in that
inviolable territory of the soul whose loneliness is the mystery
of God. It was a frightening thought. He must not be
hard with Betty, so high-spirited and swift in response. He
thought of some words of Mr. Lincoln's, when he had been
nearly thrown by a spirited horse. " Snaffle her lightly and
she'll answer you, snaffle her hard and she'll rear." Betty
was like that. He must not be so heavy-handed in future.

At four o'clock he fell asleep.

CHAPTER XV

THE ROAD TO TISZATARDOS

I

ANOTHER week fled in a whirl of sightseeing. Mátány was
constantly devising some new entertainment for Jim and
Betty. They had seen very little of Waddle, who tapped
at their door in the morning, shouted a few words, and,
apologising for his great hurry, was gone again. Sometimes
he scribbled a note, naming some café as a rendezvous, at
which he invariably arrived late, and began to scribble
letters in between conversation.

The Congress, they gathered, was a great success. They
were planning another in New Orleans, a Pan-American
Congress of Folk-Dancing. " I want to go to Louisiana—

H

I hear there are some very interesting survivals of French dances there. Just think, what a bond between the nations ! Hands across the Atlantic and all that," he said, dropping sugar into his coffee. " And, my dears, I've met a Mexican delegate, such an interesting man—he is interested in the lost Maya kingdom, and has investigated all the ritual dances of the ancient Mayas—very bloody, but most interesting ! They are supposed to be a race who lived in the lost Atlantis—you see ? There is a link—a folk-dance link right across the Atlantic, from the ancient world to the new ! "

They had lunched again with Herr Gollwitzer. They found him in a state of high excitement. He could scarcely remember his English as he tried to tell them what had happened. Hans, his beloved valet, had succeeded in getting out of Austria, and was with him. Hans waited at table, a sturdy young Tyrolean who anticipated Gollwitzer's every need.

" Eet is 'ome again, mit Hans and my leedle Friedl. Kind friends, I thank you, I thank you," said Gollwitzer.

" You owe it all, really, to Count Mátány and Mr. Waddle," said Betty.

" *Ach*—I do not vorget dem. *Nein !* My life ees owed to the Herr Graf. Und kind Herr Waddle. *Ja !* Goot friends, goot friends all," said Gollwitzer, emotionally.

They had been to the swimming pool on Margaret Island, an island in the Danube, joined to Buda and Pest by its bridge. Here they had sat in a circular pool of hot sulphur water, whose concrete reclining places were in concentric rings, growing hotter and hotter towards the central spring. They had dined at the side of the long pool, and splashed in the artificial waves. They had lunched on the terrace of the great St. Gellért Hotel, swum in the blue pool, with its Roman-Persian marble arcature, behind which rose a terraced garden on the cliff side.

The baths of Budapest seemed endless. They had also visited the Széchényi baths, and Mátány had taken Jim to the various Turkish baths, dark, and domed in the old Turkish tradition. They had motored out to the summit of the János-Hegy, with its tower and restaurant. There they looked down on the illimitable mountains of the Treaty of Trianon. In the evening light they had believed they saw the high Tátra and the faint Carpathian ranges. As the sun sank, the Great Plain turned purple, mauve, and deep blue, and the windows and roofs of Pest were burnished with the crimson light.

One morning Mr. Bowling, lingering in their room at the Pension Balaton, told them his story how, having drawn his life insurance money, already earmarked by his grabbing relations, he had decided to give them the slip and see the world. He had intended visiting the Pyramids, and had chosen Athens as his first halt, but being invited to stop over in Budapest by a charming widow he had met on the train, he had been here ever since. At the end of a month he had married the widow.

" I shall never see Egypt now, nor Athens—no, I've done for myself all right," he said, dismally. " Of course, my wife's a clever woman. She does very well here. But I never get out. As I can't do the shopping, she goes out. And she's always visiting relations—so I have to stay and look after the place. I did have regular hours in Derby—but here ! "

He spread out his hands in a gesture of despair.

" Why don't you tell your wife you must have some time off ? " asked Jim.

" Tell her ! " exclaimed Mr. Bowling. " Tell my wife ! I ought not to say it—but she can be a very violent woman, Mr. Brown. I hate scenes. Why once——"

The story of woe was cut short by Waddle's entrance.

" Well—I must not keep you," said Bowling, with a sad smile, and withdrew.

Waddle, as usual, was in a state of excitement. Did they know what was afoot ?

" A Folk-Dance Congress in Tokio ? " asked Jim, mischievously.

" No—no—I have just been talking to Tibi on the telephone. My dears, it is simply wonderful, it will be a unique experience ! Tibi's mother has invited you to Tiszatardos. Tibi, of course, will tell you himself. I am delighted. You will see the real Hungarian life."

" I thought we had been seeing it," said Jim. " Our heads are reeling."

" Oh, this is just mere sophistication ! Believe me, this isn't the real thing. Now you will see the Puszta, the Hortobágy Plain—the great herds, the *csikós*, the true village life. Quite feudal, my dears. I've stayed often at Tiszatardos—just south of Tokay. You'll love the Countess, such an old dear."

" Who ? " asked Betty.

" Countess Mátány, Tibi's mother. She's a Pole, very musical and cultured. Well," said Waddle, " I must run along now. I'm lunching with *The Times* correspondent— most important we should have a good report, there ! "

When Waddle had gone they discussed his news.

" I don't think I want to go," said Jim.

Betty stared at him.

" What ? Why ever not—it's a wonderful experience," she said.

" No—I feel we're getting out of our depth. Mátány and Zarin have been wonderfully kind to us—but we don't belong to their set," said Jim. " I don't like taking everything, knowing we can't repay it."

" What nonsense ! " retorted Betty, sharply. " They enjoy our company. And if it comes to that I don't see that I'm not every bit their equal, apart from money."

" ' Apart from money ' is quite a difference," said Jim, quietly. " I stood a round of drinks the other night that took a week's wage. I don't mind, but we mustn't lose our heads. It's not a world for a waitress and a railway-porter."

She flashed a look of anger at him, her cheeks suddenly burning.

" Thank you for reminding me of that ! " she said.

" Well, aren't we ? " asked Jim, stubbing out his cigarette.

" You are, perhaps, but maybe I'm not," retorted Betty.
He looked at her with an amused smile.

" And what exactly do you mean by that, my dear ? "
he asked.

" Exactly what I imply."

" All right, we won't quarrel about that."

" I've no intention of quarrelling, Jim. There is something
I think you should know I'm not the common woman you
imagine I am."

" I've never imagined you were common," said Jim,
quietly.

She put down the sewing she was doing as he was dressing.

" Jim," she said, in a serious voice, " I've something to
tell you. I'm not at all what you think. You've said yourself
you have been astonished at the way I've ' carried it off,'
as you put it."

" Yes—I have," agreed Jim. " You've been a marvel."

" Count Zarin wouldn't have paid me the attention he has,
or taken us about so much if he had felt we were different."

" I don't know about that, my dear girl," said Jim, a
little impatiently, as he brushed his coat. " It's you he's
after. He's one of those everlasting kiss-your-hand counts
who chase every pretty woman."

" You needn't be rude. Count Zarin's a gentleman," said
Betty, becoming angry.

" Exactly, and he knows damn well I'm not," retorted
Jim.

" There's no need to be vulgar," said Betty, severely.
" He's treated us with the greatest courtesy and kindness."

" I never said he hasn't, my dear girl, but he knows exactly
where we belong, I know that ! " cried Jim.

" Where *you* belong—perhaps," said Betty, nettled.

" Oh, I didn't know I'd married above me," laughed Jim.

He came across the room, put his hands on her shoulders
as she sat sewing, and rubbed his cheek against hers.

She drew her face away, a red spot glowing on each cheek.

" Well, it happens you have ! " she retorted.

She had not intended to say this. It slipped out.

"That's interesting, my dear. Have I married a waitress in disguise?"

"You really mean someone disguised as a waitress," said Betty, coolly. "Well, if you must know the truth, you have!"

He looked at her in astonishment. She went on, ignoring his look.

"I'm not exactly what you think, Jim. You've been giving me credit I don't deserve. What I've been able to do has not been a matter of cleverness, but of instinct. You think I've come out of a mean street, from very common stock——"

"My dear girl——" interrupted Jim.

She turned on him sharply.

"You must let me say what I'm going to say. I tried to tell you this before. I'm not a Parrish at all. My father was not really my father. He——"

"Good heavens, Lizzie—Betty," he corrected himself, "are you going to tell me again you're a bastard? It doesn't shock me, of course. I don't care what you are, but——"

"There's no need for you to be vulgar and offensive, Jim," retorted Betty, heatedly. "Do I look common?"

"No—you look quite one of the nobs. You can keep your end up, all right," said Jim, proudly.

"Thank you. It may surprise you to learn that my real father was Lord Wyford, who became the Marquis of Cranford later."

Jim stared at her for a moment.

"It surprises me quite a lot," he said, quietly.

"I see you don't believe me."

"Well, it takes some swallowing. You always were an imaginative kid."

"Call me a liar and be done with it!" she said, indignantly.

"That isn't very aristocratic," he retorted, and then, with a good-natured smile, "Don't bother your head what you are—you're my wife, and I'm proud of you."

"I'll say no more," replied Betty, coldly.

" All right—we'll let the barometer settle," he said, and
went into the bathroom to do his hair.

Betty sewed so angrily that she stabbed her finger. Then
she rose and put her sewing away. It was foolish of her to
quarrel with her husband. After all, he belonged to a different
class, and she should make allowances.

" You don't really mean to refuse Tibi's invitation ? "
she called, after a pause.

" If you're so keen to go, we'll go," he answered. " But
we haven't been asked yet."

He put down the brushes and came into the bedroom. His
wife, standing in front of the long mirror, was fitting on a
small hat. It rested most becomingly, at a saucy tilt, on
her neat head. He put his arms round her from behind.
She half turned her face to him. He kissed her full on the
mouth. She laughed. Her eyes softened. He kissed her
again.

There was the sound of a car stopping outside. Jim went
to the window and looked down. It was Madame Balaton,
setting forth for Margaret Island.

" I think she might take Bowling out for a change,"
commented Jim, as the car went off.

" He's a little worm—he can't wear the trousers," said
Betty, contemptuously. She glanced at her watch.
" Heavens—I'll be late for the hairdresser ! "

" What, again ! You had your hair done last week,"
exclaimed Jim.

" And a frightful mess they made of it."

" Well, I like it."

" And I don't," retorted Betty. " I'll be back here at
twelve."

She put on her hat, picked up her gloves and handbag.
Jim gave her an approving glance. She certainly looked
charming. He watched her go down the street, and she
waved to him as he leaned out over the flower-box.

There was a tap on the door.

" Come in ! " called Jim.

It was Bowling, with three letters, two for Jim and one

for Betty. He was not wearing his apron and looked quite different in a brown suit.

"I say—what about having a drink at the corner now we're both off the chain? My missis has gone off for the day."

Jim laughed. He liked little Bowling. He felt sorry for him; there was no doubt Madame Balaton was a forceful woman.

"Right," said Jim, getting his hat. "But I must be back at twelve."

It was obvious that they knew Bowling at the café on the corner, overlooking the Danube. He ordered two glasses of lager, and with them they brought him an English paper on a reading-stick. He had a few pleasant words with the waiter.

"Now, that fellow's seen life," said Bowling. "He's a Czech, and at the end of the war he was in the Russian army and found himself stuck right away in the North. Of course they'd ceased to be Russians, they became free Czechs again, with a country of their own, when the war ended. There they were, and the Russians went Red, while they stayed White. Do you know, him and his whole regiment fought their way right through Siberia to Vladivostok, and were picked up there, and so got home to Ruthenia!"

"Where's Ruthenia?" asked Jim.

"It's now the eastern part of Czechoslovakia—in the Carpathians. It's a regular mix-up, I'm told, of Ukrainians, Russians, Poles, Roumanians, Slavs, Magyars, Armenians and Jews. It used to be part of Hungary, though they never bothered about it, except as a grand place to shoot in. The people there are all woodmen and peasants who can't read and write. The Allies took it from the Hungarians and gave it to the Czechs. This chap's a Ruthenian Slav——"

"What do you talk to him in?" asked Jim.

"Oh, a little bit of Magyar—I'm getting the lingo slowly. My, what a language! Well, to tell you about that chap," went on Bowling, looking at the beer in his glass. "Seventy

thousand of 'em set out for Vladivostok and about half of
them got there—the Bolshies picked off the rest. And here
he is—a Czech by nationality, a Slav by birth, speaking
Magyar, and married to a Roumanian girl, with five kids
who are all little Hungarians ! That's the sort of mess you
get into in this part of Europe. Now look at me. My
wife's a Hungarian, but a British subject by marriage—since
she married me. And do you think she'll call herself Mrs.
Bowling ? Oh, no—she's Madame Balaton, of *Pension
Balaton* ! Now I say," emphasised Bowling, putting down
his glass with a bang, " she's Mrs. Bowling, and it ought to
be called *Pension Bowling*. It's humiliating, downright
humiliating—and ungrateful ! "

" Ungrateful ? " repeated Jim.

" She married me so as she could get an English legacy—
that's where most of her money came from."

" And why did you marry her ? "

" It wasn't the money—if that's what you're thinking,"
answered Bowling, taking a pipe out of his pocket, and lighting
it. " I can't smoke the damned thing in my own home,
what do you think of that ? No, it wasn't her money, not
altogether. You see, I'd got some of my own. I've always
had a mania for seeing Athens—all those Greek temples, you
know, and the Pyramids—have you ever read *The Secret of
the Pyramids*, and what the British Israelites say about them ?
No ? Well, they say——"

" Your wife, you didn't marry her for money ? " asked
Jim, prompting. Bowling never kept to the line of conversation.

" No ! I married her for love—and, of course, a few con-
veniences. This place went to my head rather. She's a
nice little business in the Pension—and she can be a very
fetching woman when she wants to. But my, she's masterful ! She's put an apron on me, and I'm degenerating into a
housemaid without a Sunday off. She's bought a car—
you've seen it ? Do you think I've ever been out in it ! Not
me ! I'm not allowed to touch the blinking thing, although
I worked in the Rolls-Royce factory for fifteen years ! I

can tell you, I've had about enough of it. Here I am, stuck halfway to Athens, answering bells and carrying trays—a regular kitchen slut."

" Why don't you strike ? " asked Jim, amused at little Bowling's indignation.

" Strike ! You don't know my wife ! "

" Have you still got your money ? "

" Some of it ! " gulped Bowling, draining off his beer.

" Then I should put my feet down. I'd insist on her being Mrs. Bowling, of the *Pension Bowling*. I'd carry no more trays and answer no more bells. Make the maids do it, and failing that, make her."

" Ah, she's a masterful woman," repeated Bowling, gloomily. " You should see her temper—a regular Hungarian rhapsody, I can tell you. You've seen how they fiddle like fury ? Well—that's only an indication of what they can do if they let themselves go. I tell you—and it's no nice thing for a man to say about his wife—that woman scares me stiff when she get's going ! "

" Then get going too, and wear her down," retorted Jim. Bowling looked dolefully at his glass.

" Ah, it's easy to say," he commented.

" Have another ? " asked Jim.

" Thanks. I mustn't stay too long. Do you know, when she goes out for the day she rings up to see if I'm in ? "

" Then I'd be sure to be out. If she won't stay on the job, why should you ? Take a few days off and let her find out how valuable you are."

Bowling stared at Jim. The idea struck a spark in his eyes. Then they went dull again.

" No—you don't know what a scene there'd be," he answered, sadly. " And I hate scenes."

He finished the second glass, and puffed at his pipe, watching the steamers gliding down the Danube.

" It could be heaven, this place. I like these folks," said Bowling, meditatively. " But I've put my head in a noose all right—just when I thought I'd got out of one."

" That's life," said Jim. " We're always going to live

to-morrow, and to-morrow's never what you thought it would be to-day."

"I see you're a philosopher," observed Bowling, knocking out his pipe. "I really think I ought to be going," he added.

II

As predicted by Waddle, they were invited by Mátány's mother to visit her for three or four days at Tiszatardos, their home near Tokay, a village close to the winding river Tisza, and on the edge of the great Puszta. They would be able to see a native wedding, to be held on the estate, and there would be horses to ride if they wished to visit the great plain.

Jim repressed his reluctance to go. The whole thing made him feel nervous, but Betty was quite determined. Unfortunately, they would not have Waddle's company as he was in the midst of the Folk-Dance Congress. He was delighted to hear of the invitation, and Jim knew quite well that, on Betty's prompting, he had put the idea into Mátány's head.

Since their host wished them to see the costumes of the people at Mezökövesd, *en route*, they left early on the Sunday morning, for eight o'clock seemed early after the routine they had been following. Mátány called for them in his car at the Pension Balaton. Bowling saw them off, and at the last moment Madame appeared also, with a bouquet of flowers for Betty. Their room would be kept for them until their return.

The way out of Budapest followed the flat road eastwards. Gradually the houses of the city fell behind them and they began to pass small villages, chiefly of mud-brick bungalows with tiled roofs, built end-on to the street, so that their inhabitants' lives were enclosed from public gaze. The village High Streets were all alike. Long, straight, cobbled tracks, flanked with acacia trees and ditches in which geese squatted, if they were not straggling across the road. Betty wondered how these men and women supported lives lived in such dreary surroundings. There was a church, a communal hall, and three or four miserable shops. That was all.

The road now became little more than a beaten mud track across the monotonous plain. The cornfields began to close in round them, the wind sent waves of shadow across the golden sea. In lush meadows, beside a clump of trees and a church steeple, lay small hamlets, squat and still in the bright morning sun. On and on they went, through the villages of whitewashed cabins, most of them now thatched, and inhabited, it seemed, by as many white geese as by human beings. It was Sunday morning and the peasants were in their best dress, the men in sombre black, the women in starched linen petticoats and heavy boots.

" They're losing their native costumes and taking to cheap factory products," said Mátány. " It's a pity—but what can we do ? Later, as we get farther away into the plain, you'll begin to see the traditional dresses."

The air was soft, the sun brilliant. A pair of storks, long-necked, with trailing legs, flew over them, and settled in a nest on a chimney. There was a crimson patch of poppies amid the green, and some plantations of sunflowers. The road stretched on and on across the undulating land. Very occasionally they came to a level crossing, and quite frequently they were held up for a road toll at the entrance to the villages.

" It's antiquated, I know. We're trying to get these silly tolls abolished—but the villagers cling to them as a source of revenue," said Mátány.

He explained how, in Hungary, there was no middle-class. They were still a people of peasants and aristocratic land-owners, both classes equally proud in their relation to each other. The system of entail prevented all the great estates from being broken up. There was little or no money. Many of the farm rents were paid in kind. It was still a life of communal bartering. The peasants lived in the utmost simplicity, tilling the land, rearing horses, cattle and poultry, making their clothes, taking their produce to market, and dancing and drinking when the week's work was done. " A month's wages of one of your London policemen would keep a family here for a year—and spoil all its contentment with unsettling ambitions," said Mátány.

" And you have no troubles, no risings ?" asked Jim, thinking of the money that flowed through his host's fingers.

" No—why should we ? We had a troublesome agitator among the peasants—he promised them heaven, like all those fellows, so we exiled him. These agitators want the entails abolishing so that they can smash up our large estates. It's been done in Czechoslovakia—it's a Bolshevik idea," said Mátány, contemptuously. " The soil is the mother of life, and Hungary has a great soil. The moment men build up from it, get their feet off it, they begin to sway. Can you honestly say that that old fellow "—he pointed to an old man smoking his pipe—" is any less happy than his enterprising nephew who has emigrated, and who schemes and slaves to keep a thousand discontented wage-earners clocked and whistle-driven in a dull factory, and who can only just satisfy his wife by living in a ten-thousand dollar duplex-apartment in Park Avenue ? No—this old fellow takes a good cut off his flitch, carves a goose whose neck he has wrung, and knows the loveliness of a sunset, and the sweetness of the wind coming across the land of his fathers. If I am not what I am, I would be what these good people are here."

Jim did not agree with his host, but he kept silent. He wondered if Mátány would really have liked to change places.

About half an hour from Mezőkövesd Betty had her first thrill. They passed three young horsemen in all the splendour of their gala attire. They wore round felt hats, rather like a Homburg with the crown pushed up, with a large feather, the Orphan Girl's Hair again, standing stiffly up at the side. Under their green sleeveless jackets, open in front, and cut short at the back like an Eton jacket, showed white, frilled shirts, embroidered in vivid colours down the fronts. These shirts had wide billowing sleeves with diapered edges. Their trousers, made of white cotton, were very voluminous and looked like petticoats, tucked in over black top-boots. They also wore fancy cloth aprons, heavily embroidered.

"You'll notice they're riding without saddles," said Mátány, as their car went slowly by.

Aware of the interest they had aroused, the three cavaliers waved gaily, their broad, bronzed faces puckered in smiles.

Mezökövesd lay ahead. In a few minutes they had entered the broad central street of the small town. A feast of colour met their eyes everywhere. The car stopped in front of the inn at which they were to lunch.

"Why! all the town's on parade!" exclaimed Betty, as troops of young girls walked by. Their coloured petticoats, pleated and worn six or seven deep, billowed out, crinoline-fashion, as they swayed past.

The Beau Brummells of the town were taking the air also. These were local bucks in vivid blue blouse-shirts with hand-embroidered collars, cuffs and fronts. They wore black, shining aprons, with embroidered hems that flapped down over their leather top-boots. Little hats, with small brims and high green bands, gay with feathers or flowers, were perched on the crowns of their heads, being held in place by elastic bands behind.

"And boots!" cried Betty, not knowing which way to look. "I never saw such boots!"

"Well, the women have it over the men there!" said Jim, watching some belles walk by. They had high crimson leather top-boots, which gave them something of a Russian air. The girls not wearing top-boots had vivid stockings with elaborate floral clocks embroidered with coloured wools. Their shoes also, somewhat like Turkish pattens, had embroidered toe points. As an offset to this blaze of coloured petticoats, head-dresses and boots, the older women kept to sombre black.

"I must have a look at one of those head-dresses," said Betty, thrilled with the gay scene before her.

"Then here you are," said Mátány, motioning to a girl in the inn doorway.

The girl came forward laughing, and curtsied.

"This is Ilonka, the youngest of the innkeeper's five laughters and seven sons," he said, introducing her. "She has just said to you, ' I kiss your hand, gracious lady.' "

" She is lovely ! " cried Betty, looking at the dark-eyed, olive-skinned girl who smiled at her. Her black, plaited hair was parted over her smooth crown. She wore a head-dress of blue silk, netted in silver thread, with three straw-coloured streamers, stiff with coloured needlework. There was something Russian in the effect of this head-dress.

Betty examined the embroidered apron. The smiling Ilonka held it up for closer inspection.

" But it is marvellous—how long did it take to embroider ? " asked Betty.

" She says two years," translated Mátány, " and her mother and she took six years over the petticoat."

" And who embroiders the men's rig-out ? " asked Jim, enviously.

" Their sisters—it's a winter's job, when they're not working in the fields. You are in a sad way as a village buck if you haven't a bevy of sisters to embroider for you ! "

They followed Mátány through the heavily raftered inn, to a courtyard behind, with a pergola giving shade from the hot sun. In a corner there was a *tzigane* band, with a youth playing a cimbalom, a flat dulcimer whose plangent wires he struck with cloth-headed hammers. The gay dance tune called for lilting feet, but Mezökövesd was busy gossiping at long wooden tables. The women sat apart, and watched with big eyes the preparations for lunch.

They had an excellent meal of broth, with egg macaroni, roast chicken and rice-meat in stuffed cabbage. They drank an excellent red wine. The *primás* of the band came and serenaded them.

The lunch finished, they strolled through the little town, but the beauties and the beaux had all gone home. Shortly before two o'clock they set off on the second half of the journey. The roads deteriorated, the villages grew more and more scattered, but they encountered the gaily attired horse-men, and farmers and their families going in their long, low truck-carts, drawn by a pair of horses, to pay Sunday calls,

They bumped dreadfully over the rough, beaten-mud roads. Sometimes even this track had become too bad where a stream had broken down the low embankment, and car and carts had to make a detour over the rough meadow-land. Mátány drove remorselessly over the road, regardless of the springs. The dust rose in clouds behind them. Sometimes the cars they overtook moved in a pillar of dust before them. The monotonous country scarcely changed. On their left there was a low range of mauve foothills where the ground began to rise to the distant Carpathian mountains, across the Czechoslovakian frontier.

About four o'clock they crossed a bridge and ran through swampy flats. Later they came to Tiszadob, a village on a broad river. The car turned northwards, the road had changed to a mere dust-track. The reed beds filled the river islands. They crossed the Tisza again, turned aside into a grove of beech trees, and saw ahead of them something that made Betty give a cry of delight. There, drawn up in the shade of a tree, before a pair of massive iron gates, stood an open landau, and five cream-grey horses. On the box-seat sat a coachman, with a crimson coat, embroidered on the front and sleeves with heavy gold braid. He wore a round felt hat, with long, green streamers falling behind. The groom at his side was similarly dressed, except that his hat was of astrakhan with a high, white aigrette. At the sight of the car the groom leapt down, and went to hold the bridle of the outside horse of the leading trio.

"We all change here," said Mátány. "I'm not going to let you arrive at my home in a motor-car, we'll do it in true Hungarian style — we'll arrive with horses."

He helped Betty into the landau, and left the car to be driven by the young groom.

And so it was that, with cream manes flying, silver harness jingling, with hoofs thudding, and a resplendent coachman on the box, Jim and Betty swept up the mile-long beech avenue in the family landau, until, at a bend by a lake sparkling in the sunshine, they suddenly saw ahead of them the

Mátány home, a long, white building with a colonnaded front.

They swung briskly around the circular gravel drive, and pulled up smartly in front of an open portico, whose columns were clad with white and purple convolvulus. A pair of Borzois came out with a rush, joyously barking, as a servant opened the double glass doors.

They followed Mátány into a glass-domed entrance hall, and there, awaiting them, stood Mátány's mother, a slight dark little woman of about sixty, with silvering hair and beautiful grey eyes. Mátány presented them after kissing her.

" It's a pleasure to have English friends here—how kind of you to come," said the Countess, holding Betty's hand. " We are very quiet here, we ride and read and talk—poor Tibi can't endure it for long."

She spoke in excellent English. Oh yes, she had had an English governess. There was one in the house now, for the grandchildren. " Oh—did I say English ? Scotch, or I shall get into trouble ! " she said, laughing. " And now you are dusty and tired after your journey—Tibi shall show you your rooms."

They followed him up a wide staircase. Giant antlered heads hung on the walls. A long, wide passage, with skins on the shining maple floors, was hung with life-sized oil portraits of soldiers in uniform, their breasts decorated with medals and slashed with the ribbons of Orders.

" I call it the Way of Reproach," said Mátány, with a slight smile. " They did something, and I——"

He shrugged his shoulders and laughed. Then he stopped and opened a door. It was an anteroom, out of which two other rooms, their bedrooms, opened. The walls were hung with flowered silks, the furniture was painted with Hungarian colours. Rugs covered the board floors. The bedcovers and hangings were of native embroidery.

" Oh ! " exclaimed Betty, in ecstasy.

Three windows opened on to a verandah, with a striped awning. Below, a wide, green lawn led down to a silver lake on which floated black swans. In the distance, crowning an avenue of beech trees, rose a belvedere, with sculptured figures dark against the brilliant sky.

" And this is yours," said Mátány to Jim, leading him into the adjoining room, which also opened on to the flower-laden verandah. " Now I'll leave you to have your baths—rather primitive, I fear. Don't dress. We dine at eight."

He left them. Jim went into Betty's room and they held one another in the excitement of this experience.

" Pinch me—do I wake or dream ! " cried Jim.

" Those horses ! "

" Those johnnies on the box ! "

" And Tibi's always complained he's so poor ! "

" Perhaps he has no cash," answered Jim.

A noise in his room made him turn. He released Betty, and went into it. He came back in a few moments.

" Betty—this can't be real ! "

" Why ? "

" A lad's been and spread a rubber sheet on the floor, and two girls have arrived with enormous copper jugs filled with hot water—and what do you think ?—the water's scented ! "

A maid tapped on the door and at Betty's cry entered. She curtsied and smiled, a rosy-faced peasant girl in embroidered blouse and apron. She, too, carried a rubber sheet.

" That's for your performance—I'll vanish ! " said Jim, and hurried into his room, closing the door. He found a servant unpacking his bag, a sturdy, thick-fingered youth with a powerful brown neck, and a somewhat Mongolian face. His name, Jim discovered, was Béla.

Betty had half undressed before her eyes fell upon a letter for her, lying on the small table with the bowl of roses. She was so surprised to see the stamped letter that, for a moment or two, she stared at it. It was not from England. She examined the stamp. It came from Czechoslovakia. Who on earth could be writing to her from that country ? She did not know a single living soul in it. And how should anyone know she was staying here ? The handwriting, too, was strange.

She tore open the envelope. The heading on the blue note-paper was *Plecs, Mukačevo, Ruthenia*. Still puzzled, she rapidly turned over the letter and glanced at its signature. Her heart gave a leap, from shock and excitement. It was from Count Zarin. Trembling slightly, she turned over the letter and read it, slowly, for the heavy writing was difficult.

Dear Mrs. Brown,

> *It was charming of you to send me that letter of thanks. I have done so little, and hope yet to do so much more to make your visit to my country pleasant. Your letter has come to me here, my place in Czechoslovakia—once in Hungary, that is what the Treaty of Trianon did to us—where I have been for some days. I am very glad to learn that you are visiting Tiszatardos. Tibi is such a good host, and I hope the Puszta will put its spell over you. It may be I shall see you there, for I may call on my way back to Budapest on Tuesday, but if not, I shall await your return most eagerly. I have yet to show you Lake Balaton. My very kind regards to Mr. Brown, who, I hope, will be able to indulge his passion for riding.*

> > *Most sincerely yours,*
> > > *Károly Zarin.*

She read it through twice. Should she show it to Jim? There was no reason why she should not, it was a most polite and formal letter. But after a moment's hesitation she decided not to show it to him. She had written, quite properly, informing the Count they were leaving on a visit to Tibi's, and thanking him for his hospitality to them in Budapest. She had not told Jim because she felt he was a little antagonistic to Count Zarin.

There was a tap on her door. Hastily she tore up the letter. In response to her call, the maid entered and helped her to dress.

CHAPTER XVI

PUSZTA CAVALCADE

WHEN Betty and Jim went down into the hall they found two young folk there.

" How do you do ? " said a slim-legged girl of seventeen, with long, dark lashes and her blonde hair plaited in two pigtails. " I am Fritzi, Tibi's niece—and this is my brother Mihály."

Mihály bowed. " I kiss your hand," he said. He was slim and blond like his sister, with the same beautiful eyelashes and dark eyes. He was dressed in a polo jersey, black riding breeches and soft, green-leather top-boots. Betty thought she had never seen such a striking-looking pair anywhere. The boy was finely bred, with his expressive eyes, his sensuous mouth, his long hands and proud carriage. His sister had a fascinating, husky voice, and an air of challenging independence.

" How well you speak English," remarked Betty.

" French, English, German, Italian, Polish and Russian," said Mihály. " We've so many foreign relations we have to— or they'd cut us out of their wills ! "

" We've a powerful Scotch governess," said Fritzi.

" Powerful ? " laughed Jim.

Mihály did imaginary dumb-bell exercises.

" She's verra Scotch—and she nearly breaks our backs with her gymnastics. She's played hockey for England," said Mihály.

" Scotland ! " corrected Fritzi.

" England ! " repeated Mihály, firmly. " She wears a rose on her jumper, not a thistle."

Mihály and Fritzi asked them if they had seen the house. There was half an hour before dinner. They would show them over it quickly.

" We'll miss out the schoolroom—it's full of noise and children," said Fritzi.

" Children ? " repeated Betty. " But whose children ? "

" Ah, whose ? " cried Mihály. " There was an old woman who lived in a shoe, she'd so many children——"

" That was the first thing Mihály learned. He's frightfully proud of it," interrupted Fritzi.

" Shut up ! " said Mihály.

" I see you've had an English governess," observed Jim, laughing.

" There are five children—and us," went on Mihály. " Seven grandchildren in all, and we're a mixed lot. Two Poles, that's us, a German, that's Karl——"

" He's an Austrian—Uncle Fritz is an Austrian ! " corrected Fritzi, stoutly.

" No, he isn't, he's a German now—Austria doesn't exist ! "

" Well, he hates being a German, and says he never will be—and poor little Karl cries if you shout ' Heil Hitler ! ' at him," said Fritzi.

" It all sounds very confusing," commented Betty, as they walked down a corridor.

" Oh that's nothing—poor little Stanislas doesn't know what he is. Uncle János was Hungarian, born in Munkács, which is now in Czechoslovakia, so he's a Czech——"

" Don't you let him hear you say it," warned Fritzi.

" Well, he is anyhow, and poor little Stanislas, whose mother's a Pole, is really a Sub-Carpathian Ruthenian, for he was born in Ungvar."

" You mean Uzhorod," said Fritzi.

" Very well, Uzhorod—that's what the Czechs called it after they stole it," retorted Mihály.

" You make me feel a war may break out at any moment," laughed Jim.

" It may—and time, too ! " said Fritzi.

" You haven't got to fight in it ! " retorted Mihály.

" And this ? " asked Betty, as they entered a room.

" The library—where Uncle Tibi works—when he does work," said Fritzi. " Look—there's a lovely view."

They crossed to the windows. The sun was dropping behind the beechwoods. A line of mauve mountains caught the evening light They were the Hegyalja Mountains on whose slopes grew the famous Tokay wines, explained Mihály.

From the library they went into the drawing-room, where they found the Countess and Tibi, together with Mihály's mother and her husband, to whom they were introduced. They were Poles. The conversation at once became a mixture of Polish, Magyar and English. Further sightseeing was vetoed by Tibi.

" Dinner's ready—and we're all famishing," he said, opening the door for his mother.

The dining-room was a long, sparsely furnished room, with four French windows opening on to the terrace. At one end of the room, standing up around a separate table, there were five children, presided over by a grim-faced, solid lady in black, who could be none other than Miss Mac-Pherson, the gymnastic governess. During the dinner she kept hushing the hubbub that mounted around her. At the close of dinner, before their elders returned to the drawing-room, the children were presented to Jim and Betty. They could all prattle a little English.

Mihály's mother and Jim were soon on friendly terms. She talked excellent English and seemed to have read everything. Fortunately, Jim had read Hardy and Galsworthy. He felt very grateful now to Mr. Lincoln, of the Lads' Club, who had taught him to ride, and to read something better than Edgar Wallace. Jim looked across the room at Betty. She seemed completely at ease with the Countess, who was showing her a great collection of miniatures in a cabinet. Her fairy-tale was growing more wonderful every day. For himself, he was not quite happy. Through chance and Waddle they had been swept into this expensive Society world in which they could have no real part. Supposing some of them came to London ? He felt he was being placed in a false position. He had not wanted to come here, but Betty beat down all his misgivings. It was the chance of a lifetime, she declared.

II

The kindness of this household quite overwhelmed Betty and Jim. Mihály had found his hero. He was an Englishman to begin with. He could ride a horse superbly, he could box, he could swim and run. Jim became Mihály's unofficial tutor, and in return the boy followed him everywhere, admiration shining on his eager, young face.

" Were you at Eton ? " asked Mihály. " My father wanted to send me there, but Mother thought it was too far off. I wanted to go."

" No—I was at Craven Street," replied Jim.

" Cravenstreet ? I'm afraid I've not heard of that," said Mihály, as he stroked the muzzle of his horse.

" No—I don't expect you have," said Jim, repressing a desire to laugh. He could see now the thirty-six of them, jammed in the Pimlico class-room, with its factory-like windows, dyspeptic-faced master, and smell of half-washed, ill-clad bodies. " It's one of the more public schools," he added, feebly joking.

" Oh—you must be very proud of it," said Mihály, politely, oblivious of the irony.

Never had Jim seen such horses, had such mounts. His conscience oppressed him a little for leaving Betty so often to her own resources, but she scarcely noticed Jim's absence. Mihály's mother and the Countess were showing her the village life and the surrounding country. She was an enormous success with Mihály's father, who was the immediate slave of any pretty woman.

Early on Tuesday morning a small party of riders set off for the Puszta They were lunching at Hajdunanas, in the great plain, where their horses had been taken overnight. At five o'clock, when the wide-winged sunrise had already filled the earth and air with pearly light, they motored south, past great cherry orchards, then through meadows of ripening corn and leafy maize. The flat, uncultivated steppe now opened up as far as the eye could see, until the earth vanished in the horizon's curve. Never had Jim known such a sense of illimitable sky and space. The high clouds floated through a serene heaven. Below, the flat plain seemed to mirror the sky. It was too early yet for them to witness the Délibáb, or Fata Morgana, the mirage of water and shady trees that so often, in the hot season, tricked the shepherd and herdsman. But as noon grew on, as they rode their horses over the flat scrub, there was a shimmering of heat towards the horizon, and in the sky hung a mirage of tress, water and meadows. For a few minutes it lingered and then dissolved.

The party consisted of Mátány, Mihály, riding like a youth from the Parthenon frieze, with his blond hair blown back from his delicate, eager face, a neighbour's daughter, Jim, Mihály's father, and Fritzi, slim, firm-breasted, one with her mettlesome mount, and two *csikós*, the native horse herdsmen of the Puszta, with their lassos and thirty-foot leather whips. They rode their horses with girthless saddles, simple woven rugs, with stirrups attached thrown loosely over their mounts. They wore their *szûrs*. which kept them warm in winter and cool in summer, long cloaks of thick white felt, with large square collars, heavily ornamented with bright embroidery. They did not put their arms in the sleeves, these being sewn up at the ends and used as pockets. A round, feathered hat with chin strap, and leather top-boots, completed the attire of this magnificent pair.

Here and there on that boundless grassy plain they saw the only landmarks, the wells for watering horses and cattle. As in Biblical scenes, these were the meeting places of the lonely herdsmen. The wells themselves were primitive objects. Each had a tall pole. Across it, like the yard of a ship's mast, swung a beam with the bucket at one end, and a weight, to counterpoise it, tied to the other. The beam was swung, weight upwards, by pulling down the bucket cord, and when the bucket filled the counterpoise brought it up, full of water, to be emptied into the trough. Jim had seen these primitive wells in the centre of all the villages through which they passed.

All that morning, in the invigorating air, they watched the *csikós* manœuvring with their great herds of horses. They stampeded to the cracking of whips like pistol shots and the barking of dogs, a hundred horses at a time, with manes and tails flying in the wild rush. What poetry of motion and vigour the scene made, with the congested rush of brown bodies, thrust-out necks and hammering hooves, through the bright air! Jim envied these clear-eyed boys, with their open, bronzed faces, their superb health and unsurpassed horsemanship.

Later, in the *csárda*, the small inn where these horseboys forgathered, and where his party took a picnic lunch, Jim talked to one of them. As a boy he had migrated to Texas with his people, but when they died he came home again, a mere youth, to his relations. He remembered a little English. He took Jim outside to show him his special horse. He talked in a soft, gentle voice that matched his dreamy, blue eyes. Was he happy here, did he ever want to go back? Oh no, he answered, laughing and showing two even rows of white teeth. "This is a good life—except in winter." Jim offered him a cigarette. He took it delicately with his strong, brown fingers.

"*Lucky Strike?*" he asked, with dancing eyes.

"No," laughingly replied Jim. "English cigarette."

He made Jim feel his horse, running his hand lovingly over its glossy flank and down its strong fetlock.

"A beautiful horse, a beautiful girl—two great fortunes, eh?" he asked, smiling.

"I hope you've a beautiful girl also," answered Jim.

The young man grinned, with roguish eyes.

"Girls very short here in Puszta—perhaps better so," he answered. "Much trouble for boys, I guess."

Inside the *csárda*, where they rested during the heat of the noon, Tibi took Jim aside.

"I want you to look at that fellow by the door," he said.

Jim looked and saw a weather-hardened *csikós*, short in stature, leaning against a post as he smoked his long-stemmed pipe with a metal cap.

"That fellow killed his rival in a lasso duel," said Tibi.

"A lasso duel?"

"Yes. Some years ago they quarrelled over a girl, and challenged each other, *csikós*-fashion. They took their horses out on to the plain, there they circled round each other, waiting a chance for the fatal throw of the lasso. That fellow got it. A swift cast, a jerk, a gurgle, it was soon over. The other had loved and lost."

"But the law——" exclaimed Jim. "Surely——"

Tibi shrugged his shoulders.

"Not here in the Puszta—the primitive law holds here. No one interfered. It's *csikós* chivalry," he said. "Anyway, there he is looking peaceful enough, though perhaps he now wishes the lasso had gone round his own neck."

They left the inn in the early afternoon. There was a cloud of dust ahead. It came nearer. A great herd of long-horned cattle drew towards them, driven by horsemen. They were herded over a small bridge spanning a watercourse, magnificent oxen, wide-horned and strong, for use on the farms. Four *gulyás*, native cow herdsmen, kept them together. Next to the proud *csikós* were these *gulyás*, masters of the round-up, who controlled the stampedes and the gallops. Sometimes, stung by the virulent gad-fly, the herd went wild.

"Then you should see them go—and get out of the way!" said Tibi. Unlike the *csikós* they had long-handled whips.

In the late afternoon, as they rode northwards, the plain changed. Great flocks of sheep were grazing lazily, watched by the shepherd. One of them, looking like a sheep himself, in a fleecy sheepskin mantle, seemed to unroll himself as he stood up to watch the party ride by. He was wearing the *suba*, said Tibi, the best friend of the plain-dweller. He wrapped himself in it on bitter nights; it kept out the rain and the wind, and the heat in summer. There were more elaborate *subas*, reversed, with the yellow hide embellished with peacocks' feathers, tulips and roses, in cotton embroidery.

Nearer home they passed a clump of pines with a gipsy encampment. Half-naked boys ran out, and dark women in vivid coloured skirts, with babies sucking at their full breasts, watched the riders pass.

" Oh—I thought so ! " laughed Tibi.

He referred to three youths, handsome rapscallions, wearing only trousers, who scampered out, waving violins. The next moment, lithely dancing, they kept up with the horses, drawing a gay tune from their instruments.

" What is it ?—I hear it so often," asked Jim.

" That's the famous song of the Puszta—the *Debreczen Turkey Song*," said Tibi.

He motioned the tousled youth with the copper-hued torso to him, and ordered him to play it slower. The cavalcade halted.

" Sing it, Mihály," he said to his nephew.

The boy tossed back his blond hair, and in a pure, boyish voice, having set the key, sang it—

> " We will go to Debreczen Fair
> For we must buy a turkey there.
> Driver, pray, the road is jerky,
> Look out, or we shall lose our turkey ! "

The song finished, Tibi tossed the gipsies some coins, and they rode on.

" Just how big is this plain ? " asked Jim, looking across the immense grassy plain with only a few shepherds' huts in sight : they seemed to be riding in an uninhabited world.

" About three hundred square miles—but more and more is being put down to wheat and maize under modern cultivation," answered Tibi. " But they still keep a herd of fifty thousand cattle and forty thousand horses at Hortobágy. One day they'll drive motor-roads over the Puszta for tourists, and then good-bye to the Great Silence."

A pair of storks rose suddenly before them and flapped clumsily away. A flock of wild geese went over. The sun was rapidly falling towards the horizon. Shortly before seven, with the golden evening glowing over the vast, silent plain, they came to the small village where the cars awaited them for the journey home. They parted with their *csikós*.

" I kiss your hand," they said, gallantly, to the ladies, as, dismounted, they doffed their round felt hats with the arrogant sprig of the Hair of the Orphan Girl.

III

Jim had a shock on his arrival home. As he came out of the stable-yard and passed the great shed used for a garage he saw a familiar object, Zarin's Mercedes-Benz racing car. Tibi noticed it too.

" Why—if that isn't Károly's car ! How splendid ! " he exclaimed. " He must be on his way back from Plecs."

" From where ? " asked Jim, not at all pleased with this development.

" Plecs—that's his shooting place up in the Carpathians, near Mukačevo. It's in Ruthenia, which once belonged to us."

They gained the house. Yes, Count Zarin had arrived an hour ago. He was out somewhere in the grounds with the Countess and Mrs. Brown.

Jim went up to his room to have a bath, and change. He was tired after this glorious day on the Puszta. It was sad to think they had only two more days before their return to Budapest. Strange to believe, but in little more than a fortnight he would be back in London. How unreal that old life had become ! He looked at his brown hands. They were growing soft, and had lost their callosities from handling luggage and pushing trucks. Yet it would be a good thing to get back to reality. This soft life was no good for him, or Betty.

So Zarin was on the scene again ! It was odd the fellow should turn up here so suddenly. He had hoped they had got away from him. It was not jealousy but simply a dislike of the fuss he made over Betty. Her head was half-turned already by this mode of life, and Zarin's persistent and extravagant hospitality was contributing to the building of her impossible castles in the air. Well, soon they would be home to penny buses, and the morning milk on the step. He heard Betty come in as he was almost undressed. He opened their communicating door.

" Hello, darling ! " he cried, approaching to kiss her.

" Oh, go away—you smell sweaty," she said, irritably, pushing him off.

She gave him a quick glance, her face flushed.

" What's wrong ? " he asked, chided.

" Nothing—but I hate horsey-smelling men ! "

" Sorry—but I don't—— "

" You don't think you are horsey—but you are ! I'm thoroughly sick of your beastly horses. Horses ! Horses ! Horses ! You talk of nothing else. I could scream ! " she said.

" What do you want me to talk about—charming Counts ? " asked Jim, stung. He regretted the question the moment it was spoken, but it slipped out.

" On—I expected that ! I suppose you think I've sent for Károly ? "

" Károly ? "

" Count Zarin, then ! " snapped Betty.

" Betty, whatever's the matter with you ? " protested Jim.

" It's what's the matter with you," she retorted, with an ugly pouting of her mouth. " Why are you such a fool when I'm straining every nerve not to let these people know what we've escaped from ? It's not the men—I can manage them, it's these ferrety women. I heard Fritzi's mother pumping you at dinner last night. Why on earth must you tell her you've never been to Court ! It's nothing to boast of ! "

" Well, I haven't."

" Neither have I. But I wasn't going to let her know I'd never been presented, when she started asking if I didn't think our Courts were so impressively done. That was a feeler, and she got no change."

" If you're going to start lying about things, you'll get into a mess, my girl," said Jim, brusquely.

" There's no need to call me a liar," retorted Betty, her eyes flashing. " I only implied that I'd been presented. On the way here I heard you telling Tibi that you'd never had more than ten day's holiday."

" And what's wrong with that ? "

" Gentlemen don't have holidays—not a few fixed days like office workers," said Betty.

Jim paced up and down the room, while Betty began changing.

" Look here, my dear girl," he said, after a painful silence between them, " will you just explain what we are supposed to be after ? We meet Waddle, and then his fine friends, and before we know where we are, we're hobnobbing with Society people, foreigners at that, and staying in houses where, at home, we'd be going in by the kitchen entrance. What good can it all do ? They're very kind, and all that, but we don't live in their world, and I find it a strain watching my steps and my words."

" You've done splendidly—but for a few silly things," conceded Betty, feeling she had gone too far. She shook out her evening frock, a crimson muslin, cut low in the throat, with flounced half-sleeves.

" Maybe—but I'm not at my ease, I can tell you, and I hate the deceit," said Jim. " They're themselves, and we are only acting a part—and what for ? "

" Isn't this something worth having ? " demanded Betty, sweeping her hands over the room out to the flower-laden verandah with its vista of the lake and the swift sunset. " I've always belived that something would happen. We're here, in one of Hungary's best houses, and two months ago where were we—what were we doing ? "

" And in a month we shall be back again—in a confectionery business," retorted Jim, satirically.

" No, we shall not ! " said Betty, firmly.

" Oh, and what do you propose we should do ? "

" I don't know, but I do know something will happen. I was never destined for a sweetshop in a back street. I believe in my blood ! "

Jim stared at his wife. There were times when she said the most extraordinary things.

" You needn't stare, Jim. I'm not off my head. I know I was not destined to be choked down in a horrible street in Pimlico, among a lot of vulgar people. I married you because you were different—there's something about you——"

" I thought you married me because you loved me," interjected Jim.

" I did, and for something more. I felt you had it in you to rise up—a natural refinement. That's what your Mr. Lincoln at the Club felt—why he had you down at his country place, taught you to ride, took you to places. And you've got It."

" It ? "

" Appeal. The women are mad about you. I can see it in their eyes. Oh yes, you needn't look so surprised ! And the men like me, quite properly—that's why we're asked."

" You put it very crudely," said Jim. " We're floating on sex-appeal ? "

" There's no need to scoff at sex-appeal—it accounts for more in this world than brains, or mere money. It always has done, through history," said Betty.

" Well—I'd better go and change," said Jim, struggling to be natural despite a deep, inner confusion.

She raised her mouth for him to kiss. He did so, listlessly. She caught hold of him and kissed him, full-lipped, her hands holding his face.

" Don't be faint-hearted. I believe in my star, Jim. Something will happen. I know it ! " she declared.

He went into his room, where his hip bath awaited him and his dress clothes lay spread out on the bed. He looked at them, feeling they were the clothes of an actor, a very bad actor.

CHAPTER XVII

THE WEDDING FEAST

I

IT was the end of flaming June, and in the plain and up the hill-sides the scene was worthy of the adjective. The acres of cherry orchards were heavy with their ripe clusters. The peasant girls, barefooted, clad in loose, printed frocks, were busy shaking the laden branches until the cherries tumbled into the baskets. Lads, bare-throated and sunburnt, carried huge burdens of melons, paprikas, strawberries and red currants, loading them into the long four-wheeled spring-less carts that went bumping over the sandy tracks. Soon the rapidly ripening corn would be ready for cutting, and across the great waving plain a hundred scythes would sweep in line, while behind them, bootless, with their heads bound in vivid scarves, and red-skirted, the women would follow, binding and gleaning.

Later, would come the maize harvest, and the autumnal gathering of pears, peaches, apricots, apples and plums ; the pears for compotes, the black plums for preserve, the apricots for *barack* liqueur. Many of the apples would be kept for winter use, wizening on the great beams in the houses. The vineyards on the slopes, nurseries of the grapes that made the world-famous Tokay, already gave promise of a grand vintage. And it would be a splendid nut year, said Tibi, for the trees were heavy with almonds and walnuts.

But to-day no one laboured, except the horses harnessed to the long carts, filled with men, women and children riding to the wedding of the bailiff's daughter. They made a blaze of colour as they collected in the village, to await the bridal procession, which would come on foot. Already through the streets the friends of the bride had paraded, displaying the treasures of the wedding chest: fine-hemmed sheets; down-stuffed feather beds; and those gorgeously handworked pillows, the bride's work and present to her husband, not for the bed, but to be piled up in the parlour, admired by all.

The village buzzed with news. Two *tzigane* bands had been hired for the dancing in the yard. Eighty people were to sit down at the tables laid out in the shade of the orchard. In the evening there would be fireworks. Helpers had been working since dawn, drawing and carrying water from the village well, chopping and lighting wood to make the cauldrons boil in the farmhouse kitchen. The milking, the herding, the rubbing down of ponies, the killing and dressing of calves, pigs, geese and chickens had all been done before breakfast.

The village had to be dressed also. Festoons were hung from gable to gable, even the gates and railings of the yards in front of the cottages had been painted in green, yellow, red and blue to give them a festive air. Giant jars, filled with madonna lilies, spaced the route to the church. The cottage windows had a frame of crimson and green paprikas, hung in strings joined with yellow maize cobs. And to keep the dust from rising and smothering everybody, since so many hoofs and feet would stir up the dry mud, men had been busy pouring buckets and buckets of water on the road.

The party from the Mátánys did not attend the wedding, which was a peasant affair. They went to the evening festivities, having had an earlier dinner, and arrived about sundown at the courtyard behind the bailiff's house, where over a hundred guests were assembled. A pageant of moving colours greeted the eye as Matány's party entered the courtyard. The whole countryside was there in gala costume. There were women dressed in their billowing, starched petticoats, seven deep, and the colours of the rainbow. They had balloon sleeves, and tight flower-embroidered bodices, with vivid silk shawls binding their straight tresses.

The men, not to be outdone, wore coloured boots, immensely baggy linen trousers covered with heavily embroidered aprons. There were *csikós*, who had ridden in from the Puszta, with white lawn sleeves, short jackets, and

I

little hats with bunches of flowers or tall stiff feathers. Some of them wore white felt *szúrs*, falling to the ankles, a mass of coloured needlework over the wide collars and down the long lapels.

There were magnificent belts and girdles of wire-worked leather, or beaten metal, gorgeous silk shawls in the Magyar colours, and silk-embroidered ribbons, cherished from mother to daughter. Many of them wore boots of black, crimson or yellow leather, reaching to their knees, and short pleated skirts. The head-dresses, frilled with lace, piled up in row upon row of fine-coloured needlework, and were crowned with ropes of golden seeded pearls. Every girl seemed attired like an Oriental princess, every man might have stepped out of a ballet by Bakst.

Jim and Betty, gazing on this human kaleidoscope, had soon exhausted their adjectives of delight. At the long tables in the orchard the guests were still eating and drinking. There was much shouting and laughing and horseplay, but no one was drunk or unseemly. The bride sat under a cherry tree, a buxom, red-faced girl, with an elaborate head-dress. She had a little court of bridesmaids round her. The bridegroom, a hefty lad, swaggered in top-boots and gorgeous apron, his long white sleeves trailing. He threw them back over his wrists, and clapped for a couple dancing to a merry little tune on a shepherd's pipe.

The bride's father, seeing the new guests arrive, came down from a veranda, on which the older members of the family were sitting, to greet the Countess.

" I kiss your hand," he said, bowing low. Then he led her into the courtyard. Many of the guests caught at Tibi's hand and kissed it. There was nothing servile in the act ; it was a symbol of homage to the overlord. The company was presented to the bride. The Countess kissed her, the bridegroom came forward and made a little speech of welcome to the guests. The bailiff escorted them to some chairs under the trees.

The *tzigane* orchestra began to play again, sitting by the barn. The couples formed up for a dance.

"Now watch," said Tibi, his eyes sparkling. "A folk-dance of the district. The *Tekercs*. The tekercs itself is an embroidered ring-pad, like a doughnut, that the girls wear on their heads when carrying baskets in from the vintage. It gives its name to this dance."

Tibi selected a portly maiden and lined up for the dance. He was known to them all, and greeted with cries and smiles. The band began a lively air. Up and down went the dancers, skirts swirling, boots clumping.

Darkness began to fall. The little coloured lamps, hanging in the trees and over the doors and windows, were lit. About ten o'clock there was a sudden rush to the meadow. Against a background of chestnuts the fireworks began, each successive splendour, as it burst in the sky, being greeted with cheers. Then, after a grand finale, back they all went to the dancing in the courtyard.

Tibi was everywhere. He constituted himself a master of ceremonies, found partners for everyone, and primed the band. The dancing became more and more boisterous. There must have been a hundred people in that crowded courtyard. The Countess, led by the bailiff, a big-bellied fellow with a magnificent, fierce moustache, headed a processional dance. Then the orchestra struck up a new tune. The *Csárdás*!

"Come along!" cried Zarin, catching at Betty's hand.

"You must try it, Mister Brown!" cried Fritzi.

"Yes! Yes!" shouted Mihály, having seized a rosy country lass.

Fritzi caught Jim's hand. Into the throng he went. The dance began, solemn, stately at first, half a march, half a polka. The women rested their hands lightly on the men's shoulders. The men firmly held their partners by the waist. The *tempo* began to increase, the boots slithered over the sanded floor, there was a swift turn, and suddenly, as if a gust of wind had struck them, the dance changed to a furious gyration. The women's petticoats swelled out, revealed frilled knickers, bare knees, and white-clocked stockings. Faster and faster grew the music, faster and faster swirled the dancers. They swayed, they rolled, they raced, swirled giddily, boots thumping, breath shortening.

The *primás* in the band goaded on the players. Their flashing bows chased the notes up and down the strings, with weird variations and little quips of sound. A youth hammered on his cimbalom, sweat pouring down his face. The swarthy fiddlers tossed the fallen black hair out of their eyes. A groundswell of brown dust rose in the air.

Then, as quickly as it had begun, the frenzy ceased, the mood changed, it became slowly rhythmic, cautious and stately. A pause, and once again, in a storm of music the dance was galvanised into furious activity, mounting and mounting to a terrific crescendo. There was a fierce, piercing cry of the violins, and the dance ended. The breathless, perspiring dancers stood laughing at each other.

Completely exhausted by his efforts, Jim let Fritzi lead him to a chair. He saw Tibi panting, and wiping his brow with a handkerchief. Betty, hanging on Zarin's arm, was crimson with exertion. The company went towards the tables. The drinking began again. The full moon came up above the chestnut woods. The coloured lanterns flickered. It was carnival in June.

At midnight there was no sign of slackening in the activity of the guests. The dancing went on, as fast and furious as ever. Fresh cooked meats appeared on the table. An ox had been roasted over an open fire, and was served piecemeal on long skewers, dusted with powdered chestnuts. Rows of chickens, on wooden spits, were cooked over charcoal fires on the ground. There was an endless supply of all manner of sweets, almond, vanilla, paprika and chocolate. The wine flowed in rivers.

There were now some solo dances, and various Hungarian dances, performed singly, or by couples and quartettes, dances in which the performers leapt, spun, clicked heels and clapped hands, the rhythm being taken up by the audience which also clapped and stamped. Then came an astonishing solo from young Mihály, his blond hair flopping on his neat head, his lithe figure making terrific leaps. It had a Russian character, it seemed to Jim and Betty, particularly when he went down on to his knees, shooting out his feet. It finished at a terrific *tempo*.

After a time Jim became aware that he had not seen Betty for some time. He looked among the crowd of guests, but could not find her. In that lanterned darkness, it was amost impossible to distinguish individuals. He asked Tibi, whom he encountered, and Mihály. No, they had not seen Betty.

"She's dancing—or under the trees. I saw her dancing the *csárdás* with Károly, and in fine style!" said Fritzi. "Dance this with me, Mr. Brown—I'll show you!"

He entered the rout. The assembly was getting noisy. No one was drunk, but the wine was now having effect. The young men began to manhandle the girls, who cried in delight. Couples were going out into the darkness of the orchard. It was there that Fritzi led him after their dance. Under one of the trees she suddenly flung her arms around Jim's neck and kissed him. Her hair was intoxicating, her young body stirred in his arms, maddeningly alive. He kissed her in turn.

"Oh, I love you!" sighed Fritzi.

Jim pulled himself together. The place went to one's head.

"Don't be silly—you're only a schoolgirl," he said, pulling her arms away from his neck.

But she clung to him, her face upturned and dappled with moonlight through the branches.

"I love you! I love you!" she repeated passionately, her eyes closed, nestling her face against his.

He looked at her, the long lashes, the wet, red mouth, the fresh, sweet flesh of girlhood's beauty, amid this enchantment of distant music, laughter, moonlight and the black network of boughs for a canopy, and his restraint broke down. He kissed her passionately, their lips sealed in wordless ecstasy. They stood thus, locked in each other's arms for long moments in which they felt the beating of their hearts. Then, abruptly, Jim flung back his head and looked at her.

"Fritzi, we're crazy," he said, kindly. "You're only a kid—and I'm a married man. Come along now!"

He began to pull her along, but an expression of ecstasy still lit her face.

"I love you, I love you! And nothing matters!" she cried.

"Oh, doesn't it!" laughed Jim. "It's time you went to bed, and I put my head in a bucket of water!"

"You are so beautiful, so——" went on Fritzi.

"Now be quiet—you'll get over it," he said, brutally. "It's a good thing I'm off to-morrow."

"No—no—no! I shall follow you!"

"Good Lord!" laughed Jim. "So that's Polish love!"

She stopped suddenly, her eyes flashing, her body shaking with passion. He thought she was going to strike him. In that moment her young loveliness was even more stirring.

"I tell you—I tell you——" she began, and then, her words failing, she burst into tears.

He pulled her into the shadow of the trees again, embarrassed, afraid that they might be seen.

"Fritzi, my poor little kid," he said, "you mustn't get it like this! I leave here to-morrow, I shall go back to England. I'm married, on my honeymoon, with a girl I love. Fritzi, my dear——"

"I love you, I love you, beautiful, beautiful Jim," she repeated, choking with tears. They streamed down her face.

He pulled out a handkerchief and began to wipe them away. She gazed at him, miserably, shaken by her sobs.

"Now, now," said Jim, soothingly. "We're going back, and you're going to smile and be good."

"Yes—yes," she replied, tearfully.

"That's right!"

"Please—please—I kiss you, for Good-bye," she said, gravely.

"For Good-bye," said Jim.

They kissed each other, solemnly, in silence. Then he led her back towards the crowd of guests.

Mihály came up to Jim soon after he had rejoined the dancers.

" You've lost Mrs. Brown—Károly's run off with her in a trotting-car," he said, laughing.

" In a what ? "

" A trotting-car—he's taken her off for a drive. She's brave, he drives like the wind ! Let's hope they don't have a spill."

The expression on Jim's face made him regret the last remark.

" Oh—she'll be all right, he's one of the best drivers in Hungary," he added, reassuringly.

Half an hour later, Betty had returned, only just in time. The Countess was collecting her party for the return home. It was nearly one o'clock. Jim said nothing about her adventure until they got back to the house, and were going to bed.

" I hope you weren't nervous ? " she asked.

" Well—just a little. You were so long coming back," answered Jim.

" I wouldn't have missed it for anything ! " cried Betty, ecstatically.

Jim thought he detected a forced gaiety in her voice. She talked vivaciously all the way upstairs, telling him about the wonderful roan ponies, the speed of the trotting-car, the long grey avenues through the moonlit woods.

" You've got some dirt on your frock," said Jim, as she stood unpinning her hair. It was covered with short pine bristles, which he proceeded to brush off her.

" The ponies threw up a lot of dirt," answered Betty, shaking her frock.

He stopped and then started, as if he had run his hand on a pin. But she did not notice and he made no comment as he patted her frock. Her satin shoes were wet and stained with grass and earth. She must have walked in the woods. The back of her frock was covered with pine needles also. Obviously she had got out of the trotting-car. She had walked through long grass and sat down in the woods. It was foolish of him to feel perturbed. Why shouldn't she walk in the woods with Zarin? But the knowledge of it worried him, and he felt guilty himself.

For a long time he lay awake, a little demon probing him. A vague fear began to possess him. They must get out of all this. It was a false world for them to live in.

II

The radiant morning flooded in through the windows when Béla, answering the bell, came and drew back the embroidered curtains. Jim entered his wife's room. She was already awake, trying to converse with the smiling maid, who was preparing her bath behind a Japanese screen. Jim, in his blue and white pyjamas, squatted on Betty's bed. The worries of last night had all evaporated. She looked so lovely, with her loose hair tumbled about her shoulders, that he buried his face in it, and gave her pink ear a playful bite."

" Go away, Jim—the maid'll be in again."

" Well, I'm your husband—as well as your lover."

" Silly boy ! "

He laughed. There was a discreet tap on the door from the maid. He jumped off the bed.

" Bye-bye—I'm going to do my canary stunt in the tin saucer," he said.

But back in his room he went to the window and looked over the veranda, beyond the lawns and the lake, sparkling in the sunshine. The world was a lovely place to-day. He felt sad at leaving.

Footsteps on the terrace made him peer over the parapet. It was the Countess Mátány, walking with her grandson, the Borzoi dogs springing around them. Young Mihály was vivaciously describing something. He was rather like a stork, with his long, slim legs encased in crimson riding-boots. His grandmother laughed with him. If Mihály was a stork, then she was a swan, moving with such proud grace.

Jim withdrew, slipped out of his pyjamas and stepped into the " tin saucer." Béla, standing by with a jug of water, looked admiringly at him.

" Sport ? " he said, grinning, and pointing to Jim's muscular chest and shoulders. " The box ? "

" Yes—box ! " replied Jim, striking a sparring attitude.

Béla grinned, his Mongolian eyes almost disappearing in their deep sockets.

" England—sport ! " he exclaimed, delighted at his progress in English.

" Water," commanded Jim, stooping.

Béla poured the jug of warm water over him. It was about as messy a business, reflected Jim, as his ablutions at the sink at home, without a valet assisting. But here the water was scented.

III

Zarin was the first to leave, and then, about ten o'clock, Béla piled up their bags on the grid of Tibi's car. They took their farewell of the Countess.

" You will come again, I hope," she said, smiling.

" Thank you—we should love to," replied Jim.

But he knew he would never come again, never see this beautiful house, ride these lovely horses under the great dome of a sky piled with shining clouds. It was good-bye for ever, but the memory of it all would be imperishable.

" We hope to come next year," said Betty, gaily. " We love Hungary so, we'll never be able to keep away ! "

There was one missing from the farewell group in the portico.

" I can't think where Fritzi can be ! " complained her mother.

" She's been missing since breakfast," said Miss MacPherson. " She's nowhere in the house."

" What awful manners !—I apologise for my sister," cried Mihály. " But she's odd that way."

They all laughed. But Jim knew.

" I can't think why you ever want to go away from here," said Jim to Tibi, as they went down the beech avenue, after a last glance back at the long white house.

" It's not what you have, it's what you want that keeps you going," replied Tibi, at the wheel. " Fresh faces, fresh scenes, and the lure of the horizon. When you've been living——"

He broke off and pointed towards the wide flat meadow stretching between the woods and the river. A figure on horseback was riding madly towards them.

" That's Fritzi ! " he said. " She's coming to say good-bye."

She crossed the meadow at an angle, riding splendidly, intercepting them on their track. She was flushed and hatless, and leapt down from her magnificent mount. Slim, in her riding breeches and boots, her blonde hair frayed by the wind, she made a lovely picture of youth in that bright morning scene. She mounted her horse again as they parted, and waved until they were out of sight.

" What a charming girl ! " commented Betty.

" Yes—but she's like a wild colt. I've an idea something's upset her—I thought she'd been crying. I wonder ! "

But Jim did not wonder. He made no reply. His heart felt heavy for that poor girl riding back to the house.

They came to the banks of the Tisza and crossed the winding river. Southwards the plain glimmered flat and immeasurable under the brilliant sky. Not a human being was in sight. The world lay virgin before them in the growing heat of that June morning. Only the purr of the car, with its following cloud of dust, broke the complete tranquillity of the scene.

CHAPTER XVIII

BELGRADE INTERVAL

I

SOON after they had arrived back at the Pension Balaton Waddle came in to greet them. He was very excited and exhausted. The Congress had ended in triumph. He wanted them to dine on the terrace of the Ritz with him, to celebrate the end of his labours. He had asked Tibi to join them. "And be damned to the expense," he said, recklessly. So after they had changed, they went with Waddle, and sat on the terrace overlooking the Corso. Tibi had not arrived. Waddle ordered cocktails.

"Oh, what a relief!" he exclaimed, removing his hat and wiping his brow. "I saw the last of the delegates off at the station an hour ago. So that's over! But it's been a great success. Not a hitch, not a quarrel, and seventeen nationalities! There's a real League of Nations, not a highbrow, mischievous thing like that ramp at Geneva, where they talk such pompous nonsense about peace and goodwill. Make 'em dance, and then they've no breath for such twaddle."

"I suggest a slogan—Waddle not Twaddle," laughed Jim.

"Ah—here's Tibi. Now I want to hear all about your visit to Tiszatardos."

As they talked the light began to fail. Waddle surveyed the terrace with its crowded small tables, its low parapet with boxes of geraniums and petunias, the leafy Corso with its promenaders, the river, the palace-crowned hill.

"Just look at all that! I don't know how I'm going to tear myself away next week. I've to go to Munich," he said. "I've never known anyone who didn't lament leaving here."

" That's exactly how I feel—I never want to go," agreed Betty.

" If you took all this away," said Waddle, " there'd still be the people holding you. I only pray it'll go on."

" Go on ? " echoed Jim. " What do you mean ? "

Waddle gave a sigh and looked across the river.

" There's a man sitting over there, the Regent, up in that Palace, who must be feeling worried. Germany's swallowed up Austria. Now she's on her road to the East. And Nazi propaganda's busy with the peasants here ; they'll perhaps not be wise enough to know that National Socialism is Bolshevism in a brown shirt."

" It's begun already," said Tibi. " You perhaps thought we all looked very peaceful at Tiszatardos. But we've some young men infected with the Nazi virus, stirring up the village. You see, they've plenty of grievances to work on. There's a ferment all over Middle Europe. So stay and enjoy Budapest before it gets bitten with the bug."

The Palace on the hill grew blacker, the lights began to flicker coldly along the terraces of Buda, then the tower of the Fishers' Bastion, the slender spires of the Coronation Church above, and ramparts of the high Citadel were picked out by flood-lighting. At the *Hungaria*, next door, the band struck up an air that had haunted Betty since she had heard it that first evening in *The Green Cockatoo*.

" What is it they are playing ? " she asked, interrupting their political talk, which bored her.

" Ah—that ! " exclaimed Tibi, listening. " It's *The Dog Song*—all the rage this season."

He sang it softly to the plaintive, despairing accompaniment.

> " Gyerünk Bodri, kutyám,
>   Szedd a sátorfádat,
>   Megcsaltak bennünket,
>   Kövesd a gazdádat."

" It is the song of a man who had lost everything, the woman he loved, his money, his friends—so he took to the road, with only his faithful dog.   That's why it's called *The Dog Song*."

" Oh, so that's what you men think of us—we haven't the faithfulness of a dog ! "

They all laughed.   It was time to dine.   They moved across to a table and Waddle ordered dinner.

II

Betty was the first to wake the next morning.   She looked at her wrist-watch, Gollwitzer's diamond gift, and saw it was half-past eight.   She got up and drew the blinds.   It was a radiant morning.   All Buda lay shining on the hillside.

Jim was fast asleep.   His pyjama jacket was unbuttoned, showing his brown throat and chest.   Crossing to his bed, she leaned over, twisting one of his curls.   His eyes opened and looked into her face, dreamily.   Then his lips parted in a smile.   He pulled her down on him and kissed her.

" Morning, darling," she said.

" Darling," he answered, drowsily, holding her closer.

" No—we must get up, Jim.   It's half-past eight."

He did not answer but lay happily, holding her to his chest, one hand stroking her.

" Darling, we must get up—it's a quarter to nine," said Betty.

" You said half-past eight."

" That was a quarter of an hour ago.   Jim, let me get up."

" This is nice," he said, dreamily.

" If you don't get up——"

" Well ? "

She bit his shoulder, leaving a red mark.

" Have another bite," he said, laughing, and released her. She went into the bathroom.   He heard the water running in the bath, and then her splashing in it.   He got up and went in to shave.   She looked like a naiad, a piebald naiad, soft limbs golden brown, with white patches where the costume had covered her. He slipped off his jacket, and pulled at the tape of his pyjamas. The next moment he was in the bath. The water spilled over.

" Jim, there isn't room ! " protested Betty.

" That's the idea ! "

" Brute ! " she said, struggling up.

He caught at her legs to pull her down, but her soft, wet flesh slipped through his hands. She was out with a scream.

" That's the way to treat your women ! " he cried.

But the next moment she had seized his hair from behind and pushed him under. She escaped with a cry of triumph.

Suddenly there was a knocking on the door.

" Yes ? " called Betty.

" Please, I come to speak to you. Very quickly," said a voice.

Betty opened the small trap. Madame Balaton's face peered in, but a face Betty had never seen before. It was white and haggard. Her eyes looked frightened.

" If you please, I want to speak to Mr. Brown."

" But he's in his bath," protested Betty, herself still clad in a dressing-gown.

" Oh, if you please, I want to speak to him at once. It cannot wait. No ! I am in great trouble ! "

" Whatever's all that ? " cried Jim, standing up in his bath.

" Madame Balaton wants to see you—I tell her you can't see——" began Betty.

" My husband—he's gone ! " wailed Madame Balaton, through the trap. " He's left me—early I think ! "

" Good Lord ! Ask her in ! " exclaimed Jim. " Close that door."

Betty closed the bathroom door. Jim reached for a towel, and dried himself. He could hear the two women's voices. Evidently Madame Balaton was in a state of excitement. So Bowling had bolted. The worm had turned.

Clad in his dressing-gown, Jim emerged from the bathroom. Madame Balaton, an amorphous mass instead of the stately dame who had overawed him, sat pitiably on a chair, dabbing her face with a handkerchief.

She gave a pathetic bleat at the sight of Jim, wringing her fat, heavily jewelled hands.

"Oh, Mr. Brown, Mr. Brown, I am unhappy! You know my husband—I come to you, you know him. You are a good friend for him. He speaks of you often."

"Yes, yes," said Jim, impatiently. "What's the matter?"

"He has gone! He's left me! It is so cruel. I love him. I love Percy! Why does he leave me, Mr. Brown!" moaned Madame Balaton, swaying from side to side.

"How do you know he's left you?" asked Betty.

Madame Balaton dabbed her eyes with a little silk handkerchief. Then, out of the palm of one fat hand she produced a crumpled piece of paper.

"You see what he says?" she cried, passing it to Jim.

Jim smoothed out the piece of paper.

"He goes quietly—I do not know. He pins it to my—what you say——"

Either she could not translate the Magyar word, or it seemed too indelicate. She pointed to what must have been some lower garment.

"I sleep heavily—he sleeps weak. I don't hear him. I wake, and he's not there," went on Madame Balaton, between sobs. "And I love him! I love Percy. Why does he go, *mein Leiber!*"

Jim read the crumpled piece of paper. Percy Bowling was not a very good writer. He had smudged the ink also.

Dear Mimi,

I can't stand this any longer. Don't worry; I shan't. Good-bye.

Percy.

"Well, what do you want me to do?" asked Jim, after he had read the note.

"You are a good friend—he will come back with you!" said Madame Balaton, tearfully.

"I'm not so sure. I scarcely know him."

"He likes you. Always he talks of you. He'll come back for you," persisted Madame Balaton.

" But do you know where he is—perhaps he's gone to England," said Betty. " Really, there's nothing my husband can do ! "

" Yes, yes ! He can ! He'll bring back Percy. Please, I know ! "

" But we don't know where he is ! " declared Jim.

" I know—he's gone to Athens."

" Athens ! "

" Always he talks of Athens."

" But how do you know ? " asked Jim. " That doesn't prove anything. He may even be here still ! "

" No ! " said Madame Balaton, decisively. " Why does he leave early—before seven ; why does he take thin clothes, and boots ? Yesterday I found a drachma piece on the floor —he has Greek money in readiness ! I know he's off to Athens—this morning. It goes 7.15."

" But even supposing he has gone to Athens—you surely don't expect me to go to Athens after him ? " protested Jim, to the tear-raddled face before him. " And let me be frank. You've driven him to this—no wonder he's bolted, dressing him up in an apron like a slavey, and making the poor devil run up and down with breakfast trays while you gallivant around ! You've married him, and yet you won't call your-self Mrs. Bowling ! "

" That's because of business—my *pension*," sobbed Madame Balaton.

" Well, you could still call yourself Mrs. Bowling. You've hurt the chap's feelings. You've collared his money——"

" Collared—what is that you say ? "

" He means you've taken his money," explained Betty.

" *Ach nein !* I have not taken it for myself. It is for him—it makes more money for him," protested Madame Balaton.

" Well, he doesn't get any of it. He complained to me about it," said Jim.

" He kept some, I know. How else does he go away ? " asked Madame Balaton.

" Then he's a wise lad," retorted Jim.

Madame Balaton rose, her eyes streaming, and turned to Betty.

" You are happy wife. You love your husband as I love mine. You will help me, please ! Mr. Brown, he will go for me ? I have a plan. I'll give Percy all his money back, I'll be Mrs. Bowling, I'll call this the Pension Bowling, if he'll come back. I pay all it costs for you to go. Please ! "

" My husband can't go to Athens ! " interrupted Betty.

" No, I did not mean to Athens. Mr. Brown flies now to Belgrade. He sees the train, with my husband in it, and takes him from it, and brings him home. Yes ? Oh, please ! "

" Impossible ! " said Betty, firmly.

" Now what's this—let's have all this over again," asked Jim. He felt sorry for Madame Bowling. There must be, somewhere in that fat, agitated heart, a real love for little Bowling despite her ill usage of him.

Madame Balaton explained all over again, with detail, what she hoped he would do. The Athens train, on which she was certain her husband had left that morning at 7.15, arrived in Belgrade at six o'clock in the evening. There was an aeroplane service to Belgrade, leaving Budapest at 10.45, and arriving soon after noon. He could, by leaving at once, be well in advance of Bowling at Belgrade, meet the train, and persuade him to leave it. They could return the next day by train, for Bowling was too afraid to fly. Madame Bowling had the plan clearly worked out. She produced a five-hundred pengo note. There were nearly two hours before the plane left.

" But why don't you go ? " asked Jim.

" No, no ! He'd not come for me, he'll come for you. You talk to him, he listens. I know ! Please ! " wailed Madame Balaton.

" The whole thing's quite ridiculous ! " said Betty.

" That's what tickles my fancy. Come on, Betty, we'll go ! " cried Jim.

" Oh, thank you, thank you ! " exclaimed Madame Balaton.

" I wouldn't dream of it ! It's too absurd," said Betty, firmly. " We would like our breakfast, Madame Balaton."

Within half an hour a car had deposited him at an hotel in a wide street, with trams and taxis, and a crowd lining the pavement. There was a procession of some kind. He heard the sound of distant music, and then saw a cavalry detachment riding down the street. A revolution ?

" There's been a review. The King is going back to the Palace," explained the head porter. " Stand here, m'sieur, and you will see him."

The horsemen came down the street, a glittering cavalcade passed. Then, alone, at the head of another detachment, rode a solemn-faced boy who saluted the cheering people. Suddenly, Jim knew who this young King was. It seemed only yesterday that a timid, small boy had left Victoria Station, returning home after the assassination of his father. Jim remembered that scene vividly, for he had searched hurriedly through a pile in the luggage van for a rabbit in a box, at the behest of an agitated governess. She had given him half a crown, beseeching him to find a lettuce, of all things, for the rabbit on its long journey. He had found it just in the nick of time. He remembered the little Prince's anxious face at the window, and the glad smile that broke over it when the governess came up with the rabbit and the lettuce. Then the whistle blew, and the Prince solemnly bowed to the bigwigs on the platform as the train drew out. Prince " Sixpenny " they had called him at school in England.

And now here he was, a boy-King, riding with his troops. Jim cheered with the crowd, and felt his eyes grow misty. All very silly, but it brought a lump into his throat to see that small boy riding by.

How odd life was ! Here was he, the railway porter, come to fetch a runaway husband from Belgrade, and cheering a boy-King for whom he had once found a rabbit and a lettuce !

He lunched at a pleasant open-air restaurant overlooking a park, and then set out to view the magnificently situated city. It had seen more battles under its walls than most fortresses in Europe, for it had been ravaged and possessed by Romans, Huns, Franks, Bulgarians, Greeks, Hungarians,

Turks and Austrians, and it was here that the Great War had begun with a bombardment by the Austrians in that fatal July of 1914.

But as Jim walked its streets now, and wandered through its beautiful gardens, and along the promenade with its river panorama, the old capital was peaceful enough. He had four hours before he went to search the Athens-bound train for a runaway husband, and the time passed on winged hours.

The Serbian language presented difficulties, but he derived more amusement than discomfort from his efforts to make his wishes known. And here, as elsewhere, he discovered that there was always some native returned from the United States, who was glad to practise his somewhat singular, and often unintelligible, English. But with smiles and pantomime Jim contrived to make himself understood.

At a quarter to six he arrived at the station in readiness for the arrival of the train from Budapest. It had taken over ten hours to make the trip he had accomplished by air in an hour and a half. The train arrived punctually, and as Jim walked down the platform he wondered what the chances were of finding Bowling. There was no positive proof that he had taken the train, but Madame Balaton had an unshakable conviction that he had left Budapest early that morning, and that Athens was his destination.

The train stopped, the doors opened and the passengers stepped down, some having completed their journey, some desirous of stretching their legs. It was not the chief Athens-bound express, and there was half an hour before it proceeded on its journey. It gave Jim time to search the train, if necessary.

He was wondering whether he should allow the passengers to leave the platform before he began his search, which he now began to think was futile, as Betty had insisted, when his disbelief was wholly shattered by the sight of little Bowling, carrying two bags, coming towards him. His light felt hat was well down over his head, a cigarette was between his lips, and he did not see Jim until he heard his name called. He gave a start, and turned apprehensively.

" You! You! " he repeated, stunned by the sight of Jim.

" Yes—surprised to see me ? " laughed Jim.

" But what are you—why—how did you get here ? " stammered Bowling, in his confusion.

" I flew here, this morning."

" Flew! But—but——"

His speech failed him, the cigarette slanted down, sticking to his fallen lip as he stared at Jim.

" I've come to fetch you back," said Jim. " Here, give me one of your bags."

He took a bag from Bowling's nerveless hand.

" So you were going to stay here ? " asked Jim, as they walked to the barrier.

" For a night—I want to see the place," answered Bowling.

" It's a fine place," commented Jim.

As they came to the ticket barrier, Bowling stopped and put down his bag.

" Look here, I want to get this clear. Did she send you ? " he asked.

" Yes—naturally, she's in a great state," answered Jim. " As soon as she'd found you'd bolted she came and implored me to fetch you back."

" But how did you know I was on this train ? I might have gone anywhere. How did you know that ? I didn't tell her, and I didn't give her time to find out ! " exclaimed Bowling, a frightened expression on his face.

" She seemed to know you were making for Athens— you dropped some Greek money on the floor. You seem to have talked about Athens a lot. She was certain you were going there, and that you'd caught the first train."

" That woman—she's a witch," complained Bowling, putting down his bag again to take off his hat and wipe his brow. He felt for his ticket. " But make no mistake— I'm not going back. I've had enough ! "

" Well, we'll talk about that later," said Jim, as he picked up Bowling's bags and led him through the barrier.

Jim had no idea little Bowling could be so obstinate. All that evening, before dinner and after dinner, he argued with him

"Why, man, you've married her; you can't run off like that. She really is fond of you. You've hit her hard, so hard I feel sorry for the poor woman. She'll do anything you want. She'll call herself Mrs. Bowling, she'll call it the Pension Bowling, she'll give you control of your money, and let you run the place. There's no doubt about it," said Jim, "the woman's madly in love with you."

"If I could believe it," replied Bowling, twisting a cigar he was smoking, as they sat at a café on the pavement.

"You can believe it, all right. She went to pieces when she'd found you had gone," emphasised Jim. "Now tell me, where did you get the money to bolt with?"

Bowling gave a sly smile, and puffed at his cigar before replying.

"Oh, I'm not such a fool," he said, after a pause. "When I took a share in her business I only told her half of what I've got. She'd have cooked my goose completely if she'd had the lot. I may be soft in spots, but——" He puffed again, and preened himself. "So you think she loves me, eh?" he asked.

"For some extraordinary reason, yes," answered Jim. Betty was right, the man was a worm. It was possible he would end by bullying his wife, if she was fool enough to let him see she was in love with him.

"Well, then I'll go back, on the clear understanding I wear the trousers—and without an apron," he added, with a chuckle. "So she'll call it the Pension Bowling, eh? That just shows you, you've got to be firm with women!"

"And not run away from them," commented Jim, unable to resist the retort.

A clock struck eleven. The brightly-lit thoroughfare was crowded with people and all the cafés were full, with their orchestras playing gaily.

"No one seems to go to bed here. Shall we take a

stroll ? " asked Jim. " How are we going back to Budapest, by train or plane ? "

" Oh, I don't want to fly; I don't like it, and it's expensive," answered Bowling.

" Then we'll go by train in the morning. There's one at
eleven-thirty, getting in at nine at night. I'll send a wire
to my wife," said Jim.

They rose, paid the waiter, and left the café.

" You know, all my life I've wanted to travel, and to
see Athens, and now I don't suppose I ever shall," said
Bowling, plaintively.

Jim looked down at the little man perspiring at his side.

" Oh, you may if you take Mrs. Bowling with you," he
replied, satirically.

CHAPTER XIX

LAKE BALATON

I

BETTY was awakened at eight o'clock by someone tapping
on her door. She got up and opened the trap. Madame
Balaton stood there, very agitated, holding an envelope in
her hand.

" There is a telegram for you ! " she said.

" Do come in," said Betty, opening the door.

Madame Balaton stepped in, and waited breathlessly,
while Betty tore open the envelope.

Arrive nine to-night with Bowling.   Jim, she read.

She gave the telegram to Madame Balaton, who took it
with a shaking hand and read it. Then, with tears welling
in her eyes, " How shall I thank you, how shall I thank

you ! " she cried, and, putting her arms around Betty, kissed her. " Your husband, he is a kind, wonderful man. I knew he would bring back my Percy. Oh, oh, how I am happy ! "

She read the telegram again, and placed it to her lips, the tears streaming down her round face.

" I'll go to meet them. I'll give them a welcome," cried Madame Balaton.

" We'll go together," cried Betty, moved by the Hungarian woman's emotion.

" Yes—yes—we'll go together ! " echoed Madame Balaton.

" I shall be out all day—but I'll be back at half-past eight," said Betty.

" Yes, yes," answered Madame Balaton. Still exclaiming, she left the room, her face radiant.

Betty began to dress, but first she looked out of the window, down over the city. It was a perfect day. At eleven o'clock Count Zarin was fetching her to spend the day at Lake Balaton, where he had a sailing-boat. He had rung up yesterday suggesting the trip, for which he would make a party, on the morrow, and expressed his disappointment when Betty said her husband was away for two days.

" Ah—that is too sad. I wanted to show you Lake Balaton," he said.

" I want to see Lake Balaton. There's no reason why I shouldn't come—Jim won't be back until late," answered Betty. " I've nothing to do."

" Then, of course ! How delightful ! If I call for you, to-morrow at eleven ? " asked Zarin.

" At eleven," answered Betty.

Punctually at eleven o'clock the red Mercedes-Benz drew up at the Pension Balaton, the Count driving. Zarin found Betty awaiting him, dressed in a white frock with a small blue and white straw hat, with little silk streamers. He thought he had never seen her look daintier, with her dark eyes, red mouth and exquisite complexion. She wore red shoes and red gauntlet gloves, and a blue-spotted, sleeveless blouse, laced at her throat with white cord and red tassels.

He kissed her hand and placed her in the car. They both had an air of suppressed excitement.

"What a perfect day," he said, gaily.

"Perfect." she echoed.

"I thought we wouldn't trouble with a party—I can show you so much more. We can sail, and lunch at Balatonfüred I hope you will like that ? " he asked

"Oh yes, thank you," she answered, trying to appear calm It would be better now to say nothing to Jim of this excursion. She would be back before his return. His ridiculous suspicion of Zarin might provoke a scene.

The powerful car rumbled through the streets out to the Balaton highway. The houses began to thin out, then the villas vanished The rocky outcrops shone boldly in the fierce light as they roared upwards through the wide cuttings They came out on to a high plateau, with the undulating landscape fading into the horizon under the brilliant sky. The light became so fierce that Betty put on her sunglasses. There were a few farms scattered across the plateau. In the distance rose bluish-purple peaks. The concrete road, wide and straight, lay like a ribbon, rising and falling across the land.

Zarin put his foot down on the accelerator. The great car leapt forward, the pointer on the speedometer moved round the dial. Eighty, one hundred, one hundred and twenty, one hundred and fifty kilometres, and still they gained speed The wind sang a heat mirage danced on the road. They roared past yoked oxen pulling a heavy cart.

"One hundred miles ! " shouted Zarin.

Betty's radiant face turned to him. He liked her for showing no fear.

"Look ! " he said. pointing ahead.

The road fell below them through the hills. Afar there was a long sheet of silver-blue water, lost in a heat haze in the distance.

"Balaton!" he cried. "We'll be at Siófok in twenty minutes."

They roared on. The soft air whipped their faces. The immense dome of heaven, cloudless and azure to its depth, spanned the treeless, smiling earth. They ran into Siófok, villa-dotted along the flat shore, spaced with bathing huts, and wooden jetties. Men, women and children, mahogany-brown, strolled about in bathing costumes, or sat reading and sewing under coloured umbrellas.

Zarin pulled up at a small hotel, where he left his car. His sailing-boat, with a green hull, and white sail, lay ready for him at the jetty. He looked at a mast where a flag flapped idly. There was very little wind, but it was blowing in the right direction, from the south-east across the lake. They could see the far shore, with the purple hills rising hazily in the noonday heat. It was half-past twelve.

"We shall reach the Club House just in time for lunch," he said, helping Betty into his boat. He showed her where to sit, and, after raising the sail, went to the tiller, and headed out into the lake. The calm expanse of blue water was dotted with white sails. The villa-fringed shore receded behind them. Sometimes they were almost becalmed, so light was the wind. On their port a thickly-wooded promontory almost closed in the lake. It grew nearer and nearer, until Betty could see two steeples, shining above the dark woods from which they emerged.

"That's Tihany, and the old Benedictine monastery," said Zarin. He had taken off his white drill coat and sat, now, clad in a thin, silk vest embroidered with his monogram, his strong brown arms bare almost to the shoulders.

"It looks an interesting place," said Betty, shading her eyes against the light. There was no wind now, the sail flapped idly.

"This will make us late for lunch—very hungry?" he asked.

She shook her head. The smiling blue water, the white yachts, and the pine-clad promontory, with the hills rising into a blue haze across the lake, made an enchanting setting.

She trailed a hand in the warm water. As she half lay on the cushions, her head against the bright sky, her beautiful eyes glowing with lazy pleasure under their long lashes, Zarin thought what a perfect complement she made to this summer's day. He smiled at her as they drew nearer to the promontory with its twin towers.

"That monastery was something of a fortress once," said Zarin. "It was one of the few places the Turks couldn't take when they invaded Hungary in the sixteenth century. The abbot must have been a tough old boy. The Turks had a camp on the other side of the lake, and used to cross the ice in winter to kidnap the Hungarian women on Tihany. The abbot would sally forth and kidnap the Turks, whom he impaled, sticking them along the shore, as a warning."

They began to draw near Balatonfüred, which looked a prosperous bathing resort with its promenade, bathing huts and hotels, standing in pleasant gardens. A long, wooden pier ran out through the shallow water. A steamer from Siófok lay alongside. Zarin did not steer for the pier, but for the yacht club-house, with its moored yachts and launches. He had to row the last half mile. The wind had completely dropped. The village lay baking in the fierce heat. The lake was like glass.

A club servant came out and made fast the yacht. They got out, walked through the club-house, on to an acacia-shaded street. In a few minutes, perspiring in the sweltering heat, they came to a row of pleasant hotels, set back in terraced gardens, with pergolas and palm trees beneath which bathers, having finished their lunch, sat idly chatting. Some lay in long chairs, taking a siesta. They turned in at a gate.

The manager came forward to greet Zarin. They did not go into the hotel, but followed a vine-shaded path leading into a cool pinewood. At the end of a sandy path they came to a clearing, where stood a small chalet, built Swiss fashion, with a wide terrace shaded with a striped awning. Through a vista of pine trees they looked on to the sparkling lake. A table with covers for two had been set on the terrace. A young waiter was in attendance.

Zarin showed her over the chalet. It had a sitting-room, a bathroom, and an out-of-door shower. There were two bedrooms upstairs, very sparsely furnished, whose little shuttered windows looked south across the lake.

"Sometimes I come here for a few days—it is so quiet. No one comes into the wood, and I have my meals sent across from the hotel," he said.

The window-boxes were full of petunias. On the lawn below there was a green marble basin, with a dolphin spouting water, which rose glittering like diamonds in the bright air.

"Let us eat," said Zarin, going to the table.

"What a perfect nest!" exclaimed Betty.

He looked at her quietly and smiled.

"That English word just suits it. 'Nest.' I must remember that!"

He placed her facing the view of the lake. The young waiter began to serve lunch. Zarin got up and turned on a radio in the sitting-room, very softly. The music floated out over the terrace. It was the only sound in the hot afternoon. Presently the *tzigane* orchestra in Budapest played *The Dog Song*.

"I want to take home a record of that song," said Betty. "It will bring all this back to me, the most wonderful time I've ever known. I can't believe it's all going to end so soon."

She raised her long glass of amber-coloured wine, and the sadness in her voice was in her eyes also.

"You'll come back again—everyone comes back," said Zarin.

"I don't think so," she answered, slowly.

He raised his glass and smiled at her, surprised to find so sad an expression on her face.

"To your return! Of course you'll come back! We couldn't think of not seeing you here again, Betty. You must make your husband bring you next year."

She made no reply and toyed with the *fogas* on her plate. If he only knew the truth about her circumstances! For a moment she felt tempted to tell him everything, of the

sudden turn of chance that had enabled them to marry,
and come on this honeymoon. But her instinct warned her
that a man like Zarin would not be interested in any story
of hardship. He wanted only pleasant people around him,
with no worries, nothing to mar the pleasure of his day.

He leaned forward and placed his hand over hers as it
lay on the table.

"Very pensive," he said, smiling. She looked ever
lovelier with that shadow in her eyes. "I give you—how
do you say—a penny for your thoughts!"

She did not answer for a few moments, then her lips
parted in a sad smile.

"I suppose it's impossible to expect life to go on like
this? I never imagined the world could be so beautiful—
with such a setting, such nice people, such lovely clothes,
music, food—oh, everything!" She broke off, unable to
find adequate expression of all she felt.

"But you have a charming life in England. Your country
houses, they are so beautiful, with their gardens and their
trees. And London—it offers so much. I am always excited to go there. I shall look forward to seeing you there."

"I don't think I could bear to see you there," replied
Betty.

"No?"

She knew then by the expression of his eyes that he had
quite misunderstood her meaning. He could not know, of
course, that the last thing she wanted was for him to dis-
cover her sordid circumstances in London. But she could
not explain that.

The waiter changed their plates. They watched two
motor-launches racing on the lake. They hummed over
the water like angry bees, leaving a white wash breaking the
smooth surface. On their right lay the promontory of Tihany,
its thick woods rose like a dark green wall against the sky.

"You know—that monastery saw the last phase of the
Austro-Hungarian Empire," said Zarin, playing with the
stem of his glass. "Our unhappy King Károly fled there
from Budapest, after his second ill-fated attempt to regain

he Hungarian throne. They practically shut him up there,
ightened of what might happen if he succeeded The
llies dared not take any risks. Our Regent, Admiral
orthy, found himself in a predicament. The situation was
ull of danger, so, of course, you British had to step in."

He twisted his glass again, and sighed. Betty thought
e sounded depressed, his voice had a sad tone she seldom
eard in it.

"How did we step in?" asked Betty.

"You put him on a British gunboat, and took him down
he Danube, into exile and poverty. He died in Madeira,
f a broken heart, I'm sure. We never loved the Haps-
urgs, except the beautiful Queen Elizabeth, who preferred
o live among us. It was a sad end for the Hapsburg
ynasty—that miserable lodging in Madeira, the winter's
old, the loneliness, the poverty. Poor Károly!"

He was silent for a few moments, and gazed at the monas-
ery of Tihany. Then he turned, smiling again.

"I mustn't be so depressing—it's too beautiful a day,"
e said.

"Please do tell me more—it's so very interesting. Do
ou think the Hapsburgs will ever come back? You have
Royal Palace, you keep the ancient crown in it, you are
uled by a Regent who holds the office temporarily—it all
uggests the return of your king?" asked Betty.

Zarin shrugged his shoulders.

"Who knows? We are a strange people. We never
ose our faith. The Turk came, he oppressed us for one
undred and fifty years, then he was driven out. The
Austrians put their crushing hand upon us, destroyed our
rmies, sent our leaders into exile—we have survived even
Austria. We exist—she does not. We survived the war,
dismembered, it is true. We survived the Roumanian
occupation, the Bolshevik nightmare—and to-day? We
ave lost provinces dear to us—but they are not lost here!"
He tapped his heart. 'Nem, Nem, Soha!' You've seen
hat declaration everywhere, on our doors, in our tramcars
—everywhere. No, No, Never! Have you heard the credo

that follows that declaration ? ' 1 believe in one God. I
believe in one Fatherland. I believe in one eternal Divine
justice. I believe in the resurrection of Hungary.' Every
day, in every school, the Hungarian children recite that
belief. The Magyar blood cannot be diluted ! "

There was a ring in his voice, a fire in his eyes as he
spoke, and then, as if ashamed of revealing so much emotion, he laughed, raised his glass, and exclaimed :

" But what folly ! Here I am, on a beautiful July day
lunching with the loveliest woman in Hungary. Forgive
me, we are propaganda-mad, I fear—but you cannot understand that, for you've not had your own proud land cut
into pieces. And now let me be Mr. Cook. You are now
sitting on the shores of Lake Balaton, fifty miles long and
ten wide. It is very shallow on the south side, and here
on the north, it is deeper—hence these yachts and launches.
But nowhere is it much deeper than ten feet. There are
some sixty watering-places on its shores, many possessing
curative springs. The hills on this side of the lake are
volcanic in origin and the soil produces some of our best
wines. For any further information apply to our local
guide, Károly Zarin."

He laughed gaily, and, the lunch finished, held out his
hand to help her up.

" Shall we go in the pinewoods a bit, and after that
suggest a bathe," he said.

" But I've no costume ! "

" You'll find costumes up in that room," he said, pointing
to one of the chalet's bedrooms.

II

It was quiet in the pinewoods except for the shrill cry
of the cicada. There was not a breath of air. Below them
the lake, misty with heat, sparkled through the pines. They
did not walk far, it was too hot, so they returned to the
chalet, changed into costumes, and bathed. The water
was deliciously warm. He was surprised to find how well

she swam. They went out a long way, and lay floating in
the blue water. "It's heaven!" said Betty.

It was half-past four when they got back to the chalet,
and lay down on the sun mattresses. She looked lovely
lying there, her smooth brown limbs set off by the tight,
pale green costume she wore, with peaked breasts, and firm
thighs, curved like the lines of an amphora. He drew a
finger down her brown arm, scratching a white blur over the
tan, then his hand caught hers, and, leaning on his side, he
put it to his lips and kissed it.

She turned her head and laughed at him. As he hung
over her, his face had a provocative, faun-like expression.
She noticed the breadth of his shoulders; for once his crisp
hair was ruffled.

"I needn't tell you what a really lovely thing you are!"
he said.

"Thing?" she queried, laughing, swinging one leg in the
air.

"I beg your pardon—I thought that was good English!"

"Well—it's rather familiar."

"Can't I be rather familiar?" he asked.

She laughed up at him, his face over hers.

Again he kissed her hand, and then ran his lips lightly
over her flesh, up to her shoulder. She caught at his hair
and held him as his eyes looked into hers, provocatively.

"You are like a faun in the wood," she said.

"You are Diana, resting after the chase."

"The swim," she corrected.

"The swim," he repeated, leaning closer.

Her hand fell from his hair. The mottled shadow of
an acacia tree, near which they lay, played over her throat
and face. Suddenly he bent and kissed her full on the lips,
his mouth lingering on hers. She lay quite still. Then he
raised his head and looked at her, smiling.

"You should not do that," she said, quietly.

"Why not?"

"You know quite well."

He did not answer, but continued to look at her as she

K

lay, her face upturned towards his. His hand slipped over her thigh. She pushed it away. He laughed.

"You are to be good," said Betty, admonishingly.

His foot touched hers, he dropped on to his back, with an exaggerated sigh, and then rolled towards her.

"I want to sleep," he said.

She laughed. Never was a man more awake.

"Then sleep," she answered.

"Thank you," he said, pillowing his head against her shoulder. But after a few minutes of silence he stirred again.

"It's too hot here—shall we lie in the chalet? The waiter's gone."

She did not answer. She was aware of his eyes watching her face.

"Betty darling! Please!" he whispered, kissing her throat.

"No!" she said, closing her eyes. "I want to sleep —here."

He made no reply. His hand began to caress her, and she had to catch it and hold it.

"I shall go if you are not quiet," she said.

He sighed and snuggled against her. She let him remain there. She did not feel angry, or surprised. It was all so obvious. This chalet in the wood, with its rooms, its private service. She wondered how many women had been here. She was playing with fire—and she had deliberately sought the fire. She had no right to be angry with him. But she was married, on her honeymoon. If only—if only—if only what? She did not answer her own question. The Betty Brown who lay here was not herself, it was another woman who was faced with the problem that every woman with a suppliant lover must answer, wisely or adventurously. The answer should be very easy—and it wasn't. Her heart pounded, she closed her eyes. She felt his damp hair against her breast, the slight odour of it, drying.

The stillness was broken by a sudden rustling of leaves. It made a pleasant, cooling sound. The sun had gone in.

Again, but noisily this time, the branches swayed overhead. Then, afar, there was a low rumbling.

Zarin raised his head from her breast.

" There's a storm coming," he said, looking up at the darkening sky. The lake had changed to a leaden hue, ribbed with white wavelets where the wind stirred it.

" A storm ? " asked Betty, incredulous. It seemed impossible on such a perfect day of blazing heat.

" We get very sudden storms on the lake. They sweep down like a cyclone."

As he spoke there was a deafening crack overhead. Then the wind beat the trees with a frenzied gust. Big rain drops fell, chilling, on their bodies.

" We must go in—look ! "

He pulled Betty to her feet. In those few minutes the whole scene had changed. The distant lake was black, the sky leaden, with white streamers of torn clouds. There was a vivid flash, as a wicked tongue of lightning darted through the sky, and struck down into the wind-lashed water. It was followed by a deafening peal of thunder. Then the rain fell as if a cloud had burst.

They raced to the chalet and reached it just as the storm, in tremendous fury, struck them. The wind howled, the bent trees groaned, the rain hissed, the lightning stabbed, and stabbed, followed by the tearing thunder.

Betty went to her room to change. The storm increased in fury. Beyond the window she could see nothing. The lake, the hills, the woods, were all blotted out. The rain hammered on the roof, and danced in white spurts on the terrace. It was almost night. Overhead the lightning flashed, and raced in splitting veins of cold flame over the black world. The cannonade of thunder rose above the hurricane-shriek of the wind and the drumming of torrential rain.

Zarin tapped on her door.

" Are you all right ? " he called.

Betty had pulled off her costume, and was wiping the rain from her limbs.

" Yes," she replied, as another crack of thunder split the heavens.

" Not afraid ? " he asked. " May I come in ? "

" No."

The door handle softly turned. She had slipped the bolt. The handle revolved again. She watched it, her ears filled with the drumming of the rain. A gust of wind struck the chalet and upset a vase of flowers on a table by the window. Somewhere a loose shutter gave a tremendous bang. The rain increased.

He had gone from the door. Betty switched on the light, and having dried herself, began to dress. The storm showed no sign of abating. In intensity and duration it surpassed anything she had ever known. Fortunately she was not nervous.

When she left the room Zarin was waiting for her downstairs, standing by a window, smoking, and gazing out on the flooded terrace. They looked at each other with some embarrassment. Then he offered her a cigarette.

" I am sorry about this," he said, as he lit her cigarette.

She was not sure whether he was alluding to the storm or to the incident upstairs.

" I've never known anything come on so suddenly," she answered.

" We get very rapid storms on this lake," he said. " You look cold."

" No—I'm all right, thank you."

" I've ordered a closed carriage—to take us to a *thé dansant* at one of the hotels here. It'll be a couple of hours before the lake's calm enough for us to cross," he said, " and there's not a steamer for Siófok until seven o'clock. Sometimes they suspend the service after a storm like this."

" Shall we be late ? " asked Betty.

" Not very, I hope, if the wind's right."

The young waiter came in to tell them the carriage had arrived. It was a hooded landau. The storm had abated a little. They drove through the wind and the rain for about five minutes. The dark interior was illuminated by flashes of lightning.

" Not afraid ? " asked Zarin, catching Betty's hand.

" No."

" Splendid," he said.

The moment of their embarrassment had passed. He was as suave as ever, the perfect cavalier.

They arrived at the hotel. All Balatonfüred seemed there. The dance floor was crowded, the tables packed.

A *tzigane* orchestra was playing dance tunes. Zarin was recognised at once. The head waiter had a table brought in for them, and set at the edge of the floor. Betty thought all the women watched her. Doubtless they were jealous. There was no one in the whole place to compare with Count Zarin. The band was excellent, the floor good. They scarcely missed a number.

" I think we must go now," said Zarin, at six o'clock.

The storm had ended. There was a glimmer of sun-shine over the wet roofs as they drove down to the sailing club. The lake was still angry from its lashing, and swirls of white cloud lay low above it. The yachts bobbed and chafed at their moorings. Zarin was not very pleased with the wind.

" We'll have to tack," he said, as they left their mooring. " I'm afraid we're going to be late."

They were late. It was nearly seven when they got into Siófok. To make matters worse no one had covered over the car, and pools of water lay on the leather seats, which had to be wiped down. It was a quarter past when they started off along the rain-soaked road, in a stormy sunset light.

" I must be back by half-past eight, not a moment later ! " said Betty, really worried.

" I think I can manage it," replied Zarin.

He glanced at her, and her face confirmed his guess. She did not wish her husband to know of this excursion. He had wondered at his absence until she had told him of the extra-ordinary mission on which he had gone to Belgrade.

The Count drove at a terrifying speed along the straight, shining road. There was no traffic.

" Not afraid ? " he asked, smiling, as the speedometer registered one hundred and forty kilometres.

She answered, but the roar of the wind carried her voice away. A quick glance showed him her eager face, with parted lips and bright eyes.

They had left the lake shore now, and were crossing the undulating plateau. Everything had been drenched in the storm. They approached the bald limestone cliffs through which the widened road had been cut, and, turning, saw below them the city lights, like diamonds flashing on level plain, where heavy clouds hung, crimson-tinged with the stormy sunset. To the west, Venus, in a clearing of the blue sky between thunder-black clouds, glittered with her pure, cold light. They began to descend the winding road, splashing through patches of white mud and pools of rain-water which sprayed up over the windscreen.

Zarin drove magnificently. The powerful car roared onwards, the wind screamed past them. The speedometer needle touched one hundred and sixty kilometres.

She looked at the clock on the dashboard. It was a quarter-past eight.

" We'll be in Balaton in twenty minutes—the Pension ? " asked Zarin.

She nodded. Madame Balaton would be waiting for her anxiously. It was a narrow squeak.

CHAPTER XX

THE DOG SONG

I

" It's all right," said Percy Bowling, sitting at his favourite café with Jim, a few days after the return from Belgrade. " I've taught her a lesson. You'll see the new electric sign up to-morrow—'Pension Bowling.' She doesn't say a word now when I go out in the middle of the morning, like this. I don't get up till half-past eight. By the way, you're getting your breakfast all right, I hope? That new lad's a bit slow. Say what you like, I was quick at the job."

He puffed at a cigar he had lit, and pulled at a fancy, striped waistcoat he was wearing, together with white shoes and white flannel trousers. He had blossomed into something of a dandy.

"And I've got control of some of that money she had. You know, my wife's a clever woman! She owns two shops, she's got some houses, and she's making a handsome profit out of the Pension. She's giving me five per cent—that's good, these days, so I'm letting her use my money—wouldn't you?" asked Bowling. "When you've money——"

"When you've money you've got more worries than when you've not," said Jim, decisively. "I'd never have believed that once—but I do now. There's something about money that gets a stranglehold on you. It changes you, it makes you afraid of something that will happen for the worst. It changes other people, in the way they behave to you, and what they want of you. I used to laugh when my old mother called it the root of all evil. She was right!" exclaimed Jim.

"My word! It has got you badly! But there's a lot in what you say. Don't I know it!" said Bowling. "When I came into my little bit——"

"I must get back," said Jim, getting up.

He called the waiter and paid the bill.

"Your missis been a bit——?" asked Bowling, as they left the café.

"Not at all!" said Jim, firmly, resenting Bowling's curiosity.

But it was Betty, despite his denial. At this moment she was out somewhere, having put on her hat after a scene between them. Waddle and Tibi had tactlessly said something about an excursion they were making down the Danube, to Varna on the Black Sea. It was a wonderful trip and it wasn't expensive. Why shouldn't they spend a little more of their capital, asked Betty. It was the chance of a lifetime. But he was resolute. They must be home next week. There was the shop to take over.

" I hate the idea of a shop. I don't want a shop. I've had enough waiting to do ! " cried Betty.

" But it was your idea ! "

" Well, I've changed my mind," replied Betty.

" And what do you propose we should do for a living, even if we can get out of buying that business ? " asked Jim, in exasperation.

" Something'll turn up better. You'll never get any-where, because you've no sense of adventure. You can be too cautious and you get nowhere ! " declared Betty.

The wretched argument went on. She was obsessed with the idea of adventure. Finally he told her they were leaving next Tuesday, definitely.

" Then you'll go alone ! " cried Betty, defiant.

" And leave you to go motoring with Zarin, I suppose ? " asked Jim. It was out before he could check himself. He had never intended to say anything about the Balaton adven-ture, which had come to his knowledge in a curious fashion.

Betty turned a sharp, surprised face towards him.

" Oh—so someone's been talking ! And you've been very willing to listen ! " she cried furiously.

" My dear girl, can't you see that this place is going to your head ? Instead of being happy——"

Betty picked up a hat, and thrust it on her head.

" I'll come back when you've regained control of your-self," she said, contemptuously.

The next moment the door had closed with a bang behind her. He was sitting miserably with his head in his hands when Bowling had come to his room and suggested going out for a drink. He wondered now, as they went back to the Pension together, whether Betty had returned.

Their room was empty. She had not returned. Some letters had arrived. He recognised his sister's handwriting on one of the envelopes. It had an air-mail stamp. He opened it.

Dear Jim,

I have hesitated to tell you earlier because I did not want to spoil your honeymoon, but Mother has not been well for over a week. Two days ago she was taken very ill. I got her to bed and sent for the doctor. Last night they took her to hospital. I think you should come as soon as possible. Love to Lizzie.

Nellie.

P.S.—It's appendicitis, they think. They may operate to-morrow.

He read the letter twice, stunned. He looked at the date. It had been posted early on Tuesday. To-day was Wednesday. He could get home to-morrow, by flying. But that was not possible. Betty would not fly.

He opened the Continental Time-Table and found that the Orient Express left on Thursday morning at ten o'clock, and he could be in London by half-past four on Friday afternoon. It was the best he could do.

Going upstairs, he found Waddle and got him to send off a telegram. When he came down again Betty had returned.

" Betty ! " he said, quietly.

" Jim, it is so silly of us—don't look so tragic, darling ! " She slipped into his arms, and kissed him.

" I'm sorry—we mustn't go on like this, Jim dear—but oh, it is so wonderful here ! To be free, to see life, to——"

She broke off and looked at him keenly.

" Jim, you're not going to sulk, just because I can't bear the thought of going home yet ! " she cried, smiling up at him.

" I've had a letter, Betty, about Mother. Read it," he said, giving her the letter.

She read it through slowly, and then looked at him.

" Poor darling, so that's what's worrying you ! How awful ! Well, we couldn't do anything, even if we went at once. They will have operated by now."

"We're going at once—in the morning," said Jim.

"In the morning!" echoed Betty. "But surely, Jim, if we went on Tuesday, as you planned, it would——"

"Are you quite mad! Do you realise my mother's at death's door? Do you think I'll stay here an hour longer than's necessary? My God, Betty, I simply don't understand you! Here's my poor mother——" cried Jim, passionately.

"Now don't get panicky! You can't do anything. We'll go on Tuesday, of course, even if it does wreck our honeymoon, cutting it short. I did so want to see Venice, but still——"

Jim stared at his wife, and in that moment he felt he hated her. She was cold-blooded, hard, utterly selfish. He felt outraged. There was a flood of indignation, the accumulation of a hundred little things, dammed up within him, and ready to burst. But, with a supreme effort, he gained control of himself. His mouth quivered, he was in a cold perspiration. Something in his eyes frightened her for a moment. Then, with a swift movement, she went to him and put her arms round his neck and kissed him.

"We're going in the morning," he said, coldly, his face averted.

"Yes, Jim," she said, quietly, and kissed him again.

II

They had said their farewells, they had packed and paid the bill, and had their breakfast. The luggage was down in the hall. It was a lovely, sunny morning, like all the golden mornings they had had in this hospitable city. There was a bouquet of flowers from Madame Bowling, and a box of chocolates from Tibi. Waddle was going to the station with them, where Tibi would join them. Last night they had dined with Herr Gollwitzer, who would be in London in October, conducting. He looked forward to a reunion. "You must never, never go out of my life. Eet is someding I never vorget," he said, grasping their hands. He was very apprehensive about their travelling through Germany again. " Eef they know what you haf done for me," said Gollwitzer, " they would——"

" Oh, don't worry, Herr Gollwitzer," laughed Jim. " The baby's disappeared off the passport again—they've no proof."

Gollwitzer shook his head slowly.

" I would not trust them. Vell, goot luck," he said.

Jim looked at his watch now, as he stood in their room. There was an hour yet. Betty had gone out to make some purchases. There was time for him to get a shave down at the corner. His last blade had proved impossible this morning. He put on his hat and went out. Over the door swung the new electric sign—" Pension Bowling." As Bowling had gleefully pointed out, it had been easy to change, for his name had the same number of letters.

Jim walked down the cobbled streets towards the hairdresser patronised by Bowling, who said he was ten *filler* cheaper than the places on the avenue. He felt happier this morning, he was going home. He wondered if they had operated on his mother. Betty assured him that an operation for appendicitis was nothing these days. But his mother's age made any operation serious.

He was back from the barber's in twenty minutes. It was now ten minutes past nine. They were leaving at 9.30, for he disliked being rushed at the station. He had always been hurried by other people ; he liked to set a good example. Back in their room, he was surprised to find Betty had not returned. She had a habit of rushing things at the last minute.

Jim sat down, but felt fidgety and excited. Waddle would be down any minute. He opened his cigarette-case, and at that moment an envelope on the table caught his eye. It had his name written across it. It was in Betty's handwriting.

He got up, and tore it open, his heart pounding, and read the brief note it contained.

Dear Jim,

It is no use. I cannot go back to that dismal life again. I must live. Forget me, and forgive me if you can. You will be better without me.

Betty.

III

A little before half-past nine Waddle came down and knocked at the Browns' door. Getting no answer, he opened it gently and peered in. He saw Jim, sitting in a chair, his head buried in his hands, sobbing quietly.

" Your mother ? Oh, my poor lad," he said, going up to him, and putting a hand on his shoulder.

" No—not my mother," said Jim, in a strangled voice. " My wife—Betty—read that ! "

His head still bent, he gave Waddle the note. He read it.

" My dear boy—I—I——" stammered Waddle.

Someone tapped at the door. Waddle hesitated for a moment, and then went to it. He found Bowling there, in an excited condition.

" I say—has anyone fetched any of the bags ? I've just got the taxi, and there's only two in the hall. I took three down, and a hat-box—and I can't find them ! "

" Oh—oh—well——" said Waddle, hesitatingly, before the excited Bowling. " Go downstairs again—I'll find out."

" The taxi's waiting. It's very odd ! I'm certain I——"

" Yes, yes," said Waddle, " I'll find out."

He closed the door, and looked at Jim, who had got up from the chair.

" I heard," said Jim, quietly.

He took out a handkerchief, blew his nose hard, dabbed his eyes, and then picked up his hat and raincoat.

" What are you doing ? " asked Waddle, breathlessly.

" Doing ? I'm leaving," said Jim, in a hard voice. " The taxi's waiting, isn't it ? "

" But—but——" began Waddle.

" We've no time to lose," said Jim, curtly, and strode past him out of the door. His face silenced Waddle.

CHAPTER XXI

CRISIS IN PRAGUE

I

THE holiday season at Brighton was obviously drawing to an end. The visitors were leaving, and now, in the last week of September, the esplanade and the beach were less crowded. Jim's mother had always loved Brighton. She liked its bustle, its crowds, the animation of its streets, promenades and piers, and, quite as much as its shore, the view across the Channel, and the background of the Downs. It was here, nearly thirty years ago, when Brighton seemed half its size, she had come for her honeymoon. The old place had happy memories for her. So that Jim, in suggesting convalescence at Brighton, after her operation, could not have made a happier choice. A month here had restored her wonderfully. Now, as she sat on the front, with Jim at her side, watching the folks go by, she felt like her old self, and ready for London, to which they returned to-morrow.

But the people this morning were not in a holiday mood. They looked worried, and walked with a preoccupied air, as well they might. Every hour the newspaper boys were shouting astonishing and alarming news. The war clouds had suddenly gathered over Europe. Hitler was moving again. A deluge of abuse and allegations poured forth from the German radio stations over Czechoslovakia, its President, and people. Troops, guns, tanks, and aeroplanes were massing on the Sudeten frontier. By day and night Germany toiled

to raise an iron wall along the Rhine. The hysterical Dr.
Goebbels screamed and threatened. Herr Hitler presented
an inflammatory spectacle of persecuted Sudeten-Germans to
his roaring audiences. A carefully organised hysteria swept
the country. An avalanche of propaganda and mass hatred
was sweeping Europe towards the abyss of war.

Suddenly the British Prime Minister had startled the
world with a flight to Hitler in his mountain eyrie at Berchtesgaden. Would reason prevail ? The world caught its breath
at the spectacle of this man of sixty-nine, the spokesman of a
great Empire, making his first flight to talk with the ex-house-
decorator of Munich. It was magnificent, cried the world.
It was humiliating, murmured the old guard.

For five days the world waited with bated breath. The
Prime Minister was home, in conference with the French.
But all this time men were arming, troops were marching,
and feverish activity seized the War Departments of Europe.
Chamberlain was back again with Hitler at Bad Godesberg.
A shift in the terms of peace stunned him there. The door
of 10 Downing Street closed on him again. The doom of
youth and civilisation seemed sealed.

The Czechoslovak nation set its jaw, manned its forts
and prepared for the massacre. France moved up a million
men to its frontier, Italy secretly mobilised, the British Navy
swiftly slipped from its moorings and set forth in force.
Russia, imponderable, secret, gave her pledge. France
declared she would honour her bond. England supported
her and gravely warned Germany. An incensed Hitler
thundered across the world. From Washington came the
weighty counsel of the President. The roads towards
Czechoslovakia were thronged with troops and guns. Germany
would not wait—not one day, not one hour. Czechoslovakia
closed its frontiers. The little men of Europe, from their
homes in the cities, their farms in the plains, their chalets in
the mountains, looked out with frightened eyes, and spoke
in whispers, while their despairing wives held their children
to them. No one wanted war, yet the whole world marched
to war. The deluge of blood was upon them.

Calm in the vortex of the maelstrom, the Czech put on his knapsack and shouldered his gun ; a little nation stood resolute at its battered door.

A newsboy came rushing down the parade with a new edition. Jim bought a paper and scanned it.

" What does it say ? " asked his mother, anxiously.

" Oh, the usual—more scrapping between the Sudeten-Germans and the Czechs. The Germans are smashing up the Customs stations. The Poles and the Hungarians are trying to grab something now. The Czechs have rounded up a lot of Hungarians trying to raise a revolt in Ruthenia. Well, we're in for it, all right. When we get back to-morrow I'm going to enlist in the Air Force."

Mrs. Brown gave her son an anxious look, the look that every mother was giving her son these days. She put out a hand to his.

" Oh, Jim," she said, simply, and lapsed into silence again.

They watched the people. Nearly of all them carried newspapers. They looked out to sea, expecting to detect the grey wraith of a warship moving down-Channel.

" Well—what's anything matter, anyhow," said Jim. " Shall we go ? It's nearly one o'clock. You've done a good walk this morning."

She rose, taking his arm. She made no reply to his question. He had been so wonderful through all these weeks, but she knew he was eating his heart out. It seemed a long time since she had been aware, one morning, of him standing at her bedside, and for a week she had not learned the truth. In a sense her illness had been a blessing. He had attended to her devotedly, and her needs had occupied him to some degree. But under his forced cheerfulness she knew the battle he was fighting. In all these weeks there had not been a line from his wife, or any news of her. She had disappeared as if she had never existed. There had been a terrible scene with the Parrishes, who had put all the blame on Jim. Her son had shown the dreadful old father to the door. But he came back a week later, very quiet and downcast. They had heard from Lizzie. There was no address, only a Hungarian postmark. It was a very brief note, completely exonerating her husband. The old man broke down as Jim read it.

" She's no good, Jim. You're better without her. She was allus ashamed of us," cried the old man. " I never want to see her again."

And what could the future offer Jim ? " I'll have to think," he replied one day, when she had tried to open the subject. But he sat hour after hour, listless, saying very little. He insisted on taking her to Brighton as soon as she was out of hospital. " But the money, Jim ? " she had said. " Oh, don't worry about that. When it's gone, it's gone," he replied. But she did worry. The shop project was dead. He would have to do some work soon. It wasn't good for him to sit about like this, brooding, without any interest in life.

On the morning of their return to London he went straight to the enlisting station.

" Well ? " she asked, as he came in.

He threw down his hat, dropped into a chair, and laughed. Mrs. Brown looked at her son anxiously.

" We're a fine lot—we're digging trenches like mad all over the parks, we're rushing the kids out of London because we're going to be bombed to death, and we've nothing ready. They don't want me yet ! I've filled in a form with twenty questions. They're very busy—and I shall hear later ! What do you think of that ? What's the matter with this country ? " demanded Jim, angrily.

Later in the afternoon Nellie came in. She looked at them excitedly.

" Have you heard ? " she cried, flinging down her hat. " The war's over. Hitler's invited Chamberlain to a conference at Munich. He's off in the morning. Mussolini and Daladier are going too ! "

" We're not out of the wood yet," commented Jim, gloomily.

II

They were having tea the following day when a tremendous rap-rap on the front door made them start.

" Now, whatever——" began Mrs. Brown, teapot in hand.

" I'll go," said Nellie, getting up.

When she came back she had a telegram in her hand.

" For you," she said, giving it to Jim.

He opened and read it. They watched him in silence.

" Is the boy there ? " he asked.

" Yes," said Nellie.

" Tell him there's no answer."

Nellie went to the door. Jim sat down again, putting the telegram in his pocket. The last time Mrs. Brown had seen him receive a telegram it had been about his football pool.

" You've not had another winner ? " asked Mrs. Brown, smiling, as she passed a cup to Nellie.

" No," said Jim, laconically.

Mrs. Brown looked at her son. He was pretending to eat, but she saw that his hand trembled.

" Jim, what is it ? " she asked, suddenly. " Can't we be told ? "

He looked at her sullenly, then his eyes watered. He got up abruptly and put the telegram on the table.

" Read it," he said, and left the room.

" Why, whatever——" began Nellie.

" Where's my spectacles," said Mrs. Brown, looking round, " No—you read it."

Nellie read it out aloud to her mother.

Betty dangerously wounded. Condition critical. Asks for you. Suggest fly Friday. Will meet plane. Wire confirmation. Waddle. Hotel Wenceslas, Prague.

" Goodness gracious ! " exclaimed Mrs. Brown. " Dangerously wounded ! Whatever's that girl been doing ? And in

Prague of all places—why, that's where all the trouble is ! "

" Who's Waddle ? " asked Nellie, reading the telegram again.

" On that's the man they met in Paris and went to Hungary with," replied Mrs. Brown. " Give me the telegram."

" Why, what——" asked Nellie, looking at her mother, as she went to the door.

" I'm going to talk to Jim. Leave us alone," answered Mrs. Brown.

She found him in the front parlour, seated on the lounge, with his head between his hands. He looked up as she came in.

" Jim—you're going, of course ? " asked his mother.

" No—why should I go ? She's made her own bed—let her lie on it," he replied.

Mrs. Brown sat down beside her son.

" Jim—whatever she's done, and whatever she's suffering, there's one fact remains : it concerns you, it's your duty, you're her husband."

" Oh, am I ? How do I know ! Why should——"

" Jim, my boy. I know all you're feeling. But you must go to her. You are both young. She's headstrong and silly—but she's not a bad girl at heart. She must be regretting it now. Whether you still love her or——"

" I don't ! " cried Jim, fiercely.

Mrs. Brown looked at her son. He turned his face away, his mouth quivered.

" I think you do—but that gets us nowhere. I feel you should go," said Mrs. Brown, quietly.

There was silence in the room for a few moments as she sat looking at his bent head. Then he turned and looked at her with misery in his eyes.

" You think so ? " he asked.

" Yes, Jim—at once, or it may be too late," she said, putting her arm round him and drawing him to her. Suddenly the pent up emotion burst its bonds.

" Oh, Mother ! Mother ! " he sobbed, his head buried on her shoulder.

The office of Imperial Airways was just round the corner by Victoria Station. There was usually a plane to Prague, he learned, leaving at 8.45 a.m., but owing to the crisis the service had been suspended. It was possible to fly from Paris by Air France. The plane left Paris at 8 a.m. and reached Prague at noon. He could leave Victoria to-night.

" I know that train—8.20, Newhaven-Dieppe route, arrive Paris 5.30 a.m.," said Jim.

" That'll give you ample time to make the connection," said the clerk.

" Thanks, that's what I'll do."

Eight-twenty, Victoria. It was now 6.30. He went across to the telegraph office and wired to Waddle.

He left a London, solemn-faced, anxious, but grimly determined in these hours of trial. All day the stations had been crowded with children, carrying their small luggage, being evacuated from a city almost defenceless against a rain of bombs. What was happening in that room in Munich on which the eyes of the whole world turned ? The minutes and hours fled. The world waited. As his boat reached the harbour at Dieppe, in the morning darkness, Jim went up on deck and learned that an agreement had been reached at Munich. There were smiling faces around him in the train to Paris. But at the aerodrome, as he entered the Prague-bound plane, he saw a man in tears. He was a Czech. " They have massacred my country—they've deserted us," he said, a newspaper shaking in his hand.

III

Waddle had always lived adventurously, but nothing in his past could compare with the astonishing events of these last few days. The crisis had caught him in Prague, the city of his lost Martha, and that memorable room off Husova-street. He had been *en route* for Dresden, for a folk-dance festival. All around him, by day and by night, the streets of the Bohemian capital had been thronged by marching troops, grim-faced, proceeding to that wall of death behind which Czechoslovakia awaited its hour of destiny. Singing and shouting, demonstrators paraded with a sea of banners ; there was an every-growing, pitiable army of refugees from the Sudeten border : Czech peasants, refugee Germans, and terror-stricken Jews.

The stations were thronged. Thousands of homeless people squatted by their bundles, which were their pillows by night. But no panic touched these people, hemmed in by hate, menaced by cracking frontiers, threatened by vacillating allies. At Berchtesgaden, at Bad Godesberg, and now at Munich, the statesmen played ball with their destiny, in which they were allowed no voice. Shut out from the council room, swamped under a deluge of insulting propaganda from Germany, snarled at by Poland, threatened by Hungary, they resolutely stood their ground. Up there in the vast castle-palace, under the shadow of the cathedral, the President resolutely steered the ship of state through the storm.

Amid the tumult, while the earth was about to split open under them, and the heavens rain bombs, Waddle, one afternoon, was called to the telephone. It was Count Zarin speaking. Could he see him at once ? Ten minutes later Zarin was at his hotel.

" I got your address from Tibi, who told me you were in Prague. I couldn't get through to him direct. I had to telephone via Paris—we're cut off from Budapest. If war breaks out I'm trapped—but that's of no account. It's Betty I've come about. She's dying ! "

" Dying ? " repeated Waddle. " Dying—but—I don't understand ! What are you doing here in Prague ? "

" We've been caught by this mess," answered Zarin. " Waddle, you're the one person who can help me. It's a terrible story ! "

He walked up and down the hotel bedroom, wringing his hands. Nothing remained of the sophisticated Count Zarin Waddle had known in Budapest. He watched him now trying to smother his dislike of the man.

"I don't understand, Zarin. I really don't know why you should come to me, or any of us, after your outrageous conduct," said Waddle, coldly.

"I deserve all you say, but this is a matter of life and death," said Zarin. "Surely—surely for Betty's sake——"

"Have you ever considered anybody but yourself? Have you—but never mind—what has happened, why is Betty dying?" asked Waddle.

"I'll tell you as briefly as I can. Betty and I have been living at Plecs—that's my place in Ruthenia," said Zarin. "When the Sudeten trouble grew menacing—I decided we'd better get back into Hungary and——"

"How long had you been there?" interrupted Waddle.

"Nearly a month—we thought it better to be away, to be somewhere that——" faltered Zarin.

"Of course," said Waddle, acidly. "Go on."

"Well, we tried to get back, but we'd left it too late. We found the frontier closed at Cop. We rushed on to the next Customs place, to Satoraljaujhely, and I thought we were going to get across when we discovered we had run into a sniping battle. You see, some of our soldiers, in mufti but armed, had crept over the frontier, to conduct propaganda among the Ruthenians——"

"With bullets?"

"It was our territory once," retorted Zarin. "The Czechs caught some of our fellows, and firing began. I don't know now what happened, exactly. I was in the Customs house, arguing with the control officer, when I heard the firing. Betty was in the car. I ran out, and saw two gendarmes fall. Betty had jumped out of the car and was coming towards me when there was another burst of firing. All at once she fell. I picked her up and got her into the Customs house."

"She was hit—badly?"

"Yes—I didn't realise it at first. I thought it was shock. But she was unconscious from the start."

"Where was she wounded?" asked Waddle.

"For a minute or so we couldn't tell. Then blood began

to ooze from her breast. Waddle, it was terrible, terrible!"
cried Zarin, clenching and unclenching his hands. Then he
moistened his lips and continued his story.

"The nearest doctor was at Uzhorod, the capital of
Ruthenia. The place is right away in the plain at the
foot——"

"I know it. I've tramped all over the Carpathians,"
said Waddle, "it's the end of the earth."

"I put Betty in the car and we motored there, straight to
the hospital, such as it is. The journey took an hour. It
was a nightmare. Uzhorod was almost in a state of war.
There were only two doctors, worked to death. There'd
been a clash with the Poles on the northern frontier, the
beds were full of casualties. Betty was half-conscious all
the time, and losing blood. They found the wound, over
the heart, but there was nothing they could do. We'd only
one hope—to get her to a hospital where they could operate.
It meant the best surgeon in the country. I found there
was an air service to Prague, and rushed off to the field. The
service was suspended, they said. But there was a plane in
the hangar, and a pilot. He refused to fly. Finally I
persuaded him, when he heard Betty was English. He was
a Czech, and didn't like me. At four o'clock we were in
Prague."

"What day was that?" asked Waddle, as Zarin paused,
and wiped his brow.

"Yesterday. They decided they must operate at once—
the bullet was embedded near the heart. I saw poor Betty,
just before they took her in—she was conscious, but she
couldn't speak. Somehow she'd scribbled on a piece of
paper, which the nurse gave me. They operated at six
o'clock."

"What had she written?" asked Waddle.

Zarin took a piece of paper from his wallet, and passed it
to Waddle. It was a note, crumpled, and written in pencil.
Waddle read the scrawl with difficulty:

Jim darling—I love you. Forgive me. Lizzie.

After he had read it Waddle passed it back. " Will you keep it, please—for him," said Zarin, quietly. Waddle put it carefully in his wallet.

" And the operation ? " he prompted.

" It was a long job. They got the bullet out at last. But, Waddle, they don't think she's going to live ! I've just been to the hospital. Last night I tried to get through to Tibi in Budapest, but it was impossible ; to-day I tried via Paris, and finally I got him. I wanted Jim Brown's address—all our luggage is in the car at Uzhorod. Tibi didn't know his address, but he gave me yours here, and said you knew it."

" Yes—but what makes you think young Brown will come ? " asked Waddle. " The last time he wrote to me he said he never wanted to hear of her."

" She's asking for him," said Zarin, simply.

" Very well," said Waddle, after a reflective pause, " I'll telegraph him. But whether he'll come, or can come, even if he wishes, I don't know."

" Don't mention me—I think it better—it would——"

Zarin faltered and moved his hands expressively.

" I shall certainly not—at present," replied Waddle, curtly.

So he had telegraphed, and for the rest of the evening did not leave the hotel. Twice Zarin rang through to know if there was an answer. Betty was sinking. The third time he called up, Waddle had received a reply. Brown was arriving at twelve o'clock in the morning.

Waddle went out to eat at his favourite café. The streets were crowded with people. Everywhere the conference between Chamberlain, Hitler, Mussolini and Daladier was being discussed. Prague, braced for war, resolved even to see its historic beauty doomed to a fate like Madrid's, was filled with misgivings. Czechoslovakia had already been forced into heavy concessions. Would further humiliations be demanded ? She was not even invited to discuss her fate, she could only wait outside the door of the conference room.

As Waddle reached the main thoroughfare he encountered a great procession, quiet and orderly, proceeding to the palace of the President. Czechoslovakia would not be coerced or betrayed, declared the banners. It would stand firm before the German menace. It relied on its Allies. It showed an iron front to all aggression.

Waddle found a seat in the crowded café. What were those four statesmen planning in Munich? Rumour after rumour passed over the assembly. Hitler's bluff was called. Hitler was adamant. Mussolini was backing out. Chamberlain was firm. Daladier was incensed. The conference had split up. The conference was still sitting. They could not agree. They had agreed.

At midnight Prague still debated its fate. Waddle went home to bed.

In the morning, coming down to breakfast, he was stunned by the news. He had never conceived such humiliating terms. Out in the streets the people passed with the air of mourners. The threat of impending doom had not shaken these people as much as this catastrophic defeat by dictation. He heard of the wild surge of refugees from the Sudeten land, thousands fleeing, ruined and homeless, before the vengeance that would pursue them because of their loyalty to the State.

" We've been crucified on the cross of Peace," said a man, in the motor-bus proceeding to the aviation field.

" You mean on the Swastika ! " retorted an old woman, sitting in the corner.

" Well—it's peace, anyhow. I don't want any young men mangled for me," mumbled a passenger.

They looked at him with contempt, and turned to Waddle for his opinion, but he only shook his head, and remained dumb. He was glad to get out of the bus.

The Paris plane was on time. Waddle watched it descend to the aerodrome. He waited by the Customs barrier, scanning the figures anxiously as they came through the gate. Yes—there was Jim Brown. In a few moments he was through, their hands met.

" A good journey ? " asked Waddle, reduced to banality to hide his feelings.

" Yes, thanks. Waddle, you've seen Betty ? What is it ? Why is she wounded ? Why is she here ? " asked Jim.

Waddle motioned for a taxi, gave the hotel address, and opened the door.

" I'll tell you all I know, Jim," he replied, as soon as they were seated, and the taxi moved off. " It's a sorry tale."

" Zarin's in it ? "

" Yes, he's very much in it," answered Waddle. He recounted Zarin's story as they drove through the streets of Prague.

IV

They were in the hospital at three o'clock. A nurse showed them at once to the room in which Betty lay. Jim was shocked at her appearance. Her face was drawn and white, all the blood seemed drained from her. She lay, motionless, unconscious of their presence.

From the street below came the sound of voices singing in unison. It was a solemn, stirring song, rising and falling in the autumnal afternoon. Waddle tiptoed to the window and looked down. There was a procession with a sea of flags moving slowly along the street, singing the Czech National Anthem. A doctor came into the room. Waddle acted as interpreter. There was no change in the patient.

" She will live ? Ask him," said Jim to Waddle.

The stout little doctor in white overalls looked at the young man standing before him. He said something in Czech and smiled sadly.

" He says there is always hope," interpreted Waddle.

The doctor left them, the nurse came and went. Jim sat with Betty's hand in his, vainly hoping for her eyes to open, for one glimmer of consciousness to tell him that she knew of his presence. Waddle had left them. He returned soon after four o'clock. They could come back again, he said. He persuaded Jim to go out with him to a neighbouring café.

They were seated there when, shortly before five o'clock, there was an announcement on the public radio. Someone was talking. The whole café listened with rapt attention, and as Jim looked at their intense faces he saw men and women quietly crying. Then the voice ceased, and the life of the café flowed on again. They got up to leave.

"What was that about—why were they crying?" asked Jim, as they passed by the Karlúv bridge, and looked across the river towards the immense palace and the cathedral of St. Vitus rising from the castle precincts. The massive pile, with its long tiers of windows, its level roofs and massed spires, crowned the opposite hill, against a sky crimsoned with a stormy sunset.

"It was the Prime Minister speaking to the nation," answered Waddle. "He said he had experienced the most tragic moment in his life, the most painful duty ever laid upon him, a thing worse than dying, by surrendering to the forces against them."

"What do you think of it?" asked Jim. "I feel rather ashamed. We've let them down. And yet——" He paused and gazed on the old city with its river and bridge, its castle-crowned hill and all the beauty of its palaces and spires. "And yet I can't believe that all this should be laid in ruins, and millions be killed because a madman insists on keeping to his time-table."

Waddle did not reply for a few moments, and watched the fading pageant of the sunset.

"There's no simple answer to it all," he said, at length; "except perhaps in our readiness to feed on old wrongs, and to nourish hate. It's easy for demagogues and adventurers to inflame patriotism until a country forgets its larger duty to the world. That doesn't apply to this nation. They are well-governed, hard-working, honourable. But twenty years ago there were too many of the rotten old timbers of foundered ships built into theirs, and they couldn't stand the gale, and their allies were caught napping. But that's only my opinion," added Waddle. "It's difficult to sort it all out. The dictators have no morality, and the democracies have no self-discipline."

They crossed the bridge, to get a new view of the city, and then returned to the hospital. Waddle let Jim go up to the room alone, and came back for him at seven o'clock.

" Waddle, she knew me ! " said Jim, as they went down the stairs, his voice unsteady.

" She spoke ? "

" No—but her eyes opened, and she saw me, and pressed my hand. I know she saw me, Waddle," he avowed, as the tears gathered in his eyes. He fumbled quickly for a handkerchief. " I can come back to-morrow at ten, they said."

" Good ! " responded Waddle, patting Jim's back.

V

Early in the morning, just before six, Waddle was awakened by the tinkle of his bedside telephone. Half asleep, he picked up the receiver. It was the night porter downstairs. The hospital wished to speak to him.

" Put them through," he said, his heart thumping.

Two minutes later, in dressing-gown and slippers, he went along to Jim's room, and tapped gently. The door was unlocked. He went in, switching on the light. Jim sat up instantly.

" Yes ? " he asked, apprehensively, dazzled by the light.

Waddle advanced to the bedside, and put his arm across Jim's shoulder.

" Betty—she's gone, my dear boy," he said gently. " Five minutes ago. She was quite unconscious—she just slipped away."

CHAPTER XXII

ANOTHER DAY BEGINS

It was such a dark February morning that Mrs. Brown switched on the light in the kitchen, after she had laid the breakfast for Jim. Then she glanced at the clock. It was ten minutes to eight. He was on duty at 8.30. As usual, he would cut the time to a minute.

" Jim ! " she called, going to the foot of the stairs, and nearly tripping over the cat. " Jim ! " she repeated, hearing no response. " It's ten minutes to eight ! "

" Coming, Mother ! " said a drowsy voice.

Mrs. Brown went into the scullery and put the frying-pan on the gas stove, to cook his bacon and egg. She mashed the tea, and made some toast under the grill. As she carried these into the kitchen her son appeared, in vest and trousers.

" Dark this morning," he said, rubbing his curly head.

" There's fog about," responded Mrs. Brown.

Jim ran some cold water into the tin basin on the sink. It was not shaving morning. He pulled off his vest, and rubbed his hands over his firm white flesh. Then he flexed his muscles, working his arms to and fro. He was a bit stiff this morning. Last night there had been a boxing fixture at the club and he had fought three times.

Mrs. Brown, coming into the scullery, looked at his strong wide shoulders, and his knotted backbone, as he bent over the sink, spluttering.

" You've no black eye this morning, I 'ope ? " she asked, regarding her son with pride.

" No—I came through all right last night."

He rubbed himself vigorously with a towel, his flesh pink, his face glowing. Then he dragged a comb through his dank curls.

" Here's your clean shirt," said Mrs. Brown, taking it off the line, where it had been airing.

He put on his sleeveless cotton vest, and then the flannel shirt, undoing the belt around his slim waist, and tucking it into the blue corduroy trousers. When he did this each morning he remembered the remark of Julietta Molnay, on that first evening at *The Green Cockatoo*. " Every time I went to a station I smelt and smelt and smelt them. Your streets smell of beer—yes, on street corners at ten o'clock— and your porters of lovely corduroy. I shock you ! "

He would never see her again, or that strange world into which he had been plunged. He never wanted to see it again. For two months after Lizzie's death he had sat about, dull-eyed and listless, refusing to discuss the future, hurt with life. Then one day Mr. Lincoln, down at the Club, had talked to him. He came away, angry at the advice he had received, but he knew now how right it was. It wasn't money, it was work, regularly and enjoyably done that kept a man sane and happy, work among people he knew and in the place where he had grown up.

So one morning, crushing his pride, he had gone back to the station, and been received with a kindness that broke him down. He put on the familiar cap, and felt he was on earth again. He felt he was nearer, then, to those happy old days when he had called for Lizzie at the staff entrance of her restaurant, and she had come out, looking so pretty, with her eyes shining beneath a new hat. Poor Lizzie, he thought of her now only with a sad tenderness.

Jim glanced at himself in the mirror and tied his tie. He looked the same, and yet what he had gone through! He ought to look a hundred. Was it possible that all that was only five months ago? It seemed ten years.

He picked up the comb again, and carefully made a parting. Then he put on his jacket, and felt a letter in the pocket. Oh, yes—it was from Waddle, yesterday. He must answer it. Funny old boy, writing on odd bits of paper, never from the same address. He was in Athens, now, pursuing new folk dances. Dear old Waddle, he would like to see him again.

"Now come along, Jim!" cried his mother, from the kitchen.

He went in and sat down at the breakfast-table, with its blue-and-white china and white cloth. He looked proudly round the kitchen. It had new furniture. It was their own home. Mr. Simkin, their lodger, had been got rid of. They now had their own parlour.

"Nellie gone?" he asked, alluding to his sister, who worked at a telephone exchange.

"Yes—she's on duty at eight," replied Mrs. Brown. "She thinks they're going to make her a supervisor," she added, proudly.

"That reminds me—I've a bit of news for you," said Jim, pouring out his tea. "Your son won't be a porter after this week."

"What?" exclaimed Mrs. Brown, startled. "Oh, Jim—you're not giving up the station!"

"No—but they sent for me yesterday and offered to move me into the Goods Department—it might mean anything in time. So I said 'Yes.'"

Mrs. Brown looked at her son, her face puckered in a smile.

"There, I knew it!" she declared. "I knew they'd find out you'd got it in you. They've been very kind—taking you back after—after——"

She hesitated, not knowing how to put it.

"After I'd come such a cropper," said Jim, quietly.

Mrs. Brown said nothing. She rested her hand on his shoulder, and then, stooping, kissed his temple, with its falling chestnut curl. He turned, smiled at her, gave her a pat, and continued eating.

She went into the scullery and picked up his shoes to clean them. It was a forbidden thing, but she liked doing it. Unfortunately the blacking tin rattled as she dipped the brush on it.

"Here! You leave those shoes alone!" called Jim.

"Well, you're a bit late, Jim," she replied.

"I've time for that—you put 'em down, Mother!"

"Oh, very well," she said, defeated.

He was all ready at twenty past eight. She brushed his cap in the old familiar way. He stuck it on jauntily, one crisp lock escaping over his ear.

"Bye-bye!" he said, cheerily, catching hold of her waist and planting a kiss on her cheek. The next moment he had opened the kitchen door and leapt up the area steps. As usual, the two empty milk bottles were there. He turned, laughing, and looked down at her. Then, picking them up, he rattled them together and did a little dance.

"Rum-tiddly-umtum, rum-tum!" he sang.

"Get off with you!" admonished Mrs. Brown.

"*Auf Wiedersehen*," he called, putting down the bottles and with an elaborate bow, was gone.

Mrs. Brown closed the kitchen door. Then she cleared the able and carried the breakfast things to the sink. It had een good to see him so light-hearted again. The old Jim as returning. Time was doing its healing work.

> " The King of Love my Shepherd is
> Whose goodness faileth never——"

ang Mrs. Brown, sprinkling soap-flakes into the washing-up water.

THE END